MERCIFUL VOWS

THE GIANNOTTI WORLD BOOK ONE

VANESSA LUISA

Dear readers,

Firstly, Merciful Vows is a full-length standalone novel set in The Giannotti World. It is the first novel in the inter-connected series and therefore it's recommended you begin here first to gather context and understanding, and then follow on to read the proceeding novels in the inter-connected series.

As a romance book lover, I have always reached the end of the novel and grinning ear-to-ear at the epilogue. But then one day, during one of the darkest times of my life, a question arose in my mind…I became intrigued by the idea of what happens when the epilogue doesn't always go to plan…and so I wrote this suspenseful, emotional love story.

Merciful Vows is a story of two people needing each other more than they need themselves. A story of strength, of vulnerability and of loving without any limits. A story of healing to breathe freely again, of hope to never let go of what truly matters and of second chance to be guided out of the darkness and into the light.

This is a story from my heart, and I give it to you wholeheartedly to take along with you during your own journey in life, wherever you may be.

Because you matter. You really do. All of it is you.

Happy reading!

Vanessa Luisa x

To Mamma,

My love for you is infinite.

To Nonna and Nonno,

Entrambi siete e sarete sempre nel mio cuore e nella mia anima,
in tutto ciò che faccio e in tutto ciò che sono. Vi amo entrambi
per sempre. Sempre.

"I love her and that's the beginning and end of everything…"

F. SCOTT FITZGERALD

PREFACE

Unknown

OUR HIDDEN IMPERFECTIONS SAY A LOT ABOUT WHO WE ARE AT THE surface. It's unnerving, the way people simultaneously pace through every day of their lives feeling resolved. Demanding success. Obtaining desires. Uplifting hell.

I know why I did the latter tonight. I know why I kidnapped *her*. It's because deep down inside I had a calling. I *needed* to do this. I needed to ruin the Giannotti family.

They will never know the horrid ticking bombarding inside my chest. My wildly racing heart pumps boiling blood, as if time is running out and my entire life depends on this—*because it does.*

A few hours have passed since the incident and once Blue Eyes hands me the baby, I bid his exit with a nod. Dark garments contrast against those bright slate eyes that unlock a corrupted world of deception—one I proudly control. A breeze of cold air swirls around the poorly lit room following Blue Eyes' departure.

As I set Addilyn Giannotti inside the makeshift bassinet in the basement, I realize I actually got away with it. *I fucking did it.* Best thing of all, they will never know or suspect me. Liars make the best promises.

I drown out Addilyn's bloodcurdling screams and leave her right there as coldness magnifies through the soles of my shoes at every heavy tread up the concrete stairs. A cold metallic sting ripples across my palms as I grip the railing to steady myself up into the world as I now know it.

The soundproof walls will drown out her tears. The operation undertaken tonight will diminish my identity. The police will never find me. I'll make sure of it. No one can stop me.

I'll give it six months. Six long months to wait it out and submerge myself in normal life. Six months to analyze every single movement of the Giannotti family. To watch their grief. Their agony. Their greatest loss become reality.

I want them to break right in front of my eyes. I will raise hell for them and watch it all unfold. I will test their limits. Just like a gripping movie, only this time I am the writer. I am the director. I am the cast and the closing credits. I write the fabricated lies. I direct the intoxicated evil. I hire the assistants. I am public enemy number one and they don't even know it. They will never be able to escape me, no matter how hard they try.

For six months they will live in my unrest, not knowing if Addilyn is dead or alive. It doesn't frighten me to do just that. It's who I am now. So I'll keep on waiting, writing their story from a distance.

Predicting their every move.

Constructing the epitome of their hell.

Until I go after them too and end it all...*for good.*

CHAPTER ONE

Giulio

"YOU CAN'T STAY IN THERE FOREVER! COME OUT!"

He's wrong. My father and I both know how long I can withstand his torture. I don't know how long exactly I have to fight his presence, but I'll give it my all.

Heavy thumps outside my door carve my heart to stone with every footstep. Through the gap below, I catch an inch of my father's brown leather shoes. They're new. He bought them specifically to wear to the funeral.

I despise them.

I despise him.

"Unlock the door, Giulio!" His rough voice digs another wound in my chest.

"No!"

"I said unlock the door or I'll do something we'll both regret."

I cannot control my pulsing rage. It's too much. "You already ruined everything! You ruined Mom. You let this happen. You let her die while you were with a woman that wasn't Mommy. I hate you!"

"You do not get to speak to me like that. I'm going to—that's it, time's up."

My bedroom door bursts wide open and in a flash, my nine-year-old frame is flung into the air. I hit one of the cream walls with a loud thud. My back aches and my hand is scraped, but I don't say a word. No. I don't care how much my father hurts me, I will never show him fear. He will never break me. Never

I know that look in my father's light eyes. The one of utter destruction. The one I see haunting my dreams every single night. The one my mom stared into and saw nothing but gold. He was different back then. He liked me when Mom was around.

My father's jaw clenches and alcohol slurs his words. "What? Do you think you're stronger than me, Giulio? Is that what it is?"

"I didn't say that."

"Don't fucking talk back to me." He crouches beside me with a vengeance, and the lines between his brows deepen. "Listen to me, kid. Your mother's dead. That doesn't mean I'm going to be here to pick up the pieces. You're not my life anymore. I have Clare and we have a child on the way. One that isn't you. Do you understand?"

Nod.

"I didn't even want you. I've never wanted you."

Nod.

"Remember that when you cry yourself to sleep like the weak little boy you are. That's what you are, Giulio. You're weak. You'll never be strong."

Once again my head inclines.

"Stop crying, weak boy." My father tugs my injured hand towards him. I didn't see it before, but now I can't miss it. Argent lighter with

his initials. **P.G.** *The warm embers entice and scare me all at the same time. I already know what will happen next, which is why my eyes slam shut and I pray to my mom in heaven. I pray for it all to stop. I wish she was still here instead of the man I'm forced to call my dad.*

Please don't hurt me.

But he does. Of course he does. Why wouldn't he?

"Open your eyes and face it. Face it like a man, Giulio."

Tears cascade down my cheeks as the flame licks my skin. It taunts my palm and curls up until my knuckles endure the brunt of the pain. The intense heat builds rapidly until I'm squirming against the wood oak floorboards. My father never allows it to go beyond the point of scarring or burning me severely, but it does blemish my skin and ego for days after.

Please, Mom.

Come and save me.

Darkness is all I'm met with. It's all the nightmares in one. I cannot call out for help because this is supposed to be the man who defends me. The man who loves me. The man that should do anything for me. But ever since Mom died, he's become the devil she'd always protected me against.

I wait in pain until he's satisfied enough to let me go. For now.

"You don't understand how much it hurts me to see your mother every time I look at you. I'm sick of it." My father grips my jaw, forcing me to bore into those devilish eyes. "It makes me feel as though she's still here and I don't want that fucking feeling. Most importantly, I don't want you. One of these days...I'll have my way. One of these days you'll see what I'm capable of. One of these days you'll despise me more than you do today. Mark my words, Giulio." And then he's gone. Leaving me sobbing with an empty heart and no place to call home.

"Daddy!" I look away from the orange tulips to my daughter's doe eyes. Slonne is pulling on my charcoal slacks with a wolfish grin. "Daddy? Didn't you hear me?"

Fuck.

How long have I been out of it?

The memory of my father ends in waves. I need to forget

about it right here inside this florist, no matter how tight my chest aches. My father will never gain that control over me. He didn't back then and he won't right now. That nine-year-old boy has grown into a thirty-two-year-old man. I am not nor have I ever been *weak*.

"Sorry, darling. What did you say?"

Slonne's giggle reenergizes me as I lift her into my arms. She matches the sweet, holistic smell of the flowers. "I said the lady asked you a question, silly!"

I arch a playful brow. "Did you just call me silly?"

"Mmhmm."

"Oh, you're going to get it now." I attack my daughter in tickles. Her laugher bounces off the walls and I can't help but see Valencia in her.

Valencia.

My father's voice plays in my mind. *You don't understand how much it hurts me to see your mother every time I look at you. I'm sick of it.* But unlike my father, I'll never get tired of seeing my separated wife in my son and daughter's eyes, no matter the constant agony in my heart.

A shallow breath escapes me as I set Slonne down. She runs off to the back of the store where Oscar is playing with the owner's slender ginger cat.

I turn to the cashier. "I apologize for earlier. What did you ask me?"

She motions to the deep red bouquet of roses I purchased before zoning out. "No need to apologize. I only asked if it was an anniversary gift. If so, I have some cards to choose from, that'll sure make your Mrs. happy."

My Mrs...

I don't have it in me to admit the truth. That today *is* an anniversary in itself, but not the one any parent wants to have. Today marks six months since my youngest daughter, Addilyn, was abducted. Six long months with no leads. Six months of hell.

I settle for a courteous smile. "No, thank you. The roses alone will do."

Oscar groans on the way to my Porsche. "Why did you have to find the flowers straight away? I wanted to stay with Ginger Rodgers!"

Ginger Rodgers? "Huh?"

"Ginger Rodgers." He blinks innocently with a shrug as I assist him into the backseat. "That was the name of that lady's cat. It was so cute and fluffy!"

Once the twins' belts are on, I round the car and slip into the driver's seat. Those damn roses taunt me as they rest by the passenger seat. "Ginger Rodgers is also an actress famous for films in the late 1930s. That's why I was confused at first, buddy."

In the rearview mirror, Slonne's eyes light up. "An actress? Wow! Was she beautiful?"

"Yes. She was."

"Like Mom?"

"Nobody will ever be as beautiful as your mother." I rush a hand over my stubbled jaw and suppress a sigh. "Nobody will ever compare to her."

And with that, we're off to Helena, my sister-in-law's house. The same house Valencia has been living in by choice ever since everything went south. The constant daily reminders of the crime that took place in our Madrona home were too much for her, and I don't blame her for it, but at the same time I'm giving Tom Hanks a run for his money for being Sleepless in Seattle… *literally.*

Although the answer may have been long forgotten between Oscar and Slonne, it burns deeply through me. *Nobody will ever compare to her.* Valencia and I have been separated for five months now, yet she's still the most beautiful woman I know. Nothing will ever change that. Nothing.

Valencia was my rock. The only person that kept me going when I didn't think I had it in me. The only person who loved me for me. Fuck, she was my everything.

Stop thinking about her, Giannotti. I'm trying, I tell myself. I'm trying not to think of those perfect hazel eyes and the way she— great, now I can't stop thinking about her.

A silver Mercedes I noticed when I pulled out of the florist distracts me. It was only seconds ago I pledged to stop thinking about the love of my life, and now I want to return to the thought because the car behind me keeps a suspiciously close distance to mine.

It trails behind me even when I carefully weave through traffic and take the side streets. *Is this person following me?* I pump on the accelerator and my heart echoes the motion.

My eyes flicker to the twins who talk amongst themselves and then to the car behind us. I can't make out the features of the person because they're losing momentum. *I think it's a man.* I slow down against the curb of an unfamiliar house and he zooms past me so fast I don't even catch a glimpse of the plate number.

Shit.

Perhaps it's all just in my head?

I settle for that because I don't need any other disturbances tonight. Tonight, after five months, Valencia and I are finally going to have dinner together as a family with Oscar and Slonne.

I flick on my indicator and turn the car around. There's another way I can get to Helena's, but whichever way I plan to go doesn't alleviate the persistent vice on my heart at the thought of seeing Valencia this evening.

I pray tonight runs smoothly. I want us to stop being angry at each other and simply *be—even if it's just for one night*. It's all I want. It's all she wants too. Sometimes we get so caught up in the notions of life that we forget what we're fighting for and begin the blame game.

When I founded Notti Designs at twenty-three, I didn't have the responsibilities I have today. Nine years later, my architecture and interior design company is an award-winning business expanding across the globe. I thought I had my life in control. It was only six months and a day ago when I was a devoted husband to a beautiful woman and a proud father of three. Everything changed when the clock struck March first this year.

I'm not the same man I was before. *It's for the better.*

Yet, deep down, my heart of hearts calls me a liar.

I ignore it.

Valencia isn't only my wife—she was my best friend, the mother of our children, and the only family I know besides them. I can't be any more damn serious when I say I still can't live without her and our children. Even now—*I can't.* They give everything purpose. I should have never taken our unconditional love for granted.

A numbness overtakes my right foot as I touch on the brakes and park in Helena's driveway. The dry orange leaves will crush under my feet the moment I step out and by that time the numb sensation will subside. What won't settle is my regret of not pouring myself two fingers of scotch before driving. It would have settled my mind right about now.

If I didn't have the kids, I would have.

The roses in the passenger seat grip me. I stare and stare until I am transported into a new wave of bleakness. Swirls of red cloud my vision and just like that, I'm back to that dreaded night in April, the one that marked a full month without Addilyn. The one that slaughtered every chance of being a complete family again. The one that ruined me completely.

It was on darn April Fools, yet the events swallowing us whole couldn't have been any more real. I remember it so vividly. How I stepped into our timeless home with one thought in mind—making everything right between Valencia and me. We were at the point of doom. The one where if we didn't fix things then, we would only continue to break. Roses in hand, I knew they wouldn't be enough to fix it all, but it could be the beginning of something.

Then I saw her wedding ring set on the dining room table, alongside two tall glasses of red, and…*I knew.*

Valencia's face said it all.

The tears wouldn't stop streaming down her cheeks and within that moment nothing would ever be the same. I was too late to fix everything between us, but I would be lying if I said I didn't suspect it.

It was my fault. My lost ability to grasp hope and my screwed up reasoning that I couldn't escape. I didn't believe Addilyn was alive and I still don't. Valencia does and ultimately it's led us to a lack of communication and a lack of love. We could be in the same room together and not mutter a single word. Whenever we were forced to, our words soon turned to rage.

No words needed to be said that night as the roses fell by my derby shoes. It's been that way ever since. We haven't been the same people since our baby was taken from us. It's destroyed me. Ruined me. Killed me.

That night…*Dio*.

My heart split in half and when she turned my way, one single glance was enough to bear witness to the strings in her own heart snap. *Separation. Equal custody. We can't do this anymore.* They all meant the same thing in the end—a life without her. A life without *us*.

Neither of us wanted to do it but we couldn't continue living like we were. It needed to be done for the greater good—our children. It was why I didn't retaliate. Why after our decision I slipped off my own wedding band, along with the nearing seven years of our history.

A godforsaken silence emerged between us. I remember it feeling as though a wall had been raised between us. I couldn't get through to her nor could she get through to me. Just like ghosts in the night, Valencia went off to our bedroom and I remember standing in the kitchen feeling everything and nothing.

I remember the first tear slip.

I remember throwing the rings against the wall in agony.

I recall the bourbon.

The sleepless nights.

My father's voice ringing in my ears, telling me how weak I was. I couldn't get him out of my mind, no matter how hard I tried and despite him being dead for almost eleven years.

Now, it's my own children's voices that call me. They tell me to unlock the doors because they can see their Aunt Helena and their two cousins, but my entire body is so tense that I can't fucking reach the button. I'm engulfed in numbness. I cannot move.

My chest tightens and every breath seems like a year. When I glance down at the roses now, a knot lodges in my throat. One that can't be freed no matter how hard I swallow. I see these roses and I'm the nine-year-old boy letting them fall loose over my mother's casket. I'm the twenty-five-year-old groom with the flower neatly pinned to my suit pocket, prepared to devote my life to Valencia Leitner. I'm the thirty-two-year-old man honoring the abridged life of my dear Addilyn.

Gripping these roses, I'm lost.

CHAPTER TWO

Valencia

"W"HEN WAS THE LAST TIME YOU FELT ALIVE?" DR. Michael Eross asks, peering over at me.

His navy glasses are positioned on top of his salt and pepper comb back. There is a softness in his stare and I wonder if it's because I broke down at his last question.

I wipe away the last of my tears. "I have no idea, Michael."

"When tragedy strikes a part of the brain seeks to shelter and protect. We often forget all about the good and focus on desolation instead. But goodness is still there. Dig deep, Valencia."

Dig deep.

That eerie night in March burns through the back of my head at its every memory. If I close my eyes hard enough, the embers are in sight. A glowing flash of auburn crosses in a millisecond. All the pain, glory, and fear is there. Rumbling. Set alight. Elusive. Then, just like that, the fire is replaced by pure darkness. Nothing but numbness overtakes my body. I cannot feel. I cannot breathe. I cannot simply be *me*.

"I feel alive when I'm with my children. But I haven't felt... *entirely alive* since I had my entire family together."

"Is Giulio included in that picture?"

My gaze falls to my left hand. *Holy hell. I thought I could deal with this.*

When I look up, my therapist fades and I have to blink twice to comprehend if this is reality or just another fantasy.

There he is.

The man who used to be my everything, Giulio Giannotti, sits adjacent to me. He leans back in the lavish jade armchair, his broad shoulders expanding as his forearms lean on the armrests. Giulio is irresistibly handsome with that slow, sexy smile and in that tailored navy suit, just like the one he wore when he proposed.

"*Do you still want me, Valencia?*" My name is pure velvet on his tongue.

This has to be a fantasy. Giulio cannot be crashing my therapy session!

My mouth parts to speak but there are no words. His alluring gray-blue eyes hold me in a trance, rendering me incapable of seeing anything else *but him*. The promise held within his eyes takes me back to a time where it was just us. Where we were wholesome and nothing could ever break us.

It's not enough when Giulio kneels in front of me and his hands slither through my chestnut waves. A part of me wants more. *Needs* more. It yearns for him to scrunch up the ends of my hair and scoop me into his arms. To simply kiss me hard and tell me I'm his.

The other part is wary and broken. It advises him to stay clear. To leave me alone forever. That he will never be the one to convince me we'll make it out of this alive.

The devil's advocate tears at my subconscious. We'll never be the same again. Only tantalizing distractions laced with barriers exist between us now.

"Do you still want me?" Giulio's smile is gone now, yet the sparkle in his eyes remains. Unease grows in my core as I spare an extra second to take him in as a whole. A broken man who has lost it all...*just like me.*

"You're not good for me, Giulio."

"No, darling. We're not good for each other," he whispers, his voice both rich and warm. *"No matter how hard we try, even if one day our hearts tell us there's another chance, we'll always be broken.*

"I—"

"Goodbye, Lencia."

"WAIT!" I reach forward but all I'm met with is my glass of water on the coffee table. Heavy breaths greet me and I'm left staring into the space Giulio was only moments ago.

We're not good for each other.

"Valencia...it's okay, you just had another vision." My therapist says, but I'm so mortified I can't even look him straight in the eyes. "Have you been taking your medication?"

I nod. "Sorry. He...Giulio *is* included in that picture, but the people we once were. The way we are now...the lives we lead... it crushes everything we once believed to be true for ourselves."

"It's normal to want someone we once could grasp so easily. It means the person was important to us. Perhaps, still is. Giulio will always be a part of your life. You have two beautiful children to look after with equal custody..." He pauses for a moment to hand me a ripped sheet from his notepad. I ward against it, but for a second I want to correct him on the fact that we have three children. *Three*, because Addilyn is still out there. "Valencia, this is something I would like you to work on in preparation for our next session."

Reluctantly, I glance down.

I, Valencia Giannotti, will maintain amicable behavior with Giulio Giannotti from here on forth. There will be

no arguments. I promise to take time with Giulio to privately sit down and tell him exactly how I feel at this current stage of my journey.

Signed by:
Date: September _______, 2016

"This is to be signed before next week's session. Now, is there anything you would like to add prior to concluding?"

Yes. Tell him. My blood sears in my veins at the very thought. Six months into therapy and I still can't quite grasp the concept of being vulnerable in front of a stranger.

"No. That's all for today."

"I'm more than happy to go over time if you need to…"

"Thank you, but I'm okay for now."

If only it were the truth…

Giulio and I have entered the pits of purgatory. Our torches have been snuffed and only cruel darkness follows. Every single day for the past six months since Addilyn's disappearance, I pray for her every breath. I still feel her warmth give life to my heart, just like when the midwife laid her on my chest for the first time.

When I exit the building, I notice a text from my sister.

Helena: Sorry, I know you're at therapy but it's important. Text me when you can.

Seattle's cool, refreshing air has me buttoning up my trench coat. My boots slam against the concrete as I cross the road in a jog. I'm about to reply when a mother pushing a baby in a dusty pink stroller pulls my attention. I grin at the baby girl whose eyes soften in adoration. Deep unforgettable wounds cloud my every step away from them.

That could have been Addilyn and me.

Valencia: Hi honey, is everything okay?

Helena: Oh, you're out already?

Valencia: Yes. You best believe I'm at your service!

Helena: Serving me is exactly what you were born to do! Haha! Anyway, it's a long story but Ben's parents invited me over for dinner. I'm on my way now with my kids, but felt bad to leave you on a night like tonight, so…I asked Giulio and the twins to come over to keep you company.

I'm hoping I didn't see that last part correctly…but I did.

Facing Giulio is the last thing I want tonight. I've spent the entire day calming myself down from the overbearing weight inside me. I thought that perhaps therapy could stabilize me, now with the news of Giulio coming…well, it deflates me.

Valencia: Send them all my love. It's been so long since I have seen them! I appreciate it, however, you didn't need to invite him. I would have been okay on my own…

I slip inside my white Jeep SUV just as a thought strings in my head.

Valencia: P.S. I hope you're not texting and driving. Tsk…tsk…tsk….

Helena's name flashes on my screen. *Just as I thought!*

I answer with a slight smirk. "Hmmm. So I *did* catch you red-handed, didn't I?"

"Oh, shut up!" She laughs. "I was dictating while Weston was typing. You know teenagers and their ability to win the fastest text championships. If there was such a thing, Weston would receive an F for all the abbreviations he *thought* he could put in them. Boy, who do you think you're texting? Trying to crack the Da Vinci code or something?"

"Mom, stop!" Weston groans in the background.

I smile at my godson's ability to always cut short his mother's sarcasm. He was so wise at times, he seemed eleven going on twenty-one.

"Don't worry. I've got your back, champ. Your mom can be a little *excessive* at times, can't she?" I tease.

"Yeah, tell me about it!"

Helena gasps dramatically. "Hey, I'm right here and I *am* loving all the attention, but still…"

Our laugher feels refreshing.

I send virtual hugs to both Weston and Daisy before asking Helena if she was serious about Giulio coming over. The first indication that it isn't a joke is her silence. This woman *always* speaks, even in her sleep when we were kids. And as much as I love her for it, there are times I search for a remote to mute her.

"You and I were supposed to have a quiet night in, right? I thought maybe if you had the kids over instead it wouldn't make tonight so hard. I'm sorry, lovely, I should have asked first."

"Don't apologize, honey. Of course I want to see my kids." There is nothing more I want in this world. "It's alright; I'll face him. Just don't feel bad, okay?"

"Okay. Well, Giulio was already cooking when we left—Daisy, please don't mess up your hair!—Valencia? Sorry. They are driving me insane—NO! You didn't just throw my Ray-Bans OUT THE WINDOW! GIRL, IT'S NOT FUNNY!—ahh, now I have to turn back. Lencia? Sorry again. Um, what was I saying?"

I can't help but smile. Helena's strength to continuously put on a brave face for her two children as a widow and successful travel agent always inspires me, especially in times of havoc like right now.

"God, I love you! Don't worry, I'll let you go."

"Love you too. Please pray a car hasn't gone over my sunglasses. They're vintage!"

The delightful whiff of basil and fresh sauce welcomes me into my sister's midcentury modern house—it's been home for me ever since the separation. We split all the grocery and utility bills in half, even though Helena threatens to kick me out if I pay them. *She hasn't yet!* Helena says she has it all covered, but paying my portion for me and my twins when I have custody is the least I can do.

I couldn't stay in the house Giulio and I once called home after the abduction.

Even during a separation, there are aspects of oneself only a woman's husband can detect. Like the small differences in my movements or the feelings expressed with the eyes alone. Tonight, I fear that a part of me will give Giulio too much. I fear I'll appear vulnerable and even though I *am,* because of what today signifies, I don't want him to see that.

Giulio is my beautiful undoing.

I met him the day I turned twenty-one. We were married with twins before my next birthday. October fourteenth will mark seven years since we first laid eyes on each other. He knows everything about me, so it's hard to shy away from how I truly feel when he knows me so well.

You cannot hide from your best friend.

In the bright mudroom, my hazel eyes travel down to my Levi jeans and worn out gray sweater. I've seen dozens of women exit therapy doors with cashmere blouses, new season slacks, and superficial smiles. Their hair glows in high buns or sleek fresh blowouts. Mine retains its long wave style 365 days of the year. I'm not like them.

"Mommy's here!" Oscar and Slonne cheer from the hall, their small feet thumping against the whitewash floorboards. My six-year-olds come into view—grinning first graders as of today. I swear they grow tremendously in the three and a half days a week they're with Giulio.

"Hello, my angels! Look at you both!"

Their embrace draws me back to my therapist and that dreaded crumbled paper tucked into my back pocket, simply waiting to be peeled out and signed.

"Daddy said you were at a doctor. Are you sick?"

"No. I'm not sick, darling." I slither my hand through Slonne's soft brunette hair. "He's a different type of doctor who helps me with my problems, just like Melanie helps you and your brother. That's where I was up until now. So, how was your first day back to school?"

"It was good. I loved it!"

Oscar rolls his eyes at his sister's optimism. "She's lying. It was *so* boring."

"Am not." Slonne's smirk is the spitting image of her father's. "I'm smart. That's why I like it."

"Don't make me tell on you!"

"I have no secrets!"

"Yeah, you do…"

"Don't." Slonne instantly deflates at her brother's arched eyebrow. "Don't you dare tell on me."

"You're both equally intelligent." I kiss their foreheads, idly glancing between them in awe. "So, Slonne's got a secret, huh?"

"Yep. She got married."

"Did not. He is my *friend*!"

"He kissed her on the cheek!"

There's a pause and then, "Is that so?"

Him.

I know that soothing, deep husky voice. *How can I not?* It's the same voice that used to comfort my every fear, a voice I could have listened to forever. Now…hearing it whirls me in a pit of angst.

Giulio's playful tone towards Slonne has her smiling awkwardly. "Uh…yes."

"A boy kissed you?'

"Only on the cheek, Daddy! Then he told me he loved me."

"Come here, *carina*." His body shifts in my periphery until he's crouched down beside our daughter. I'm still incapable of glancing over. "Come here so Daddy can tell you something."

It weighs on me that if Addilyn were with us today, we would have never had a falling out. Our marriage would be stable. I would be able to look him in the eye without any reminders.

You can do this, Valencia.

Slonne steps forward and gives Oscar an evil eye.

It's only when Giulio wraps her in the solace of his arms that I look at him. His black hair is slicked black perfectly and his signature short stubble makes my heart swell. *I'm a sucker for stubble.* Giulio is elegantly dressed like the dapper gentleman he's always been. A crisp white dress shirt with a couple of buttons undone brings out his eyes. He wears charcoal slacks and his signature pointed Italian black leather shoes. His sleeves are rolled to his forearms, exposing his Rolex and that beautiful olive skin.

It feels like yesterday when those arms were wrapped around me. The reminders of what we used to have come crashing down violently. So much so that I draw a hand to my throat, stabilizing how dry it's become. I still feel the tip of Giulio's fingers skim over my tender skin. The sensual kisses. The chaste ones. The security. The honesty. My best friend. My *husband.* Everything that once was the Giulio Giannotti I fell in love with and married.

Before the complications.

Before we both changed for the worst.

Before we ended our marriage and everything that came with it.

I know what it feels like to be on the opposite side of that smile—it's *contagious.* Almost intoxicating. I used to be willing to give anything to be the one who made him happy. The twins are those lucky people now, and I hope they never grow sick of our devotion for them. *The same applies to Addilyn.* They will always be on the other end of our smiles, even if we never look at each other in that same way again.

"So, what's this boy's name?"

"Samuel."

"You're far too young for that, darling. I'm the only man who can kiss you." She giggles at Giulio's attack of cheek kisses. "No other boy will do that until you're older and until it is truly what you want. Understood, *carina?*"

"I promise, Daddy."

"Good."

"Don't worry, Ma." Oscar winks and nudges the dip of my waist. "All the girls try and hold my hand at school but I don't want none of them. You're the best hand holder."

"No, you're the best. I love you!" I hold onto him tightly, never wanting to let go.

When I do pull back, Giulio's hot gaze lands on mine and it's all over. The pact I made with myself to reserve all my nerves shatters into a million pieces as those eyes burn straight through me. They're heavenly fire. A perfect concoction of gray with specks of powder blue in the center.

It's as if he can see me. *All* of me.

The twins run off down the hall, and as much as I want to pull away, I don't. I'm trapped in his stare, at his mercy from all the emotion it brings. We remain in silence, inactive in clutching our past, and so instead, we simply stare at one another as if we are in foreign lands. Our bodies are inches apart, so much so that I can feel his hot breath tickle my lips. It shouldn't affect me this much. I should be able to stand and venture into the kitchen.

Instead, I stay.

And so does he. For now…

The vision of him during therapy replays in my mind. *Do you still want me?*

As much as I want to say yes, I can't. Just because I'm still attracted to Giulio doesn't mean we have a resolution. Our sentiments are and always will be laid out on the table. I still feel that beat in my chest when I see him, but it's not for complete infatuation, it's for disappointment. It's heartache and devastation all in one.

Giulio answers the question for me as the muscles in his jaw tighten before he retreats.

I thought these five months would have provided me with a small comfort or some sense of security at least, but it hasn't. Our daughter is still missing and I'm just as heartbroken that we can't see the entire case eye to eye as the first day.

The large tear in my heart mimics the sound that comes from ripping the paper from therapy into shreds. I should have been honest and told Dr. Eross that I couldn't comply. Not only have I let him down, but I've let myself down too.

My mouth waters in the kitchen from the sweet aromas of Giulio's homemade cooking. It soon turns bitter when I open the trash can to throw away the paper, only to find half a dozen red roses.

"Were these for…"

"You? Yes, partly. They were for Addilyn too."

"What happened?"

Shards of smoky glass circle his eyes as Giulio opens and closes his mouth. A sharp, staggered breath escapes me and when I finally do open my eyes again, his back is to me. He's slowly stirring the pasta and by the white noise between us, I know our conversation is over.

This is certainly not what I imagined life would be like marrying the man of my dreams. The cracks only appeared after we became skin deep in a missing person investigation.

"I'm cooking your favorite."

Spaghetti Bolognese.

"Thank you." I fail to mention every single one of his dishes is my favorite. They still are because they remind me of him. *Of us.* Giulio has always been a passionate cook; it's the Italian in him.

In an attempt to distract myself, I focus on the accents of brushed brass and white marble surrounding us. My gaze flickers to the cream herringbone backsplash tiles. The kitchen is dim and moody, producing an elusively false sense of romanticism.

I despise the way my eyes are drawn back to him to analyze his jawline and straight nose. His attractive features, that narrowed waist, and his impressively toned body plunges me from my thoughts as he turns to face me. Giulio should be miles away and I should be able to breathe properly.

"How was therapy?"

"It was…progressive."

"Good to hear. Is everything else okay?" His voice comes out softer than I expected.

Giulio's question remains in the air when I grasp two wine glasses. *No. Nothing is okay.*

"Yes. Why wouldn't it be?"

"You seem different tonight."

"You can judge all that based upon the two minutes we've seen each other?"

"No," Giulio rejects sternly. "I can judge that based upon the seven years I knew you."

I knew you.

The words are toxins against my ears. Past tense. They have no meaning. None.

Giulio fell in love with the type of woman I once was. Before all the shit got in the way. Now, he is left to adapt to the changed person I am. I know this because I find myself doing the same with him. That's what makes it harder, that we have to accept that perhaps we'll never be the people we once were. Coincidentally, it's also the equalizer between us, the only thing that *is* fair as we're both struggling to comprehend it.

I take a step forward and grip the necks of two wine options. "Red or white?"

He gives me nothing.

"Red or white, Giulio?"

Silence.

"Red or whi—"

He interrupts me. "You've known me for nearly seven years, you already *know* which one."

That damn seven-year itch.

I thrust the Merlot bottle into his chest and put away the other. "Pour it yourself."

Leave.

I wish I could tell him to go but the words get stuck on my tongue. I tread away from him in fury to the open plan dining room and set down the wine glasses.

Why is everything a battle with him?

Why can't we see Addilyn's disappearance in the same light?

Giulio believes it's best to let go of the torment and accept her fate. *She will always be in our hearts.* I cannot live like that. I've tried. I did. For him, I tried to accept it, but I can't see it like him nor let go of hope.

Giulio attempted to have faith after the abduction like I did. *She will come back to us.* He tried. He did. For me. Yet, it all came crashing down and he can't part with his gut instinct. And so our diverse outlooks on our daughter's case has caused us the tragedy of a broken marriage. We speak less. Love less. Give up over and over again.

How can he lose hope in finding our baby?

If I thought I escaped the tense waters we call legal marriage separation, I thought wrong. Giulio's warmth consumes me in areas it shouldn't. I'm still by the dining table when his hard chest presses against my back. Electricity awakens my skin as his hands find their way to my shoulders and he massages the knots of tension away. It's the first time he's touched me in months. We mold into one as his fingers dance their way to my exposed neck and my resilience slips ever so slightly as those warm lips reach the shell of my ear. I feel myself slowly sinking into Giulio's world, one where I know if I dip my feet in for too long, I'll never want to get out.

"Valencia," he whispers softly. "Please, tell me what's going on."

See? I knew his innate knowledge would come to bite me in the ass.

Giulio knows my mind and how my body reacts to both dilemmas and pleasure. He knows the little ways to have me come spinning inside his world, and although we're separated, although I shouldn't feel this way towards him, I still do. I'm *home* in the warmth he projects.

"It will feel too real if I say it out loud."

"That's an even better reason why you should tell me."

"Why? What would it help?"

I know it's me. It has always been me. I'm the problem. My desire to hold onto hope caused the fracture in this damned marriage. But I'll be damned to say that I regret holding onto good faith in this investigation. I will be damned if I give up on Addilyn too. I can't.

It hurts too much.

Concern laces his every word and it makes it worse. "Please, Valencia. Talk to me."

Even when Giulio's touch fades, his masculine cologne remains lingering in the air. It's fresh with Italian hesperidium fruits of tangerine and bitter orange. A touch of musk enriched oak and subtle sandalwood creates the perfect blend of sensuous sexiness. It taunts me. Enough to onset the heavy palpitations of my heart.

I turn around so we're face to face. His pulled expression demands something more from me; I decide to set myself free. "I lost my job on Tuesday." The shallow breath I take is hardly enough to fill my lungs. "The truth is I haven't been concentrating at work. With summer ending and Addilyn...I thought I had enough in me to persevere, but parents had meetings with me before the break and voiced their concerns. High school is critical. Art is the most creative aspect of young minds and so during a meeting with the principal the other day, we concluded it would be best if we parted ways."

"Oh, I'm so sorry to hear that. Is there something I can do to help?"

"Not at this stage, but I appreciate it. Thank you."

"It will take time, but you'll get there again. I know you will."

"Thanks. Everything seems just so..."

"...Surreal?"

"Yes, exactly! It hurts knowing nothing will ever be the same until we find her again. I mean, it's six months today, but I haven't been okay since the first day. Addilyn...she has to be out there somewhere."

It's done.

My thoughts are black and white laid out on the table, the same ones that have Giulio back away, *our sweet Addilyn.*

"I'm sorry..." The warmth in his eyes fades until it all comes crashing down. "I can't tell you what you don't want to hear."

Wow.

I can't believe this!

I shake my head the second he walks away and follow him back into the kitchen. "Well I'm sorry, but I still can't believe you don't have one inch of hope that she could still be alive."

"We have to face reality, Valencia."

"This *is* reality, Giulio."

"For *you* maybe."

"And for you?"

The tension between us escalates with a sharp sigh. "To me, this is false hope. You know that. You *know* I feel that way. The hope will only get worse. It is not good for any of us."

The '*not good for us*' line sets me off and I don't know if it's solely based on my vexation or my hallucination of him earlier. "I cannot just forget about her. This, *you* know."

Giulio switches off the stove. It takes two strides for his six-foot-one frame to tower over me. His voice remains composed, but I know that I have pushed him enough. "I never said that. See, this is the issue. You accuse me of things I never say. All I'm saying, all I have ever said, is that we are slowly losing our minds over it."

"Dead or alive I'm still losing my mind over it! There you go! I admit it! I *am* losing my mind over it! That's what happens when depression takes over. It's bleak. It's cold. It makes you feel as though you are on the edge, but at least I have emotion! At least I feel *something!*"

"Do not," Giulio grits with flared nostrils. "Do not throw around a word like that."

"What word, huh? Depression? Is that the word?" Tears form in my eyes as I swallow my pride and open a cupboard, raiding it until I find my small orange plastic bottle. I shove it into his dress shirt with a growl. "Here! Here you have it! I have a fucking right to say the word because that is what I am. Depressed."

Loud thumps of anguish thud in my ears.

Time slows as he takes the bottle from me.

"I'm sorry, Valencia," he whispers after a while, breaking

the silence. "I didn't know you started taking anti-depressants. I didn't mean to cause any…What were you diagnosed with?"

"Clinical depression."

Head still low, his eyes flicker from the label to me. "When?"

"Last month."

"Why didn't you tell me until now?"

I cross my hands over my chest and shrug. "I guess I was too busy catching false hope according to you. While you were out there forgetting, I was—"

"You know how much I loved Addilyn. How much I cared for her. How much I still do."

"Then why don't you believe me?"

"Valencia, please. Let's not do this right now."

"I need to know!" I beg him in a fit of hysteria. "There's this pain inside me and it intensifies every time you shut me out. I needed you and you were never here. You are still never here. Why can't you have faith? Why can't you admit that there is a possibility she is still—"

"BECAUSE IT'S BEEN SIX MONTHS. HOW DO YOU SUPPOSE SHE'S ALIVE?" Giulio's outburst has him slamming the pills against the kitchen counter. Orange plastic shatters and flies everywhere with pills scattering in every direction.

Oh my god.

My heart splits in two, all over again.

I know his actions were unintentional from the way his face crumbles. He was only blindly motioning his hands and didn't expect this as a consequence. *Yet it happened.* Giulio's heavy breaths intensify the anarchy between us. Regret is there, but his anger doesn't subside. Neither does mine.

I'm numb by the sight against the kitchen tiles. At the sight of myself. At the sight of us.

We're nothing but a distorted reality.

I can't hear the television in the distance anymore. It only means one thing: the twins have heard us. We were too loud to even question it. I wouldn't be surprised if a neighbor or the police soon knock on the door with their concerns.

This is what a missing child does to a family.

One of two things is bound to happen. You unite or you fracture.

This is all too much.

"You didn't believe it from the first day. I want you to leave, Giulio," I whisper.

"I didn't mean to…" Remorse paints over his face. "Let me help clean up at least."

I wipe away the tears with the sleeves of my sweater. "No, I'll do it. Please, just go."

Giulio's face weakens and his eyes turn red and glassy. When he runs a hand over his mouth, it doesn't rub away our grief for that absent place in our hearts our love once lay.

We're not good for each other.

Sorrow overthrows his bare whisper. "I'll take the twins with me."

"Okay. It's your night with them anyway."

"It's best if you don't say goodnight. They'll see right through us."

Giulio's right. As much as it pains me, I know that I will be unstable in front of them. I want nothing but security displayed in front of our twins. They deserve to be uplifted by us, even when we don't support one another.

We stare at each other for one last moment before he steps over the pills and plastic. In the distance, I hear our children's faint voices asking if I'm okay. Giulio's response is inaudible, but whatever he does say is the opposite of everything I'm feeling.

My chest tightens the moment the front door slams shut and I'm on my own with nothing but a disaster surrounding me. My sobs lead me to sweep away the plastic and salvage the white circular pills.

They're my only chance at serenity.

The agony at the back of my throat continues as I prepare the pasta dish and store it away. I don't want it now. Perhaps Helena and her kids can have it tomorrow night for dinner.

I pour myself a glass of Merlot and storm through these

cursed hallways to the front porch. I shouldn't have listened. I should have said goodbye to Oscar and Slonne.

The hell with Giulio Giannotti.

The wooden porch step grazes against my jeans as I take a seat. I need to clear my mind from all the nerve endings exploding at this derailed stage of my life. Seattle's air is now damp and blankets of ominous clouds banish the dark blue skies. It disturbs me. It was exactly like this when Addilyn was taken.

Addilyn.

I take a gulp of wine every time I feel a sob surface. The mix of dry and rich flavors blend into a pit of nothingness. I feel nothing. The thoughts cultivate. I miss her so much. *I need her.*

At first, I don't register the movement across the street, but when I do I see an unrecognizable man standing beside a parked gray car. I can't decipher the make, but the bright orange cigarette embers burn deep into the evening. His gaze is straight ahead, studying me.

The tears make him blurry and I take it as a warning to hurry inside. But when I peer out the front facing window, he's already gotten into his car and takes off.

What did he want?

Who is he?

I realize the pounding in my head has been there all night, but my rapid heartbeat took over at some point. I had managed to silence both of them while in company, but now all that answers me is white noise, shattered vows, and the tears which continue to flood my cheeks, begging me for something beyond this suffering.

CHAPTER THREE

Giulio

THE WORDS MY MOTHER TOLD ME ON HER DYING DAY WILL ALWAYS be engraved within me.

All good things end. It is okay because they existed and will continue to exist in your heart, even if you cannot see them. Live in the now. Love in the now. Trust life, amore.

I was only nine years old at the time and it wasn't until I first laid eyes on Valencia that I completely understood the severity of her words.

I recall the day we met, how Valencia entered my company with two dozen of her eager high school students by her side, ready for their art field trip. It was her first year teaching and she had blindly chosen my company, Notti Designs, as their excursion to learn how architecture and interior design can be incorporated into young minds.

That day, which also happened to be her twenty-first birthday, our hands touched for the very first time and the feeling electrified me. We both knew it was more than just a professional handshake. It was more like locking gazes and seeing our entire life in each other's heated eyes. I never believed in soulmates or love at first sight before her, but Valencia changed all that. We looked at each other so intimately, and amid her warm grin and the wave of emotion dictating my heart, I just knew I was going to marry her.

With Valencia, I had finally found somebody to love. Somebody who knew me better than I knew myself. Somebody to share life's achievements and nostalgic moments with. Life works in fucked up ways though. When I married the love of my life, I imagined only death would part us. I never thought we would be saying goodbye to each other and going on to live separate lives without one another. To me, it's worse than death. It's freaking torture because the arguments will stay with me forever, constantly echoing in my mind and manipulating me beyond repair.

We used to be so perfect together.

The fact that I needed to walk away from Valencia last night when all I wanted to do was hold her, was one of the hardest things I've ever done. I didn't mean to yell. I didn't mean to break her bottle of anti-depressants. I didn't mean to be the inadequate man I was to her.

There were so many thoughts circulating in my mind, when Addilyn dominated our conversation, I struggled to get the right words out...*again.*

I just keep on making everything worse.

"Bye, daddy!" Slonne waves goodbye to me by the school gates and scurries off to greet her friends. I keep an eye on this Samuel kid who plants a sloppy kiss on her cheek, his firm arm slithering around her neck.

Watch it, kiddo. That's my daughter.

I'm not ready for it, no matter how cute it may be.

"Dad? I wanna ask you something."

Oscar is still by my side gripping his backpack straps. It's the green dinosaur one he couldn't take his eyes off of during first grade shopping a couple of weeks back. Oscar is the passionate type of kid, the one who doesn't let go of what he truly desires until it's in his little hands. He's a fighter.

They both are.

I fall to one knee with a smile. "Yes?"

Hesitation crosses his expression before fading. "Why were you…"

"What's going on, buddy? We don't want you to be late for—"

"Why were you and Mommy fighting last night?"

Shit.

I pull him into a tight embrace. *Fuck. Fuck. Fuck.* A pang hits my heart. Deep down, I know these little white lies will do more harm than good. Valencia and I aim to be as honest as we can around them; however, there's things they're too young to understand.

"I'm sorry if it scared you, Oscar. There were some issues Mommy and I needed to resolve and we couldn't come to an agreement."

"But you told me to never yell at Slonne. Why did you yell at Mommy then?"

"I made a mistake. A big one." My stubbled jaw grazes his knitted sweater when I kiss his shoulder. I feel so bad. There's a weight in my chest that won't subside. "I let my anger come out instead of talking to Mommy properly. I'm going to apologize and make sure it doesn't happen again."

I stand and take him with me.

He sinks into my right hip and pats down my black tie. "You promise?"

"I promise, *amore*. I'm really sorry I let you down."

"It's okay. I guess everybody makes mistakes sometimes. Even grown-ups like you."

Behind my forced smile, all the strings mastered by the puppeteers who abducted Addilyn snap.

Managing a team and managing my own children often blend into each other. All the grit, compromises, and good judgment is there. With my children, however, I have to be careful with the habits they pick up. Last night wasn't my proudest moment, and I take note of the promise I made to Oscar. Mostly because it's the same one I conjured in my mind all night, lending me yet another restless night.

"You're right." I start. "We all fall off track sometimes. The important thing is to come back up even stronger than before. I promise to be better at navigating my emotion with Mom."

The warning bell buzzes across the schoolyard.

"Okay. Bye, Daddy!"

"I love you, buddy."

"Love you too!" Oscar runs off to class.

Surrounding me, parents scramble to get back inside their cars to begin their days. It's the second day of first grade for the twins and tomorrow marks the beginning of Labor Day weekend. For almost seven years straight we've always embarked on some type of road trip to celebrate the three-day weekend as a family...*that won't be happening this year.*

I slip inside my black Porsche Cayenne SUV and dial my younger half-brother's number.

Marcus' line goes straight to voicemail.

Typical.

Whenever his phone is off in the morning, it means one of two things: he has some farfetched excuse and isn't coming into the office, or he simply hasn't yet *thought* of the farfetched excuse and subsequently never turns up to the office. Either way, he's degrading my business and wasting clients' hard-earned money.

You could say that my half-brother and I have never gotten along. But with my children, he always makes an effort to be part of their lives and he treats them well. I respect that, and at the end of the day, he's part blood. Those two reasons wouldn't stop me from firing him, but I can't because...*well, there is something else...*and so I've learned to deal with it.

Amanda, my assistant, used to follow up with Marcus for me during the day, but it's become apparent that it's a waste of energy to chase a man who can't dedicate his time to a career he supposedly wants. And so the nagging from me stopped, partly due to Amanda taking personal leave. It was a family matter. She opted for two weeks, but I saw the pain in her eyes.

She needed more time.

Amanda has been part of the team since the beginning and has always been a loyal employee. She told me it was her mother and that she was the only one who could take care of her. Without any hesitation I signed her leave for six weeks that very afternoon, not caring that it went against my own policy. I would've given anything to spend more time with my mom. These weeks for her will be tough, and so I assured her that her position at Notti Designs wouldn't go anywhere.

With this, I can't add Marcus Giannotti's bull to my over-flowing agenda today. The one that's already filled with site visits, design renderings, a midday meeting with Tate, and in the afternoon I need to welcome the intern due to take over Amanda's place while she's away.

My turbulent promise to Oscar rings in my ears the entire drive to my office.

Valencia is also on my agenda.

The words I wish to say to her scatter free in my mind. I need to make this right with her. I need to apologize for every-thing…but *how* without causing even more turmoil?

You'll figure it out, Giannotti.

Figure it out.

I'm so perplexed, I almost miss the turnoff.

Almost.

It could have all gone differently.

Addilyn's abduction shifted my entire outlook on life as I knew it. That horrid night forced my family to slip through my fingers. *My fucking family.* I had lost my grasp on the ones I needed to protect the most.

I wasn't there when it happened. I had just touched down in London for a work trip to meet with a developer and estate agent with plans on expanding my company to England, when I received Valencia's distressed call. Addilyn was gone in an instant. Marcus, Helena, and my in-laws had dinner at our single-story house with Valencia. The time came to put the twins to sleep and Addilyn down for a rest. They were all together in the living room after coffee and had innocently mistook Addilyn's soft cries as normal.

Now, we know they weren't.

Just as they stepped out of the house for a brief moment to walk Helena to her car and bid her goodbye, our CCTV showed a male dressed in all black with gloves and a covered face carefully breaking and entering through Addilyn's window. As SPD outlined, the operation was calculated because, as Marcus, Valencia, and her parents reentered moments later, the figure rushed to the front of the house, over the side gate, and slipped inside an awaiting unlicensed getaway car with *my daughter*. The car was seen speeding off, but then disappeared from the purview of surrounding house cameras in the area—a complete Twilight Zone moment, and still to this day the car hasn't been spotted ever since.

SPD worked with determination, but their results ended in no arrests, no leads, no possible suspect, no clues, or even any indication that Addilyn Giannotti was still breathing. With the case now classified as cold, faith was lost on me.

Addilyn was gone.

We didn't even get to kiss our baby goodbye.

I had felt helpless. I was almost five thousand miles away when my family needed me the most. It's my gravest nightmare and not being there is my biggest regret. *It could have changed everything.* Because as soon as Valencia broke the vile news, I told her promises I never kept.

I vowed to her everything inside my aching heart during that call...

We will get our daughter back.

Whatever it takes.

I promise you, darling.

…but days later, I wasn't so sure.

I feared that soon those words would be the very ones to destroy us. That they would be our undoing. And as much I didn't want to be, I was right. Nothing has been the same since. So, for my own sanity, I *have* to accept that Addilyn is in a better place. A place where my mother resides. Up above. Watching over. Protecting us from the looming heavenly flames.

After all, for every single vow spoken, there's a price to be paid. And deep down I have a feeling that ours will endure the ultimate sacrifice—life.

⬥

"A wedding band won't reappear on that finger, no matter how hard you look."

I don't deserve a ring. Not after everything she and I have been through.

I'm not in the mood for Marcus' sarcastic remarks full stop, but especially not on a Friday afternoon. He *finally* arrived not too long ago after claiming he had a *personal emergency*. By 'personal emergency' he means curing his hangover. *Go figure.* I'm almost glad he *did* come in late and missed the meeting with our joint client, Tate, because this is NOT the way to represent Notti Designs.

Oh yeah, that's right. Let's shift the focus on that.

I flick my gaze from my left hand to his deepening smirk. "Couldn't you have at least postponed the bar hopping until this long weekend? Nothing big, just you know *save my company's reputation from collapsing* due to your unacceptable responses to clients, the unpredictability of your house parties and spontaneous trips to Hawaii during a deadline…as I said, nothing *big*."

"You still can't say her name, can you?" He leans against the sandstone desk in the boardroom, a brow arched in challenge. "You're still in love with Valencia, aren't you?"

"Marcus…" I warn.

"What?"

"Let's circle back to your explanation for the house party I suspect you hosted while I was up last night finalizing the meeting for today."

He scoffs at my statement. "You knew from day one that I handle business differently."

"And how is that? Care to enlighten me?"

Oh, how I'm looking forward to his answer the second his eyes roll. His gray button down is fine, but his ripped jeans violate *all* aspects of the company dress code. It also doesn't escape my notice that he's wearing a prohibited Seahawks snapback on backward, taming his short dark curls.

"Well, I deliver differently on deals…*real* different…"

"Go on."

Marcus shrugs, unchanged as he lets it all loose. "Well, while you gift clients Dom Pérignon for their housewarming after a project is complete…I congratulate them by drinking the hell out of it myself."

My heart sinks.

Someone. Tell. Me. I. Did. Not. Hear. That. Right.

Cocking my head to the side, I lean forward in my seat with narrowed eyes. "You do *what?*"

There is no way in hell that he would do this to me. *Well, this is Marcus after all…*

The idiot bursts out into rumbling laughter. "Oh my god! You should see your face right now!"

"You should feel my heart! Please tell me this is some sick joke."

Wiping his eyes, he comes to and nods. "Don't worry. I'm only messing with you, man."

"I can only hope so." Relief doesn't begin to explain it but I'm still staring him down, fuming he would play his card like that. "But don't joke around like that if you want to continue working here, *Capisci?*"

That dampens his sarcasm and rapidly alights a tense glare

of his own. Like a raging bolt in the middle of an unpredictable storm, flashes of our tattered past fester as Marcus' face darkens. The monstrous issues we usually reserve for outside office hours come alive. "The hell you will, Giulio."

"You think I won't?"

"You should think twice before pulling a stunt like that."

"*I should think twice.* Really now?" I challenge as Marcus rises from his seat adjacent to mine and rounds the circular table until he's right behind me. The smooth soles of my derby shoes pivot against the sleek concrete floors as I swivel my chair towards him.

My half-brother is smirking, arms crossed over his chest as if he owns the joint. "Oh, are you forgetting about something, *brother*? You're smarter than that. We both know how it will go when it comes out that businessman Giulio Giannotti is—"

"That's enough." My jaw ticks as I stand, towering over both him and his goddamn ego.

"*Oh*, but I don't think it is." He chuckles coldly and for a flash of a second, I see my father standing before me because their grayish-brown eyes are identical. "If you fire me, you also fire your damn right to freedom. Remember? You *can't* fire me or go against my wishes here. You *owe me* big time. So don't you for one second think you've got the upper hand."

"That doesn't mean you mess with my company!"

"Why, yes it does. I thought you were a man who handles it all, are you not?'

"I am," I hiss, feeling my shoulders tensing up. "I can handle anything you give me."

"Good. Then handle my day to day *and* what Mr. Bryce McCarson is currently doing..."

Marcus knows he'll never win this battle between us, yet he always attempts to raise my blood pressure with his calculating advances. Every fucking time he takes the left field *this* is what he resorts to: blackmail, and lucky for him, it's enough to have me shut my mouth and keep him at the company.

My yellow gold Oyster Perpetual Rolex reads 2:45 P.M. but

I need to confirm with the clock hanging in the hall outside the glass-walled boardroom before I fire somebody else instead. Bryce McCarson and the new intern, Miss Aguilar, are fifteen minutes late and I have yet to receive one phone call explaining why.

A classic McCarson move.

"McCarson is late because he's praying to God. I can learn to handle your ass, but not his. He's not family and has nothing in the slightest to do with our..." I clear my throat, shaking my head in disgust. "...*agreement*. You best believe today's his last day if he's a no show."

"While he has nothing to do with the agreement, he's still my mate. You can't fire him."

I almost laugh. "The hell I can't. He's been in for what? Three out of the forty hours this week?"

"Don't care. You know the consequences...you *owe* me. And forget about what Bryce is doing right now..."

Right now?

Why does he keep on saying that?

Both Bryce and Miss Aguilar aren't here...no...they couldn't be...

"No..." I shake my head repeatedly with an unconvinced laugh. "He wouldn't go there."

"Wouldn't he...?"

Fuck.

He. So. Would.

I take off rushing to the elevator and stab the eleventh floor button. *Prove me wrong, McCarson. Prove me the fuck wrong.* The second I'm in the interior design level, I almost crash into a man carrying a wooden side-table and quickly apologize before sprinting to his office.

This Brit is going to be the death of me. I have no words for this behavior. None. If my instincts are right, this will be the third time in the last two weeks he's tested my patience in this exact manner.

Every move McCarson makes affects my business. My reputation is in the hands of the employees I hire. They're highly educated, dedicated performers, and ace every single client brief... All except for one, Bryce McCarson.

I knock on his frosted glass door. "Are you decent?"

A woman's giggle comes first, prior to Bryce's unintelligible murmur.

For fuck sake.

Bryce has made me see red from the first day he strolled into my company, six hours late. Yeah, I *wish* I was lying. I never expected to meet somebody who appeared at 4 P.M. on their first day on the job. His disregard breaches all my expectations. Every single fucking one.

Damn Marcus and our damn agreement.

I don't have time for McCarson's excuses and step in.

In a rather compromising position, Miss Aguilar is spread out on his desk with only a bra in sight. McCarson is standing behind his desk, his arms laced around her waist and he's laughing at something she said. Bryce, who's usual attire is a charcoal Harley Davidson t-shirt or a sweater and distressed jeans, is from East London. He supports a rich, Cockney accent and has an innate talent of doing the opposite of what anybody says.

His arrogance withers the moment his eyes flicker to mine. "Yeah, about that meeting..."

"May I have a word?"

"Can't ya see I'm preoccupied?" Bryce's disdain towards me shifts and dissolves as he stares down at *my potential intern* with a wolfish grin. "Don't worry, babe. We have all the time in the world."

I'm forced to avert my eyes when they continue going at it. My jaw can't clench tighter, any more and the bone will launch out of my skin and boomerang across the room, knocking this Cockney out. *But now that I think of it, that wouldn't be such a bad idea.*

No.

Get your head in the game, Giannotti.

"Mr. McCarson. A. Word. *Now.*"

"I said wait one fucking minute."

"Miss Aguilar, if you could kindly give Mr. McCarson and I some privacy."

"She's busy too. Get out! We'll tell ya when we're done."

A string of Italian curses spill from my tongue as I leave, slam the door shut and move up in the hallway to cancel their exaggerated moans. *He's doing it all purposely. For the love of God.*

Luckily, I brought my phone to kill time.

Giulio: Let me fire him and I'll give you anything you want.

Marcus: Okay, give me planet Mars.

Giulio: Grow up. Fuck it, I don't need your permission. I'm firing him.

Marcus: Then I'll call the police and tell them everything I saw... EVERYTHING.

And just like that, he wins.

Marcus has my entire life on a string because of one single action when I was younger. One move and now I can't even terminate the contract of this Brit banging a woman at work.

Giulio: You owe me for this.

Marcus: You owe ME.

A few moments pass before Bryce McCarson's door swings open and I intercept Miss Aguilar as she steps out. She glances up at me with a small smile, adjusting the chain of her bag. "Sorry, Mr. Giannotti. I don't think I was cut out for the job anyway."

We were supposed to sign the contract today. Now I need to find a replacement before Tuesday. It's virtually impossible on its own and then if you add the fact it's Labor Day weekend... *Thanks, McCarson!*

"I respect your decision."

"Thank you. Goodbye, Mr. Giannotti."

Inside Bryce McCarson's office, I stare right through him. *Unbelievable.*

I'm beyond livid.

Bryce slips on his infamous vintage t-shirt, failing to cover up his heavy inked chest and full sleeves of tattoos. My patience snapped the first day he worked here and now that I can't even get rid of the guy, I'm climbing the walls. Nevertheless, he isn't going to win this. He made it clear that last time would be the *last time.* Now Bryce leans by his desk, arms crossed, with a smugness in his distant green eyes. "She's really something, aye?"

"Sit down."

Bryce's smirk enlarges and his arrogance leads him to an assertive head shake, all the while whisking a hand through his dark brown hair, the same color as his short tamed beard.

"Sit down."

Nothing.

"Why is it that my children listen better than you and they're six?"

"It's the way to live. You should try it sometimes. You'd probably like it."

I step closer and cock my head to the side, intensifying the bad blood between us with one look. "What did you just say?"

"Ya need hearing aids?"

His rumbling Cockney accent vexes me. The fact he believes he can speak to *anybody* in this manner has me appalled to have him represent my business.

"Maybe if you found a woman to—"

"BRYCE!" I sneer, grinding my molars at every letter. *Is he serious?* "The next time you seduce one of my potential employees or existing clients and act smart about it you'll have the most nominal fragment in correlation to my company. Is that understood?"

"Now, is that supposed to scare me?" Bryce scoffs with a

wide smirk. "Because it's not doing the job…which has me ask, does Marcus Giannotti know about your little scheme?"

"This is *my* company."

"And *Marcus* hired me. If and when he sees fit, *he* will be the one to fire me. Not you."

It doesn't matter what I do, I can never get through to this man. Once he has his trademark smug smirk in place, it doesn't depart from him, along with his dedication to consume me in rage.

Looking out the window, I focus on my heavy breaths. "You drive me insane. You really do."

"Boss," Bryce mocks, "well, that's the first time a man has ever said that he—"

The neckline of his t-shirt is fisted in my grip before he can finish. The cords in my neck tighten, threatening to explode any second now with the amount of animosity coaxing my tongue. Our stubbles cross amongst the commotion, two flickering flames on the edge of engulfing at one more stroke of the match.

"Get. Out. Of. My. Fucking. Building. Now." My lips meet his ear in a staccato hiss. "Go home, screw your head on, and come into the office Tuesday as a proper thirty-year-old man."

"I already did the screwing part."

The unnerving comment has me release my grip and take a solid look at him. Bryce is solemn now, but I know it won't last long. "You'll return Tuesday morning dedicated to your job. Anything less and you'll suffer the consequences. I won't go lightly on you. End of discussion."

"Nutter!" Bryce snarls, always needing to have the last word, and his shoulder intentionally slams into mine during his departure. I don't have the time nor the energy to react.

Not today.

I need to pick up the twins.

Bourbon soothes my throat, numbing my mind and plucking away the strings holding my heart together. I need to call Valencia. I know I do. Now is the perfect time with the twins in bed. My shoulders are tense and I don't know if it's due to the thought of her, the workday I've had, or because I'm in Addilyn's nursery. Yet I fall into the wingback chair and take another swig.

It took weeks for me to step inside this room and now it's the only place I can find refuge. The dusty pink walls. The lingering scent of vanilla. The abandoned bassinet. The godforsaken window. This is where it happened. This is where we lost her.

It still doesn't feel real.

I pick up my phone and call Valencia. The line rings and rings. It draws out. All into one.

She doesn't want to talk.

Why should she after how I acted? After all, I'm just a man. A man not happy with the world. Forced to hate it by external sources. Doing my best to accept it without falling into a conscious pit of terror.

"Giulio?"

She answered.

"Valencia."

"Sorry, my phone was charging in another room. Are the kids okay?"

"They're perfect." My fingers drum against the rim of my glass. She sounds placid, not enraged like I initially expected. "I want to talk, but if you're busy—"

She cuts me off. "No, it's okay. We can talk now. Let me…go to the living room."

"Take your time."

Valencia's hum vibrates straight down my body. The wave travels to my heart first, my abdomen, and then even lower.

"Okay. What is it you wanted to talk about?"

I exhale sharply. "I fucked up last night. I deeply regret speaking to you the way I did. Nobody deserves to be spoken to like that. Especially somebody who is battling through so much. I mean, slamming the pills like that…you know I don't do that type of thing. The last thing I want to do is cause additional suffering. I'm so sorry and I know these words at times are not enough; if there was a way to demonstrate it I would, but it's all I can say now."

There's a moment of silence until her voice cracks through the phone. "Thank you. However, you're not entirely to blame as I was the one to initiate it. Last night was tough for both of us…I'm sorry."

"It still doesn't make it right that I acted that way."

"We just really miss her, Giulio. We miss her and we take it out on each other."

Valencia couldn't have said it more perfectly. That's exactly what's happening between us. It kills me to know that as much as I someday hope we can be on the same team, all I see in our path right now is uncertainty.

"Exactly. Especially the way she was stripped from us."

"It was the worst possible way."

"I feel you." I have a death grip on my phone, as if somebody is seconds from pulling it away, and I won't ever be able to speak to Valencia again. "There's…something else I'd like to discuss."

"Sure, go on."

Now or never, Giannotti.

"Would you be interested in working with me at Notti Designs?"

Silence greets me.

She wasn't expecting this.

She's going to say no.

"You want me to work with you?"

"Yes. Temporarily as my assistant with hours adjusted to suit," I confirm. "It's a six week paid contract. Amanda is on personal leave and issues arose with the internship program."

"Giulio…I don't know."

"I know how it seems, but there's no catch. Perhaps this will be…a good thing."

Perhaps it will change everything.

It would mean seeing her almost every day as apposed only

Sunday afternoon where we swap custody. I pick up the kids from school on Thursdays and have them through to Sunday noon. The encounter is always brief when I drop them off. Sometimes we barely speak.

Her voice softens. "How do we work together when we don't agree on a single thing?"

"For our kids."

"They would love it. The problem is apart from logical reception duties, I don't have the skills. Even I were to say yes, I don't want to be treated with leniency."

"I know it's not your field but no other company understands *our* situation. Nobody will judge you and everybody respects you. If you're struggling with concentration, perhaps this can help it. If it doesn't, then after the six weeks we don't have to ever speak about it again."

"That's the appeal."

She's considering it.

Please, say yes.

I clear my throat. "The job would accommodate to finish before school hours on the days you have custody of the twins. On Thursdays and Fridays, I would expect a 5 P.M. finish."

"When would I start?"

"Tuesday."

"You mean *this* upcoming Tuesday? The day after Labor Day?"

"Well Tuesday typically comes after Monday, but yes that's the one..."

It warms me to hear her beautiful laugh. It's been so long. "You just had to add that in, huh?"

"You know me; I couldn't let it slide." I smile in the dark like a fool. *A fool still in love.*

"I'm glad you didn't." Valencia murmurs. "Can I think abou—you know what? I'll do it!"

The fool's grinning now. "You will?"

"I will. Only because you need the help and I've been losing my mind doing nothing all day."

I can hear the hint of a smile in her voice and it brightens every part of my being. With every single thing that went wrong today, she's the one thing that's right.

"Thank you. You won't regret this."

"Can I ask you something?"

"Of course," I say, my voice low. "Anything at all."

Beats pass, those that match my heartbeat.

"Before we met and you were taking anti-depressants too, did you suffer from insomnia? I have the occasional dizziness, nausea and sometimes my energy just isn't there, but I'm talking *extreme* insomnia. Like some nights I'm okay, but others I'm lucky to get four hours. I haven't spoken to my doctor yet but have heard it's a normal side effect. What do you think?"

My heart aches for Valencia.

Our suffering should have never reached this far.

"I used to be the same. For about a whole year there were only a couple good nights. I had to avoid coffee, imagine how hard that was for me! If your doctor approves, take them in the morning. It'll give your body more time to adjust. Anti-depressants generally take four to five weeks to kick into the system, so never just stop taking them; give it some more time to work."

She breathes out a sigh of relief. "That's everything I needed to hear. Thanks, I'll suggest that to her. As you know it's hard. You can't sleep with all these worries clouding your mind and when you finally do sleep it's always so disrupted. All I want is for them to help me out."

"I want that for you too. I'm always here if you need to talk. You know that, right?"

"I do…and I'm here for you too. Anytime, Giulio."

"*Grazie.*"

"I knew you would understand."

A lump forms in my throat. I can't believe I broke something so precious to her. "I would understand regardless. I took them for years until I felt like myself again and subsequently met you months later. You became my permanent cure. My reason for being in the aftermath of my past and what it led to. You loved me when there was no one else, Valencia." I need to pause to swallow the emotion and the fact that my voice broke when I said her name. "You accepted me with all my flaws and I'm glad you know that even though times are rough…talk to me. I don't want you to go through this alone. Never feel ashamed for taking anti-depressants. If they are helping you to overcome these problems, then that's all that matters. Promise me you'll remember that."

"I promise, Giulio."

"Good. It's getting late. I should let you go."

"Thank you for the job and for calling."

Don't hang up. Think of something else to say.

"It's okay."

Way to go, Giannotti.

"Giulio?"

I launch upright in the wingback chair. "Yes?"

The silence feels like years pass, but in reality, it's seconds; seconds that can change an entire lifetime. If we only shared similar views or could accept each other's, she would be here. We would be confiding in one another, not miles away from each other all tattered and bruised.

"I want to be transparent with the kids about our struggles, but I also want them to be secure and have faith. They don't know about the pills. I'd like to keep it that way for now."

"I won't say a thing."

"Appreciated," she says. "I really have you to thank for the times you were vulnerable enough to show me taking pills doesn't define who you are. It's okay to seek help. Essential, even."

"That's exactly right. Don't listen to what anybody else thinks. You know how your body…" I need to halt my words. The visual alone has me rubbing a hand over my face. "You know how your body feels and so listen to it on the days you need a rest. You're also entitled to unlimited personal days within these six weeks."

"I want to be treated like everybody else but I appreciate it."

I appreciate you, amore.

"It's the least I can do."

"I won't keep you up any longer. I'll see you on Sunday. Goodnight!"

"Goodnight, Valencia."

I hang up the phone with a heavy heart, replaying every single word we just said. All I want to do is talk to her all night long, just like we used to when we were dating, but I fear that if I didn't end the call there, our peaceful conversation would soon devolve into an unforgivable one.

God.

I take a cold shower, each droplet reviving every inch of my body until I'm calmer. I'm sitting on my bed in sweatpants, replying to emails when I sense I'm not alone.

Slonne stands by my doorframe, tears cascading down her cheeks and dripping onto her pink cupcake flannel pajamas. The despair in her stance has me tossing my phone and scooping her in my arms.

"It's okay." My lips press against her forehead in a warm comfort. "I'm here, darling."

"I wanna sleep here with you," she sobs into my neck and I hold her even tighter.

"Of course, my darling girl." After wiping away Slonne's tears, I set her on the bed with her puppy slippers dangling over the edge. My large hands clasp her soft small ones and peer into her dismayed eyes. "Did you have a bad dream?"

"Ye-Yes. Monsters were in my room and then bad guys took Mommy. We couldn't find her and she got lost forever!"

Her nightmares have become much more frequent since the abduction. Some days were more optimistic than others. Group therapy with Dr. Melanie has helped them tremendously and although Slonne frequents it more than Oscar, it settles me to know professional help is there whenever they need it.

"It was only a dream, baby. Mommy's safe."

"But what if bad guys really do something to her?"

"Daddy's not going to let anything happen to her, you, or your brother." I kiss her nose and smile. "I promise. It wasn't real, *carina*. Now you're awake and everything is okay."

I mean it.

I still want the best for Valencia; that will never change.

Nothing is going to happen. *Not again.*

"How do you know nothing will happen again?"

"Because I know what to do now to prevent it, but there's one thing we can do right now."

Slonne's eyes brighten. "What is it?"

That's my girl.

"I have a way to take away the monsters. Think you can help me?"

"Let's do it!"

On the way out of my bedroom, I pick out the classic hand-bag shaped perfume bottle with a deep green python print and gold chain on the dresser. *Decadence* by Marc Jacobs. It's one of Valencia's signature scents, along with the floral vanilla one. But the Marc Jacobs is the only one she mistakenly left here. I guard it like a knight in the middle of a violent battle. Simply opening the lid gives off enough of a sophisticated, woody whiff that I become engulfed in her world.

I check underneath Slonne's bed, the closet, and then in her chest of draws. "There's no monsters here, *carina*, but we have to make sure."

Slonne inches by my side and points at the bottle. "That's one of Mommy's perfumes!"

"Yes. Do you know what else it is?"

Her adorable face forms an innocent smile. "Nope."

"Something very special!"

"Tell me! Tell me!"

"This right here is not only a perfume." I take off the lid and ignore the tightness in my chest at the familiar aroma. "This is also a bad dream spray. All we need to do is spray it a few times and you won't have any nightmares. It only works if you think of nice and happy thoughts."

"Wow! That's so cool! I want to do it."

And so the erratic spraying on Slonne's behalf begins. She runs up and down the room, spraying at every angle. She tells the monsters to leave and go into Oscar's room instead. I ward against that and say how we simply want them to perish, not relocate.

It's a little white lie that doesn't intend to hurt anybody.

I want her to feel secure and have something to cure the heartache in her chest. I know it's there and even though the group therapy is helping, it will take time to reach 'normal' again. Fortunately, our twins have some form of refuge from this madness. Life works differently for me. There is no spray to resolve the questions circulating in my mind.

Who would want to hurt Addilyn?

"If you do have any nightmares, then we need to re-spray it. It helps."

"Thank you. It smells like Mommy." A cheeky grin overtakes her and then I'm being sprayed to death. "There you go! Now you smell like Mommy too. Haha, you smell like a girl!"

I can't help but belly laugh.

Slonne is feeling much better after we slip into bed. Well, partly because she managed to spray my bedroom while I was away to check on Oscar. *Welcome to reminder central.*

It's just past eleven o'clock when she lays her head on my bare chest, her fingers fanning across my abdominal muscles. "Wow, you have six! Are you Superman or something?"

"Not quite, darling. I just want to be a good person."

"I think you and Mommy are the best people in the world!"

"That's very kind. I love you, Slonne."

"Love you." She giggles and pulls the sheets up higher mid yawn. "I miss Mom and Addilyn."

A knot forms in my throat. "Let's try and get to sleep, okay?"

"Okay. Will you save me just in case the monsters still come in?"

"I promise you they won't come in, but if they do, I'll turn into Superman just for you."

That sets her off in a fit of laugher triggering mine.

"Yeah, and Mommy can be Wonder Woman!"

The knot intensifies.

"Sounds good to me. Goodnight, *carina.*"

"Night, Superman."

I already know I won't sleep tonight. A persistent tightness renders me too uncomfortable to simply lie here. To be still and stable, without resistance. But I need to push right through it for Slonne; she needs to get some rest even if tomorrow isn't a school day.

My fingers thread through her soft waves and just like that, every single moment of our past comes crashing down. It has me holding onto her tighter. I want Slonne to know that I'm never going to leave her. That she is safe.

Right here.

In my arms.

In her mom's.

With all of us.

Valencia's scent lingers in the air around me. It torments my every breath and has me yearning for an escape. Some type of way out of constantly thinking of her. Yet, all I'm capable of doing is thinking of her and that platinum diamond wedding ring. Just the thought is enough to transport me back to when I promised her a lifetime of my love and reverence. I would do anything to witness that diamond sparkle on her finger now, for it to catch a glimpse of the luminous moon creeping through the French doors' sheer drapes and fill the ceiling with rays of kaleidoscopic shapes of the night.

It's here where the persistent ticking of the alarm clock terrorizes my mind. *Tick tock. Tick tock. Tick tock.* The same fastidious sound is resonating in my chest. *Thud. Thud. Thud.*

It beats wildly for several different reasons. All of which are significant. All of which I love. All of which hurt so deeply, that it has me hopelessly whispering into the dreary darkness.

"I miss them too."

CHAPTER FOUR

"I HEARD ON THE NEWS THAT LAST WEEK MARKED SIX MONTHS. It must've been so hard on you." Zoe smiles sadly, observing her freshly red manicure against the sunlight. "Do you think I should have gone for a brighter color?"

"No. I think it looks good."

"Hmm…true. So, have there been any more leads that the press won't reveal?"

"Not currently, the case is virtually cold due to the lack of clues. It's just been a nightmare!" I push through a smile, ignoring the bitter taste pooling in my mouth. "I'm sorry. I have to go, Zoe."

"I can imagine it's tough for you and your husband. Well… separated husband, yeah?"

I nod.

I had just dropped off the twins at school and was about to get inside my car when Samuel's mom, Zoe, stopped me. It's not my intention to cut her off, especially since the twins only started first grade under a week ago and I *do* want to get to know everybody, but being late this morning, my first day working for Giulio, isn't in my plans.

"Is he seeing anybody?"

I arch an eyebrow. "Who? Giulio?"

"Yes! Who else?" She deadpans with a wicked smirk. One that makes me uneasy. "Yes, of course I mean Giulio. We've never spoken but I've seen him a few times during pick up and drop off. Samuel and Slonne are friends after all… Damn, he's sure a heavenly sight!"

I'm taken aback.

Okay…how do I respond to that?

"Oh come on, I thought you guys were separated anyway. What's yours can be mine too, right?" Zoe throws her head back with a laugh. It reels me in for all the wrong reasons.

Since we first met last year there's always been something about her that was odd. Something I couldn't quite pinpoint, and to be frank, I don't appreciate her having her cake and eating it too.

A gust of cool breeze fans her perfectly curled blonde hair. She's gorgeous and from our brief conversation last year, *married*. She had moved to Seattle with her family ahead of the kindergarten year from San Jose when her husband was transferred. Weeks after settling in, his work needed him back in California and Zoe hadn't wanted to move and so he's been flying back and forth on weekends for the past year.

So, it's understandable when Zoe looks at me with those perfectly curled lashes and tight pink bodycon dress *asking about Giulio*, I don't get the best feeling.

"Look…I'm sorry, but I have to go now."

Her glowing expression dims. She crosses her hands over her chest, spilling more cleavage than I needed to see. "I wasn't joking, Valencia. Some days are tough. I'm not going to steal him from you…just a little something something. I want to organize a play date for Slonne and Samuel with him. You know, so the kids can play together on a Friday afternoon. You're not together anyway and it's just a *play date* for the kids, Valencia."

What?

A little something something?

Hell no. I'm sensing ulterior motives for this 'play date' cover up.

"I don't think he will be interested, Zoe."

"In me?"

She seems offended and I suppress the urge to roll my eyes. This entire situation is ridiculous! She's married! "No, I meant in general. We both have a lot on our plates and—"

"And Giulio can be the judge of whether he's interested or not. This is for the kids; don't you want Slonne to have a friend beside her brother? Come on! Now, are you going to give me his number, or do I have to wait until I catch him picking up your kids one day?"

There's no way in hell!

I'm not jealous, but Giulio will see right through the 'play date' motive with her protruding love heart eyes and far from subtle *wedding ring*. He would decline any offer simply because it's not our objective. Technically we're still married and we made a deal to not venture into new waters until we formally decided if this separation would resume or end in divorce.

My heart beats furiously as I grip my car handle. Never have I had to associate with anyone like her. "I don't think it would be a—"

"Are you really that delusional, Valencia? Can't you see it?" Zoe hisses coldly. The space between us narrows until her cheap perfume runs through my airways. "Giulio doesn't want you. That means he can go around seeing whoever he wants. That woman can be me. That woman can be somebody else. I'm sorry about Addilyn's disappearance, but freaking pull yourself together, girl. You have to move on sometime, and for god sakes, smile more often!"

"You better—"

"What? Watch my mouth? No, babe, I won't. But you better keep an eye on those windows. Ha!" She taunts with a victorious snarl. "One of these days I'll invite Giulio to a play date with the kids and then you and I can have a little chat. Goodbye, Valencia."

Buh-bye.

I'm too taken aback by her words to say anything. I despise confrontation, and although Giulio and I have stepped over the line, I would never make a scene with somebody I barely know.

My jaw remains on the ground as she proudly sashays to her car.

What the hell just happened?

"For the third time, I cannot permit you to enter the premises any further."

"Sir, you don't understand. I don't have my ID because this is my first day!"

"I've heard that before."

I clench my fists at the security guard. His stare degrades me, threatening everything I pushed aside on the way here. After Zoe, I had managed to calm myself down. Some people aren't worth the time and if she likes insulting others, that's her issue to deal with.

Just when I thought today could be looking up, the guard won't allow me access to Notti Designs. He stopped me at the downstairs lobby, right by the elevator. I already flashed my license but what he seeks is a keycard. *One I don't have!* I've never seen him before, meaning he must be a new guard with no clue that I, in fact, *am* Mrs. Giulio Giannotti.

Nerves drill at my weak spots. It happens whenever I'm on edge.

The guard remains calm during the entire altercation, his hands never once straying from his hips. I should know better than to push my luck. His fingertips are brushing his holster and

I'm not looking to start any chaos, but I *do* need to get through him.

"I'm technically married to the man who owns this company. You have got to believe me when I say this is my first day!"

"I've heard that one before too. Look lady, why don't you go home and start a fan club for Mr. Giannotti instead. Okay?"

My jaw involuntary drops.

He can't be serious!

What is wrong with people today?

"I don't know what else to say."

The guard glares at me pointedly. "How am I supposed to know you truly work here? Oh, that's right I don't. I can't help you without a keycard. Is that clear?"

"But I—"

"I said is that clear?"

"No." Giulio's voice comes from behind. "She's with me. That's the only proof you need."

An aggravated Giulio approaches from behind me, gripping a leather suitcase. The guard wordlessly allows him entry and I finally feel secure enough to step through behind him.

I thought wrong.

The guard reaches out a hand towards my shoulders. "Lady, you can't enter."

Giulio's narrowed gaze drills deep into the man's shaven head as he grips his outstretched wrist, preventing the guard from touching me. "And I said *she's with me.*"

"Sir, when you hired me you specifically stated security was a crucial factor. My conditions are every employee needs identification. Every client or associate must present confirmation of their meeting. She could be a fraud! I—"

"I am *very* well aware of the conditions as I am the person who made them. I have three things for you. One…" Giulio whips out his phone and begins to scroll. "Do not *ever* make the mistake of nearly touching her again. Two. You're fired. And three…" The security guard tenses as the device is shoved in his face. "Valencia Giannotti is no fraud. She is my *wife.*"

"Oh…" The man glances between the phone and me. "Oh, I'm extremely sorry."

A glimpse of the white lace is enough to launch my trembling hands inside my coat pockets. The photo Giulio showed him was one from our wedding day. *Holy…my heart is pounding.*

Breathe.

Giulio disregards the apology and only reiterates that this is the man's final day.

Well…I didn't expect that.

I'm glad Giulio's hand falls to the small of my back as he guides me to the elevator because if it didn't, I would still be standing in shock. After our discussion the other night, I felt we took a progressive step forward and now I feel the same inside this elevator. Although I can't quite meet his eyes and my lips are pressed shut, our tension is eased—peaceful almost.

But how long will it last?

I needed to get my feet back on the ground after losing my teaching job and although working for him could be another mistake, the appeal is blinding. Giulio was right. Nobody else will understand my uncontrollable outbursts of emotions. Nobody else will say; *talk to me, I don't want you to go through this alone.* Nobody else will understand the intensity of my heartache like he does. He will accommodate me and as selfish as it may sound, I agreed for those exact reasons.

I want to be a better mother and woman; that means stepping up and taking opportunities that scare me. I haven't taken many steps into the unknown during my life and the first is always the most frightening one.

I only hope everything works out as planned.

"Valencia?"

I turn to Giulio, blinking away my thoughts. "Yes?"

"The first thing you can kindly do for me this morning is contact backup security guards on the system. I permit you to hire the most proficient guard to commence effectively immediately."

"Of course. I'm sorry to have caused so much trouble already."

"None of this is your fault."

I massage my throat. "Maybe you shouldn't have been that tough on him. He was irritating me, but in the end, he was only doing his job. Are you sure you want to fire him?"

When Giulio rushes a hand through his dark tousled hair, his bicep tenses through his black button up. The coat he wore seconds ago is draped over his right forearm and I get lost in his perfect morning stubble.

Giulio takes a good look at me and nods. "Yes, I'm sure of it. He deserved it. The moment he made the mistake of even thinking he could touch you, he deserved it."

I have nothing further to say because I'm mesmerized by just how electrifyingly potent his gaze is. It's a tug-of-war between what my head says and what my heart wants. It's for all the wrong reasons, and as much as I know it, I also can't look away. So, while I'm ogling the hell out of him, I make a mental note to contact security on the system and obtain a keycard before I cost someone else their job.

God, I never wanted anything like that to happen.

Notti Designs HQ is located in the heart of downtown Seattle on 5th Avenue, inside a modern twelve floor building with exterior glass wall panels. The company shares the building with two other businesses, coincidently both in the real estate field. Each business owns four floors with Notti Designs occupying the top floors.

The last time I stepped inside of Notti Designs was half a year ago. Most of the furniture is different. Giulio is a perfectionist and strives for change, especially with weekly new hot items and seasonal design trends.

Aside from an Italian marble interior accent wall with a golden business sign, glass wall hallways run through the entire company. An emerald velvet couch and matching armchairs are the statement pieces in the open plan waiting area and surround a glass table styled with eccentric gold pieces.

Further along, the area blends into reception. Kayla is at her sandstone desk, typing away on her Mac in unbroken concentration. Her straightened dark hair is short, one side curled behind her ear to reveal a classic golden hoop earring. It complements her glowing medium dark skin and perched purple glasses. *This is exactly how I remember her.* She's been here since Giulio founded the company and we have become close through the years, which is why it has been so tragic that our friendship is yet another thing that has waned during the separation.

Kayla waves as I pass and I mirror the action with a smile.

"She's missed you," Giulio informs me.

"I've missed her."

He simply nods, his vision zoning straight ahead as we continue to his office.

Notti Designs HQ is divided into five departments across three other floors of the building; the design center on the eleventh floor, the development and marketing team on the tenth, and the construction administration, management, and human resources on the ninth.

There's also a warehouse less than ten minutes away that I've only been to a handful of times. It holds their stock, staging items, and additional storage. Giulio controls just over one thousand employees across twelve successful global firms, assisting clients in achieving their dream homes and commercial businesses.

We stop short at the end of the hall and Giulio begins explaining that this will be my work station. His office phone begins blearing and when he doesn't make an attempt to move, I urge him to take the call before he misses it. Giulio seems reluctant to leave me at first, but eventually gives in and promises he'll be less than two minutes before rushing into his office.

I stare at his door sign longer than I know I should.

GIULIO GIANNOTTI
Notti Design Founder, Chief Executive Officer and
Senior Architect

A couple of feet from Giulio's office is my area as his acting assistant. A large concrete desk expands from the sunken wall panel, and around it is everything I'll need.

I think back to after the call on Friday and our brief encounter on Sunday where during swapping custody, I signed the contract. That afternoon was the first time since the separation that we were able to look each other in the eye without it escalating into an argument.

It was odd spending time alone with the kids yesterday for Labor Day without Giulio. Every year we used to embark on a three-day road trip. Last year was San Juan Island, the one before that Vancouver, Canada. Although I loved the city, I also enjoyed escaping and roaming free with my family on adventures—a breath of fresh air.

I missed it this year.

Get used to it.

I take a seat behind the desk and swivel my chair to switch on the Mac. I'm surprised to find my name already programmed on the screen with a circular 'V' profile icon. No password is required and I wonder if that's solely based upon the countless times I've locked myself out of significant accounts in the past.

It's something only *he* would know.

Giulio steps out of his office and gives me a brief rundown of the system, all the while I struggle to find a single fitting word to say. Despite our best efforts, the growing tension is still there...but it's not awkwardness, it's something else I can't quite describe. Still, it can be cut with a knife and I hate that we've gotten to this point.

After his Ted Talk, I thank him and he trails into his office. I'm left glancing at his closed door, wondering if I should be calling him by his last name. *My last name. No. That's ridiculous.* Surely I can call him by his first name...no matter how many reminders it brings.

It's nine-thirty when Giulio's door opens next.

"Valencia?"

"What can I do for you, Mr. Gia—I mean Giulio! Sorry."

Amused, Giulio smiles slowly and I love the crow's feet that come out to play. I haven't seen him smile in what seems like months…*probably because it has been that long*. Those allusive eyes don't leave mine; they contrast against his dark stubble and hair and by the time he leans by my desk with crossed arms and I take in a whiff of that hypnotizing sensual cologne, I think somebody should arrest me for gawking.

"Giulio. I'm Giulio to you."

My lips twitch upright. "Right. Just like I'm Valencia to you?"

"Exactly. You see, we're getting the hang of things now."

Maybe you are, baby. Not me.

Ahem…I didn't just call him that in my head…

He motions towards the computer. "Need any assistance?"

"No, don't think so. I just hired a guard. His name is Lee and he's proven himself to be highly experienced based on his past employment. He has a clean background check and has been in the business for the past twenty-five years. He'll be here within the hour."

"I knew I could count on you."

"Maybe working here won't be a bad thing after all."

"I certainly hope not."

"Same." My cheeks flush as I glance back at my Mac. There's absolutely nothing I need to look at, but his hot gaze digs into me so deeply I think I may become blinded by him.

Giulio has me all flustered just by his presence alone. It's dangerous. *Very dangerous.* Because at the same time I don't agree with many aspects of the man he is now. His views. His lack of hope. His mind. Yet, his charm remains in my heart… along with his touch and the sentiments I've tried to bury. This is why determining my relationship with Giulio is such a constant struggle within me. It's odd to me, how quickly we've shifted from being in plain desolation to concordant this morning.

"Wasn't there something you needed to ask me?"

"Uh, yes." Giulio clears his throat and the smile fades. "I wanted to warn you about a new employee. An interior designer, Bryce McCarson. He may need your assistance every once in a while. Allow it *sparingly*."

"Will do."

"*Oh*, and one more thing."

I flick my attention to him at the softness of his voice. Giulio rushes into his office and returns seconds later with a piece of paper.

A smile pulls up the corners of my mouth at the drawing made by Oscar and Slonne. From what I can make out, a woman who's presumably me sits at a desk with abstract flowers sprouting from the floor. I understand it perfectly. The picture warms the parts of me I always throw darkness into. Above the woman is a sign which reads: * **Mommy's first day working with Daddy!**

"After I told them the news on the weekend, they drew this up. However, I forgot to bring it with me on Sunday."

"It's beautiful!" I set it on my desk with a grin. "I'll have to thank them tonight. Thanks!"

⁕

The day goes better than it began. Giulio and I communicate professionally with business emails and brief intercom discussions. He's had a busy office day with in-house meetings, client phone conferences, and design production.

My concentration sways from time to time to the gaping hole in my heart. Every time I think of Addilyn, my entire world stops. I'll never be able to comprehend why somebody did this to us. But I feel as though my leap of faith to work at Notti Designs is paying off. I can be myself here and that's something I truly value. I don't need to pretend I'm ecstatic or hide the tears prickling my eyes, unlike at my previous job.

Aside from Marcus' office straight across the hall, who hasn't shown up yet, Giulio's office and my work desk are secluded from the rest of the firm. It's something I love—the pure bliss of not being in an overcrowded space employees pass.

During a rare quiet moment, I make a dash to create my

keycard and I collect it just before lunch. Upon returning to my desk, Kayla formally welcomes me with a tight embrace. "Oh Valencia, it's so good to see you!"

"It's been so long, Kayla!"

"Tell me about it! I've missed you! Let's not lose touch like that again."

Kayla is like another sister to me. We used to be inseparable. When Giulio and I began dating, I would call him at work and she would transfer me. Somehow, that made me feel less flustered about calling him. Giulio had told me I could call his cell, but calling the girls always felt more comfortable in case he was in a meeting.

Following Addilyn's abduction and my separation from Giulio, Kayla and I spent months without talking. Last time I reached out to her, she had told me she didn't want to make things uneasy between knowing Giulio at work and me in her personal life.

Not anymore.

I want to change that.

During these past few months, I've lost a lot of people due to the struggles that come with depression, people I thought I would never lose. Having Kayla as a friend again means more than she can ever imagine.

We have lunch together and talk about everything we've missed in the last months we didn't see each other. It feels good knowing I can confide in her again. She tells me of how she's still in a long-distance relationship with her boyfriend, Zac, who lives in New Zealand and how her brother has moved to Vancouver, Canada to advance in his studies in Performing Arts. I tell her how I've been attempting to cope during these months and how anti-depressants have been slowly helping, but that I won't fully recover until Addilyn is back in my arms.

I'm tempted to go on further about Addilyn, wondering if Kayla shares my hope, but I derail and tell her a few stories of Oscar and Slonne which brightens the mood. I explain how I haven't touched a paintbrush this entire time except for when I was teaching. I lack both motivation and inspiration, no matter how many times I pray for those bursts of colors to rectify me.

Lee, the new security guard welcomes us with a smile upon returning. He's someone I looked at once and instantly knew I made the right choice.

"Back so soon?"

"Yes, it was only a quick chat!" I say.

"Good to hear," the guard smiles. "Oh, I'll be seeing you at 3 P.M., Mrs. Giannotti. Mr. Giannotti gave orders to accompany you to your car."

"He did?"

Lee nods, unknowing to the fact Giulio hasn't made any mention of this to me.

"I'll be okay. Thank you for the consideration though."

"Well, it's quite okay, Mrs. Giannotti. However, I'll still accompany you to your car."

"Okay." I force a tight smile. "Oh, and you can call me Valencia."

"Of course."

Kayla turns to me the moment we enter the elevator. "I take it you didn't know Giulio requested Lee to do that?"

"Not at all. I appreciate the gesture, but it also makes me feel like I'm incapable of getting to my car without something happening, you know what I mean?"

"I know, babe." She pulls me into a side hug. "But perhaps this is Giulio's way of lifting the white flag or showing that even through all of the shit happening, he still cares."

"Just like a picture is worth a thousand words."

"That's exactly it, babe."

My intercom buzzes the moment I sit down at my desk. "Giulio?"

"Not quite, babe. Take another shot." A thick Cockney accent stumps me.

Huh?

My eyes narrow, until I realize it must be the relatively new interior designer. "Mr. McCarson?"

"The one and only. Aye, why don't ya com—" He gets cut off as Giulio's voice takes over. "Valencia, please excuse him. Could you kindly bring me Tate Rogers' architectural drawing from storage? Thank you."

The entire storage room towards the design corner is filled with storage cabinets, each with their own compartment and label. I scan across the appointed section until I find the correct white cylinder tube.

In passing, some of the workers in the design center greet me while others are head down in their work. Their dedication impresses me. Crossing the hall to boardroom one, I stop short in front of a mirror. I tuck the tube underneath my arm and focus. *Breathe.* I can barely look myself in the eyes. *Smile more,* Zoe's voice taunts me, *you have to move on.*

Adjusting my black pencil skirt and tucked-in white blouse, I tell myself I can do this without anybody else's influence. Everybody copes differently and that's okay. People will always talk, but I don't care if people judge me. I can block out everybody…except Giulio.

I can't block him out.

We were supposed to be teammates, life partners.

How does the dance go when one learns a whole different routine and the other isn't willing to adapt? That's exactly what our marriage is now—an unsung melody, an absent dance step, a broken record.

Peering inside the glass-walled boardroom, Giulio sits at the end of the table with six other employees on either side. A full speed in-house meeting is underway. The brightness beaming across the entire room draws a smile to my lips. You can see the Space Needle from here and on not so gloomy days he once told me Mercer Island is also possible.

I step inside without knocking to Giulio addressing his team. "Are you certain?"

"Yes," a man responds. "It may be the only chance to advance the design."

"Go on. What will it entail?"

"Tate wants no altercations in the west wing; that leaves only the east to compromise."

"No possible amendments in the south wing?"

"No, I overlooked them. This is why I need some assistance, Mr. Giannotti."

As I turn to shut the glass door, a loud bang reverberates through the room and everything falls silent except for the immediate exclamation that follows.

"Aye! For fucks sake!"

Holy shit.

I realize the end of the tube tucked under my arm has collided with something hard and I turn to find a man with short dark brown hair, the top tousled back with sides cut to a gradual low fade, clutching the back of his head. My jaw hangs open when he swivels his chair around in my direction.

Not lucky me.

He seems like a tough guy, and an intimidating one at that. His deep green eyes focus on mine with knitted brows. "I only had one brain cell left in me head and ya killed it!" His Cockney accent is new to me.

"I'm so sorry, sir. I didn't mean to—"

"It's alright, babe." He cuts me off with a wink and his grin widens into a full blown smug smirk. The brazen bitterness from moments ago vanishes. "Ya can make it up to me one day. That's fair, innit?"

"Bryce!" Giulio sneers. "Leave her alone and enough with the drama."

Bryce dramatically gapes. "You, calling me dramatic? Have *ya* ever been personally hit in the head with one of them tunnels of death? My whole life flashed before me eyes."

So this is what Giulio meant when he said to assist Bryce McCarson *sparingly.*

Giulio's gaze meets mine. "Please ignore him. Was it easy to find?"

"Relatively."

He thanks me as I set the tube down.

I'm mortified by the accident. At least Bryce is only an employee. I don't want to imagine the outcome if instead of an in-house meeting, it was an important business deal with clients. The thought alone has me cringing inside.

Way to go, Valencia.

Across the table, two older women return to their discussion. They're in deep conversation and swiping through an iPad between them. On the left side of Bryce sits Lance Hilton, Giulio's closest friend and project manager at the company. On the right side of him is a man I don't recognize, the same one who was speaking before my disturbance.

Lance shoots a kind smile my way and I mirror the action.

"Ya leaving without formally introducing yourself?' Bryce nods towards my hand near the handle. A smirk takes over his face at my parted lips and all of a sudden those green eyes drop the length of my body, slowing at my waist and then again at my legs.

Breathe.

Out of the corner of my eye, I note Giulio watching Bryce, taking in his stance as the Englishman rises to his full height and extends a hand. I reluctantly shake it. Dark shadowed tattoos cross the back of his hand, but I can only make out a detailed rose and a thin cross.

"I think ya like 'em. Miss…?"

"*Mrs*," Giulio jumps in, a hiss in his delivery, "Mrs. Giannotti."

Bryce takes one good look at me and chuckles. "*Aye*, Mrs. Giannotti. I thought you two were separated, nah? That's what they all say, innit true?"

I nod. "We are separated. However, this isn't a conversation for the office."

"Well, in that case, a new bar opened up near—"

"For the love of god, Bryce."

"Oi, shut your mouth, Giannotti! I weren't even talking to ya. I'm talking to ya Missus."

"*Exactly*," Giulio grits. "You're talking to my *wife* about going to a *bar* during *work*."

"And the problem is…?"

"Guys! Let's just let this go, okay?" My attempt to defuse the tension between the two men does little to help. They're left glaring at each other, brooding with pressed lips. It's as if they have some sort of personal vendetta against each other.

I'm definitely missing something.

There's no denying the confidence that spills from Bryce McCarson. I've only known him for a few minutes and he's already claimed himself to be the type of man who isn't afraid to say exactly what's on his mind. A no filter type of guy.

McCarson's dominant personality intimidates me, even though it shouldn't. It's less the tattoos and rather his penetrating stare. How it begins diluted, destined to suck you in for all the wrong reasons. A hint of caramel blooms by his pupils, illuminating the lightest features.

"I ain't trying to be rude…" Bryce begins. "But is it possible to call you something other than Mrs *Giannotti*?"

"You can call me Valencia."

"Oh, does the 'cia' in ya name stand for 'cute intelligent attractive' woman?"

"*Enough.*" Giulio pushes off his chair with so much force his knees slam against the edge of the table. He doesn't react to the pain, but I know it's there in his clenched jaw. "Apologize to her right now, McCarson."

McCarson's eyes roll. "He doesn't like to share you, does he? We'll need to change that cause imma need ya from time to time, Valencia." His cockney accent thickens and so does the damn plot. It's wicked the way certain words like 'you' change to 'ya' whenever he becomes passionate. "You'll allow me in, won't ya? Allow me in ya schedule that is. I promise I ain't *that* scary."

I clear my throat.

Smile.

Nod.

Do anything!

I have never met anybody like him before, and now as I stare up at this man with this mysterious aura surrounding him, I'm pretty sure I never will again.

"Of course, Mr. McCarso—"

"Call me Bryce."

"Okay, Bryce."

"Hmm, nah. Actually, call me Mr. McCarson."

"Noted. And once again, I'm so sorry about before, Mr. McCarso—"

"Nah. I don't like it. Call me Bryce instead of—"

"JAMES!" Everybody turns to Giulio who's fuming. He rubs his face before directing one hand in the Englishman's direction. "Well, which one is it? Huh? Your first name? Your last name? Or, should we begin calling you by your middle name instead? You're being preposterous! Sit down. Don't you dare play around with anybody else, especially Valencia. Never. Ever. Fucking. Again. *Understood?*"

Woah.

I have never known Giulio to be this worked up. Especially not the way each word was presented with a staccato pause to emphasize his point. Bryce must really push his buttons.

The room is at a standstill, my heartbeat the only sound blanketed by the white noise. Everybody's gaze is on Bryce, and his is on me. That smug smirk remains, and all the while, he takes a step closer to me, his bergamot cologne infiltrating my air. "Call me whatever ya want, babe."

I need to look away and remove myself from this situation. Not because I'm entirely uncomfortable, but because of Giulio. He knows his employees better than me and if he found it right to defend me, I know better than to press it further. Giulio knows something I don't and that's enough to have me escape Bryce's hypnotic gaze.

"Giulio, is there anything else I can do for you?"

He appears so consumed in his own thoughts that he misses my question completely. He's watching Bryce James McCarson so intently that I'm left baffled as to why he would hire somebody like him in the first place when it's evident that he can't stand him. Then it hits me…I'm also his employee and I don't exactly see eye to eye with him either.

I reach for the door handle for the second time. "Giulio?"

Nothing.

"Don't worry, I'll say it for him…" McCarson winks and goes on to click his tongue. When he lowers into his seat, his left arms bridges over the back of it, purposely widening his broad shoulders. "That'll be all for now, babe."

CHAPTER FIVE

Valencia

"THERE'S NOT ENOUGH PROSECCO TO CELEBRATE YOU GOING into day two working at Notti Designs!"

"It's a full bottle, Helena!"

"And when has that seriously *ever* been enough?" My sister grins, pouring two tall glasses. "You deserve it! There aren't many women out there that'll willingly work with their separated husbands. Especially with the lurking turbulence of the abduction."

I swallow down some of the bubbly aromatic wine.

Addilyn.

Her name alone offsets the beading tension in my body. I had been okay during our Spin class this morning after taking the kids to school early, but fear always set in during the early morning and overnight. Anxiety doesn't let me sleep, and when I do, I wake up in hot sweats, shivering in panic attacks and gripping my pillow for comfort. What hurts is it's never a dream that brings it on—it's reality. My baby girl is facing this cruel world alone and it tears me apart knowing I can't do a single thing.

"I just hope it helps the dynamic between Giulio and I. Yesterday was a good day. It made me think back to when everything was okay. It was as if we were…at peace with the world."

Helena sinks into the couch beside me, her hazel eyes sparkling. We share our mother's full, plump lips, and our father's hazel eyes. Her light honey brown hair with soft, blonde balayage is tied in a low bun. We're two years apart but that's never stopped us from growing the strongest bond there is between siblings.

"That's what I want to hear! I'm proud of what you're doing. I know it won't be easy seeing him every day, but when it comes down to the wire, he isn't a bad person. He always puts you high up on a pedestal."

"I know. He's always treated me well. Always. I guess that's why it hurts that he lost hope so quickly. When Addilyn…*you know*…I thought we would have time to talk things through. Instead, it only spiraled, argument after argument."

"I know, honey."

"I so desperately want the job to simmer everything down."

"Let's cheers to that!"

Our glasses clink and I want to be optimistic, I do, but strife eats away in my stomach until all I see is bleakness. Flashbacks of my baby torment me and I play the blame game in my head. I remember Addilyn's soft reflex smiles, her adorable baby scent, and the lullabies we sang to her. *It's my fault. All my fault. I should've checked on her. Should've had the baby monitor on.* Stress eats away at me, to the point I'm forced to set down my glass to stabilize my numb hands.

Helena sweeps it right up. "You want it?"

"Take it."

Reaching my hands across towards the fireplace, an odd exhilarating feeling rushes down my spine. I got through yesterday without a single argument with *him*. That means something to me, because there was once a time where we couldn't even be in the same room together. Although we're not perfect, day by day I'd like to think we're trying to be amicable.

My sister sets down the empty glass. "Remember that year where the storms were horrid and you stayed over while Ben was on duty? Even our electricity went out! I was pregnant with Weston, so you must have been…seventeen? You were studying like crazy because you had that English paper due and hadn't even made a start on it. Remember that?"

"How could I not! That was the only time I rebelled in my senior year. No wait, I also had an oral presentation in history on the same day!"

"That's right! In order to remember the script you were telling me all these random facts about ancient Rome. You've always been a neurotic organization freak, but I love you for it!" She laughs warmly. "I remember, despite your studying, you were so passionate about making sure I was okay every two minutes. You were worried for the baby and I was like *a blackout won't hurt him!*"

I smile at the memory. "And you did the same for me when I was expecting the twins…and then Addilyn. Even when I could manage it myself, you and Giulio became a tag team. When it wasn't him cooking, it was you coming over to bring us casseroles and sugarless lemon bars."

"I would do it all over again in a heartbeat, that's what sisters are for! God, do you remember when we had the world in our hands? As kids, we used to dream of growing up, of love, and having a family. Now that we're here, all I'm searching for is a pause button."

"That or a rewind."

"Yeah, a rewind would be nice." Helena frowns and leans against the backrest, causing her low bun to droop. "Real nice…"

I so desperately want to pull her into an embrace and tell her that everything will be okay. But how is one supposed to do that when it won't?

"I dreamed of Ben last night."

"Oh?"

"Yeah. I don't remember it exactly, but just seeing him again was refreshing. Despite how long it's been since he passed, it feels like yesterday and a lifetime ago all at the same time."

Consoling Helena on the tragedy that stripped her of Benjamin Holmes seven years ago is like somebody consoling me about the abduction. As much as we appreciate it, it doesn't matter what is said because the person is still gone and grieving continues.

Helena's strength during the passing of her husband has always been inspiring. The way she continued to battle on and kept on keeping on, just like her motto. Seven years ago, Helena woke up to a knock on her door that sealed her fate. All it took was one knock and she became a widow at twenty-three years old with her almost four-year-old son in the blink of an eye. A week later, she found out she was expecting Daisy.

Ben Holmes was a firefighter and died in his line of duty. Helena Holmes is the toughest woman I know. She's passionately dedicated with a bubbly and sarcastic charm. But deep down, I know her past still haunts her, even if she doesn't always talk about it.

Helena's always there for everybody. When I was expecting Addilyn, Giulio and I used to stay over at this exact house with the twins and babysit my niece and nephew just so she could get a few hours to herself. Our parents help her out too, but I always worry what's happening beyond those sarcastic remarks and her giddy attitude.

I would do anything for Helena.

The way she has supported me these last few months…I can't thank her enough. We've been each other's rocks since day one. She made me realize I'm not alone in this, that she'll always be here for me, as I'll always be for her.

"Ben sees everything up there and he would be so proud of you for raising Daisy and Weston." Our fingers intertwine and I pull her closer. "For your strength which inspires me to be better.

For every single thing. I'm extremely proud of you too. You do so much for us. You deserve to find that happiness again."

The fireplace's glowing eruption of heat is mirrored in Helena's glassy eyes. They water and overflow when her hands loosen in my grip and instead, she embraces me. I hold her tightly, both of our agonies blurring into one. My sister's warmth provides me the strength to acknowledge it's okay to be vulnerable, right here, alongside her.

It is okay.

"And so do you. We've been through enough suffering. You deserve the world, Lencia."

"I feel as though I'm back in high school with these lunch dates!"

"Tell me about it! I'm getting the flashbacks already." Kayla laughs as she pulls up a seat by my desk and plops her sandwich down. "Sad thing is, this used to be my exact lunch order."

I draw the coffee to my lips but don't take a sip yet. Instead, I grin. "Some things just don't change, right?"

"Right! Just like my crush on my eleventh grade history teacher, Mr. Estevan. He was so young and handsome and *ah!* Anyway, guess who comes rolling into the office a couple months back? Yep, you guessed it…Estevan! He was there with his wife. I was so shocked when he recognized me. He's still the same sexy mother fuc—"

"Now, now Kayla, where did the professionalism slip off to?" Bryce's Cockney accent rumbles down the hall. He's venturing our way, beaming as his gaze moves between us. "Did it run off with this Estevan to the Maldives? Or better yet…to Timbuktu?"

"You are *so* aggravating!" Kayla teases.

"Aggravating? Well, I guess that's better than intolerable. Innit right, Valencia?"

I set down my coffee cup and lean forward, not expecting him to sit on the edge of my desk. Bryce lowers his head so we're inches apart and those green eyes bore into mine. "Uh…"

"Ya scared to come to the lunchroom and hit me in the head with something else?"

Kayla jumps in before I have the chance. "Congratulations. You've just upgraded yourself to intolerable!"

"Nahhhh." A chuckle escapes Bryce as he elongates the word with his breath. "Valencia, tell her I'm not as intimidating as I seem. Ya do believe that, right? Or ya think I'm a bad guy?"

"Well, Mr. McCarson I don't know enough about you."

"*Oh?* So ya think I'm bad?"

"I never said—"

"Uh-ah" He draws a cold finger down the center of my lips to silence me. That permanent smirk deepens into a full blown smile. "See, there's a thing you'll get to learn about me; I'm a stirrer so don't take offense to anything I say. I'm only playing, but right now you're looking at me with eyes that tell me you are intimidated by me. Why? Do I scare ya?"

Scare me?

This man doesn't *scare* me. Sure, Bryce may be intimating, but it's just that I've never crossed somebody like him before. It's my second day working with him and I still can't figure him out. There's something in the way he strings his words together that feels as though a wall is coming up and it becomes harder to zone into who he really is.

"I'm not scared," I openly admit when his finger glides away. "I just don't know you."

Bryce stares into the distance and for a moment his composure drops. "Not many people do. Not many people want to know."

"I do."

"Why?"

Why?

The question stumps me because even though it's a straightforward one, I can't help but notice the change in his demeanor. Apart from his tense shoulders, his entire body seems on edge now. The '*why?*' he muttered seconds ago wasn't in that usual cheerful tone, it was rough and toxin laced.

Kayla shrugs it off and motions for me to forget it.

I almost do.

"Because we're working together and it would be nice to get to know you on a professional level."

"Mmmm, a lot of people that are a part of my life come and go. They don't stay for long, not because they try and run, but because I don't let them." His looks to me now with furrowed brows. "So, when ya told me that you don't know a lot about me, ya didn't overstep. You got it right because even those who claim they know me, don't."

"Bryce, stop torturing the poor woman." Marcus walks past us, stopping short of his office door. "It's enough she has to work with Giulio, she doesn't need to deal with you too."

The interruption is enough to snap McCarson out of his trance and just like that the smirk returns and his body eases when he stands to his full height. "Aye, don't defend the new girl. She's got her own boxing gloves."

"And they're on tight." I wink over at Marcus who throws his head back in laugher.

"Damn, okay girl. Remind me not to get on your bad side, like *never*."

"Or mine!" Kayla adds in perfect song.

I smile. It's nice to finally see Marcus again.

Bryce looks between us. "See, I wasn't intolerable. Was I, Valencia?"

"Perfectly harmless."

"Yes, *harmless*. I like you already." With a salute, McCarson fist bumps Marcus and strides down the hall.

Kayla points her coffee at the Englishman. "Definitely the class clown back in high school."

"Nah, babe." Bryce halts in his tracks and turns back to the group. "Firstly, back in Hoxton, we called it college. Secondly, I was the school charmer. Everybody and their mothers…which did happen on occasion."

My jaw drops. "You did not."

"Oh, yes I did."

Marcus clears his throat. "Alright, I don't need to hear more. Get out of here!"

"Those who tell ya to leave are often the ones who need ya the most in the end. I'll let ya all ponder on that while I make my exit. Don't miss me too much."

"Un-fucking-likely."

"One day you're gonna love me, Marcus. One day."

Well, that was certainly something.

Marcus waits until it's only the three of us before speaking. "He can be an asshole at times. Ignore it. There's a good side to him too. Now, aren't you going to give your best and only brother-in-law a hug?"

The air is sucked out of me at the title.

I appreciate Marcus and Giulio look almost nothing alike. It would be difficult for me if they did. At twenty-three-years-old, Marcus is nine years younger. Their eyes are their greatest difference with Giulio's being lighter. Marcus' dark hair is thick with a slight wave and since all the years I've known him, he's always been clean shaven.

Kayla dramatically huffs at our embrace. "I swear men are ruining my life. Give me the lunch hour with her!"

"Don't be greedy." He smiles. "Valencia, how are you finding working for the boss man?"

"It's been…tough, but I'm glad I made the decision."

"I'm glad he thought of it. Anyway, I have a lunch meeting in ten. Catch you later."

Kayla points her coffee at Marcus' door once he's out of earshot. "He's got a point. I'm glad you made the right decision too."

Warmth works over the violently intense blues. "So am I."

"Now, let's finally dig into some lunch!"

"Not yet. Sorry, I have to steal Valencia for a minute." Giulio brushes past me when I circle my desk to sit down. I'm instantly flooded with his elegant masculinity and that citrus aroma with a hint of spice—for the first time in months, it's comfort. He continues his walk undeterred and softly murmurs. "My office."

"Do I need to bring anything?"

"Just yourself."

Kayla groans. "You've got to be kidding me, Giannotti!"

I throw her a sympathetic look and promise tomorrow's lunch will be without any interruptions. Perhaps we could go back to yesterday's café.

Once at his office door, I brush over my teal blouse and leather pencil skirt. Inside, Giulio leans back in his leather chair. It's his throne and the birthplace of all business deals and intimate discussions. The latter is why I'm here. *I know it.* Burning inside me is the curiosity to unravel his intentions. I set it aside for a moment because there's something else on my mind.

"How long has Bryce McCarson worked here?"

"About four months." Giulio watches me intently. Those azure, gray eyes have my heart skipping a beat. "Why do you ask? Has he said or done something to upset you? If he has, I'll speak to him right this second."

"Oh no, Bryce hasn't done anything. I'm just curious, that's all." My hands squeeze the back of the leather chair adjacent to his desk. "I mean, I could be wrong but I get the feeling you loathe him."

"Marcus hired him without my approval or consent. Don't ask me how or why because I truly don't know, but…I can't get rid of him. Trust me, I tried. There's just…something about Bryce I don't trust. His morals are catastrophic and he regularly flounders client briefs."

"Perhaps you can develop his skills?"

"That isn't my job."

"True but my crash course came just over twenty-four hours ago."

Giulio shakes his head. "You're different *and* you're successful in your duties. I went through everything with him once and he wasn't even listening. You're not like that. You're acing it."

Acing it.

No matter how much I try to ignore his compliment, it comes back in crashing waves. It ripples through me and just when I think it's about to seep into my chest, I reject it, but my heart doesn't.

"Well, I hope you two eventually find a common ground. Thank you for protecting me yesterday by the way. Bryce may have been a little too eager, but I can manage myself too."

"I know you can, Valencia. I just don't want him getting the wrong idea, that's all."

I let my gaze roam over every inch of Giulio as the tips of his lips raise into an asymmetrical smile. I see my past, present, and future in him. I blink, unable to run away from what we had— from what we *have—do we still have something?*

A voice echoes in my head. *He is perfectly imperfect for me now. Concentrate.*

I clear my throat. "You called me in for something?

Giulio nods slowly. "You can sit down."

"I prefer to stand."

"Okay." He studies me without the shame of looking away and that drowns me in fateful water. His stare is long, meticulously outlining every one of my poised features. "I know this isn't the place to discuss it, but it's been in my head all day. One of the terms we agreed on regarding our separation was that we would remain honest and open, yes?"

"That's right."

Part of my world ended when we decided to legally begin the process of ending our marriage. It was one of the bleakest days of my life. I don't know how it's so easy for him, to throw around a word like that without wanting to slam his head against his desk.

Because that's exactly how I feel.

"Sure you don't want to sit?"

I nod. *Please, just tell me.*

"Well, as we know, all leads have been exhausted with Addilyn's case. We never received closure and we may never obtain it."

"What are you saying?"

Giulio's eyes drop to the photo frame by his desk and I feel my insides burning. I know this is about our baby, but I don't know about *what* specifically, and that scares me more than anything. We've been doing so well. I don't want it all to blow up in flames, but we also *need* to have these complex discussions.

Gazing outside his window, Giulio's fingertips trail over the edges of the photo frame lying flat on its face. Without even seeing it, I already know which one it is. The one of us.

Breathe.

Hold it together.

"Giulio…?"

"With the case cold, the only way to honor Addilyn and say goodbye is a private memorial. I know we already had one, however what I mean is…similar to a funeral. Something intimate with close family. The press may get involved, but we deserve a conclusion. I see this as our only way out."

No.

No.

God, no.

My hands rush over my face but the pain doesn't subside no matter how hard I rub. A memorial…a *funeral*…it's out of the question for me. I know Giulio's intentions come from the heart. I know his greatest desire is to move on and accept that we'll never hold Addilyn again, but it's too much for me.

I can't believe he could even think of something like this, let alone tell me to my face when he *knows* how I feel about this subject. He knows I'll never give up on finding her. I'll dedicate the rest of my life to it if I have to. It can't be all over.

It isn't.

"I'm sorry, but I can't do that. I can't bury an empty casket."

"You're saying it like we have a choice, Valencia."

"Because we *do* have a choice and it's to keep *hoping*," I say. "If we were to go ahead with what you're saying…to have a funeral…it…it would be too painfully real for me."

Giulio pivots his chair to face me. I see the pain in his eyes. I see that this is ruining him as much as it is me. But I can't lose the only thing keeping me together—*faith*.

"I understand what you're saying, but at this point we don't know Addilyn is alive."

"Nor do we know that she's dead!"

Dead.

It's a word that raises hell for me. I don't want to think of the possibilities. It feels as though the longer Giulio and I walk down this path, the more allusive the fire grows. Like a painting without any limits of ending. With an unlimited paint supply, our story will never be complete. There will always be imperfections within each change. Covered up beauty. A farfetched motive. No silver linings.

Addilyn *is* alive.

I still *feel* her.

She's *here* with us.

Giulio stands, slips his hands into his pockets and staggers towards the floor to ceiling windows. Outside, Seattle is heavy with leaden skies. The hustle and bustle of the city downtown is washed away with the pitter-patter of rain. It wouldn't be Seattle without it.

When he finally turns to face me, all I see is how close he is to breaking down. Giulio's eyes are watery and I'm sure as hell not the only one with the sensation of impending doom in my heart. His entire body is tense and I know he's hurting. The thing is, I need to think about myself too.

I need to remain committed to what I believe is true.

"As hard as it is to let go of a part of us, I cannot live with false hope anymore," says the man I once called my husband without any thought of separation. "*Please.* I can't do this alone, Valencia." His whisper is a plea and I wish I could do more. *Be more.* I see the warmth in him. I see it all. But I'm so damn trapped inside my own head that I can't feel it. No matter how much I wish I could. "Please, Valencia. This may be the only way to take a step forward. I need this. *We* need this. Please, trust me on this."

"We're both hurting. I understand your…can we please talk about this another time?"

"When? We're *separated*. There may not be another time."

"Thanks for the reminder about the separation but the co-parenting and hovering divorce papers are enough!" The anguished words are out before I even know it. I can't seem to stop as my fists tighten on the chair. "It was cruel of you to suggest such a thing. I can live with hope, at least it's something. At least there is a question mark versus complete darkness."

I should have already known that when Giulio begins walking towards me and sets himself in such close proximity, that his warmth would electrify every part of me. *Yes.* He still has that effect on me and I hate myself even more for it.

"Exactly." He bites back. "Losing Addilyn has me questioning everything. Every single day. I'm questioning everybody's motives and it's not the way to live. I need to break out of it and so do you."

"Do not tell me how to live!"

"You're going to lose yourself!"

"I ALREADY HAVE!"

"I *NEED* TO SAY GOODBYE TO HER AND YOU'RE NOT PERMITTING ME TO!"

"BECAUSE IT WILL FEEL TOO REAL! BECAUSE I'M SCARED! BECAUSE I WILL NOT BE ABLE TO DEAL WITH IT IF ANTI-DEPRESSANTS AREN'T ENOUGH!"

The wall raised between us fortifies, rendering us incapable of comprehending who we really are at this second. *This is not us.* This hatred towards each other is not us. I don't know what we are...but I can't be *this*. Not for our kids. Not for our hearts. *No.*

Giulio and I remain staring at each other. We're nothing but panting chests and hazed visions. There's too much of everything. Too much conflict, baggage, and regret—and it's not fair. I'm not proud of the shouts, but everything I needed to say was within them.

I'm scared I will not be able to deal with it.

I'm scared it won't be enough.

I'm scared.

In the same breath, Giulio gently cups my face and draws me to his chest. He's forced to bear witness to the way I crumble at his touch. How lost I get in his smell. How much I miss him. How intimately tender this moment truly is.

Giulio *knows* me.

His arms that carry the weight of the world wrap around my waist in a tight embrace. When sobs ripple through me, one of his hands slides up to the back of my head, weaving through my hair, and he holds me even closer. It's here where my fingers clutch his shoulder blades over his cashmere sweater.

Right now, we cannot be any more connected.

I need this embrace.

Just for a moment. Just until my trembling soul stills.

"It's okay. I've got you," his hot murmur promises. "I've got you."

It's been so long that I've almost forgotten the feeling. *Almost.* The warmth that spreads across my body is a reminder of everything that is Giulio Giannotti. He knows and owns every single part of me. My heart. My mind. My body. My soul. He has since I was twenty-one and will continue to do so until I leave this earth.

That's the truth I hide myself from.

The fact that I can't control how I feel, even after all the substance we're missing in our lives, scares me. I'm scared of giving him that piece of me again and losing even more. I'm scared of confusing our children with the back and forth. I fear redemption. I fear a second chance. And equally so, I fear hope will fail me.

At the same time, this is *Giulio*.

My husband.

My best friend.

My everything.

This is the man I vowed I would do anything for. The man I would *still* die for.

It will always be him.

Even through the hollowing pain, my heart still beats wildly every time he enters the room. He should despise me. I should despise him. We should disregard how the other feels.

But we can't...

"I'm sorry. I'm so sorry." Giulio will never know the extent of my apology. Right here in the solace of his arms, I apologize for every single thing I've done to hurt him. For not loving him like I vowed. For not being here when he needed me the most. For not being able to overcome my depression and sleepless nights I kick myself for come morning.

A stiff breath escapes him. "I'm sorry too. I know how you feel about it. I shouldn't have said it. I won't bring it up again. Sorry. Really I am. I only wanted an amicable conversation."

Gentle.

His voice is so damn low and gentle.

"Me too. I'm so sorry." Tears trickle down my cheeks, and my body shivers when he wipes the tears away without regret. My voice softens. "I will never stop looking for her."

Giulio's soft touch kills me as he kisses my shoulder.

I'm not sure I have enough air in me to breathe.

Still wrapped in each other, his gaze lowers to my full lips. "I don't want you hurting. Especially for me." Forehead resting against mine, his hot breath teases me. "Never for me."

Inches apart, we become locked in each other's eyes. This is a wild game between my head and my heart. Despite our differences, my mind never fails to remind me of him. Especially with him so close right now...I cannot deny how strongly my heart feels for him.

"Giulio, I..." My thoughts fall to silence. While my mind says one thing, my heart wants another. The latter wishes I could just cup his stubbled jaw, kiss him and forget about the rest.

"It's okay. You don't have to say anything, Valencia."

Breathe.

Softly smiling, we simply live our moment in slow motion filled with nothing but *us*.

It's a tough battle inside me...I don't want to go through life with the thought of something developing between us, only to break again. This may very well be our way to a second chance, but...

What happens if it fails?

What happens when we crash and burn?

Or when our relationship hurts the twins even more than our separation does now?

It's not easy to say I could blanket our canvas with paints and start all over again. Every time we try, shades of gray sprawl over an already painted picture. A picture that continues to build over and over again, like a book with no ending or worse, with no words. If the book is in our hands with endless blank pages, how will we ever know when to stop writing?

How do we truly know it's the end?

A small part of my brain answers.

Now.

It's over right now.

And that alone is enough to convince me this is the end of us. This is where it has to stop. Yet the battle continues and heat ignites as Giulio cups my jaw and lowers his head, his lips moments away from brushing mine. It's something so familiar. How he used to kiss away the pain. Cure my hurt. Lift my pride.

But as quickly as the spark between us is set alight, it dies out and our moment is over.

Giulio can't go through with it.

It's over.

I'll never forget the apprehensiveness in Giulio's features as he retreats to his desk, just in time for a knock on the door. I'm left standing in the middle of his office mentally and physically numb.

Marcus speaks through the door. "Clients are waiting in the lounge. We could hear you both shouting before."

Knowing that once again we've let things go too far crushes me inside. Giulio and I are so passionate about Addilyn that instead of using that passion to heal, we're using it to turn on one another.

Giulio dismisses Marcus with words I don't even catch.

I fail to contain myself and take a chance.

A leap.

"I miss the people we once were." My head drops as I sniffle my lost tears. This is the conversation Dr. Eross wanted me to have with Giulio last week. The same one I crumpled and threw away. The back of my throat burns. I need a drink. But most importantly, I need to tell him this, especially if this is where our end needs to be drawn. "I miss my best friend. I miss my husband. I miss it all."

Before looking down, I catch his disgruntled pursed lips. It's not aimed at me. I know this much. It's aimed at whoever did this to us. Whoever abducted our missing piece.

"Valencia?"

"Yes?"

"I miss you so fucking much."

I feel Giulio's eyes on me but I can't meet them. Partly because his confession is stated with a broken voice and partly because I can't breathe straight. *I miss you too.* I feel the onset of an attack coming. The ones of panic that rustles with chained anxiety.

It's over right now.

The ringtone of Giulio's phone jolts me. It blurs between our truths. He doesn't answer it. Not the first time it rings and not the second time it starts again. It becomes a siren for our hate, our love, and everything in between.

It may be my anxiety playing devil's advocate or it may simply be me, but I listen to the part of me that says to let go. I would rather face the consequences of being burned now than go through it all over again later. I can't fall for Giulio Giannotti all over again. It'll only further shatter our hearts and they're already on their last leg, convulsing.

I take my leave without a single glance back.

At my desk, I almost don't make it to my chair before my legs give out. My lungs are bursting and my head can't stop conjuring evil thoughts. All of which I pray to God aren't true, but at this stage, I don't know anymore.

I push away my cold coffee and do the inevitable. Scrolling through the pictures on my iPhone of Addilyn during her first two months of life, I cave inside, one photo at a time.

I'm so sorry, my angel.

CHAPTER SIX

BY THE END OF THE WEEK, I'M GETTING THE HANG OF MY WORK coinciding with the twins' schooling. Giulio and I didn't speak about what happened between us on Wednesday at the office. I thought it would be for the better, but then that night he texted to ask how I was doing. A brief discussion followed before he had to finalize design renderings.

The following morning when I wake up from my five-hour sleep—the most hours I've slept all week—there's a knock at the front door. There I am at 6 A.M. in my silk nightgown in front of some delivery man, signing off for an unexpected package...*from Giulio.*

To say the action surprises me is an understatement. The

content inside surprises me even more. A pale yellow bow wrapped around a medium sized bound mental health handbook titled '*How to get your life back and win, the Giannotti way.*' Slipped inside the bow is a single red rose. I'm in complete shock to find the entire lengthy unpublished handbook was handwritten by Giulio. Had he written it all night instead of those design renderings? Is this the 'design renderings?' It has to be, because as I flip through, I note he's divided it into sections with all written accounts of methods he implemented to overcome his struggles and how I too can find the other side.

At the center of the handbook is a card.

Valencia,

I once read that the darkest nights produce the brightest stars.

I hope you see the light again. Until then, I'm here. I will continue to be here, even on the days you don't want me, because that's when you need me the most. That's when I need you the most. Because that is what we do. I don't want us to fall apart when things get tough. I want us to fall together.

I'm sorry for not being there when you needed me the most. You have a right to be scared but I want to remind you just how strong you are. Just like you hold on to the hope of Addilyn, hold on to the hope of a better tomorrow. Hold on to the hope that you will make it because you are enough. And after all, the opposite of hope is fear. You have hope. And you will be able to deal with anything that comes your way because you have me. Whatever we are to each other—married, friends, or simply co-workers—you will always have me.

I hope this book helps you see the light.
It helped me and will help you too. I promise.

Here always,
Giulio

I cry as I read the card twice.

A tidal wave of emotions bubble up inside because it was just the previous day where I made an oath to myself that this had to be the end of Giulio and me, but the next day when I saw him, I wasn't so sure.

Giulio was already in his office when I arrived and I didn't even bother to knock before stepping in. Those angelic eyes shifted to mine and he stood up from his swivel chair. With growing embers between us and the ghost of a smile on my lips, I rushed into the raging fire and crushed him into the firmest embrace of my life.

He held me, full of need as the unspoken devotion of what once was so natural for us intensified. No words were exchanged because all was said in the silence.

Thank you for everything.

If this is supposed to be the end of us, then why does it feel like it's only just the beginning?

On the following Wednesday, both Giulio and Bryce leave for a meeting together after lunch. Kayla predicts it'll last until 4 P.M. According to her, meetings with Bryce always run over time. It doesn't sit well with me knowing that despite their past tension, my name could be fueling spiteful words between them. I don't want to be a cause of violence, especially not at Giulio's empire.

I have come to love working at Notti Designs and although

it's only been a week and a half, it's longer than I thought I would last.

Minutes before three o'clock, Bryce calls to request I meet him at The Red Tavern to hand him the Rodney Project's design brief which is *"hanging around somewhere"* in his office. He mentioned that after a blow up with Giulio, he left him and the client without any interior design leads.

I heard Giulio mention his collaboration with Bryce on The Rodney Project before. Situated in Bellevue, the Project is set to be a luxurious ultramodern waterfront home. The Project isn't set to be completed for another twelve months, but with Giulio in charge of the architecture and assisting Bryce's interior design direction, it's set to be one of the most anticipated houses by Notti Designs to date, but it can't quite live up to its reputation with a lack of design plans. Neither Giulio nor the client would have been happy with the news.

So I help Bryce out, even though the bar he's at is only a few streets away and *I'm sure* he would've found the manila folder himself with far more ease.

Marcus slides into the elevator seconds before the doors close. "Finished for the day?"

"Almost." I smile, pressing the button for the ground level. "I need to drop off a design plan to Bryce."

"Oh? Are you meeting him someplace?"

"Yeah, the Red Tavern. It's just around the corner on Pike Street. Ever been?"

"Nah, can't say I have. Giulio there too?"

"He's in Bellevue. Apparently they had some argument and Bryce stormed off."

"Ah, yes. Now I remember." His lips twitch to a lopsided smirk. "Typical McCarson move. It probably had to do with Bryce ordering all the tiles before confirming any measurements or the style with the client. Or because he did it all before construction has even begun...and without signing off with Giulio. He went over budget by thousands and forged Giulio's signature on countless contracts before this current project they're joined in."

My jaw drops. "Are you serious?"

"Would I lie to you?"

"Never."

"Exactly." Marcus winks and steps out of the elevator first. "Well, good luck with him!"

Stepping out of the rain, a warm ambiance illuminates my every step as I enter The Red Tavern. I take the first right at the first archway, scanning the wood oak floorboards and illuminated booth sections. Each has intimate soft lightning. In the distance, a band plays a rhythmic beat.

Bryce isn't in the first section.

My heels against the monochromatic checkered tiles as I take a left. With the manila folder tucked underneath my arm, my mind wanders.

Could this be a setup?

I shake my head. *No. Why would it be?*

My watch flashes at me and I curse at the time. I walk further on and finally, I hear chattering. Behind an alcohol cabinet stands a middle-aged man with a buffalo plaid shirt and dark jeans.

"Ya look awfully confused," he says with a thick Cockney accent and laughs, all the while cleaning the edge of a tumbler. "Looking ta meet someone?"

"Ah, yes, Bryce McCarson."

"Aye. He's right behind ya."

He is?

I spin and to my surprise, Bryce's eyes are pinned on me. They drop to my legs as he waves me over with a single hand. He's sitting quietly in a closed corner nook, in the booth furthest from the entry and it makes me wonder if this is his favorite spot, away from reality.

He smiles softly as I set the folder in front of him. "Here you go. Have a good night."

Turning on my heels, the distant chatter of diners catches my suspicion. Ever since the abduction, I've consumed myself sick in the conversations I hear about my tragedy. People who state their own version of the events. I've heard almost everything there is to hear and nothing satisfies me.

"Aye." Bryce tugs on the left three-quarter sleeve of my white bodycon dress, halting my feet from progressing further. "Where do ya think ya going?"

I give him a wary look. "I need to pick up my kids."

"You're going to leave me all alone here?"

"You left Giulio."

"And?" The hand is gone yet the grin remains, widening at my raised brow.

All I can think about is the turmoil between him and Giulio and what could have possibly occurred between the men this afternoon if Marcus' assumption is correct.

"I thought you were working."

"I am working, but what's the fun in doing it all alone? Giulio most likely left minutes after me. Can't he pick them up?"

"My custody runs midday Sunday to Thursday morning."

"Peachy. Oh, come on, just one drink. It won't do ya any harm. You've got no one waiting for you, and I'm sure those kids would love to spend some time with that father of theirs."

For someone who doesn't know me at all, Bryce guesses correctly.

You've got no one waiting for you.

I consider the invitation for a split moment, until a flash of Giulio's face crosses my mind. I know better than to deceive him. I should stay far away from this man. "Thank you for the offer. Perhaps some other time?"

"Just one drink as a welcome to the team. Plus, nobody can resist the English charm."

"I really shouldn't—"

Bryce stands abruptly and disregards all rules of personal space, moving until his body is pressed against mine. Nothing changes for me. *Nothing.*

I part my lips in protest only to be met with his pointer against my mouth. It's the second time he's done it, and I'm not exactly thrilled about it. "You're not wearing a ring.

So, technically if a guy wants to have a few drinks with ya, platonically to welcome you to the team, is that considered wrong?"

My god.

The finger slips away and my voice comes out a bare whisper. "Not necessarily."

"So, are ya gonna sit with me or not? I'll give you intel on some of the upcoming project."

"That's against protocol, Mr. McCarson."

"You have Giulio's mouth, you really do. I still want ya to stay a little longer, babe."

"On two conditions."

"Hit me, babe."

"You don't call me babe, and please don't silence me with your finger again."

Bryce nods with a smirk, gloating at my apprehension. "Deal."

I show myself into the red vertical striped booth, shoving my umbrella, coat, and bag to the side. Yeah, this is *not* a good idea. He throws his head back with laugher at the grunt that escapes me.

Well, good luck with him—Thanks Marcus, I need it now.

Bryce finally calms down. "I'm gonna have another drink. What do you want?"

"A mimosa. Thank you."

"Ahh, city girl move." He gestures towards the bartender, his light wash jean jacket constricting the full movement. "Don't run away from me now. I do know where you work."

I can't help but snicker. "Yeah, well I know where you work too, so kindly be on your best behavior."

"I'm always on my best behavior." Bryce winks and turns to walk toward the bar as I pull out my phone.

Valencia: Hey honey, I have a work emergency. Would you be able to pick up my kids from school? I'll be home shortly. Thank you.

Helena's response comes the moment McCarson sets down our beverages.

Helena: More than happy to. Everything okay?

Valencia: Yes, thank you! :)

My phone dies the second I hit send. *Great.*

Bryce opens the manila folder and scans the contents inside. Drawing the beer to his lips, some froth dissolves on his short tamed beard. My attention drops to his hands and more specifically to the rose tattoo. I need to work past his thick exterior and unlock what's truly happening in his mind.

"What happened between you and Giulio?"

"A falling out."

"Can I ask what about?"

Bryce sets down his glass soundlessly and looks up at me. "We just had a falling out, alright? There's nothing more to it. We just don't see eye to eye."

"Did you really forge his signature on today's file?"

"I don't want to talk about it."

"If Gi—"

"Why did you both separate? Huh?" His eyes darken at my frown. "Didn't you separate cause ya didn't see eye to eye anymore?"

"If you want to cut the long story short…yes."

McCarson shrugs. "Ya see, same thing happened between Giulio and I. He's a nutter who can't take me lightly. So what if I over-budget at times and fuck a few women on my desk like that intern who never got hired. He has enough money to just allow it and fix it…I don't want to talk about it further. Now, drink up."

The sharpness in his voice is lethal.

Did he just say that he…

It all makes sense now with the intern. It makes sense why Giulio was so protective of me the first time Bryce and I met. He was worried Bryce would try to…seduce me.

I down the mimosa.

"Where ya going?"

"Home. I won't tolerate you speaking to me or Giulio as if we're animals."

Bryce scoffs the moment I stand. "He deserves it."

"See? This is exactly what I am talking about. I shouldn't have stayed."

"Continue to put me down, why don't ya."

"Bryce, this is not a game. This is *my* family we're talking about."

"I don't get it. You're separated, why are ya still so defensive whenever I say his name?"

My breaths quicken. "Because we were in love once and Giulio was nothing but good to me. He doesn't deserve to be dragged down for having to tolerate your behavior. So if corrupting or seducing me are your intentions tonight, I'll save you the time and leave right now."

I have never in my life spoken to somebody I barely know like this. Perhaps it's all the bottled up rage about the turbulence in my life or the fact he criticized Giulio, but it just feels right to stand up for him.

What I've come to learn about Bryce McCarson is that he doesn't back down...*ever*.

"Wait. Those are not my intentions at all." Bryce's expression softens as he reaches for my coat before I can and sighs. "Look, I didn't mean to offend you. I'm...I snap quickly and say things I don't mean sometimes. Please, stay a little longer."

"I want to see my kids. Please get out of my way."

"You know Giulio better than anyone. I need you to tell me if he likes the designs."

"I don't know much about him nowadays."

"But you did *once*; that still counts. Drinks are on me."

I let out a sigh. *This is such a bad idea.*

The bartender appears, setting down a tray of alcohol and sliders. "Happy hour begins early here! So stick around, I promise you'll love it here!"

We have been going through the designs for hours. Bryce redeemed himself and so far has listened to all the suggestions I've made. Although I don't have an interior design degree, I know Giulio's expectations and what he expects to maintain his company's reputation.

Bryce makes notes while I recall Giulio's most luxurious style. I recommend stores I remember he often visited for inspiration and assist in creating mood-boards for every room. For every piece of furniture that hits the brief, we raise a glass.

The one thing McCarson doesn't need any assistance with is drinking. All evening he has continuously filled my glass, ordered round after round, and somehow convinced me that we should be celebrating our unlikely friendship and that I deserve the new job. As much as it feels nice to come out of my element and help out Notti Designs, I also miss Oscar and Slonne.

I don't notice how tipsy I am until he pours me another glass of wine and I misjudge my mouth, spilling the red liquid all over my *white* dress.

"I think you've lost it!"

"Oh, shut up!" I laugh and reach for the napkins.

Not that they'll help.

Bryce's chuckle rumbles loud inside my head. I grip the table and launch for the napkins a second time. But every time I do, either it's in my head or I swear they really do move further away.

"Need help?"

"Nope!"

"You sure?"

My head shake ends up a circle. *God, I feel so drunk.*

Bryce can't stop laughing at me as he yanks a few napkins and rounds the table to my side. My adrenaline is high. I haven't been this far gone in a long while. I attempt to decide if the beat in my head is my own or if it's coming from the blues band that has been playing non-stop. I don't know the time, but it feels late.

Very late.

Bryce's eyes move over my body as he slides into the booth next to me. "Let's clean you up."

"What are you looking at?"

He grins. "You."

"Why?"

"I…don't have a lot of people around me. You staying around tonight and having some drinks with you really does mean a lot to me. I'm happy to be here with you."

"Same here." The drum in my heart beats wildly. Bryce is drunk. We both are. My entire body is on fire. It's all I can think about as he wipes the napkins against my dress. It's ruined though and no amount of cleaning up can fix that.

At some point, Bryce lets go of the napkins and replaces the sensation with his touch. There's an allure in his green eyes when his foreign hand fans out across my hip and slowly rises higher to the dip of my waist.

He's staring straight through me, asking for permission that I'm yet to give. "Valencia…"

"Yes?"

Bryce tosses the crumpled napkins on the table and turns so we're face to face. A sea of warmth dances across his face from flickering pendant lighting. "Don't worry. It's nothing."

"It's more than nothing, Buddy."

There's his infamous smirk again. "Who's this Buddy and what happened to Bryce?"

"Hmmm, wouldn't you like to know…" I take another gulp of wine and laugh at Bryce's amused face. Sweeping my tongue across my lower lip has those green orbs tracking the movement. I have no idea what I'm doing, but this…*right now*…it feels exciting. My mouth twitches up into a smile. "Glad to know I'm funny. Why aren't you speaking? Dog got your tongue?"

"I don't think that's the saying…"

"Boo hoo. You were going to ask me something before. Ask it."

My chest is burning as I scoot closer to him; the whiff of

alcohol crossed with his bergamot cologne takes me back to Giulio. It shouldn't. This isn't even his scent, but under these lights, Bryce reminds me of my husband. Perhaps it's the drinking or just the fact that he's here with me tonight, making me feel something other than the same torment. Perhaps it's the way his hand trails up inches from my breasts. Perhaps it's the warm, sensual lips by my ear as he brazenly asks, "Have you been with another man since Giulio?"

Shaking my head causes his beard to scratch against my cheek and I'm transported back to all the times it used to happen with Giulio. Whenever he kissed my cheek, or I rolled into him in the middle of the night or while we wildly made love…*Hmm, yes I miss that.*

"Ever thought about it?"

I come to, my eyes heavy at the uptick of McCarson's brow. "Huh?"

"Have you ever thought about being with another man?"

"I…don't know."

"Ever fantasized?"

No. The word gets stuck in my throat and just as I manage to back away into the booth, I lose my balance and lie down instead. Bryce finds a way to instantly appear, holding out his hand to pull me back up with a wolfish smile. "Now, that was a rather dramatic way to avoid a conversation."

"Thanks, McCarson, but I do it without your help."

"Oh, yeah?" He chuckles, challenging my tendency to get back up. "Now this I'd like to see."

Although he's willing to help me, a part of my brain blurs as my fingers fan out against the leather booth. I don't have the strength to pull myself back up and so I shrug and continue lying here. "Don't mind me. I'm just living my best life here."

"I don't believe that, but sure. Whatever floats your boat, babe." Bryce reaches over the table and I watch as he draws the glass of beer to his mouth. My eyes linger on the way his tongue runs over his lips after the second gulp. He must sense me looking because the moment the glass is set back on the table, those green eyes are on me and his brows are arched in amusement. "You're staring…that must mean I did something wrong. What did I do, babe?"

Now I'm the one smirking. "I told you not to call me babe."

"And did I call you babe, babe?"

"You did now."

"*Oh*. Right now, babe?"

"You're so annoying!" I laugh.

"I think ya secretly like it."

"I think ya a bit delusional, babe."

"Oh, wow. Did you just mock my accent?" Bryce teases with the brightest grin I've seen all night. Leaning forward, he slowly props his body over mine. His forearms rest on the leather by my head to separate our bodies. He looks back and forth between my eyes. "Because it's kind of hot the way you said that before."

"Maybe…" I bite my lip at my growing drunken smile. "Maybe I like your accent."

"You really are a hell of a lot beautiful. So fucking beautiful, Valencia." He cups my cheeks and breathes out a sigh, his thumb brushing over my lower lip. "Don't be like my mother who never got over my father. Don't ruin yourself for a man who can't see it like you do. Don't let Giulio hold you back from loving somebody else again. I see so much potential in you."

"Bryce…"

"It makes me want to kiss you and do whatever you want me to."

"You're not…*him*."

"I can be whoever you want if you let me, babe. I'm not saying forever 'cause I've never done love…but I can ease your pain, even if that's just for one night only."

"You want me?"

A moment passes between us. All the sound around me fades, all but my throbbing head. Bryce swallows, dead serious for the first time tonight.

"Yes. I want you," he whispers, arousal evident in his voice. "Do you want me?"

The moment our drunken eyes meet, I keep on blinking flashes of Giulio in my mind. It's as if he's the one on top of me, not Bryce. He's the one smiling down with his perfectly sculpted face and toned muscles I want to run my hands down. That lower lip I want to erotically tug before kissing him like he'll never forget. Those alluring eyes I want to never lose sight of as I devour him.

Giulio.

That's who I want right now in his drunken state.

"I think I'm too far gone to answer that."

McCarson bites his lip when he catches me staring at his hand tattoo. "You like the ink?"

I shrug.

"Don't leave me hanging. Do you like it, babe?"

I giggle. "I'm not your babe…and still deciding."

"Fuck the decisions," he whispers in a chuckle and drops his lips to my neck. They hover over my hot skin, silently asking for permission. "Sometimes you've just gotta live in the moment." His unsolicited kisses evoke a thrilling sensation as they trail down my neck to my collarbone. It's there where he swirls the tip of his tongue and bites down with a playful growl. "Let me help you move on."

No.

We've taken this too far.

The alcohol buzzes inside me. "No, I…"

My hands shove at his chest, needing him off of me. Bryce backs up to study me for a moment. I'm not sure what he sees in me, but adrenaline kicks in when he lowers his body on mine again. It leaves me to rest to my hands above my head and that gives him gives him the upper hand.

Bad move.

My thoughts of Giulio must have provided the silence he mistook as a 'yes.'

"Bryce, please get off me."

"Forget all about Giulio tonight. You don't deserve a man who doesn't stand by you."

"No."

His rough beard grazes against my soft skin. That spicy bergamot has my stomach churning. I need him off. *I don't want to forget all about Giulio.*

Bryce is still by my neck, roughly kissing my fragile skin. His hands remain away from my body, but this is still too much. I don't want it and if he was sober enough, he would notice it. But he's too far gone and so am I.

"Please, stop. Don't ruin our progress."

"This would improve our progress."

Why can nobody see us?

I flutter my eyes open to tears spilling and whimper against his kisses against my skin. Thrashing my limbs does nothing. I shove his shoulders, but still, he doesn't budge.

"Maybe you want this, babe. Deep down you want this with another man," he says, all while I'm shaking my head. "You do. I know you do. You deserve better. Tell me the word and we'll forget about everything else."

This can't be happening.

I should have never stayed. I shouldn't have drunk this much.

I am about to protest further when Bryce is violently yanked off of me. The distant music falls off key and then stops altogether. The chatter dies down and I finally summon the strength to sit up to observe the scene.

"WHAT THE FUCK DO YOU THINK YOU'RE DOING?" Giulio has Bryce in a headlock against the wall. His roar is so distressed the entire bar turns to look. My vision blurs and it takes a second to see clearly. I can just make out the pulsing veins in his neck in my dizzy haze.

I think I'm going to be sick.

"Nothing." Bryce has the audacity to laugh it off. "I wanted to show Valencia what she's missing, but she's still hung up on ya."

It all happens so fast. Blood sprays between them and the confidence dissolves from McCarson's face. Giulio punches Bryce again and an unpleasant groan escapes the Englishman, who attempts to retaliate, only to be slammed against the wall once again, his head crashing against the tiles.

"That's what you get for touching my family." Giulio grits, gripping the collar of his worker's bloodied jean jacket to emphasize his point. "What did you do to her? HEY! I said what DID YOU DO TO THE LOVE OF MY LIFE?"

The love of his life.

"Fuck, man! I think ya broke my nose!"

"I will break every single bone in your body. What the *fuck* did you do?"

The middle-aged bartender rushes towards both men. Acting as a barrier, he turns to Giulio with an irritated look. "Ya better leave and I advise ya to never step foot in here again."

"Are you seriously taking his side—"

"Giulio," I call out, my cry a small plea. "Please can you…"

There is nothing more I want than to leave this place.

I can still smell the lingering bergamot against my skin when Giulio nears me. His entire composure breaks at the sight. When his secure hands pull me into a gentle embrace, it doesn't feel strange or foreign, it feels like home. *My salvation.*

"It's okay. I'm here. You're safe. You're safe with me."

"Giulio…I'm sorry."

Our prolonged touch and vigorously beating hearts is all I need to know I'll be okay.

I breathe in Giulio's husky smell and it transports me to a place of comfort. A place beyond my spinning head and clouded vision. Giulio is right here. *He came for me.* He found me. In this moment, he's all I need.

"None of this is your fault. Please never think something like this can be your fault. Ever." Giulio tucks a strand of hair behind my ear, softening his gaze before the only lips I'll ever love meet my forehead. "You're coming home with me, darling."

CHAPTER SEVEN

Giulio

THE BASTARD KNEW EXACTLY WHAT PLACING HIS HANDS ON *MY WIFE* would do to me. This is it. The final straw. Nobody fucking touches Valencia. Nobody fucks with my family. This is personal and he will get everything coming his way.

After receiving a call from Helena stating Valencia had asked her to pick up the twins but still hadn't returned after *six* long hours, I backtracked every movement. Marcus told me she mentioned meeting Bryce at The Red Tavern and I immediately sensed something was wrong, especially when all my calls went to her voicemail.

Lance offered to collect the twins from my sister-in-law and look after them at my house since it's my custody night. I needed to be the one to find Valencia. As I enter my house now, Lance's jaw drops at the sight of us; a passed out Valencia in my arms, bridal style. That manila folder…it's somewhere on the ground, between my Porsche and the door exiting the garage.

This is going to be a night I'll never forget.

"Giulio…I'm sorry."

I hold onto her tighter. This is one of the first times in months that we've been this close. I surrender to her. I need her, just as much as she needs me. Her vanilla scent reminds me of a time when life was tranquil. Not this nightmare.

"None of this is your fault. Please never think something like this can be your fault. Ever." I sweep her soft waves behind her ear and soften my gaze. My lips gravitate to her and I kiss her forehead. "You're coming home with me."

"I br-brought him a folder and was helping him. I didn't expect him to…"

"Do we need to file his sexual misconduct as sexual harassment or sexual assault?"

She shakes her head, sobbing. "No. I don't want to deal with th-the police again."

"Let's take it slow. Can you tell me what happened?"

I can hear Bryce shuffling behind us, speaking with the bartender. I'm not a violent man, but Bryce brought me to another level tonight. I want to finish him. Right here. This time with my words. But Valencia is my priority. I need to take care of her first.

Valencia tells me everything in detail. Twice she stops and I accompany her into the bathroom. I rub her lower back and hold her hair back when she throws up.

The first time we return, Bryce is gone.

The second time, the whole place is shutting down early.

Valencia tells me she feels better after emptying her stomach, however, I know it's not over. She's still tipsy. I get her a water, shove the damn manila folder between my belt and dress shirt, and scoop her in my arms. She falls asleep as I slip her into my car. Her Jeep is parked in front of mine. I'll collect it tomorrow—after I hunt down Bryce McCarson and treat him like the coward he is.

"What happened, man?"

"Bryce McCarson happened. You should have seen him."

Lance brushes a hand over his light crew cut, before locking the front door and rushing by my side to ensure I can make it up the stairs with her. *Of course I can.* If this was any other occasion I would be rejoicing that she's in my arms and this close to me…

Not tonight.

I'm beyond pissed off.

I should've got there quicker.

Lance weaves past us at the landing to open the door to my bedroom. I can always count on him. He was my best man and my closest friend since we attended the Washington State University together, which is also why I hired him as my project manager at Notti Designs after we graduated.

Valencia whimpers in my arms as I lay her on what used to be *our* bed. Her peaceful expression crumbles. Those full lips I used to kiss press together in silent protest.

Oh, Dio.

Half asleep, she doesn't let me go and I don't want her to. My body relaxes when her hands slither around my shoulder blades and she pulls me into her hair. It drives me deeper into *her,* into everything I once had.

Valencia needs me tonight. I know more than ever not to ruin it.

No talk of Addilyn.

No talk of Bryce.

Just comfort.

"What did he do?"

I do my best to brief Lance with my turned head. "Almost sexually assaulted her—actually, it was more than that. Not one fucking person in there intervened. I asked and they thought they were a couple. Can you believe that? Marcus saved me on this one. If it wasn't for him…I would not have known where to look."

His eyes widen. "Did McCarson…?"

"The bastard was close."

"Oh, shit! I'm sorry, man. Did you manage to speak to him?"

"He left before I had the chance to. They were both drunk. Bryce had her pinned down, non-consensually kissing her neck and attempting to convince her that she deserves better than me. My first reaction was to pull him off and punch him in the face. Fuck. I'm losing my mind. I could have done more. I *should* have done more."

"You did what you could, Giulio."

"But what if my best isn't good enough?" I shake my head, causing Valencia's arms to fall. *No. Hold onto me, baby.*

She stirs in her sleep and curls into fetal position. I loathe her wine stained dress and the whiff of Bryce I get from her.

How dare he fucking touch my girl?

Yes.

My girl.

Rising from the bed, I walk to where Lance is standing but can't look away from Valencia Giannotti. I'm too worked up. Too preoccupied something will happen to her even if I blink. "I was in London on a business trip the night Addilyn was abducted. Tonight, I was too late..."

"Hey, look at me." Lance levels with me. "Don't blame yourself for something you can't control. You weren't the bystander; I imagine you put him in his place. There's nothing more you could have done. Nothing at all. It's okay, Giulio. Valencia needs you right now. She needs your comfort and strength. Be there for her. Be the real man that you are."

A long breath escapes me. "You're right. I needed that. Thank you."

"You'll both get through this." Lance nods, squeezing my tense shoulder. "It'll all be okay. Oh, and the twins were good. Slonne was having trouble sleeping. I hope you don't mind I made her a hot chocolate."

It draws a smile to my lips. "No, I don't mind you practicing your fathering skills."

Lance chuckles softly, careful not to disturb Valencia. "The more practice, the better. Right? If my future children are anything like Slonne or Oscar, then life will be a breeze."

"Don't speak too fast," I advise him when we make our way to the front door. "I still have a few years to determine that. Elementary can be a breeze but Valencia's taught the older years and they say high school is when you truly understand your children's demons."

"Well, in that case, how about this…" He slides on his work boots and bites back a smirk. *Ladies and Gents, here comes the real Lance.* "Whenever I have children, I'll grow them up until the end of middle school, give them to you during the demon stage, and you hand them back a week before graduation. You know, just to show I actually was a part of their lives."

"Ahem…sorry, do I know you? Who are you again?"

"Wow. I see how it is. Thanks for helping a brother out."

It feels incredible to laugh in the middle of this unrest. "Anytime."

"In all seriousness, I'm at your disposal if you want me to get a hold of Bryce."

My lips twitch upwards. "I appreciate it, but I should be the one to do it."

"All good. Night, man."

"Goodnight, and thank you for everything tonight."

I'm back in the bedroom the moment Lance's car fades into the night. Soundlessly, I lie beside Valencia who's still passed out on top of the sheets and pull her head to my chest. My fingers weave through her soft hair. It's something I always used to do that calmed her.

It isn't until after one o'clock in the morning, after checking on the twins numerous times and updating Helena, that I return to find her awake. Valencia sits at the end of the bed, head bowed with her fists gripping the hem of her dress.

I stop at the doorframe. "How are you feeling?"

"Like a winery."

"I should have been there."

"It's okay. I feel sick. I think I'm going to…faint." She launches up to stand, only to lose her balance and tumble back. Stabilizing her fall on the bed, I aid her hands and create a small divide between our bodies with my propped up forearms, laying all my weight off her.

Those flawless hazel eyes blink up at me, the ones I promised to devote my entire life to. Now they brim with tears, while the rest of her sinks into my touch.

"You're not alone in this, okay? I'm here."

"I know you are."

"Then trust me when I say Bryce isn't worth it."

A sense of desperation consumes me. I don't know if she can see or feel it in her drunken state, but it's there. *This* isn't Valencia. I can count on one hand the number of times she drank this much since the day I met her.

Did he put something in her drink?

There's a darkness in my heart. A seeping wound. It eases a fraction when she tells me she saw every one of her drinks hit the table and Bryce didn't spike anything. His name slipping from her tongue ruins me. *He* ruins me. Hell, this entire situation does.

"I'm su-such a—" she hiccups, struggling to find the words to say, "—an idiot."

"No, you're not."

"I am. You sa-said in the billboard that I'm enough, but I'm no-not. I can't be."

I draw her hands to mine and kiss them. *Slowly.* There's a weight in me. One so strong I don't even have in me to correct her on the fact she said billboard instead of letter. I only hope she's been reading the handbook I sent her.

The weight has me lowering her hands away and warming the coldness by the small of her back with my touch. "You *are* enough. Being you is enough."

Valencia stares up at me, biting her lip. Her eyes are dull and tired. Although she slept for a few hours, it's not enough to restore her. When she cups my jaw and brushes her thumb over my rough stubble, I swear all the air is sucked out of me.

How can I breathe when this is the first time she's voluntarily touched me in months?

I can't act as if it doesn't affect me when it's so obvious it does.

Her delicate touch is potent. The way her hand slips away to the nape of my neck and teases its way down to my dress shirt… *Holy hell.* When she struggles to undo the third button, I snap back to reality. It's as far as I'll let it go and I clasp her wrist to stop her movement.

"Please…" she softly whispers, "I don't want to feel him."

I know you don't, darling.

"We can go about this another way."

I have to admit I'm relieved to breathe in her sweet scent, it's the same perfume on my dresser. It reels me in deeper, urging me to protect her from anybody who plans to hurt me by going through her.

I help Valencia to her feet and we stand there in the middle of the bedroom in the middle of this sexual tension. The way she's looking at me…the way I'm feeling…*shit.*

"Giulio."

"Yes, darling?"

In her drunken state, Valencia steps closer to me until our bodies are flush. So many things rush through my head. One stands out. The desire that burns in her eyes and how it makes my entire body throb. I should look away. I should avert this conversation…But my heart wins.

"Make me forget him. Make love to me."

For. The. Love. Of. God.

My heart picks up speed and I'm left parting my lips. I want nothing more than to hold her. To make this right. To sink into her after all this time. But I am not going to touch her. Not until she is sober. Not until we resolve all of our issues and sex is something we both crave.

Not until she wants me again like I want her.

"I can give you everything but *that* tonight. You're under the influence, Valencia."

Although that didn't stop one fucker.

"Fine." She sniffles, reeking of wine. "A shower."

"It's not the best idea while drunk."

She frowns. "I don't want him on me."

Dio.

"I'm scared that you'll fall and god forbid break something." I brush her hair away from her neck, mentally kicking myself that he was right *there*. I'm somber for her. For everything she endured. "Okay, fine. You can shower, but I'll wait outside the door just in case you need me. Call out if you need help."

Valencia smiles weakly. "Giulio?"

"Mmhmm."

"Thank you for always being a gentleman."

Now it's my turn to smile. "Yeah, you're definitely drunk if you're complimenting me."

And that's how it goes. I assist her into the bathroom and slide closed the pocket door. I'm left holding my breath until I hear the water running. *She's safe.*

I can't believe this happened.

After this, Valencia needs to get some rest. In my bed. I'll take the guest bedroom.

Raking a hand through my hair, I play out the entire night in my head.

I want her.

All of her.

I don't expect myself to admit it, but something changed for me the day she told me she was scared that she wouldn't be enough if the anti-depressants don't help. The comment felt like somebody stabbed me in the heart and I finally saw Valencia's depression in the same light as she did. I saw the pain in her eyes and the way her body trembled when I wrapped her in my arms. That's why I sent her that book and wrote those words. I know it won't solve everything, but it's a step.

It's something.

Something to remind her that I'm right here with her; I'm not going to run away. I'm not going to give up. No matter how hard some days will be—I will always be here for her.

Valencia wants to push me away because she's scared. She

trusts hope because she fears the opposite…Addilyn being dead. She's an artist. A creator. Somebody who always believes in silver linings. I'm the opposite. I give in to the most probable prospect because that is what my career relies on me to do.

I realized something holding her moments ago. She thinks the anti-depressants will be her cure, and although they will help, from experience I know they won't be enough. I want to be her cure, but I can't. Ultimately, it's *Valencia* herself. She needs to be her own cure. She needs to be the one to rise above. I know it's easier said than done. I get it. That's why I'm going to help her through it and will never let her go, especially not when she's pushing me away.

I need Valencia.

Our children need Valencia.

But most importantly, *Valencia* needs Valencia.

My body freezes at a crashing sound beyond the door. "Valencia! Everything alright?"

A few seconds pass with my heartbeat in my ears.

"Yep. Just, walked into the stool step."

You mean step stool, darling. I knew this wasn't a good idea. For her sake, I persist, however, the damn anticipation's going to kill me. *Wait…*why is she even outside the shower when the water is still going?

Give her a few minutes, Giannotti.

She's okay.

She'll call out if she needs anything.

I haven't checked on the kids in the past half hour. That is what the abduction has driven me to; checking on them over and over again. I check on them now, kissing their foreheads. I hope they never know the man I am when people hurt the ones I love, the man I was days after Addilyn's disappearance, the man I was earlier at The Red Tavern.

I was able to put myself together again for them.

For Valencia and them.

I have flaws. Deep lies I have kept hidden, even from Valencia. My only hope is that if I ever do choose to speak about it, it will be on my terms.

Twenty minutes have passed now. I lean against the door, my fingers fanning out against the cream paint. "Valencia? You okay?"

I get nothing and become concerned. The water is still running. I call out her name louder for a second time. *Perhaps she didn't hear me the first time.* There's still no response. I don't wait a third time and slide the door open.

Thank God.

Valencia leans against the shower wall. Her hands press against the charcoal tiles, as if they are the only things holding her up. She hasn't seen me enter, but her sobs deliver straight to my heart. I know they aren't only for what happened with Bryce. It's for Addilyn too. A selfish part of me wants to say they're also because of *us*.

It aches to witness her pain and agony unfold in front of me. If warmth and comfort are all I can provide tonight, hopefully it will be enough to settle her turmoil and the desperate pieces inside me.

Her nakedness is on full display. Her light olive toned skin, those soft, ample breasts…It's another first in a long time. I don't gawk. I don't take advantage. I keep my gaze on her face and unbutton my shirt. I shrug it off and keep going, stripping away every last piece of clothing.

This can ruin everything.

It can make it worse.

Or it can change everything for the better.

My mind is in shreds. I will never forget this moment for the rest of my life. *Never.* Not the way my arms wrap around her waist. Not how her body relaxes at my touch. And especially not how her heat transfixes me. It's so fucking familiar—the feeling of her.

Warm water trickles along my back, shielding Valencia from impact. We're blanketed in steam. It's some type of make believe. I make it reality and kiss her freckled shoulder. "Let it out. It's okay to feel this way."

"I…" Valencia's turns to face me. Her hair is darker, slicked back from the water. "I need you to hold me."

It takes a moment. A single second. A hitched breath. I pull her into the securest embrace of our lives. She clutches onto me tight, as I do her. The sweet nothings I murmur while rubbing her back in circular motions take me back. Water sprays in my eyes, but I don't dare move.

The softness in our voices has me yearning for her more.

I kiss the side of her head and note her hair smells like me. "I'm not going to let go."

"I want her, Giulio. I want our baby back. *Please.*"

It's difficult to suppress my own pained tears when she cries out for Addilyn. In a perfect world, I would give Valencia everything. Anything she wants, I'd find a way for it to be hers again—*ours* again. In a perfect world, I would devour her against these very tiles for the way her naked body surges against mine with those stunning breasts making both my heart and cock feel. But this is no perfect world. One wrong step and our marriage will be further damaged.

Even if we were to get back together, our differences are bound to set us apart again.

"The twins. We need to—"

I place her mind at ease. "Nobody is going to hurt us. I won't allow it. I'm going to protect you. I'm going to protect Oscar and Slonne. Whatever it takes."

"What if one of us has to die to save our family?"

It's haunting. Eerie. I know exactly how she feels.

We're experiencing the same tragedy but in completely different worlds.

My silence has Valencia looking up. Her hazel eyes are dim as water drips from her long lashes. With my free hand by her waist, I cave to the feeling of her fingers around my neck. I know they won't stay there for long. It's the hardest part. That's why I cherish it the most I can now.

"Please, don't talk like that," I whisper.

"But what if it's a part of the 'whatever it takes?'"

I know it's not the alcohol speaking now. It's her. And so I tell her the only thing I can vow. "Then I go down protecting our family. But it won't be you. It will be me."

"I don't want that. I don't want anybody to die."
"It's a wicked world out there. I'll do what I have to."
"How can you be so sure it'll be you, not me?"
Some can't guarantee it...
"Darling, I just feel it."
But for her, I can.

CHAPTER EIGHT

Valencia

I WAKE TO THE DISTANT SMELL OF COFFEE BREWING.

The morning sun illuminates my vision as I turn over to glance at the bedside clock. 10:47 A.M. *Oh no.* My throbbing head is a reminder of last night.

Bryce McCarson.

The ugly crying.

Giulio. *Telling him to make love to me. Ugh!*

I groan and sit up to lean against the bedrest. When I lower the gray bamboo Lyocell sheets from my chest, I notice I'm wearing a dark oversized sweatshirt and navy pajama pants.

They're both *his.*

One whiff of Giulio's alluring aroma and flashes from last

night resurface. Bryce's advances and how Giulio rescued me. The following events become blurry until I focus and recall crying in the shower. I remember the concern laced in Giulio's voice when he called out for me and I didn't reply. I couldn't. I was too numb.

He called me darling.

I remember the way he held me closely and how our naked bodies pressed together. I felt better after his comforting touch. Wordlessly, Giulio had dried my hair, carried me to the bed, and had helped me get dressed. When I slipped under the sheets, on the verge of falling asleep, I swear he kissed my forehead. I'm sure of it. But I missed what he whispered seconds before leaving.

Ugh!

This used to be *our* bedroom. *Our* house. Now, it is a reminder of everything I have lost.

My marriage.

My daughter.

Myself.

I hold onto the familiar vanilla smell of the sheets and how it transports me to the past. *He still uses the same laundry detergent.* Things like this shouldn't get to me, but they do.

A soft knock has me glancing towards the door. A smiling Giulio crosses the room and sits on the edge of the bed. "Good morning."

"Morning." I smile, flustered.

He hands me ginger tea in a floral mug with the words; *We love you Mommy!* The sentimental mug is one he bought on the twins' behalf for me one Mother's Day. I guess I had forgotten to take *everything* to Helena's.

I do my best to not react and thank him for the two pills that follow. I down them quickly, for a second forgetting how to swallow at the sight of his broad shoulders, narrow waist, and the lush charcoal colored towel around his hips, framing his toned body and naturally lightly tanned skin.

I never thought months without him...without *this* sight

would affect me so deeply…boy, was I wrong. One glance at the sexy thin trail of trimmed dark hair that runs down the center of his defined V muscle and disappears beneath the towel has me taking an extra-long sip. Steam filters into my vision as my gaze hovers over the mug.

So not obvious, Valencia.

Fresh out of the shower, Giulio's damp hair is tousled in that sexy kind of way I love. Handsome doesn't even begin to describe him. Not in the slightest. He most likely went to the gym after dropping the kids off.

The kids!

I snap out of my trance and expect to meet his gaze…apparently, I wasn't the only one checking somebody out. His slate eyes burn through my sweater and further flicker down to where the sheets begin at my waist. It takes a full minute for Giulio to realize I'm watching him too because he seems to stare at my lips for the longest time while I ponder what his mind could be brewing.

It's only when I take another gulp of ginger tea that he comes to and clears his throat.

I guess we're both just going to act as if our moment never happened.

I set down my mug. "I'm sorry I put you in that situation with Bryce last night."

"There's no need to apologize."

"For me, there is."

Giulio stands up, but it takes a full second for him to face me. Crossing his arms over his chest proves an error as my gaze involuntarily lowers to his biceps, abdominal muscles and then that v-line for the second time this morning. I stop myself from going any further. This is not healthy for either of us.

Girl, you were pressed up against it last night.

I mentally facepalm.

"I stopped by Helena's after taking the kids to school and picked up some clothes for you. They're in the bathroom. It doesn't mean work has to be in the equation today; that's up to you. Your clothes from last night are at the cleaners and your car is at Helena's."

I'm mortified. "I don't know how to thank you enough."

"You don't have to. I made breakfast for us. Come eat soon, okay?"

"Okay. Thank you for everything."

Giulio flashes a warm smile before leaving, but his cologne lingers, clouding my every thought.

I finish my tea and go to the bathroom to find a neatly folded pile of my clothes, just as he promised. I bypass my reflection. After all those tears last night, I know my eyes will not be their usual vibrant color. To be honest, they haven't been since Addilyn was in my arms.

I opt for another shower, seeing as last night's wasn't quite complete. Warmth streams down my body. The humid air and steamed glass doors are heavy indications that Giulio was in this same space not long ago. I used to love this sleek modern bathroom Giulio designed. It was unique and special; easily the favorite part of our house. Now I hate it. I despise the way the solitude of the room makes me feel so excluded, as if I've lost my place. How the gray step stool by the sink is a persistent reminder of my children. The way my heart anxiously beats at the memories of the infinite sex Giulio and I have had against these very tiles.

I want it all to stop, but it never ends. Especially not the moment I'm forced to use his bodywash as it's the only thing I have. Last night I went overboard with it. I lather the blue substance all over me and it reconfirms I've erased all of Bryce's mouth-works.

Being naked in front of Giulio last night did draw upon my vulnerabilities. I had a traumatizing labor with Addilyn. She was a breech baby. My cesarean scar is another reminder of what I've lost. When you bring life into the world, nothing compares to the connection between a mother and newborn. With Addilyn being stripped from me I have lost touch with what it means to be a woman. I disregard myself and never see my body as something worth praising like I'm sure other women do.

Giulio never knew this and following her disappearance I didn't want to be touched. I didn't want him to see me because I didn't love anything about myself without her with us. Last night our situation caused a physical reaction. We clung onto each other as if it was life or death. It felt different. A part of me wants to say a *good* different.

My fingers grip the pressure changer, yet I'm incapable of switching it off when fingertips graze my hand. I gasp. Giulio's hard chest presses against my back, his left hand working its way to my waist.

"I'm sorry for everything I've done…"

My breath deepens. "It's okay."

"No. It's not okay."

His touch runs up my body, leaving hot prints of his passion. "Giving up on us was the biggest mistake of my life. Being apart has been the worst decision of our life. I want you back."

"Giulio, I…" I want to say more but I am incapable of thinking straight. My head is spinning, and for the first time this morning, it's not only because of the alcohol.

"Set us free. I want you to set us free, Valencia."

My eyes open and I spin around to find nobody. Giulio isn't in the bathroom. It was a fantasy. A hallucination.

I gather the strength to shut off the shower. "Oh god."

I need to take my pills.

My body is hot all over and I struggle to grip the black bra and underwear he picked out for me without clutching the countertop. *Holy cow.* It was only a vision. *But it felt so real.*

I slip on the black cigarette pants with a thick belt and a tight gray top. Seattle weather dictates the revival of a coat, and placed neatly on top of the kid's stool, is a nude pair of heels. I slip the rather comfortable outfit on, drying off my hair the best I can, and use a spare toothbrush. I have to go without makeup, despite my puffy eyes.

Giulio glances over when I enter the sleek contemporary kitchen. He sets down the newspaper in one hand and lowers the espresso from his lips with the other. He's standing on one side of the luminous marble island. Breakfast is presented perfectly on it. There is orange juice, neatly cut fruit, and my favorite: honey on toast. My anti-depressants also make a feature.

Giulio Giannotti looks straight out of a GQ cover. The way he leans by the island, ankles locked and giving me his undivided attention—*my good god!* His black hair is slicked back with one single strand fallen on the side of his face. The dapper look is complemented by its slightly messy element, reinforcing its alpha feel. Most importantly, he's changed into a black turtleneck and elegant pinstriped charcoal slacks.

He looks too good.

Giulio gives a slow, sexy smile. It's the first time in a while. "You look gorgeous, Valencia. I didn't do a bad job with the outfit, hmm?"

I bite my lip. "I'm afraid you're right."

"Is that permission to add fashion stylist to my office door?"

"Sure. Right under smartass in the making."

"*Oh,* really now?" A smirk crosses Giulio's face. I like it when he's happy. "Well, should I add your number as my referral?"

"I'm afraid I would have to change my number then, Mr. Giannotti."

"Mmmm. Although I shouldn't say it, I like your tactics."

"I'm glad you do." My heart flutters at our playful banter. I set the mug on the island before it has the chance to slip from my sweaty grip. Sliding onto one of the steel kitchen stools, I take a bite of the toast. *It's pure heaven!*

"What are you going to do about this personal vendetta against my style eye?"

I wave the toast. "This may have just bought you immunity."

Giulio chuckles and leans towards me. With his head resting on his hands, he's teasing me and knows it. Those thoughts from the shower intensify the moment he arches a brow, only to sweep his tongue across his lower lip. "Only if you'll give me a taste of that immunity."

"I respectfully decline."

"Request denied. What are you going to do about it now?"

My cheeks heat. "I guess I'll have to come up with something."

Giulio rounds the island slowly, positioning himself inches from me. Those irresistible eyes I once fell in love with enrich the temptation to forget the barriers between us.

"You do that, Mrs. Giannotti."

Mrs. Giannotti.

I set the toast down and reach for the napkin but Giulio beats me to it. He takes my sticky hand and draws it to his lips. My legs cross as our uninterrupted gaze never drops and Giulio's warm tongue swirls over each finger, running across the tips and sucking off the honey. The highly erotic moment is drawn out by his meticulous motions.

Holy hell.

His touch drives me wild and when Giulio sets down my hand, his lips draw inches from my neck. It's allusive. Lustful. Our problems are placed on pause. He's going to kiss me, right *here*, just when I need him the most. I'm sure of it. So certain that I yearn for it.

Instead, Giulio's mouth skims to my ear. There's no kiss. His voice becomes a raspy, sensual whisper. I wish I had the will-power to ignore the effects it has on my body, but I can't. "Next time another man touches you, they will not again see the light of day. Even on the days we disagree and disregard each other, you're still my wife. I'm still your husband. The hell with the ones who get in the way. The hell with anybody who even *attempts* to break us down."

Energy swirls in the room. Sexual and emotional tension. I never imagined that such a bleak night yesterday could turn into such a thriving positive. It feels as though we have finally progressed and taken a leap forward. My mind repeats what I told myself the other day: *it's over.* The thing is…it isn't. It sure as hell isn't over from the way we're acting. I don't know how long it will last, but for now, I want to stay in the present.

And so I kiss his cheek and smile as his eyes darken.

Yes.

I take our promises to heart and enjoy this breakfast with him. We talk about work, the twins, and how I have begun the handbook he gifted me. I've been loving it and knowing it came from the heart...it does something to me. We both need serenity today and I'm feeling much better than I did last night.

"Thank you for everything you did for me, Giulio. For everything you are doing now. Especially with the kids. You know I'm not the type of person who goes out drinking like that. I don't know what happened. I lost track of time and myself."

"It isn't your fault. Any person with human decency would have done what I did last night. I still don't understand how nobody came to your aid before."

"I know." I fold the towel as we finish drying the dishes. "What do we do about Bryce?"

"I'm going to fire him." Something flashes in his eyes and he sighs. "I...I *want* to fire him."

"You have every right to, but he's not a bad man. Yes, he was drunk and what he did was illegal, but...before that he genuinely wanted assistance to better your company."

"I'm prepared to do whatever you're comfortable with. It's just that with Marcus..."

"What about Marcus?"

"We have this..." Giulio rubs the back of his neck and begins shaking his head. "What do you want to happen to Bryce at work? How about we call the police and report him?"

"I don't want him fired or reported. I think he deserves another chance to prove himself."

"But he was trying to persuade you. He was making advances, and if I hadn't gotten there when I did...god knows what would have happened. I know he was drunk, but that isn't a reason. Seeing you like that last night...it ruined me. If you don't want him fired, I can suspend him until your contract ends. Whatever you want to happen, I'll see it through."

I shake my head. "That will only prove he's winning. I'm not scared of seeing him."

"Are you positive?"

"Positive."

Giulio blows out an unconvinced sigh. "Okay. If that's what you really want, but I want you to think about it. There's always time to change your mind. Always. I'll talk to him this morning."

"Thank you." I stay on track with our conversation, appreciating that for once we're dissecting something without restraint. "I decided to drink. Everything would have been different if I hadn't stayed there so long or continued accepting those glasses."

"That's even more of a reason why this is on him. It doesn't matter how much you drink; it doesn't mean others can advance on or take advantage of you. Yes, he could have gone much further than he did, but either way it's wrong and I'm almost certain Bryce did it in spite of me. He knows how fragile we are at the moment with everything going on."

"I know…Last night he noticed I don't wear my ring anymore. He said something along the lines of it technically meaning him and I can spend time together without anybody talking."

Giulio's jaw clenches. "Is this guy serious?"

"Apparently nobody can resist the English charm. His words, not mine."

"They say the same thing about Italian men, but I don't go around raving about it. Maybe I should. Maybe I should get a gun and shove it up his ass for even thinking let alone saying such a thing—"

"Damn. Somebody woke up on the wrong side of the bed." Marcus' voice has me clutching my chest and screaming in shock. *Oh, my heart.* My brother-in-law chuckles from the entry of the kitchen at Giulio who responded to my reaction by instinctively throwing the sponge at his half-brother and protectively stepping in front of me.

The moment we see who it is, we both let out a sigh of relief.

"Fuck, Marcus!" Giulio curses, rounding the counter to collect the sponge. "Why did you have to scare us like that? There's such a thing as a doorbell!"

"Why ring the bell when you have a key? If architecture ever gets exhausting at least I know I have a secure job in home invasions." A cackle escapes Marcus, who winks in my direction. "Isn't that right, Val?"

I feel as though I've received a blow to the stomach.

Addilyn. The home invasion. The abduction.

The havoc in my head must be evident in my eyes because Marcus' expression falls and worry replaces it. "Oh shit, I'm sorry. I'm such a dick. I didn't think."

It's not his fault. It's mine. My incapability to detach everything that has been happening to us. Especially the fact that last night was the first night I actually slept well under the same roof since everything happened...well, I have the alcohol to thank.

I gulp down my glass of water.

Giulio glances my way and his jaw locks when he looks back at his half-brother. "That was a low blow. Do you ever think before you speak?"

"No need to get so defensive, bro. I admitted it was a shit move."

"Wrong move or not, you knew better."

"I thought that after all these months you wouldn't tense up at every single thing associated with my goddaughter."

"A parent's pain doesn't go away. Especially not when your child is taken like that."

I don't see what unfolds next between the men because my eyes stay on my hands. I take in my ring finger and swallow harshly as I recall Bryce's words from last night. I never thought of it *that* way. Giulio and I decided to take off our rings to make it easier for us—I never considered the possibility of it meaning I'm open for business. I certainly am not. I am simply *being*.

Marcus scoffs. "I still don't know why you're going on about this!"

"You *know* why. Don't play dumb with me," Giulio growls in disgust.

"You're the one acting like a lunatic! I said I'm sorry!"

"Me? Lunatic? I'm not the one spending my entire weekly pay all in one single day."

Marcus' reddened face turns livid. "Fuck you! You don't have sex for half a year and all of a sudden you have no filter! Wow, talk about low blows. I can't believe you just said that!"

"All I'm saying is the truth and you know it. I have always helped you. *Always.*"

I step in between them feeling lost. "Wait. What are you both talking about?"

What did Giulio mean about Marcus spending his entire pay in one single day?

Marcus must be ashamed to tell me what's going on with him, but he knows the type of woman I am. I don't judge. I will always willingly listen and help the best I can.

Marcus' expression weakens at my furrowed brows. "Now is not the time."

"No, now is perfect," Giulio says, "I think Valencia has the right to know."

Marcus mocks the suggestion. "Oh, is she your best friend now?"

"She *was* my best friend."

"Until you both fucked things up."

Giulio loses it, his composure cut prematurely short. He's face-to-face with Marcus in three strides. "What is wrong with you this morning? Huh? You think you can come into my house and bad mouth my relationship? Let me tell you something. I loved Valencia, you know that. She was my best friend. My lover. My everything. Then in an instant, she was gone, along with Addilyn and my entire purpose. A family broken by the touch of evil. Have you ever felt that? Huh? The feeling that you could have it all and then suddenly you've lost it all?"

She was my best friend.

My lover.

My everything.

My throat tightens at the poetic melancholy.

"Give me a couple years. Maybe I'll get to that point too, brother."

"Marcus!" I gasp at his attitude. "Giulio has done nothing but help you. He's funded your studies, flew you across the world, and gave you a successful position at his firm. I know your relationship is messy because of the past, but he's always been good to you."

"I'm not the issue. *He* is," Marcus hisses, "Something has got him so uptight and it all started the moment you began working for us, Valencia."

Giulio silences any further accusation. "Don't you dare go there. Why are you here, Marcus?"

He glances between us, eventually calming down. "Tate called and needs to move the meeting an hour ahead. We are due to be there in fifteen minutes."

"Was Bryce at the office?"

"Haven't seen him all morning. Are you ready to go? We don't have much time."

I take their plans lightly. Although his words are directed at his half-brother, Giulio turns to me with a frown. "Since Bryce is not in the office, I'll work from home today with Valencia. Can you go without me, Marcus?"

"No. I need you there."

"Go," I encourage Giulio with a soft smile. "I'll be okay if you drop me off at home."

He doesn't take it lightly. "I don't know…"

"What's going on with you two?"

I let Giulio take the lead. "I was hoping to speak to Bryce. Apparently for him, if there isn't a wedding band on a woman's finger it's a green light saying come and fuck me."

Marcus' jaw drops and he looks my way. "What?"

"After I met Bryce at the bar last night, he was adamant for me to stay. We had a few drinks and…he went too far."

"As in?"

Giulio steps in. "Unwanted advances. We're talking border-line sexual assault."

The tension between us all simmers. I'm still adjusting to the fact that I'm in Giulio's house and recovering from a hangover.

"So you're telling me he's a threat?"

"I think you were out of your goddamn mind hiring him. The man doesn't have any interior design skills. Last week I brought him along to a client's house, and do you know what he suggested for a contemporary design? An orange granite kitchen counter-top and a mint backsplash?"

Marcus shrugs, unfazed. "Maybe it's a common trend where he's from. Don't be so hard on him; he's worked hard to make it to where he is now. Remember what I said? *Deal with it.*"

Giulio shakes his head. "I can't just *deal with it* when I'm questioning his ability to perform well in my company and his intentions with my wife."

"She's not your wife anymore."

You are enough.

Being you is enough.

My heart drops into my stomach. I can't take the drama anymore. "Giulio, please take me home. You need to go to that meeting and I will be fine on my own. Come on, let's go."

I can see it in his stance that he's torn. He eventually gives. Marcus leaves without saying goodbye and ignores mine. *That's nice.*

Giulio and I don't say a word as he drives me to Helena's. Our new normal is something we've been involuntarily forced into. I can barely tolerate it on top of all the angst. The tension between the half-brothers sparked a tension that renewed our new normal, back to that tense silence.

Before Marcus intervened, we were two different people, caught inside a make-believe fantasy, one without the water rising. Despite all of the chaos, this morning our laughter and smiles blanketed out the worries.

But that isn't real life for us…not anymore.

Call me delusional but I somehow make it to Notti Designs an hour after Giulio drove me home. He wanted me to rest and take it easy, but I couldn't stay cooped up at home any longer. The dizziness turned to guilt and I don't want to let go of my dedication to my job.

Helena's the first one to deconstruct my plan in a phone call during her lunch hour. "Girl, why the hell are you there? You should have stayed home!"

"I couldn't stand it any longer," I admit, flashing Lee my keycard. He smiles and allows me through to the elevator. There are a few people already waiting. "Plus, it's the least I can do for Giulio. He's done so much for me."

"True, he's been incredible with you. That Bryce must have been a nightmare. What an asshole! I had a terrible feeling when you didn't answer my texts. I wanted to come over last night, but I figured you needed the rest."

"Yeah, trust my phone to die. It was…up there with one of the worst experiences in my life, next to having Addilyn taken. I couldn't get him off me and I know he was drunk but—"

She cuts me off. "That's still no excuse to act the way he did."

"Exactly. It's never okay." I blow out a breath, waiting for the elevator doors to open. "But as I was saying, last night with Giulio was so raw and intimate. We haven't been like that since before the separation. It just proved how much I miss him and the people we once were."

"I truly believe that with time you'll get there again with him. If he didn't care, he would have never gone to the extent you described before. Lencia…it's obvious Giulio still cares."

"But everything is so different now. He cares because I'm the mother of his children."

"We both know it's more than that."

Deep down, I know that too.

Silence overtakes me until I push through. "So, how's work going?"

"Nah, ah! We're still on you, girlfriend. I would eliminate all interaction with this Bryce."

"Oh, I will. Whenever Giulio and Bryce are in the same room there was always this tense energy. Now I know it's because of Bryce straying from schedule and forging Giulio's signature. Oh, did I forget to tell you that the reason the intern set to replace Amanda didn't work out was because Bryce and her got it on in his office?"

"Oh my god, get out! Giulio caught them?"

"I'm not sure what exactly happened but it was Bryce himself who told me that the incident occurred. Apparently he doesn't see it as a big deal and we both know what that means…"

"That he doesn't give a shit about the company." Helena finishes my thought with a scoff. "But that's between them so don't worry about a thing, hun. You do what's best for you."

"I know, I just hate being in the middle of it. *Oh*, I have to go. He's walking up to me."

"Who? Giulio?"

"No. The one from last night." My rushed words come out as barely a whisper as Bryce nears the elevator. I don't think he's seen me yet. The elevator doors answer my prayers and the second they slide open, I rush inside.

"Bryce? Oh my god. Let me speak to him and give him a piece of my mind!"

The reception begins breaking up. "It's okay, honey. I have to go. I'll see you later!"

Her words bring a brief smile to my lips. Helena is my sanity. One of the only people I can openly speak to without feeling judged or overwhelmed. I would be so lost without her.

I stab the twelfth floor button, but then I watch Bryce's white Converse enter the elevator and it's all over. Confined anywhere near him is the last thing I want to be.

At least we're not alone.

Bryce's broad shoulders brush against mine when he steps in. Those distant green eyes linger for a fraction too long and for a moment I debate stepping out and taking the stairs. Hesitation has never blinded me more. There is nothing I want more than to be away from this man. Giulio is right. I feel it too, the mystery that looms above Bryce's head from the first moment I met him

The elevator stops on numerous floors before the top floor

permitting Bryce and me to create a distance between us. Silence floods the space. Instead of a quick elevator ride, this one is beginning to be the longest of my life.

There's still another man dressed in a navy business suit, and he seems to be heading for Notti Designs too. I recognize him as Mr. Jermaine, one of the realtors set to meet Lance.

"Aye...I won't bite, Valencia."

Oh, here we go...

"I don't know that." I raise my chin high, displaying my resistance is not based upon Bryce's reputation, it's wholly based upon last night. He went too far. "I don't want to talk about it."

"Fine. But you can't escape my existence. We work together."

Not for long. I'm out of here in six weeks, McCarson.

His words reel me in despite his cruel gaze, but I stare ahead, unable to look at the dark bruises around his eyes and swollen nose. It doesn't seem broken, but it's obvious Giulio did some damage.

"So last night was something else, huh?"

Mr. Jermaine glances our way and bites back a smirk before he turns back to his phone.

Perfect. Now he thinks the absolute worst about McCarson and me. Just what I need.

"I had too much to drink."

"Same. It didn't surprise me *ya know who* ruined the night. He has a tendency to ruin things."

"He didn't ruin it."

"He did in my book."

"I beg to differ, Bryce." I shake my head and turn to him, noting the way his jaw clenches when he rubs his beard. It's a long steady stroke. His lack of speech falls on white noise and when the elevator doors slide open; I excuse myself to step through to Notti Designs first.

My heels slap against the concrete floor, but Bryce is right behind me. I want to be alone. I want a couple of moments to simply recenter and come to terms with the consequences of working here.

Kayla steps in my direction, oblivious to the reason I'm speed walking. "A couple letters came in for you and Giulio. I've left them on your desk."

I force a smile. "Thank you."

In the distance, the normal chatter comforts me. *Nothing can happen here.* I drop my bag on my desk, eyeing the two ivory letters. Each has our names in printed blocks.

"Aye! Valencia!" I keep my head straight towards the desk, disregarding Bryce's deep, rumbling accent. "I'm sorry if ya felt as though I was forcing ya. It wasn't my intention. I was drunk. It felt good but I wasn't gonna go any further. Not more than what you wanted. I thought ya wanted a change. Give me a chance to start over. Maybe we could have some lunch together today to talk everything through, yeah?"

"That wouldn't be a good idea."

"Okay. How about dinner then?"

"Bryce, please stop this."

"Stop what?"

I spin on my heel and find myself trapped by my desk and his hard chest. It's barely enough to stand straight, let alone think clearly. My heart shifts to a place of uncertainty.

I miss my kids.

It's hard to glance up at Bryce and not feel as though my head is on fire. "Look, maybe last night was an off night. I'm not saying it's what you do to women but you did it to *me* and so I hope you can respect I need time to recover."

"Is that a no to the dinner?"

"You're…being friendly, I get it, but I'm not looking for a relationship. I'm not looking for somebody to satisfy my needs, no matter how strong the desire can be at times. I'm going through a rough patch in my life, the separation and abduction have destroyed me. I need time to find myself again. So pl-please, I don't feel comfortable with how close you're standing."

McCarson makes a brief effort to stand back, but I can still smell him. That rugged, bergamot scent. He cocks his head to the side, brows furrowed. "So, you didn't enjoy last night?"

For the love of…

"Your body was involuntarily pressed against mine! What part of that statement do you not understand?" I hiss. Enough of being nice. I decide I'm not taking this any further. "I don't want anything to do with you. Am I clear?"

Bryce grinds his jaw. It reveals the type of man he is. Feisty. Cunning. Manipulative. Redness pulls across his face, settling at the base of his neck. "Is this Giulio telling ya to say all these things? Because I swear that man is gonna do me nut in if he—"

"No, I'm saying them myself! Giulio doesn't control me! And while we're at it, what the hell does *do me nut in* even mean?"

"I honestly don't believe that he isn't contributing and it means to drive someone insane."

"Well you're wrong because I'm speaking my own truths and I would appreciate it if you'd respect them, Mr. McCarson."

"And how about *my* own truths? I have no idea how many lies he's feeding ya about me. I'm not the type of man who jumps on any woman. I admit that I was wasted and shouldn't have gone that far last night, but everybody makes mistakes. Right?"

An apology.

It's all I ever wanted, but it gives me no assurance that he wouldn't try this stunt again or that he truly means what he's says.

I take a different approach. "I don't think you should bad talk your boss, Bryce. He's the one holding up this company. He can drop you at any time."

"Actually, he can't. It's exactly why I associate with Marcus and not him."

"What do you mean he *can't*? He's the CEO! What really happened between you two?"

"Nothing happened, it's just fucking impossible for us to get along. That's all."

"Well, you could try to change that."

"Nahhh. I've got better things to do. Besides, I don't need to do anything for Giulio's benefit. I'm not the one who decided to marry and have three kids with him…"

"How dare you say such a thing!"

"Oh, come on. Don't give Giulio the respect he doesn't merit."

"He deserves the respect much more than you know! Giulio built this company from the ground up. If you don't feel fit to work here, then don't. But don't you dare drag him down like he's undeserving of success. He deserves it. He worked hard to be where he is now. He's a good man."

Bryce arrogantly scoffs. "Is that why ya got separated? Because he was a *good* man? Obviously he isn't because he couldn't hold his family together. He lost the end of that deal."

My eyes widen.

Screw him!

The malice laced in Bryce's voice leads me to one conclusion: perhaps his drunken actions last night were solely to get back at Giulio or some type of payback, even though he's the one happily breaking every single rule here…*could that be it?*

"You just don't get it, do you? You don't understand how much your words hurt me or my family. You don't know what either of us have been through, or who I really am."

"I know that he doesn't deserve ya. He doesn't deserve his success, his children, or—"

Bryce's face jerks to the right. The slap is quick. Hard. My lungs deceive me at my shallow gasp as I recover my assaulting hand and his eyes shut for the briefest of seconds.

Oh my god!

What did I just do?

Bryce's gaze flickers back to me and I note something's changed. They're glazed in speckles of defeat. "I…I deserved that."

I don't stay to witness him further.

Racked with emotion, I tightly grip the letters and round the unpredictable man who does nothing but stare. His feet remain planted on the floor, yet that doesn't guarantee a thing.

I can't believe I just did that.

Giulio's office acts like my refuge. I scramble to lock the door and sink into his dark leather chair. His lasting scent shouldn't calm me…but it does. *I'm safe now.*

I need to get myself together.

There are two picture frames on Giulio's desk. The first is of him with the twins and Addilyn a couple of weeks after her birth. I remember taking the photo. Giulio is grinning at the camera, his arms securely holding Addilyn. The twins are seated on either side of them. Oscar is gripping a paper plane, the picture taken seconds before putting it on his father's hair. Slonne is captured mid-giggle, kissing her baby sister's forehead as Addilyn's smiles.

The second photo frame is face down and I know why.

Giulio must still be with Marcus and their client, Tate. I have no reason to call him, but a deep part of me wishes he was here, especially with the harsh knocks on the door, followed by Bryce's persistent pleas to open the door.

No.

I ignore it and fight the urge to feel any type of sympathy. I'm so used to attending to everybody's needs…the kids, my students…now I have to block it out for once.

The knocking stops and I make the mistake of turning over the frame.

Our wedding day.

We're grinning at each other as he has me in a dip, holding the small of my back. Our passion enthralled in heavenly fire. I remember the feeling it brought. Security. Honor. Forever and always.

The memory flickers alive so vividly.

Giulio's hands slip in mine, distracting me from the marriage officiant's words.

This will be the greatest moment of my life. Right here. Right now. Standing face to face with Giulio Giannotti. The man I would die for. The man I love more than life itself.

"You look beautiful," he mouths.

"Thank you."

My cheeks sting from the smile that hasn't wiped off my face since last night. That was when everything hit me and it no longer felt surreal. There's that familiar warmth within Giulio's eyes. It tells me that we will be inseparable, that this will only the beginning.

Giulio's hands squeeze mine and all I want to do is kiss him. I need to wait though. We are getting married after all!

I want to take it all in. Every single detail. From his perfectly slicked back hair, to my fluttering heart, to the ocean waves crashing behind us that intensify the excitement bursting inside me. A destination wedding is something we always wanted, especially to escape the December cold in Seattle.

Fiji.

"Valencia?"

I snap back to reality and everybody is looking at me. Giulio is wearing that mind-blowing smirk that I love. The marriage officiant smiles warmly, "Your soon to be husband was about to say his vows…"

"Oh gosh, sorry."

Guests laugh at my mishap. I smile at the faces of friends and family who have devoted their time to us. My parents catch my eye and then Helena, my maid of honor, tugs at my side. "You've got this, girlfriend."

"She won't be your girlfriend for too long now." Giulio winks over at us.

I giggle, followed by the rest of the guests.

Helena smiles at her soon to be brother-in-law, "Oh, really now?"

"Yes. Lencia and I did something about that."

"That's right." I squeeze his hands in mine. "We sure did."

As the laughter fades, Giulio squeezes back. "Valencia." He starts over, adoration in his tone. "Before I lost my mother, she told me something. That all good things end and so I should make the most of life. I promise to support you within our best moments and within our worst. I vow to love you even after death do us part. Because it will not mean that our journey is over, it will still continue to exist inside us. I vow to appreciate every single moment of my life with you by my side. I vow to give you the best of myself. To respect and cherish you. To be there and support you. To do anything for and love you more than life itself."

My heart clenches at his perfection. The words. His heart. Our love.

Giulio kisses my forehead just as a tear escapes my eyes.

"Giulio," I grin. "Every day I wake up and cannot believe we found each other. I vow to love you unconditionally. To give you all of me, even the crazy. I vow to wholeheartedly put us first and never forget how deeply you complete me. With you, I'm whole. When times get tough, with any challenges we may face, know that we will conquer them together and will always find our way back to each other. Your mother is with us, baby. She's here and is so proud of the man you've grown up to be. The man you are now. The father you are going to be… very soon."

Still smiling, Giulio's jaw drops. His eyes drop to my flat stomach. "Are you…?"

I can only nod for half a second before he crushes me in a tight embrace. His lips press against the side of my head and both our bodies vibrate in pure emotion.

Happy tears trail down my cheeks as guests begin to cheer, clapping at what I've been concealing for the past few weeks. It's the perfect moment to share in front of everybody who means so much to us.

I'm wrapped in affection.

"Oh my god." Giulio's eyes are glossy when we retake our positions. "You better announce us husband and wife before I kiss the heck out of her!"

I will never forget this day.

The moment comes where 'I do' means much more than just three letters. It's a whole life commitment. Within a second we have confirmed everything we have been fighting for. All our sacrifices will be worth it because he will be right by my side.

Giulio Giannotti will be the one I turn to when times get rough. He will be the one I confide in during the good and the bad moments in our lives. Together.

"You may kiss the bri—"

We don't need any more permission. Our passionate kiss is fueled with heated desire. Guests clap and cheer, and it brings everything alive.

Giulio's soft hands slip over my stomach and I feel whole. "I love you, Mrs. Giannotti."

"I love you more."

"Impossible."

I miss having somebody so close to me, however, I can't forget the reasons we ended everything. Those reasons were washed away during this morning's breakfast, but now they're hung up in front of me.

Distraction.

I need a distraction from these unnerving thoughts.

The letters.

My name is printed in bold on the first letter. I'm perplexed there is no return or sent address. Even more so when I find it's a typed up letter. Then comes the sinking feeling at what I read.

Valencia,

Under no circumstance may this be shared with anybody other than who it is addressed to. No police. Nobody. If you do, you risk it all and it will be game over.

Be the smart woman you are. Rearrange the letters in each word.

ENALVCIA, UYO REA ETXN.

I rearrange them carefully.

VALENCIA, YOU ARE NEXT.

I thrust the letter away from me and fall back into the seat.

My dear god...What is this?

The noise that escapes me takes everything out of me. Everything. The banging comes alive again inside me and my heart pounds a distant tune, one of panicked turmoil.

I'm next...

A letter addressed to Giulio follows. In anticipation I grip it, searching his drawer to use a letter slicer. At first, my trembling hands shake the paper so hard it blurs and I am unable to rearrange the letters.

GIULIO, YOU ARE NOT FAR BEHIND.

There's another sheet behind it.

To O&S.

Oscar and Slonne.
My stomach is not holding up with the mixture of my parting hangover, the medicine, and my nerves. *Yeah, not the best combination.* I swallow down the lump in my throat and attempt to convince myself this is all a dream.
This is not real.
Not real.
Not real.
But it is and that's what gets me the most.

BUT BEFORE ALL, IT IS YOU BOTH.

I jump from the seat and brace myself against the desk for assistance to stand.
No.
I can't do it again. I can't watch helplessly as something else happens.
I need to lie down.
I need to calm my aching body.
I need this to all go away.
I drag myself to Giulio's sage ottoman bench by the floor-to-ceiling windows, overlooking the gloomy Seattle afternoon. I need a few moments to comprehend that this war between my family and evil has only just begun.
This is the beginning of the end for us.
It's only going to get worse from here. *I know it.*
I clutch my stomach and lie down on the bench, curling my

knees to my chest. Simply staring up at the merging clouds does nothing. I can't handle this.

Who is doing this to us?

What do they want?

Why?

Get me. I want to scream. *Get me.* I don't care what they do to me. All I want is to protect Oscar and Slonne. They don't deserve to suffer so young in this cruel world.

Because that's exactly what this life can be.

Cruel.

CHAPTER NINE

Valencia

"**V**ALENCIA?"

The soft whisper wakes me as steady hands wrap around my waist. Somebody's screaming in the distance. It turns to wailing. I want to know who it is, but can't open my eyes no matter how hard I try—something's wrong.

"Shh, it's going to be okay." Giulio reassures me with his mouth pressed against my ear.

A twist just above my heart forces me to launch up from the ottoman bench and clutch onto something blindly. A cold glass of what could belong to a window shoots through my fingertips.

The scream halts.

I realize that it was me all this time.

It's me.

I can't swallow down my pain. It feels too heavy. Everything's too tight inside me. It's as though I've been thrown into a deep blue ocean, incapable of taking one breath without the pinching sensation in my head.

"Giulio, what is happening?"

"I need you to listen to my voice, okay? Can you do that for me?"

I nod.

"Let's try and lie down." Giulio presses my shaking body to his and lifts me up. Chest to chest, he sits on the bench before lying down on his back with me on top of him. "That's it. Slowly."

Then it hits me.

A bolt zooms through me at the flash thought of Addilyn.

All I see is her and the fateful cries that follow.

Our baby is gone.

"No! I can't do this. I can't forget her. She's a part of us." I cry, struggling in Giulio's grip until I lift up to my knees, essentially straddling him. "Now they're coming after all of us. They're going to hurt the only things I have left! Giulio, they're going to kill us!"

"I won't allow that. Breathe. We'll figure this out."

"We won't! It'll be too late!"

"You're thinking too far ahead, concentrate on the now. One step at a time, okay?" he murmurs against my neck, seeking to calm my distressed state as he sits up. "I saw the letters. Nobody is going to hurt us. Tell me one thing you've read from the handbook I wrote you."

"That when things happen you don't forget the tragedy, but in time it gets a little easier."

"Yes, that's it. That's perfect. Now, let's try and lie back down again."

"I don't know if I can…"

"I *know* you can. I've got you, okay?" Giulio's gives my hands a tight squeeze. "Now, let's do this again. Nice and slow…that's it." I give him my whole body as we lie down against the ottoman bench again. I snuggle into his neck and whilst his left hand remains clasped in mine, the other rubs small comforting circles on my back. "Some deep breaths in together. A deep one. Hold it… good…now let's release."

We count ten breaths.

"Tell me about your ocean."

"Giulio, I don't know if it will work."

It's something we used to do whenever I had panic attacks throughout our marriage. They happened rarely but increased to frequent after the abduction and even more after my diagnosis. Before our separation, Giulio advised me to think about an ocean and everything going on there. It was a tough solo mental game, but it helped.

"We can only try."

"It's a calm day." I start, well aware of the air caught in my throat. "There's a boat in the distance. A few actually, but I can only see one clearly. It's the closest."

When my breaths crash, Giulio responds by letting go of his right hand and slips it through my hair. Just like old times when he played with it, easing me. "What type of boat?"

"I'm not good with boats…"

"Whatever comes to mind."

"A sailboat."

"Can you see the sailor?"

"Umm." I try to think. "Yes. A middle-aged man."

"Glasses?"

"No."

"What's his flaw?"

"He can't work a compass correctly."

Giulio's chuckle electrifies me. It produces a long awaited smile on my lips. "I love that answer. What do you like most about your ocean?"

"The serenity." My lungs contract and steady in a space of tranquility. I'm grateful as the tension leaves my shoulders. When I my eyes flutter open, heaviness is still persistent, but the burning sensation has lifted from my unsettled body. I wipe at my wet cheeks. "I think I'm okay now. Thank you."

He helps me to my feet and to the guest chair next to his desk. "You don't need to thank me, darling."

There it is again—*Darling.*

Giulio exits his office and returns with a glass of water for me. The cold, refreshing liquid soothes my throat. When he sits on his leather seat, the one I occupied earlier, he folds the letters back into their envelopes.

"What time is it?"

"Just after one-thirty. Do you know what time it was when you passed out?" Giulio's gaze flickers from mine to our wedding photo, and the blood drains from my face.

Shit. I never faced it back down!

He doesn't physically react and that only makes me wonder what he's thinking.

"I came into the office just after midday, so sometime after that. Bryce stepped into the elevator after me and apologized, however when I didn't accept it he began disrespecting you. I couldn't tolerate it any further and got worked up. The letters made it worse and I went into shock." My voice cracks. "I'm sorry."

I cannot believe I fell asleep and had a panic attack *here.*

Giulio frowns. "Did he touch you?"

"No, but I did slap him."

I don't anticipate his crooked smile and the wicked amusement in it. "*Woah,* hold up. Wait a minute. You did? Only *one* time?"

"Yes, I don't know what I was thinking…I just got so worked up."

"Valencia, you've just made my day! What did he say? Why did you stop at one?"

And so I tell Giulio everything, along with my greatest concerns of all; Oscar and Slonne. We can't go to the police which means we're all alone in this and the probability of something happening to the twins is high. SPD stated it months ago. If Addilyn's abduction is a targeted attack and the abductor knows who we are, it might be only a matter of time. On the other hand, this could be a case of mistaken identity or simply a sickened mind.

This is the issue with The Window Case being cold. There have been no leads in six months, not until right now with the letters. To me, they carry the hope that if this is the kidnapper sparking communication, the possibility of Addilyn returning to us could be a reality.

But can Giulio and I do this without SPD?

No. Of course we can't.

Yet we have to.

"Kayla said they were with the rest of the company mail. The words are printed and there's no indication of any other clues. That does not give us much intel."

I oppose the idea circulating my mind. "What if this is some sick hoax? Most people in Seattle are familiar with the case, right? Hypothetically, what's to say somebody out there who knows about our situation, knows that we're vulnerable and wants to place unnecessary stress in the mix of everything else?"

"It's a possibility. God, at this stage there are so many possibilities."

"*Too* many. Now we even have to stay tight lipped about the letters."

"It's our only choice at this stage. We're bound by this now." The lure in our stare that soon shifts to longing has us both look away. He lets out a forced cough, noticeably affected. "Are we not?"

I prolong our avoided gaze.

"Yes, of course we are." My chest aches at the thought somebody is playing us. Their cruel intentions make me numb. "I need to revise my will, don't I?"

"No. Last night I told you how it will go down."

"It'll go down how they intend for it to go down. We're not in control. We're the prey in their game. Their eyes could be on us this very minute. They may know the kid's school and lurk. They may even have Addilyn!"

"One thing at a time, Valencia. Deep breaths."

I try. I will not cry. Not again. Not with him here.

Valencia, you are next.

Giulio, you're not far behind.

But before all, it's you both.

"Hey, you alright?"

I take advantage of the way Giulio's hot eyes are already on mine and respond to his concern with a brief nod, but he isn't convinced that I'm okay even when I vocalize it.

We don't break eye contact...

Not when he stands and smooths out his slacks.

Not when he rounds his desk.

Not when he drops down on one knee in front of me. It brings back memories. *He knows.* Of course he knows what it does to me, otherwise he wouldn't urge his gentle hand to my chin and slowly turn it so that I fixate on him.

"I'm not going to let anything happen to our twins or you. I may not be able to promise you many things, but I *can* promise you this."

I break at the rapid reminder of everything Giulio wants to push past. "And Addilyn?"

We can't get through this.

"Valencia, I'd like you to take it easy today."

My falling concern is not even taken into the equation. It's completely ignored. My cry for help means nothing. He still doesn't believe it. He doesn't believe me or *in* me. "Please answer me."

"Addilyn will always have a place in my heart. She will always be a piece of me. A piece of you." The pad of his thumb brushes my earlobe, down my jaw, and curls at the center of my lips. Those eyes I promised my entire life to scan my features one by one. "As much as we want to, we can't bring her back. Not after all this time. I can't promise her fate and I'm sorry that I can't. I wish I could, but I *can* promise you Slonne and Oscar's. I *can* promise yours."

And I will promise yours, Giulio.

I barely know who I am within this moment, let alone the wild thoughts running through my mind—but they're there. They blossom when his eyes fall to where I'm biting my lip. It seems as though Giulio is wedged in a place between reality and fiction. *I feel it.* Oh, what I would do to crawl into that mind and rearrange the puzzle pieces I identify as my husband. I want him to be on my team. I thought that maybe the letters would provide some refuge to the tension between us. Now, I acknowledge they have only intensified our broken hearts and shattered beliefs.

"Have you eaten lunch?" I ask, changing topics.

Giulio blinks and swallows as he comes to. His response to being caught red-handed lost in thought has me bite the inside of my cheek. It's hard to look at a man who has changed so much, yet at the same time is the same in your mind.

"Yes, I ate before coming back here. I have an in-house meeting at two. Have you eaten?"

"No."

"Buy some lunch and take the rest of the day off. You should be resting."

"I know," I say flatly. His touch leaves mine, yet close proximity remains. We're inches apart when he asks me softly in parting. "You scared me back there. Are you sure you're okay?"

"Yes, I'm okay now. Thank you."

Back at my desk, I need something to *set me free*. I know exactly what…a strong ginger tea. Yes. *Again.*

Voices chattering surround me in the Starbucks waiting area. After purchasing a sandwich, my eyes fall behind the shoulders of a man in a power suit flipping through The Seattle Times. An article's title catches my attention, forcing a gasp to slither down my throat.

The man glances over with a screwed up face. "Can I help you with something?"

"Oh my god!"

"Lady, I said is there something I can help you with?"

He probably assumes I'm a weirdo. *Maybe I am…shut up.* "May I kindly see that paper?"

He stares for a long moment, shrugs, and hands it to me. "I guess so. It's always the same things in here anyway."

I grab my ginger tea just as it's called and bolt. The man calls out behind me, telling me I can't steal the newspaper but I can't control my mind. My heels are daggers against the pavement and my blood pumps nothing but heartache.

Once inside Notti Design, I opt against the crowded elevator and take the stairs two at a time. Adrenaline crawls so deep Lee must notice because he doesn't even attempt to stop me. My mind fills with compulsive voices I've heard over and over for the past months. The ones that led to my separation.

It can all change now.

This is the clue I've been waiting for!

I press my elbow down to open the boardroom door and stumble inside. Just then, my left heel slides against the shiny concrete, my balance weakens, and I overcorrect to prevent myself from falling. Tea spills onto the floor, my blouse, and ends of my hair. The sandwich compressed in its protective container flies across the room, missing the head of a businesswoman by inches.

Shocked expressions duplicate in the men and women who surround the oak desk. Giulio is the only one who stands as I brush myself off and rush to his side, at this point stumbling with one heel off.

This is so not a good look.

The newspaper is partly soaked from the warm beverage, but I'm lucky it missed the article completely. "You have to see this. You have to!" I insist, slapping the paper on his desk.

Giulio takes one look at my wide eyes and turns to his associates. "Please excuse me for a moment. Lance, continue and brief me later." Giulio grips the newspaper and I retrieve my heel before he escorts me outside with his hand laced in mine.

Preoccupation outlines his previously composed façade when we come to a halt. "What's going on, Valencia?"

"Look!" I plead, letting go of his hand to continue whirling through the pages with each turn more violent. "They say there is a new lead in the case! They say somebody saw her, read this! Please Giulio, read this!"

Thursday, 17th September 2016

NEW LEAD—THE POSSIBLE SIGHTING IN THE WINDOW CASE:

The investigation of missing two-month-old Addilyn Giannotti is predicted to resume following Seattle Police increasing their reward to $20,000 for information on the disappearance. The infant was abducted from her nursery window on March 1st, 2016 from her parents' Madrona home and has been missing for six months. Seattle Police also recently released an updated computer-generated sketch of how Addilyn, who would be eight months old now, would look today.

Security cameras were active at the time, catching a masked intruder unlawfully forcing her window open while her mother, Valencia Giannotti, and close family were in the front yard. The intruder was seen rushing Addilyn to a get-away car moments after Mrs. Giannotti and close family entered. Father, Giulio Giannotti, the successful founder of leading architecture and interior design company Notti Designs, was in London at the time.

Nobody is yet to be arrested or identified for the crime.

Yesterday afternoon, a witness on her daily walk passed an infant with a unique identifying birthmark similar to Addilyn's being held by a young woman. The witness slowed to converse, but the woman began to act suspiciously. Seattle Police are adamant to speak to the young woman and call on the public's help to locate her. She is described as Caucasian, early twenties, with short, blonde hair and blue eyes. She was wearing a white sweater and jeans at the time. Security cameras within the area have been checked, but no clear images have been found and no further leads have been made. The witness, who does not want to be identified, filed a police report early this morning.

Anybody with any information concerning the whereabouts of Addilyn Giannotti or on the possible sighting is urged to contact Sergeant Steve Flynn or their local SPD precinct.

This is *our* life. Something Giulio and I have been struggling with for so long, but this right here is reaffirmed hope—something that is set to heighten my farfetched efforts.

In late March I stopped watching the news and had to refrain from searching her name. It was too overwhelming. I know SPD would contact either Giulio or me with any new information which is why it surprises me that they didn't regarding this.

"Just because there was a possible sighting doesn't mean it was actually Addilyn. This doesn't mean anything. The witness account is lacking and they still have no leads."

"But don't you see? The letters and now this. This is fresh hope for us!"

Giulio works his jaw and looks to the side. He provides no comfort in carrying my heavily weighted heart. I know it isn't his job to console me, but any form of encouragement would help me in this fragile and delicate moment.

"Valencia...we still don't know if the letters are legitimate or a hoax. There's still no hope, only further unsettling uncertainty."

I shake my head at his refusal. "Let's go to the precinct and ask about this article. They may know more. Even if it's a little thing they failed to publish, maybe they can give us something else."

"That's not a good idea."

"Why? It's the right thing to do. Giulio, please listen to me. It could be her. Somebody *saw* her. Somebody *saw* our baby girl and the police didn't even contact us! They didn't even call!" My urgency has me grasp the paper tighter. "Let's go to them. Maybe they have something tha—"

"They called me."

What?

No.

He wouldn't do this.

He wouldn't hide this.

The air is pressed from my lungs by the heavy weight of betrayal in my chest. *"Pardon?"*

Giulio can't avoid my gawking expression any longer. "They called me early this morning with the news. You were still asleep. The description the witness gave isn't strong enough to confirm the sighting, however the police can't rule it out just yet. After the call ended, as you already know they're obligated to call your cell too because with our legal separation we're considered separate parties...They called you, but I...I answered because I didn't want to wake you up early after last night. I told Sergeant Flynn it wasn't a good time...that you'd call them back, because...I wanted to tell you first."

"How did you expect me to call them back if you didn't tell me about the call in the first place? When you dropped me off at Helena's I checked my recent call list in case I missed out on anything, there was nothing from SPD. Did you delete it from the list?"

"Valencia, I…yes."

"Why would you do that?" I screech, "When were you going to tell me about the call?"

His silence says it all.

When we separated we made a promise to never hide anything. For the sake of our kids, we would remain amicable to not jeopardize their memory of their parents' rapport. Even though at times we've fallen off track, there was never *this*.

Giulio has never deceived me like this before.

He has never hidden something this big from me.

Just last week I told him about the car parked in front of Helena's house after our fight on Addilyn's anniversary. The same one he confessed he saw of a similar description follow him from the florist. We agreed to contact SPD if it happened again.

Giulio broke our promise. He shattered my glimmer of hope. He stopped it all for me.

"How could you not tell me? I am her mother! I deserved to know!"

"I didn't tell you sooner because of this exact reason. I don't want you feeling this false hope. We have to face reality. We have to move forward and that can only be done without distractions of potentially false leads."

"Don't tell me things like that! My daughter—"

"*Our* daughter."

"Our daughter will return to us. You should have told me they called. Is this why you're so lenient with me? Why you took care of me and held me? Why you allowed me to stay the night and teased me this morning with that damn honey? Why you mended my panic attack? Was it *all* out of guilt?" Anger laces my every word because I'm so sick of people concealing the truth and deciding what's best for me behind my back. "I don't know what to believe anymore. You…you *know* this hope is what I crave and you suppressed it, pretending nothing happened. I bet you felt bad for me and thought all of what I just said could make up for it. You should have known better."

Giulio's lack of response is all I need.

Whatever passionate desire we had for each other this morning has fizzled out. *Good.* This explains everything. It was all out of guilt because he knew about this new clue and didn't tell me anything.

When I picked up that wedding photo earlier, I felt something. Now I feel nothing. There was so much love within his eyes back then. Those piercing, bluish-gray eyes can't even look at me now. They no longer hold the same warmth and richness. They are tired, owned by a broken man, looked at by a broken woman.

There's no reassurance, only a disconnection.

The memory lingers like a bitter aftertaste. I find it hard to believe that standing in front of me is the same man I married in Fiji. That we are the same couple who vowed to face any challenge life threw at us together. That we'd *always find our way back to each other.'*

How could he have looked at me all day and concealed something I held so closely to my heart? How can our tragedy be managed when lies are thrown into the mix?

Damn him!

"I'm sorry, but this..." Shoving the newspaper in my bag, I wave my pointer between us and then the office space surrounding us. "...isn't going to work. I've caused enough damage here. Kindly find somebody else to replace me. I don't want to be here. I don't want to see you. I want to be with two of the only people I have left."

Giulio comes alive solemnly wrapped in a bare whisper. "Where are you going?"

"I'm picking up Oscar and Slonne. I think it's best if they stay with me tonight."

"Okay, but you can't pick them up now. They still have an hour of school left."

Tears cascade down my cheeks. "Watch me."

I'm so lost.

Giulio doesn't trust me. He doesn't understand how much I crave this information. He's afraid of how I would have reacted, but little does he know withholding the truth from me makes everything a whole lot worse.

As much as it hurts, this only proves how different we are.

How much we have changed.

And why I need to do this without him.

———◆———

To protect me.

I know that is why Giulio hid it, but we'd committed to upholding integrity throughout our relationship, even during our separation. The thoughts will explode in my mind if I don't talk about it more. It's my own type of progression. I need to discuss it all with the two women I love the most in this world.

"If you quit, it means you did it with the best of intentions."

"I'm not so sure," I tell Helena with a sigh. "I wish I heard the news out of his mouth first."

Marissa, my mother, brushes a piece of her dark bob behind her ear. She's joining us for dinner since my father's in Austria, his home country, visiting family until mid-October. My parents are childhood sweethearts. The way they still look at each other, as if it's the very first time, fills this void inside me. Their love story reminds me greatly of Helena and Ben, who met in sixth grade and were inseparable up until the very end.

Life doesn't always go as we plan it. Nobody expected Helena to be a widow so young. Nobody expected Giulio and I to fall apart after seven good years. Sometimes life just changes, just like the night and you're thrust into this new world and forced to adapt to the new ropes.

Mom sighs. "You're right, Valencia. He won't let you off the hook that easily."

"Well, he can't bribe her either. It's her choice!"

"I should have never taken the job. I don't know what I was thinking."

"Darling, I know why you did it," Mom says, motioning towards Oscar and Slonne in the dining room playing with their cousins. "*Them*. You thought maybe this would open a door so they wouldn't feel hurt. I would have done the same, but when betrayal is thrown into the works it's better to look after your own. The twins...and Addilyn love you both regardless."

I stare down at my glass of water with pursed lips. Before picking up the twins this afternoon I contacted Sergeant Flynn, the newly appointed chief of the Seattle police department's missing person's unit, but everything he said was already mentioned in the article.

"Tell me truthfully, am I...am I crazy for still believing Addilyn is alive?"

"No." My mom threads her fingers through mine. "No. You're not crazy, sweetheart. I believe in you and in my granddaughter. It couldn't have ended that way, there needs to be more."

"Giulio's crazy for not believing," my sister cuts in. "I mean, he's this big family man and then when it comes to his own child he doesn't even want to hold onto any hope! It's—"

"Helena, enough."

"No, Mom, It's true. Don't you see my point, Valencia?"

I do.

It's the point I have been fighting for these entire six months.

"As each day passes, Giulio's reasoning is beginning to come to light. I think it has to do with his mother." I glance between them and sigh. "His mother dying when he was young possibly scarred his view on death and what it is. That's the only thing that makes sense in my mind as to why he doesn't want to delay anything. Perhaps Giulio needs to accept it, just like he accepted his mom's or else the uncertainty will destroy him. He doesn't want to be hurting."

Helena takes my free hand. "I get it. I do. But he's hurting you instead. I say wear that killer black dress of yours into his office and he'll come around faster than you can blink."

"No. Stand your ground, Val. Wait it out a few days, maybe he'll apologize."

"I just miss him so much," I croak, swallowing down my bittersweet truth. "I really do."

"He misses you too. I see it in his eyes when we have dinner together." Mom hugs me tightly and her rose perfume flutters away all my fear. "It's not just because we're the only family he knows, it's because he genuinely does miss you. It takes a brave man to admit that. It takes a brave woman to accept it. Giulio's one in a million; we all know it. He just needs some time."

A voice clearing breaks our discussion.

Helena's children stroll into the open plan kitchen. My godson, Weston, reminds me of my late brother-in-law. Reserved. Calm. Sarcastic. They share the same composed features. Despite sons typically looking like their mothers, Helena once admitted she saw a lot of Ben in Weston too.

I know it must be difficult for her to face.

Daisy is seven and began first grade a couple weeks ago with my children. Although she's a year older, Helena had wanted to wait and give her an extra year before enrolling her. My niece is like Slonne's twin and they do *everything* together—just like Helena and me. If there's one good thing that has come out of my separation, it's that my children are even closer to their cousins.

Both Helena and her kids have also been through a lot. Weston was four and Daisy lost her father before she was even born. My sister ensures he stays alive through photographs and memories; it keeps the fairytale vivid and allows them to still live harmoniously.

When Giulio and I met in October of 2009, Ben had already left this earth in March. We had only begun dating but the spark between Giulio and I was so strong that we knew there would be nobody else. In retrospect, some may say it was crazy that Helena appointed Giulio to be Daisy's godfather after only two months of knowing him, but it worked out as he was my fiancé and it was exactly a few days from when Giulio and I were getting married.

We all stepped in for Helena when her husband passed because that's what we do when we love somebody. Giulio still goes above and beyond for her kids. He flourished Weston's love for basketball and soccer while maintaining a frequent client at Daisy's hairdressing studio. When we had our own children, he continued the traditions.

What they say about falling deeper in love with your husband when children come in the picture is true for me, but sometimes love isn't enough…even when it's all I desire.

"Mom, I'm starving! Is it dinnertime yet?" Daisy hollers.

"Almost. Have you all cleaned up?"

"Yeah….?"

Helena arches a playful brow. "Are you asking or telling?"

Daisy looks up at me for refuge. I smile and crouch down. She grins up at me and gives me a side hug that puts me on reset. "It's okay, butterfly. Go get cleaned up with your cousins and we'll make sure dinner is done when you're back."

My mother is already laughing when the four cousins return, only to begin slamming their knives and forks on the table, chanting a chorus of *'We want food.'*

Helena scolds them, yet fails to suppress her smirk. "I swear they're turning into mini beasts! First Daisy throws my Ray Bans out the window, now she's leading the cult in damaging my favorite dining table."

Radiant energy jolts through me at the mention of her glasses. "Oh yeah, that's right! Did you ever find them?"

"Oh my god! I never told you! A car ran over them—hey, it's not funny! They were vintage!"

"It's called karma, my love." Our mom snickers and, seconds before joining the kids, turns to throw us a wink. "Sweet karma. That's what you get for not getting me a pair too."

"They were a onetime deal!"

"Sure, sure."

It becomes all too much during dinner when for the first time in months, Helena keeps the news on. The case flashes across the screen.

BREAKING NEWS: THE SECRET WITNESS ASSISTING IN THE WINDOW CASE.

The reporter informs us of what I read in the newspaper this afternoon that Giulio had kept from me. It's only brief coverage with the police not putting forth much information. There's no mention of any letters and for once I feel a comfort knowing that my life is not being *completely* dissected and shared with the entire world. There are still aspects that are just for me.

Then a picture flashes on the screen of me at the supermarket with Oscar and Slonne by my side. *"Her mother, Valencia Giannotti, spotted grocery shopping just hours after the news of the new lead in her daughter's abduction has shut down all interviews."*

Oscar points towards the television "We're famous! Our family is on the news!"

"Yeah, that's you," Daisy pipes in.

My veins pulse with nerves when Helena and I exchange an uneasy glance. Mom hasn't moved her gaze from the kids once.

Giulio pops up on the screen next, walking through 5th Avenue on the way to a meeting.

Slonne gasps loudly, "Look! It's Daddy!"

"Yes, baby."

It's LIVE and a microphone is thrusted into his face. The blonde-haired reporter makes fast strides as she attempts to keep up with him. It's obvious Giulio isn't in the mood to speak.

"Mr. Giannotti, do you believe this could spark a reopening of the case?"

"At this stage, we have to wait until the police make a decision."

"Addilyn's mother is refusing to take interviews, what do you say to this?"

"I believe Valencia has the right to her privacy. As you can

understand, this is a traumatic time for our family and we ask at this stage that our privacy is respected. Thank you. Please excuse me."

The news report ends with the underlying big question: *What happened to Addilyn Giannotti?*

Everybody is silent as a report begins about an influx of racketeers and young gangs returning to the streets. I take ahold of the remote and change the channel to Disney. Swirls of animated colors swarm the screen. I don't expect the burning sensation in my stomach to spread so rapidly across my body, yet it does, taking along all my pride with it. I know why my mother and sister don't say a word, mostly because I don't have any words either.

The children are a different story.

They think differently.

They have questions.

I concentrate on cutting up the chicken breast for Slonne, feeling Oscar's eyes on me. I wish I could take away his pain. I wish I could take away every single person's pain around this table.

"Mommy, so somebody saw her?" Oscar's eyes, so similar to Giulio's, survey me.

"It's possible that somebody did. The police are working with them at the moment."

"Who saw her?"

"A lady, but she doesn't want to be named. The police haven't revealed much more. We have to wait a little while, buddy."

I should use the same advice on myself.

"How long do we have to wait until we know?" Slonne's curiosity sparks as she grabs the neck of the orange juice bottle. "Until tomorrow? The weekend?"

I wish my darling angel.

I take the juice from Slonne and refill her glass. While I'm here, I pour a glass for everybody. It buys me time. I force a smile and pray they don't see right through it. Helena does. She's frowning at the end of the table, partaking in her own demons.

"Perhaps a bit longer than that."

"How long then?"

"It could be anything, darling. Perhaps a few days."

"Or a few weeks," my mother echoes her optimism. "It all depends."

"On what?" Weston pipes in. "If they saw her, then the police know the area to look. That's a pretty good place to start considering there has been no other clues, right?"

"True," I say, "but there are procedures they have to follow."

"And then the police will find Addilyn and bring her back?"

I swallow down the regret that laces my tongue. My chest feels strange. Too caged, too tight.

Our children are hurting just as much as I am—just as much as *we* are. They're not excluded in our agony. That hurts too. The fact that Giulio left the kids out of the loop. We had no time to privately discuss how we would explain this to them.

This is life we are talking about. It's not a game where we can adjust the rules. There is no manual. We're handed life in fragile pieces, forced to move forward blindfolded with no sense of direction. It isn't fair—but it's *life*. We all live and die. The cruel reality of Addilyn being the latter haunts me.

"Is that how it will work, Auntie Valencia?"

"Mom?"

"Yes. Hopefully, that's exactly how it goes." I draw out my hands, clasping Daisy and Slonne's tiny hands. "Let's say grace before dinner. Who would like to lead?"

Oscar raises his hand and so we commence. "Thank you, God, for this food. Chicken breast is the best. It helps me pass every test."

"Oscar." I peer at him with one eye and smile. "Serious this time."

He nods, and around the table, everybody's eyes are shut except my mother's and Helena's. We're all looking at each other intently until Slonne squeezes my hand and I turn to find a grin on her lips. For a split moment, I see myself at her age—*pure innocence and the ability to believe in big dreams.*

Oscar starts over.

"God, thanks for the food. Thank you for life and the

sunshine and my family. I love them heaps. Help the people that don't have food and a house. I hope you find that person's name and that the police bring Addilyn home. I miss her. When she is back home it will all be better. We can all live together with Daddy and Mommy again and be happy again. Then they can have even more babies and everything will be okay. That good, Mommy?"

The first salty tear runs down my cheek. "It couldn't be more perfect, Oscar."

"Amen."

CHAPTER TEN

Giulio

I KNOW WHY I DID IT. SOME FUCKED UP SIDE OF ME WANTED TO protect Valencia. Now I know I shouldn't have. According to her, I should have told her about the sighting and watched her suffer in front of me.

That doesn't sit well with who I am.

I don't want her to suffer. That has never been my intention. Ever. For too long now we've been blaming each other for everything. Yes, everything did crash and burn with Addilyn, but that wasn't *my* fault. It wasn't Valencia's either. It's out of our control.

I wholeheartedly take responsibility for what Valencia uncovered yesterday and even more so the fact that I was too tongue-tied to explain myself. Admitting it in my head isn't enough to fix everything. No. Of course it isn't. It's not enough to fix the constant drilling.

I'm weak.

I failed...again.

I'm incapable of gifting Valencia happiness when it's the only thing I want to do. This morning I picked up the kids to take them to school, I wanted to see them before my business trip to Canada. Valencia and I couldn't even look each other in the eyes. After kissing the twins goodbye, she stepped back inside the house without us exchanging a single word.

She should know that all those things I did for her weren't out of guilt. I'm not toying with her. I'm just a man attempting to navigate this path of separation, it's like a pit of hell between marriage and divorce. One false move and I'll be burned alive.

Dio.

Now, I have to push past it all because Valencia didn't show up to work this morning. No Friday Funday for me, *more like Friday Fucked-up-day*. My mood is completely distorted and I can't think straight. Yesterday at this exact time Valencia was in my arms through her panic attack.

She was right *here*.

With *me*.

Darling, where are you now?

"Dad?" It's Slonne. I'm in the process of slipping back into my Porsche when I notice her running to me, through the school gates and past a few parents who walk in with their kids.

"What's going on?"

Slonne pivots her foot in the gravel, her head low. "I forgot to tell Mommy last night..."

"Forgot to tell her what?" I ask with concern.

"I don't wanna say."

My brows knit. "Is this about Samuel?"

"Umm..."

"Slonne."

"Yeah...it's about him."

My protective dad radar hits one million. If it were up to me the entire police department would be on standby. I settle for a tight jaw and a smile. If I'm calm, she'll be calm. *Yeah right. I'm beyond fucking livid inside.*

Did he do something to her?

"Baby, what about him?"

Slonne shrugs bashfully, her cheeks reddening. "Just that he keeps kissing my cheek and mouth, even when I tell him to stop. The first couple of times it was okay but now it's annoying. I don't like him, even if he says he loves me."

"How about I talk to your teacher or find his mom? Stick by Oscar and Daisy, alright?"

"Thanks, Daddy." Slonne smiles.

I reel her into me and hold her hands in mine. When I look into her light hazel eyes, all I want is to protect her from this unfair world. I want to shelter her from pain and save her. I want to help her in all the ways my father never helped me. "Thank you for telling me about him. I will do everything and more to ensure he never annoys you again. Real men always stop when women say no. Never do anything you don't want to do, okay? Your voice should always be listened to. Now and when you're older. Never be afraid to tell us anything, Slonne. We will always be here for you. Mommy and Daddy will always love you. Always. You know that, right?"

"I know that, Daddy. That's why I love you both so much!"

"I love you too." My throat burns and I know now is not the time to break down outside her school. I hold it in, but *fuck* I'm an emotional guy when it comes to family.

We embrace and she kisses my cheek with a cute giggle. "I gotta go now, Daddy. Bye!"

"Have a beautiful day, *carina*."

Once Slonne's out of sight, I rise and am about to pull out my phone when a hand brushes my bicep.

What the…?

I stare down at red manicured nails and turn to find a woman around Valencia's age. Her blonde hair's in a tight updo and she's sporting maroon colored workout gear. There's a wolfish grin on her lips which concerns me more than the hand caressing my arm. Her presence aggravates me more than anything after what Slonne told me about Samuel. I hope it becomes apparent by my narrowed brows. "Sorry, do I know you?"

"Not yet, I'm Zoe!"

"Giulio." I nod, taking a step back to reclaim my space. "I'm Slonne and Oscar's dad."

"Oh, I know who you are!" She laughs, batting her lashes as if it's the most hilarious thing in the world. *Okay...*When she doesn't stop, I dig into my pocket and feel for my car keys. "I'm Samuel's mom. I've been seeing the news and hear there's a new witness in the case, right?"

"Yes. It's pretty new so—"

"Hey, listen to this." She cuts me off. "I was thinking since Slonne and Samuel are getting close, how about a play date? I can do this Saturday for lunch. They'll love that and you know, you and I could have a nice little lunch to ourselves. Just the two of us. Do you like Rosé?"

Me? Rosé?

I glance around to ensure we're not on Candid Camera.

Nope. Nothing.

I'm all for women making the first move but this woman is too much and most importantly, I'm not looking for anybody else. Even though we're on horrid terms, I already found the love of my life. No one will ever replace Valencia Giannotti, nor will I ever love someone the way I love her. The way I *still* love her, even after all these months.

"Zoe, I appreciate the offer. The thing is, I'm not interested in a date if that is what you're implying. I also don't think it would be a good idea for Slonne and Samuel."

"Oh, come on! You're telling me that you've gone all this time without Valencia and you haven't once thought about being with somebody else?"

I'm struck silent by her brazen question. How did dropping our children off at first grade escalate to her accosting me about a date and my personal life? As I'm trying to make sense of the situation, I notice the ring on her left hand—why is Zoe soliciting any sort of date with me?

I motion to my car. "Sorry, but I have to go."

"Damn, you're even more delusional than Valencia."

"Excuse me?"

The mention of my wife triggers my defense mechanisms. The fact that we're currently not talking makes it worse. I should have stayed quiet but this woman is not getting away with talking about the love of my life as if she has the upper hand. I know nothing about her and I want it to remain this way.

"What my *wife* and I have is not your business. But for your *specific* information, no I haven't been with any other woman and I don't plan to. Now, is that all?" Slonne's words about Samuel come back to me in that moment. "Actually, no. What *is* your business is teaching your son how to respect girls. My daughter has told Samuel on numerous occasions to stop kissing her. He hasn't listened. No is always no. If you don't explain the facts of life to your son, this matter will soon include the principal. Kindly stay out of my family's life. Have a good one, Zoe."

"Oh, please." She scoffs, arrogance bright in her eyes. "It's not my fault if my son likes the girl in the class with the saddest sob story. Tell Slonne to suck it up. Weak kids don't win. Like mother like daughter, huh?"

Suck it up?

Weak kid?

Like mother like daughter?

All of a sudden it feels as though my father is standing in front of me. That four letter word, *weak*, digs deeply in my mind and the words are out before I can even think about it.

"When you throw around a word like that, you are the weak one. Slonne reached out for a friend and Samuel gave her more than she bargained for. She doesn't want him kissing her anymore. Make sure he knows it. Stay the hell out of my family's life and never, *ever*, call my wife or daughter weak again."

I slip inside my car before Zoe can reply.

Christ.

My heart is racing.

Squeezing my eyes shut, I realize I told her everything I wish I'd told my father.

I wish I could text Valencia. I wish I could tell her that if Zoe has ever bad mouthed her, she won't anymore. I wish I could tell Valencia that I'm sorry and all I want is her.

It's what I'm desperate to tell her, but I fear it may be too soon. I've never not wanted Valencia, but with all the shit in the way, I've needed her in different ways. I miss the person she once was, but it would be selfish to openly admit that to her. Logically and morally, she will never be exactly the same woman I married, and I will never be that exact man. Addilyn's abduction has changed us and as much as I want to tell her I want her, as much as I want to sink inside her, I know better...*or do I?*

Even through the chaos, I'm still in love with Valencia Giannotti.

I'll never stop.

But deep down I know we need time to heal. I need time to comprehend what she truly means to me now. Valencia needs time to understand what my true intensions were when I hid that the police called. It's been too much for us. Letters. Terrors. False hope. Bryce's advances.

Bryce.

The thoughts remains lodged in my mind, alongside the next. Today, on this Friday fucked-up-day, not only am I chasing the thoughts cluttering my brain, I'm also chasing up Bryce McCarson. He hasn't shown up, answered my calls, nor responded to the knocks at his duplex. He isn't seeing clients. I'm beyond the stage of disappointment. With Bryce, I go full on Terminator.

Marcus and I haven't been on the best terms since our blow up. We stay professional with clients, but it's still tense. I don't even want to remember how catastrophic of a day today is turning out to be, which is why when Lance calls, I'm relieved.

He offers to meet me in the Seattle neighborhood of Cascade, where our assisted retirement village project is located.

While on his routine check monitoring the construction progress, he unveiled damage that needs my attention.

So much for forgetting just how messed up my life currently is.

I avert my gaze to the driver beside me at a red light minutes before I arrive. What initially captures my attention is the glossy black 1950's Chevrolet. I know it's a Styleline Deluxe because my father used to have the exact model. Pietro Giannotti was the car enthusiast and while I couldn't care less for him, the car beside pulls me in for all the wrong reasons.

It was mom's favorite car to drive around in. *The elegant Mafioso spin* as she liked to call it. Even with her declining health, she insisted we drive up to New Jersey's Coast for at least a week during the summers. Like in 92'. I still recall sitting in the backseat with the windows rolled down, that sultry humid breeze the closest I'd ever get to Sicily again before my twenties. My father with that constant brooding stare towards me in the rearview mirror and a lit cigar. My mother complaining to him about the clouds of white smoke and glancing over at me with an apologetic smile. I remember the constant changing of stations on the AM radio with my father wanting to be informed with talk radio while my mother only loved opera.

Every pedestrian turned, ogling the car. Other motorists honked in appreciation.

It was a show car, which is why when the man's gaze meets mine I give a curt nod. This stranger can't feel my racing heart or the way my sweaty hands grip the wheel at the memory. That was the last time we made it to the coast before my mom passed the following year. My anger at the discovery of my father's affair had me take a baseball bat to the car. I had only managed to dent the bumper and a small section by the Chevrolet emblem before Clare, my step-mother, stopped me.

Red fades to green and I allow the car to merge in my lane in front of me. The second I do, my body freezes up. *Oh, God.* This Chevrolet has the exact dents...*I'm sure of it.* But it's been eleven long years since his passing, what are the chances it's my late father's? The chance it was sold to somebody in Seattle? That they haven't fixed it? It's a common damage point on a car. The chances are slim. But it still shakes me, and for a second, it's as if my father is in front of me.

It couldn't be...

At the next red light, the driver meets my gaze in the rearview mirror. An intimidating lengthy stare, one I don't look away from. I stare so deep that for a second his dark eyes turn a soft shade of gray with slate blue. My father's shade. I blink and they're dark again.

I'm seeing things...

It didn't happen...

As he takes off straight ahead, I turn onto a side street. *I can't tell anybody about this.* I shake my head to rid the thoughts of what I think I saw. *That's what I get for missing my morning coffee.*

A bewildered Lance meets me by the chain-link fence. It creates a division at the property's entry where charcoal rubble spans for a good ten feet before the first duplex. He didn't tell me anything on the phone and with none of the contracted builders on site, I know it's bad.

"Lance, you're worrying me. What's going on?"

He smiles flatly, gestures to the duplexes and we begin power walking. My Oxfords violently crunch against the tiny rocks. *Thank god this is going to be cobblestone in a matter of weeks.*

"You know I wouldn't call you unless it was urgent. There's been some vandalism between last night and today."

"When you say vandalism..."

"I mean extensive damage to the interior and exterior. Shattered windows. Tiles that were installed to twenty-five percent of the duplexes are smashed in. Security cameras that we have are all sprayed over, but we can still check if they caught anything. And there's more..."

I slow in my step. "You've got to be kidding me."

Lance grimaces. "I wish I was. I really do."

"We need to call the police."

"I agree, but seeing as it's a personal attack, I thought you should see it first."

Personal?

And then I see it.

The sight has me grind my teeth and exhale sharply. The same name is written out. Over and over again. It surrounds every exterior dark brick wall in glowing crimson spray paint.

ADDILYN

BURN IT DOWN

YOU WILL NEVER FIND HER

I have no words. None. No expression but utter disgust for this destruction.

Lance is right about the interior. The entire premises is ruined. Red spray paint turns to black. Shattered glass crunches under our feet. There's this unsettling feeling inside my chest, duplex after duplex.

We walk through all fifty and even though more than an hour passes Lance sticks by me writing down each instance of damage and its extent. The whole scene repulses me. *Taunts me.* Damage like this will set us back weeks. It slaughters the promises I've made to a deserving client. The fact that this is a personal attack hurts further. Was this done by the same people who abducted and killed my baby-girl? There's too much carnage here for it not to be done by a handful of fools. This is no lone wolf attack.

Addilyn's name is everywhere, along with profanities and comments about *my* family.

This is a nightmare.

"What are you thinking?'

"That whoever did this is way over their heads if they thought this would break me."

"I'm sorry you had to see this, man."

I flash Lance a half smile and bring him into a side hug. "I'm sorry you did too, Hilton."

The police ensure me they will get to the bottom of this with as little publicity as possible. While they are present, I notify them about the silver Mercedes Valencia and I spotted a couple of weeks ago on Addilyn's six month anniversary. The one I noticed was following me from the florist, the same one Valencia suspects was parked in front of Helena's that same night. There's no real evidence to prove this man is after us, we don't even have a clear description of him other than his slim build and lack of license plates, but it's better to be safe than sorry.

The officers make note to visit Valencia with further details. I text her that the police will be there soon. She replies quickly with a curt 'OK' and we leave it at that. The officers also mentioned they would break the news to her about the vandalism. It'll be better if she hears it straight from them.

I reschedule my afternoon meetings for the late evening. I want to be on site to see through the clean-up as the bill isn't pretty. My last minute work trip to Vancouver, Canada for the weekend ends up being a blessing in disguise. *A distraction.* I don't like that it means less time with the kids this week. *I hate this part of my job.* But what it does mean is I have one final chance to apologize to Valencia and plead my case to convince her to resume her position at my company.

It's hell without her.

If I don't summon the courage to tell Valencia this tonight, it'll be pushed into next week, meaning I only have a few weeks to find a solution to our dilemma before we go back to seeing each other once a week for forty-five seconds.

I make a note to contact the tilers and delay their work until everything is in order. Those blueprints I'm meant to work on at the office have to be squeezed into my time in Vancouver, somewhere between sightseeing, networking, and virtually chasing Bryce McCarson down. As if my scheduling isn't already overflowing, the vandalism situation tests my limits further.

When the twins run out of the school and into my arms, I finally feel secure. They ask if we can go to the park before taking them to their mom's. And despite my instincts, the September chill, and the ominously heavy clouds promising rain, I give in.

I give in because I don't want to waste a single second of my life without them.

CHAPTER ELEVEN

Valencia

I SET DOWN THE PAINTBRUSH FOR THE THIRD TIME TONIGHT. I DON'T have it in me to complete the first brushstroke. Nothing soothes me to sleep as the clock strikes a quarter to twelve. I've tried it all—watched television, pace up and down the living room, music, yoga, paint. Anything to coax myself to sleep—but, I get nothing in return.

Insomnia tends to take over some nights, but it's been far less daunting since I began taking the anti-depressants in the morning. My one true savior is the mental health book Giulio gave me. It's one of the most beautiful things anybody could ever give because it is truly *made for me*. I finished it a couple of days ago and I'm already beginning to see everything clearer.

"Mommy, are you awake?" My daughter peers through my open bedroom door. Her small face searches until her innocent eyes meet mine.

I rush to lift her in my arms. "Is everything okay? Why are you out of the bed, angel?"

Slonne rests her head in the crook of my neck and I breathe in her calming jasmine and vanilla bodywash. Dread takes over me at her tears which hit my skin. "I've got you. Mommy is here, butterfly." I kiss the side of her head and sway her side to side, just like I used to when she was little. At six she's no longer that little newborn, but she will always be my babygirl.

I think back to the book and remember a saying: *In life, you're not always in control of what happens, however you are always in control of the way you react.*

"I ha-had another bad dr-dream."

"Do you want to talk about it?"

Slonne nods against my neck. "I had a dream that dragons got Daddy and put him in this big tower...Like in Rapunzel! There was no window and so me and Oscar and you were at the bottom trying to get to Daddy but we couldn't see him. Then more and more dragons came. Then...then they took away our candy and blew out fire. It was so scary because they made us leave and live without Daddy forever!"

My heart aches. Over and over for her. Slonne has been having these types of dreams for a long while. Although they are much less frequent now, they are still concerning. Especially because they all in a way relate to the subject of kidnappings.

The twins' therapist, Melanie, has expertly shown them that dreams are only fantasy and an extension of their fears. The only way to cure them is through positive thoughts and a happy mind. Giulio and I continue to separately do our best to console them and cure their pain, but some nights are harder than others.

"I can imagine it would have been scary, but it isn't real. Daddy's safe! We're all safe."

Slonne breaths out a sigh. She's cried so hard she's now hiccupping. "We're all safe."

"Yes, angel. We are." When I wipe away her tears and sit us both down on the bed, I hold her hands in mine and bring them to my heart. "We're all going to be okay. Sadly, in life nothing is promised. I can't promise bad things won't happen, but what I can say is that we will find a way through it, like we always do. When you're with Mommy and Daddy, you never have to worry or be scared. Okay? We will always protect you from every single nightmare."

"I love you, Mommy."

I hold her tightly, never wanting to let go. "I love you all the way to the stars, my angel."

Slonne eases down until her breaths normalize. "Can we still use the bad dream spray?"

"The bad dream spray?"

"Yeah, the one Daddy said. He told me that it's our secret but I really need it right now."

Bad dream spray?

I scan my bedroom with furrowed brows, unsure of what she means. Giulio has never mentioned it before and I don't want to disappoint Slonne by not helping her. I also don't want to make it seem like I have no clue what she's talking about, and so I rub her back and reach for my phone on the nightstand.

"Yes, of course. Let's just stay like this for a little while first."

"Okay."

Slonne can't see the phone in my hand with her head in the crook of my neck. I put it on silent and pull up Giulio's contact. I know it's late, but this is urgent. We're still tense and haven't spoken since the altercation. This morning when the police knocked on my door asking further questions about the suspicious man leaning against the car, a part of me had hoped they were here to tell me more about Addilyn.

But they weren't.

The news that vandals destroyed one of Giulio's sites with toxic words about Addilyn destroys me. I didn't appreciate what Giulio did to me, but I would never wish this upon him.

Valencia: I'm sorry it's late. Slonne had another nightmare and is asking for a bad dream spray? I'm not too sure what it is…Apparently you've used it with her?

Those three bubbles appear faster than I expect.

Giulio: Hey, it's okay. I'm leaving for Vancouver in a few hours. The bad dream spray is your favorite perfume bottle. The Marc Jacobs one. Spray it a little in her room and I told her she'll have sweet dreams. If she doesn't, re-spray it again. I hope that helps.

I almost drop my phone from shock.
My favorite perfume.
Decadence.
I must have left one at Giulio's. The fact that he's been using something of mine for such a delicate physiological cure for Slonne makes me see just how…compassionate he really is.
That is so touching.
Remember what he did, Valencia.
He hid the truth. He hid hope from me. I can't forget about that and it stings.
Right now, my feelings for him are so strong, but every time he makes a move I deflate. The fact that he's leaving for Vancouver doesn't help. I want to remind him to remember his passport. Six years ago, we eagerly presented ourselves at Sea-Tac Airport to begin our wedding and honeymoon in Fiji, only to be publicly mortified we miraculously both forgot our passports at home. *Call it pre newlywed dementia.* It's been a running joke between us ever since…well, until a few months ago.

Valencia: That helps tremendously. Thank you.

Those three bubbles appear and I bite my lip waiting and waiting and waiting. Then all of a sudden they disappear. I shouldn't feel this disappointed, yet I do.

What were you expecting him to say or do? Apologize?

I don't even know anymore. What I do know now is how to make Slonne feel even better.

"Okay, angel. Let's use the bad dream spray now!"

It's been half an hour since Slonne's nightmare and I wish I could use that darn perfume on me because while she's sound asleep, I'm in the living room racking my brains. Helena and everybody else in this house is sound asleep, and I can't shut my eyes no matter what I do.

My gaze darts to a basket a couple of feet away by the fireplace.

No.

I concentrate on the snapping of twigs and the mesmerizing glowing heat it projects. *I can't possibly look inside that basket.* I put in my Bluetooth earphones, adamant for something to come from it as I lie on the couch and pull up the weighted blanket. Perhaps being outside of the bedroom will help.

'I Found' by Amber Run blasts through my ears on repeat.

I shut my eyes.

Nope.

I up the volume, blurring out any source from reality. Yet my eyes trail to the basket again.

For the love of god.

In a split moment, the dusty pink photo album is set on my lap. **Addilyn Giannotti.** If Helena were to catch me, she would advise against this triggering move. My therapist once said reminders of the past don't have to be potent. The handbook mentioned the same thing and right now, I want to implement and absorb as much as I can. I want to overcome my depression, or at least know how to tolerate it better.

I glance through the pages, reminiscing our premature happiness. Addilyn on my chest as a newborn. Her first night at home. Meeting her siblings. That gorgeous little smile.

I stop at my favorite candid picture. The baptism. Giulio and I stand together. His left hand is hooked around my waist, the other settling on Slonne's shoulder. Oscar is beside me, making a face while I have Addilyn cradled in my arms. She's even more adorable in white. Giulio is looking lovingly at me, grinning. I too feel his warmth, wrapped in love.

This used to be my favorite picture. Tears build. There's no resistance in me when I reach a finger forward and stroke Giulio's face and then the children's.

I need something to take away the bitter taste in my mouth and ginger tea becomes my last resort. I don't usually have it at night because it gives me a headache and keeps me up late, but seeing as everything is becoming a role reversal, I give it a try.

The powerful chorus of the hauntingly beautiful song blares in my ears, a perfect reminder of my situation. The lyrics start off describing breaking away from the person you love and losing your mind over wanting to move on whilst your soul continues to hold onto the person. Then depending on the state of the heart while listening, the ending can either be depicted as; the couple falling back in love—or, walking out of each-other's lives for good.

I pull out the kettle and fill it up when the unexpected happens. Something hard presses against my back.

A body.

The kettle begins overflowing, but I can't reach the faucet fast enough before my mouth is covered, muting my scream.

Oh my God! What is going on?

One of my earphones falls out amid the commotion. The music stops as the hand leaves my mouth. It's only then I get a whiff of aftershave that my entire body heaves.

"I'm sorry." A soft murmur meets my right ear. "I didn't know you had them in."

Giulio.

I thought the absolute worst moments ago and now I don't even know what to say.

"Holy hell, you scared me!" I set both earphones on the

counter in a daze and turn to face him with my heart beating a million miles per hour. "What are you doing here at this hour?"

Giulio sports a classy five o'clock shadow, a crisp white shirt that sculpts his impeccable torso, and those damn gray slacks. He swallows, regretful sorrow plunged in his bright-eyed gaze. "I needed to talk to you."

"I don't want to hear it. How did you even get in?"

"I used my emergency key because I knew you may not have opened up. I don't want to get on a plane in a few hours knowing we're angry with each other. I was in a late meeting when I got your text and once it ended I gambled with the idea you were still awake."

"I think it would be best if you leave."

"Please let me explain." We're so close I feel his hot breath against me. "You see how perfect Oscar and Slonne are. We care and love them more than life itself. We'd sacrifice ourselves to have their sister back, but there's certain things in life we have to...accept."

"I can't accept that I will never see her again. She's us. She's a piece of me. I carried and nurtured her for nine months. She was safe with us. I can't let it all go now. It hurts...too much."

"I know it does. I'm sorry, I used the wrong word to explain it. But, that hurt is the exact reason I wanted to wait a few days to tell you about the sighting."

I shake my head, the heavy lump in my throat throbs just as my vision blurs with tears. "There isn't a perfect time. Whoever did this to us ruined *everything*."

An unsteady sigh escapes Giulio.

His closeness lingers even when he steps away. I lean over the sink, clutching my chest when the world begins to spin. I get that feeling I felt at the dinner table last night after seeing the report. That tight bundle of angst. The hurtful thoughts. The non-existent goodbye.

Please, not another panic attack.

Not with him.

"Fuck. I can't see you like this, Valencia."

"What am I supposed to do? I can't do anything!"

"It kills me too. You know it does! The truth is, I don't feel her."

"Please don't…"

Don't say that.

I shut my eyes to remember that ocean of mine. I need to go back to the sailor incapable of navigating his compass. Back to the clear blue waters where everything is serene.

"Valencia…are you okay?"

"Please, just go," I plead, pouring some water out of the tea kettle before placing it on the stove. I reach up on my toes to feel for a mug in the overhead cupboard, only to gasp at the sensation Giulio's body gives as he aligns himself against my back. I don't expect for his warm hand to fall by my waist, nor the other to effortlessly clasp the mug for me with ease.

His lips graze against my ear. "Here."

"Thank you," I whisper, taking the mug.

"It will only worsen us if I walk out with everything left unsaid. I owe you an apology."

"There's nothing worse than this."

"There is. You don't want me to raise hell these next four weeks without you."

I turn around, bewildered. "Wait. Are you actually accepting my resignation?"

"Never." A hopeful smile rises on his parted lips. "But at least you're looking at me now."

That gets me to chuckle and my eyes roll at his *achievement*. "God, I hate you!"

Giulio turns serious. His hands by the countertop box me in, preventing me from escaping him. *Maybe I don't want to…*It doesn't help how the overhead light illuminates his pupils and I witness them expand. "Do you though? Hate me, that is."

My head involuntarily shakes. "No. I could never. You aggravate me sometimes and I'm sure I do the same to you, but never hate. Hating you would be unfair on us and our children. I don't want them growing up in a broken family…I know you don't either."

Giulio's smile endorses my words.

I know I've hit home.

"Exactly, my upbringing was filled with animosity after my mom died. It wasn't until my father took his life that I realized some people don't need to be dead to begin grieving them. Meanwhile, others leave your life even though you've been holding onto them the entire time." His tone takes on a low cadence. My entire body comes alive underneath his enticing gaze. "I never intended to let go of Addilyn. She's my babygirl too. I was supposed to protect her, but I didn't, just like I couldn't protect my mom. My mother died believing her *devoted* husband was a man of gold. That will always haunt me."

I wish I could take away Giulio's pain. His past torments him. Seeing his step-mother pregnant with Marcus at his mother's funeral and uncovering how his father betrayed his mother during her battle. Then being forced to grow up with those who had betrayed her—he couldn't tolerate it. He was twenty-one when his father took his life. He and Marcus witnessed their father's suicide during Giulio's first trip back to New Jersey for Thanksgiving after relocating to Seattle. I can't begin to imagine what it would have felt like to lose both parents so young, and the tension of it all will always remain within him.

It's still there.

I remember when Giulio first told me the story and I saw the immense love for his mother in his eyes. *I still see it.* How moved and inspired I was by what he's made for himself. That night I knew we were destined to be together.

"I know you're hurt…I wish I could take it all away for you, Giulio."

"Nobody gets me like you do. I've always been loyal to you. Even during this separation, not once have I even thought about being with another woman. I'm not looking for that. Do you know what my priority is? The one I share with you?"

I feel our every breath colliding and it reminds me we're alive, capable of tackling anything and everything. Giulio's heat slaughters me and takes me back to when everything was much simpler. A place only for him and me. I'd do anything to return there, but I'm also scared of the perpetual limitations between us. Until we're on the same page, it won't work.

"Our priority is our children."

"Exactly." He nods with a soft smile. "My priority is being a good father and protecting them from harm. You're also my priority. I still care. God, I want you thriving. I hid something big. I fucked up. I know that now. You deserve much more than what I give you."

"Giulio, it's…"

"It's not okay. I couldn't forgive myself when you walked away from me yesterday. I was so torn. I don't want you crying for me. I don't deserve it."

If I don't get out of my head, I'll be the person dragging this moment down. My hands fall upon Giulio's chest and it electrifies me right *there*. My palms cover his crisp shirt, just above his heart and for a moment, his rapid heartbeats are all I concentrate on. I wonder if he can feel that mine are beating to the same rhythm.

Through my lashes, I absorb how attractively vulnerable he is. "You deserve something."

"I deserve nothing."

"No. You *do* deserve it."

"I'm so sorry that I let you down. You know I would never do anything to intentionally hurt you. I need you. I need you at the office and not just because of work. I promise to never hide anything again. I thought…I didn't know what I was thinking. Please. Come back, Lencia."

Lencia.

The last time he called me that we were a happy family of five.

"It makes sense. You were scared of the news impacting me and reacted on instinct. The past got in the way. I understand now…and I'll keep working with you. I forgive you."

Giulio's eyes squeeze shut in relief.

I know he's trying so hard to open up. It's something we constantly struggled with since signing our legal separation. Both of us bottled away our feelings after every argument. We need to go back to that happy place where we can speak honestly and openly.

"I'm so sick of fighting with you, Lencia. I'm sick of the back and forth. It hurts me. It hurts me right *here*." Giulio's hands slide over mine by his heart. I fan out my fingers and he laces our hands together, every inch of my body throbs at his touch.

It still gets me.

He still owns every single part of my body without even saying a word. Even when I attempt to deny it, I'm his. At the core of Addilyn missing, we have to work together and be on the same team. I have a feeling that after tonight we will be.

"It hurts me there too. We need to be kinder to each other." I express my gravest concern within our window of honesty. "No more lies, no more getting all angry and worked up. There's somebody out there seeking to destroy us, and we are hurting each other in the process which is only benefiting whoever is doing this to us."

"You're right. You are so right." Giulio's eyes open to warmth. I'm smiling through the emotional desolation and am fond of the way he mirrors the action. "How's therapy and the anti-depressants been going? The book?"

"They're helping me more than I ever expected. Especially the book, thank you once again for it. It's been incredible. The conversations with Dr. Eross are getting more…intense."

"Maybe I could come with you one time?"

Enraptured by his closeness, the words escape me. "That would be…"

"Good?" Giulio asks, detaching one hand to cup my cheek. His eyes are on my pink lips. He can feel my heart now. *I'm certain of it.* It thumps in my ears, slowly fading out the sound of the crackling wood fire across the room.

It's all him.

Entirely him.

"Yes. That would be good."

Giulio's head moves in line with mine. We challenge each

other's gaze with the light in our eyes. We're burning like an allusive flame. I squeeze our intertwined hand and his body responds by bringing me even closer. That captivating and erotic cologne is all I breathe. My throbbing heat intensifies and my nipples harden, poking through my soft silk top as I press up against Giulio's shirt.

Woah.

"When should we go?" His lips almost touch mine. Almost. His deep, sexy voice has me drop my composure. *And I don't want it to stop.*

"Next Tuesday night. That's my next session."

"That works." His nod proves a risky move when his lips brush against the tip of my nose and then my forehead. It's there where he leans in and kisses it. "Only if you would like me there. I know it's complicated, but I would like to stand by you and support you."

Oh my…Yes.

I'm in my own world of wondering thoughts with moans threatening to escape at the idea that all Giulio needs to do is lower his mouth down to my lips or neck. Even with all the obstacles in the way, tonight I see him for him. I see him as the man I married. *The man I love.*

"I need you…" Excitement molds our sensual touches and lingering gaze. "I need you at the session with me."

"I'm already there, Lencia."

The nickname again.

Giulio's presence teases my desire. He knows my body too well not to notice my roused silent plea when he hovers his lips by my neck, seconds from kissing me. *Yes, please.* The sexual tension is slaughtered by the kettle's whistle. Our touch falls away without any kiss, yet I still feel him. I will for days. This memory will be with me long after tonight. I never thought that after yesterday we'd share such an intimate moment together…*and yet…*

I don't know what this means for us, if it even means anything or if it's making everything better or worse. God, I don't even know how to comprehend the way I feel. All I know is that we were so close to becoming whole again…even if it was for a moment in time.

"I should go. Goodnight, Lencia."

I have no time to gather my thoughts let alone speak before Giulio leaves. He nudges the door shut without another word, leaving me with the roaming impression of his sensational lips lingering across my skin.

———<<>>———

I expected to feel something more than this. Something *much* more. My hopes and greatest prayers diminish the moment Giulio and I are called to the police department on Monday morning.

The little girl sighted who was believed to be Addilyn…isn't. The little girl, whose name is Madison Clark, was with her nanny taking an evening walk. It was the nanny's first day working and so when the witness approached her, nerves took over. It was all a false alarm.

I can't break out of my motionless state. I don't feel like crying. I don't know *what* I feel like. All I know is that I won't stop the desperate search for my baby. The false sighting sparks new faith in The Window Case for SPD.

We meet with Sergeant Steve Flynn and he seems optimistic, reassuring us that we can contact him anytime, even if we discover the faintest of clues. He also informs us that at the crack of dawn they arrested four men suspected to have committed the vandalism at Giulio's assisted retirement village project. They are all in their late teens and locals of the area. Apparently, they were paid under the table for the job but refused to cooperate when interrogated further, taking us back to square one.

SPD suspects there are no links to Addilyn, and that it was only a scare tactic to remind us somebody is in fact out there lurking.

Giulio doesn't say a word during the briefing and arrives at Notti Designs before me. I know because my eyes remain on his vacated Porsche as I step out of my car. He only touched back down in Seattle this morning after a weekend work trip. I haven't spoken to him properly since our *moment* on Friday night. I thought we were progressing well, *I mean he was so close to kissing me,* so why did he leave the house so suddenly after that damn kettle began whistling?

Why? Why? Why?

I conjure the confidence to brace for the day's challenges and am met with Marcus' open arms upon entering the lobby. It dissolves all the tension between us. Last week's mishap with him was a disaster. We've never spoken to each other under such tense circumstances before.

Marcus takes one good look at me and immediately acknowledges my silent pledge with a longer hug. "I'm so sorry to hear about the news, Val. We all wanted it to be Addilyn."

Despite his harsh words the other day and the disputes with his half-brother, Marcus has always been nothing but decent towards me. Giulio must have just told him about SPD's update when he arrived.

I wish Giulio held me like this at the department.

If the diamond ring was on my left hand he would have, but eggshells are constantly beneath us. They dictate everything we do.

Dan, a junior architect, walks up to us and stops by Marcus with a curt smile my way.

My brother-in-law's eyes soften as we pull away. "I shouldn't have said those things last week. I was fired up and shouldn't have taken it out on you. The separation is something between you two."

"It's okay, I get it. This is a hard time for all of us."

"You have the right to be angry at me."

I feel the urge to wrap him up in another embrace. "I don't want to be, Marcus. I just want to go back to normal. Like it was before. That's all I want."

"You're a good woman. You really are. I just have..." He pauses to rub the tip of his straight nose. "There's a just lot going on now. Work, personal life, and you know, trying to make women happy. But I need to make this right between us. How can I make it up to you?"

"By allowing me to help you with whatever is going on. It would be a good distraction."

Marcus smiles empathetically. "Appreciate it, but now's just not a good time. Look, if I do need help I know where to go. You do the same, sound good?"

"Sounds perfect. Thank you."

"Don't worry, gorgeous. They'll find whoever's behind all this. They have to."

"You believe me on this? That Addilyn's still out there?"

He nods adamantly. "Of course I do, I always have. I think Giulio is just overwhelmed and is not thinking straight. He has a lot on his mind with work. He'll come around eventually."

I hope so too.

"Well, Dan and I better head to our site. You've got this! Keep your head high, alright?"

I nod with a faint smile, desperately needing it to be true.

CHAPTER TWELVE

Giulio

"**T**HAT'S SCOPA, BABY! YOU LOSE SOME, YOU WIN SOME!" Lance hollers proudly beside me, slapping down his last card, the seven of spades, and begins fist pumping the air like a madman.

Hmmm. You shouldn't celebrate quite yet, Hilton…

"Oh, I thought this was supposed to be a friendly game. No?" Sandro chuckles with that familiar Italian-New Jersey accent and pulls his cigar from his lips. "Don't get too ahead of yourself. Giannotti still has the final turn and let me tell you, that's serious fire in his eyes."

White clouded smoke hazes Sandro's pointed eyes and sharply structured face. It clears to reveal the man who's seen just about everything there is to see in the underworld. A few long scars above his brow and along his cheek have faded to white, yet the memories they evoke never will.

I can't control my deepening smirk when the two men glance my way. It's so obvious that Lance groans and covers his face with his hands.

Ha!

I have the last card of the round to close out the game, but Lance believes he's already won with the seven he's put down. He believes my card is lower and he'll sweep up the last point and most likely win this round of the classic card game Scopa for the second time in a row. What he doesn't know is I've collected not only more cards than him, but the single card I have left is golden.

"Don't tell me you have the…"

"Alright, I won't tell you then." I smile, taunting my best man before turning to Sandro on my left. "Got a cigar for me? It may take a while for Lance to process his losses."

"A *long* while." Sandro takes another cigar from his case, lights it, and hands it to me.

"*Grazie*, Sandro." I blow out a cloud of victory, grinning as Lance shakes his head. "Go on, Giulio. Put me out of my misery."

I slap down the seven of suns and place Scopa. It takes a moment for the three of us to count our points and the second we converge our totals, I lean back in my plush dining room chair with a wolfish smirk. "Well, well, well. Look who won nine out of the twelve rounds played. What is it that I heard you say before, Hilton? Oh, that's right. *That's Scopa, baby!*"

"Shut up!" Lance fails to compress his dramatic frown and bursts out in laughter. "How do you win every time? It's like you were trained to professionally kick my ass at this game."

"Oh, that's because I was. Took a two week course on how to specifically piss you off."

"Ah, so you're a qualified con artist?"

I nod playfully, crossing my arms over my charcoal shirt and pinstriped vest. "Yeah, something like that."

Lance throws his head back in laughter. "You sneaky son of a bitch!

"Okay…*Thunderbolt.*"

Lance jumps up from his seat with wide eyes. *That did the trick.* "Alright, alright. I'll stop. I see what you're trying to do by digging back to our college days and the most embarrassing moment of my life. I'm going to get us another bottle of Dom Pérignon to drown that memory."

"Don't knock yourself out in my wine cellar."

"Oh, I won't. I'll bring the bottle here and knock myself out on the dining table instead."

"Sure, stay the night even. Won't be the first time I've tucked a child into bed," I tease.

"*Wow!*" Lance mocks, gasping mid grin while loosening his tie. He averts his gaze to Sandro who simply watches. "Sandro my man, let's schedule a meeting tomorrow morning. I need to take out this successful businessman with a qualification in sarcasm. Make it fast."

"I was only joking." I laugh, raising my hands in defense. "You know I love you and would do anything for you."

"I know. Love you too, man. I'm always here for you too. Anytime and I mean it. Now, I'll be back with one of your bottles of Dom Pérignon." Lance snaps his fingers and points to the hall. "And best believe we're playing another game of Scopa and I'll get both your asses."

"Famous last words."

We all erupt in laughter as Lance takes his leave out into the dim hallway. It always goes like this when the three of us meet up during a work night at the start of the week. It's nice to just breathe and spend a few hours with friends, rival card games, and burning cigars.

I set mine in the ashtray and collect all our cards, shuffling them into a neat pile at the center of the table. I feel Sandro's eyes on me and swallow down the harsh reality of why I also called him over. This morning when SPD revealed the girl spotted wasn't Addilyn, I did some digging of my own.

I first met Sandro a few years ago when my company designed and built one of his houses. I didn't grasp what *sort* of house it was until during one of my final inspections when I witnessed Sandro pinning a man to an interior wall and putting two in his head.

Sandro's explanation? *"It's my property and so I'll do whatever the hell I wanna do in it. What the hell are you gonna do 'bout it?"*

I never pressed it. It was a safehouse after all and what happened within those walls stayed there. An unlikely friendship formed between us though, with a foundation based on that we are both native to New Jersey.

"I've asked all my associates and none of them know anything about your kid."

"You sure?"

"Positive. You know I take care of you, Giulio. Everybody's clean. Nobody knows a thing, and trust me, I'd know if they did. No underworld organization has anything to do with Addilyn. If you want me to start an investigation, I can gather some of my men and we—"

I cut him off. "No. No, that's okay. Thank you. We'll let SPD do their job. But are you certain it isn't anybody you know? Perhaps you haven't done business with them for a while?"

He chuckles coldly. "You don't have to worry 'bout any of those guys, Giulio."

"Why's that?"

Sandro takes one good look at me and those deadly eyes flicker to the floorboards beneath our feet. "Cause they're all in the fucking burning pit below. All the guys I haven't done business with for a while are either dead or on their fucking way there. *Hai capito?"*

"Si, ho capito." I swallow thickly and glance over my shoulder to ensure Lance isn't in sight before turning back to the Mafioso. When I lean forward with my forearms on my thighs and fingers laced together, my voice stays confidently low. "You know the *thing* we said earlier?"

Sandro nods.

"I'll think I'll be needing it after all."

There's a challenge in his eyes that dims the raging light in mine. *Will this be a mistake?* I rub my hands over my face, prepared to revoke the plan when Sandro smiles. It's a lethal one that only edges on the pit of fire burning inside me. All he needs to do is light that match and I'll withstand the blaze that consumes both my versions of heaven and hell—this will be something I can never take back.

Whatever happens from this point forth, I need Valencia to know I'm doing this for us.

"You sure you want it?"

"Positive."

"You don't seem like the type of man who would make a decision without thinking it through. I trust you. I won't anymore if you fuck with me. If something happens and you let it slip that I gave it to you, you're a dead man. I'll do it myself. I'll drive you to that safe house you made and so God help you if you even dare whisper my name to the boys in blue. *Capisci?*"

Nodding, I accept that this is my only choice if I want to protect my family right. "*Si.*"

We shake on it, sealing in every one of my fateful sins from this point forth.

"Marcus! Open the damn door!"

"Fuck off!"

"I know he's in there!" My fists pound against his front door, adamant to get inside. It was a normal Tuesday morning up until Lance gave me the tipoff that he spotted Bryce's orange pickup parked in my half-brother's driveway upon passing Marcus' house on his way to work.

Bryce is inside and I'll be damned if I don't see him. Tomorrow will mark a week since Bryce made an advance on Valencia. I've been hunting him down ever since to no avail.

"Let it go, Giulio!"

"This has nothing to do with you. I *need* to speak to Bryce."

"Not going to happen."

Marcus reminds me of our father. Cunning. Ruthless. Stubborn. Pietro Giannotti confirmed all three for me on the day of my mother's funeral when he had the audacity to invite the woman he'd been having an affair with, one of my mother's at-home nurses.

I cried for my mother that night. Wept until I felt sick and complete lonely despair. If my mother were alive, she would have laid on my bed, kissed my forehead, and stayed with me until her comfort was enough for me to peacefully fall asleep. Hard to do when the person you need the most disappeared into the stars above.

My father didn't check on me that night.

I should have kept the door locked the next morning. It would have prevented the beating I received from him for acting *'weak.'* Me. A nine-year-old boy who just lost his mother *acting weak*. To him, I had been since the day I was born, only he didn't show it until I was nine. I took the beatings, every single one of them. I did not say a word or shed a tear.

I had not only lost my mother that day…I lost my father too.

Pietro Giannotti disregarding my existence continued for the next nine years. It was then I had enough money to move to Seattle, one of the best leading cities for architecture, and started *my* life. I haven't looked back since because the move was the best thing I'd ever done for myself. It eventuated in my career, my children, and *Valencia*.

I regret stooping to my father's level that fateful Thanksgiving weekend when I traveled back to New Jersey to see him. It was only him, Marcus, and me that night. His wife was working the late shift at the hospital. I remember when my father took his life…that loud bang of the gunshot…I will never forget that sound. *Ever.*

Marcus acting the way he is right now reminds me exactly of our father. He loved Marcus. Hated me. I didn't attend our father's funeral. Marcus says it was my greatest mistake, but I don't regret a thing. My father was the first person to break my heart. No father in his right mind should ever do that. No father should mentally or physically abuse his child like he did me.

"Alright, I'll go."

"Good." Marcus' footsteps retreating have me conjuring a plan.

I back away from the door, suck in a breath, and kick to the side of it, exactly where the lock is mounted near the keyhole. *The subtle art of being an architect and knowing 'weak' spots.*

I prevail, even when Marcus returns and shouts for me to stop. *Two can play that game.* The door bursts open and I stride inside like I own the place. My half-brother and Bryce stand before me, their mouths slack.

Hello, motherfuckers.

"Now…" Smugly, I brush off my blazer and cock my head to the Englishman. His bruised nose seems to be healing. "Bryce, are you and I going to have a *nice* talk, or am I going to have to do to your head what I did to the door?"

"Pleasure to see ya as always, Giannotti."

"I wish I could say the same, McCarson."

"Too bad ya can't fire me…"

"Wish I could, but you're so fucking deep in this mess I want to witness you crawl out!"

"Hey, do not speak to him like that!" Marcus grits, stepping forward to block my way to Bryce. "Get out of here, Giulio!"

"You would not say that if you were in my position."

"I wouldn't get myself in your position to begin with."

"How can you be so sure?"

"I just am." Marcus scoffs and leans against the wooden stair balustrade. His beady eyes flicker to the coat closet, then back to me. "Firstly, you know where you went wrong…now, the consequence is having to deal with me and whoever I call a friend— like Bryce. Secondly, I don't do commitment…or rather, I never get to that commitment stage. I've tried."

"As a man whose wife was involuntary kissed by this *friend* of yours, I'm kindly asking you to move out of my way before I do something *you* will regret."

"Well, well, well. The tiger comes to play when it's about this girl, aye?"

"And YOU have another thing coming!" I point a finger at Bryce, defusing his smirk with a single look. "No smartass remarks from you."

"Guess I've gotta take a number and wait in line." Bryce shrugs and turns towards the ominous looking hallway. "I'll be in the living room when you're ready to ring me neck. Don't worry, I won't run. I've got nothing waiting for me but you."

You run and I'll catch you.

I glance around, analyzing the dark timber wood floors and dark walls. I feel crowded in here. There is a distinct smell of whiskey mixed with something I can't grasp.

"I kindly suggest you get the hell out, Giulio."

A chill runs down my spine. I don't know why. There's something about this house. I get this agitated feeling inside as I follow Marcus' gaze to that coat closet again. He's quick to rush forward and take a hold of the handle before me.

My brows quiver. "What's in there?"

"Nothing."

"Doesn't seem like nothing by the death grip you have on it."

"I apologized to Valencia, okay? I got out of line with her, but we're good again. I don't need to apologize to you. Quite frankly, I don't need you."

"Open the door, Marcus."

"Fucking leave my house before I destroy you!"

"You mean the house I bought you? Father would be ashamed of you."

"No!" My half-brother sneers. "He would continue to place me on a pedestal, like he always did. You would be the one to suffer, like you always *do*. Why? Because you're w…e…a…k."

Oh, that's it.

I fight his grip and swing the door open. "Holy shit!"

I cannot believe this is happening *again*. One glance is enough to see the stashes of white power and possibly hundreds of stacked up pill containers. I rush to shut the front door, which hasn't received as much damage as I thought, and turn back to Marcus. "You're using again?"

"No. I'm not using."

"Look me in the eye and tell me again."

When Marcus does I curse at the redness crawling in them. I don't know how I missed it before. "I'm not using. I'm…selling."

Oh, Dio.

Years ago when Marcus moved states to attend college here and later work at my company, I couldn't say no because of our past. Something else that happened on that Thanksgiving night has ironically bound us to this promise…one that I resent.

We have never gotten along, but I continued to help him. He is my blood after all. There are times he's asked to borrow thousands of dollars, and thinking he'll use it for good or at least something *legal,* like starting up his own design business, I accept without question. Even though he's never paid me back, I've maintained a fraction of faith in him. Looking back now, I've been too generous. Helping Marcus is a foolishly desperate move to keep him as part of the family.

Foolish.

I stopped the additional payments when I walked in on a drug trade in his office months ago. It's irresponsible. I feel like a fucking tour guide in my own freaking building; *and on the left it's drugs in Marcus' office, down a level and to the right it's sex in McCarson's office. Take your pick.* Fuck no. It's preposterous. This needs to stop. Marcus has always pledged he's only the seller and that he'll stop. I have never believed it and how he's acting now is why.

"Do you know how bad this is, Marcus?" I can't speak sense into him, no matter how hard I try. "If the police find you—"

"They won't."

"Let's say they do. Are you prepared to throw away your entire life?"

"I'm careful with the people I sell to."

"You're twenty-three, Marcus! You have your entire life ahead of—"

"The only way the police will find out is if YOU tell them. Okay?" he hisses. I see the terror in his eyes, even if he doesn't want to admit it. "If you tell them, I swear on my mother's life that I will tell them *everything*."

"Don't you dare. They are two different situations. You promised me—"

Marcus cuts me off. *Again.* "Don't tell a soul. You owe me! You fucking owe me this!"

I don't see a man in front of me; I see hell. That wicked look in his eyes has been there ever since he learned the word 'brother.' Yes, he lost his father too, but I became an orphan that night. I admit I haven't been the best to him, but I have my reasons.

What reasons does *he* have?

Marcus took my mother's favorite pieces of gold jewelry and threw them in the river.

My father praised him.

He keyed my first car.

His mother laughed it off.

He set my bed on fire the day before I left for Seattle.

The happy couple said "it was going to be removed anyway."

That nine-year-old playing with fire grew up to be a man toying with every opportunity in his precious life.

Marcus' anger fluctuates as I stand motionless in front of him. I can't give him more than I already have. A steady job. Steady pay. A steady family through my children.

"I don't know what to say, Marcus…"

"Nobody cares, Giulio. You know where I was this past weekend? Jersey. My mom got remarried and wait a minute…oh, that's right you weren't invited."

"Good luck to her. There's no need to be childish about it, you know that I would not have gone even if I was invited after what she did to my mother. I want to talk some sense into you. I want to help you. But I can only explain it to you. I can't understand it for you, Marcus."

It happens in a split second.

He launches at me and his fist collides with my left cheekbone. I don't flinch. My half-brother doesn't stop there. He punches my diaphragm and keeps going. My breaths stagger but I don't retaliate throughout the entire ordeal. I simply stare ahead at him with a clenched jaw.

He throws punch after punch. One blow to my stomach and I'm on my knees, suppressing the groans that threaten to escape.

Not for him.

Marcus kicks my side. Once. Twice. He screams, telling me to *fight back* and then switches to insults. All of which reminds me exactly of my father. It's exactly what he used to do. I let Marcus treat me however he likes because I know the demons inside him will never stop without a release. I take it. Blow after blow. I do not care that I will wake up in the morning battered and bruised. All I care about is that Marcus wakes up tomorrow morning with at least one brain cell that tells him just how wrong he is.

"Marcus, what the hell?"

"Leave me alone, Bryce. He fucking deserves it."

There's a struggle between them. I miss it, too desperate to catch my breath.

"Get out of here! Innit enough you're a dealer? Don't add being a nutter to the title."

I clutch my side, compressing the sharp pain I haven't felt in a long while.

The front door opens and slams shut. Marcus is gone.

A hand is extended to me.

I smell bergamot.

Bryce.

It's Bryce. *Helping me?*

"Your face is alright, it's the body that will bruise up," he says with a pinched expression, his nose scrunched up. "He shouldn't have gone that far. Come on, up ya get."

I stare at him perplexed and he has the exact expression. He's just as astonished as I am that *the* Bryce McCarson is taking my side.

Has Marcus kicked me into the Twilight Zone?

I can't forgive Bryce for what he did to Valencia, but what I *can* do is take Bryce's tattooed hand. And I do, and Bryce helps me up. I thank him while adjusting my suit.

I attempt to work through exactly what just happened. Bryce stopped the altercation and as a result, made Marcus leave the house. Now he's protecting me, ushering me into the mid-century wood kitchen and pulling out vinegar from under the sink.

I came here to put Bryce in his place.

He knew this as much as I did.

Then why is he helping me?

McCarson sets out a small bowl and pours a dash of vinegar, the rest he fills with warm water. I watch wordlessly as he disappears and returns with a rag. His green eyes flicker to mine and then my torso.

"Take ya shirt off."

"Why?"

He looks at me as if I'm insane. "Because those bruises will make ya feel like shit in the morning if you don't do something about them. How can I help ya with it on? Rubbing vinegar and warm water on the areas before they appear will help the coloring and healing."

I swallow hard. "I meant why did you take my side back there?"

Bryce stays silent as I take off my shirt. He stares outside the kitchen window, shoulders tense underneath his Harley Davidson sweatshirt. I've never seen Bryce this quiet or somber.

McCarson without the sarcasm? Unthinkable.

"Have ya ever been to Hoxton, England?"

"No."

"Hmmm." Bryce nods, his gaze still on the outside. When he speaks, his accent shines through. "Well, I was born there. Now if ya ask me, my mother, or say the local bread-maker what makes Hoxton really *Hoxton*, we'll all say different things. The bread-maker would say the tight-knit communities and cloudy days, right. There's something poetic about it. My mother would say her bread and butt'er pudding with raisins. She hates nutmeg and puts so many raisins in it's basically a raisin cake. Every bite there's like sixty pieces in your mouth and you're paralyzed...but I never questioned it because it's what she likes. You see, a lot of people have different perspectives on the world. It's the same place but different things stand out. Like you in your job. Ya notice things that I wouldn't necessarily pick up and that there takes courage to notice things others wouldn't without the fear of being judged."

I take the small towel and wipe over the beaten areas. Still, I'm attentive to Bryce and keep my eyes on him. The spot near my diaphragm stings and I hiss in protest.

"Easy, mate. It'll hurt for a bit...Anyway, if someone asked me what I love about Hoxton, I would say the warmth of friendship. I had friends back there." He smirks when he turns to me. "Hard to believe that, innit?"

The corners of my lips rise. "Am I allowed to say sometimes?"

"You're allowed. All tough guys with the softest hearts, ya know how it all goes. I left them for opportunity here in Seattle. One thing I learned about my group of friends is if you fuck with one of us, you fuck with us all. I've never had a long-term girlfriend, I'm the casual type of guy. This week I hid from ya because I...I know what I did was wrong. If I was back home, all my mates would circle me and beat my ass. We love each other but we always put each other in our place too. Ya know what I mean?"

"I do."

Bryce takes a step forward and motions towards my hand. "See what I like about you, Giannotti, is what you did to me. You hit me. Valencia, she slapped me. Now, I'm not saying violence is the answer but it's needed to place things into perspective sometimes. I put myself in ya shoes; it's something I've never done, right, so I put myself in those shiny fancy fucking Italian shoes you wear and imagined myself with kids and a wife. I imagined my wife assisting her employee with important work. They got drunk and he...he thought that maybe she was sick of me and wanted to show her what she was missing."

He pauses with a staggered breath, his face flushed. There's aggravation within him and I notice now it's anger at himself. With each sentence he takes a pause, amplifying the severity.

I should be giving Bryce McCarson a piece of my mind, but he's surprising me. I never expected *this*, that he would actually have an honest conversation with me. Then Valencia crosses my mind and how distressed she was in that shower. I know this is going to be more complex than I initially thought.

"If I stepped inside that bar and I saw that, right? If I saw somebody feeling up my wife, kissing her neck...I would have killed that man. I wouldn't have stopped at a punch. I would have fucking ended him for even thinking, let alone kissing her without her wanting it. Why didn't ya go that far with me?"

"I'm not that type of man."

"Nah. I saw the havoc in them eyes. If she wasn't there, you may have gone there."

I swallow hard. *No. No, I wouldn't...not with him.*

McCarson's confidence is like no other person I have ever crossed. There's something very cynical about him. He's the type of man who rakes carnage and isn't afraid to drag everybody down with him. But right now, there's a different side to Bryce McCarson. Perhaps the side he only shows for Marcus, close friends, and particular women.

Is the arrogance just a façade?

"I needed to attend to Valencia."

"Nah." He shakes his head confidently. His pointer rests upon my chest and taps twice. "You didn't go that far because you still love her and you didn't want to face the consequences of killing a man in front of her. That's a life sentence in marriage. I know you hate me, Giulio, but every once in awhile the hero needs the antagonist and vice-versa. That's exactly what happened earlier...and now."

Bryce and I are left staring at each other. I don't know what to say because I never expected this from him. *You still love her.* The cords of my neck soften at the thought of civil ground, but I cannot let go of the repercussions of his actions and how much it reeled Valencia back into our greatest suffering.

"I have never seen Valencia that drunk in my life. It wasn't her and perhaps that wasn't you either, but you hurt her deeply and that hurts me."

"I know, mate. I am sorry for everything that went down. It was never my intention going into the night and the alcohol fucked with my head and I just felt…I don't know what I felt."

I ring the towel and wash out the bowl.

I need time to evaluate everything that he has said to me. I need to talk to Valencia about it and I already know it can't be tonight. Therapy is hot on the schedule and I'm counting on it helping us.

There was so much animosity in the air and then Friday night we confided in each other. I was so damn close to kissing her and showing her just how much I've missed her, but it wasn't the right moment and I needed to leave. It was the same feeling when she thanked me for giving her the mental health handbook. The heat in her eyes matched the blood pumping through my body, coaxed with nothing but my very much still present feelings for her. Just like on Friday, that moment had me wanting to whisk her away into the mesmerizing sunset with me and give in to every last one of our desires.

I need time to think.

You've got a lot to think about, Giannotti.

Bryce follows me on the way out. I'm wordless in my pursuit to slip on my blazer and undo a few of my shirt buttons. I can't walk straight without feeling the pressure of each blow.

I quicken my pace by the coat closet and Bryce notices. "For the record, I've only seen Marcus sell them. I don't do any of it. I'm more of a…drinks type of guy." His rough, rumbling accent has a way of making me glance towards him as his eyes widen. "Even though I know alcohol is…never…the…ahem, answer."

I'm so used to the unmotivated, cocky, persuasive Bryce.

He's nothing but wise now. I've never heard him speak so much truth. Would this bloom into some unlikely alliance?

Warmth of friendship.

Every once in awhile the hero needs the antagonist.

As Bryce slides his hands into the pockets of his dark faded jeans, I ask myself, can I forgive him for what he's done? Can Valencia forgive him?

When he slips his hood over his head, I start to say something but I'm distracted by a figure in my peripheral vision. Head low, Marcus is down the street and walking back up at a slow pace. I don't think he's seen me, but I do and so does Bryce.

"Don't worry, I'll calm him down," he says.

I eye Bryce who's still focused on my half-brother. Then something dawns on me and I stand paralyzed for a moment. *Does he know about...?* No. Why would Marcus have told him? He wouldn't have told him. It doesn't involve Bryce. *But what if he did?* I don't trust Marcus but he wouldn't do that.

Oh, Dio. Stop overthinking it.

"Thank you." There's no anger left in me. I came here intending to settle the score, but his peacemaking has derailed everything. I'm so pensive yet perplexed I can't even think straight.

"Your clients cannot be disregarded any longer, Bryce."

"I know...I promise I'll fix everything when I return to work. But if it's alright with you, I just need to talk it out with Valencia first and apologize. Ya know, make her feel okay."

I slip into my beige leather driver's seat, my left foot still pressed against the pavement. Turning towards him has my injuries ache. "Zeluci tomorrow night at 7 P.M. She'll be there with Kayla and her sister, Helena. Don't tell her I told you. Make it right with her and we'll review your position in the coming days. Okay?"

Bryce nods and I shut my door. "Okay."

With one final nod, I switch on the engine and shut the door, not knowing if I should have told him where Valencia would be. It's done now and it settles me that she won't be alone with him. He wouldn't do it again.

I have to trust Bryce McCarson.

I have to accept our truce.

Marcus is almost at the drive but stops to stare straight through me. I ignore the urge to talk to him and refocus on Bryce. I slide down the window when he taps on it. "Aye, don't forget to apply vinegar and water in the mornings, even after the bruises appear. It'll help 'em."

"Will do. I'm curious, who hurt you so bad you needed to learn all of this?"

That cunning smirk makes a return.

Bryce smiles. "A sweet little thing called the warmth of friendship."

CHAPTER THIRTEEN

Valencia

GIULIO KILLS THE ENGINE OUTSIDE OF THE THERAPIST AND MY eyes slam shut.

Breathe.

We didn't mention anything about our *moment* on Friday during the entire drive here. Instead, we spoke about the children, his run in with Zoe last week and he also then briefly mentioned he saw Bryce McCarson this morning who apologized for the drunken bar incident. It doesn't fix everything, but apparently Bryce sounded sincere and wants to make amends with me one of these days.

One point during our conversation earlier Giulio's hand laced over mine. It was of those gentle thumb caresses that made my heart skip a beat and want him even more. Even the rough tension diffused and for once the silence between us wasn't awkward. It was refreshing.

Now, as I mentally prepare myself for therapy, I attempt to drown out all my previous thoughts with positive affirmations.

I can do this.

It will be alright.

Trust the process.

"Everything okay?"

"Yes, I'm just preparing myself. It helps me get through it."

There's a soft hum to my left.

Giulio's door shuts and I wait in anticipation for the next move. His fresh, citric aroma with a hint of elegant spices wraps around me, softening the bubble I use to protect myself from the world. The same bubble he can see right through. This is my life. *Mine.* And I'm doing my best to get through before the storm. I've been burned before. I know this pain too well.

I hear my door open. "What are you thinking about?"

My eyes open to Giulio looking down at me smiling, his hands outstretched on the roof of his car. "Small nuggets of hope. Or like Slonne likes to call them, *nussets.*"

Our laughter fades and we become nothing more than two broken souls watching each other. Time stops when Giulio crouches down and his hand falls upon my right thigh. Both our gazes drop there, simply analyzing how he circles my knee and later spreads up over my light blue Levi jeans. Every single second bursts at the electric waves beneath his palm.

"*Sei molto capace di questo. Lo prometto.*"

You are very capable of this. I promise.

Giulio's hand halts at mid-thigh. It burns through the fabric. Teasing me to set me free. It's the same allusive feeling he made me feel on Friday night before he rushed out of my house.

In a matter of three weeks working with him, we've gone from broken to a place of comfort. One where both of our voices are heard. It was only last week I told myself that there had to be an end to this, that we shouldn't have any future, but now I'm not so sure. Nobody gets me like he does and we've overcome so much together.

Is it bad that I…*want him?*

That even though we still don't see eye to eye on the investigation, Giulio is still everything to me. His tendency to be strong, passionate, and kind to me in these last days…I recognize it as the man I married and I *need* that.

"I should make one thing clear, Valencia. I want only good things from you. For us."

"So do I."

"The other night…" He looks over his shoulder, his face tight. I want to reach out and hold him. I want to declare that everything will be okay if he just kisses me. That this is only a phase in our life and I can't do this life without him. But…how am I supposed to believe everything will be okay when the entire world is burning at our feet?

"The other night I wasn't ready to say goodbye." He starts. "But, I knew that if I didn't leave when I did, I may have never left. There was fire in my veins every time I looked at you and all I wanted to do was get burned. To protect you from every danger. To find a place of no fear, no hurt, no fighting. A place where we can try again and be safe within each other's arms. Where the only healing we need is each other. Where we will find some way to heal from the head down, *properly*, so we can raise our family. To allow our children to be proud and brave warriors. You gave me all of those feelings seven years ago and Friday night they strengthened. I couldn't stop thinking about it back then and I can't stop thinking about it now. I left so abruptly because I feared you may not want any of this."

Oh my god.

My hands lace into Giulio's and they assist me out of the car, into a purified state of mind. I pull his body into mine and hug him. When my cheek presses against his solid chest, I feel so alive.

Seattle's air mixes with his warm touch. I'm holding him with so much need, desire, and assurance, that when his own hands sink into my waist, everything but the truth escapes me. "That was beautiful, Giulio. Friday night I forgot about all the barriers and remembered everything all at the same time. I know it sounds confusing but...it was *us* and it felt so refreshing and inviting."

"I love *us*." Giulio sighs in relief, his face falling to the crook of my neck. "I'm going to win you back, Lencia. One of these days you'll be mine again. One of these days we are going to be happy and nothing will ever break us again. Tell me you want this too. Tell me you still feel what I feel."

"Yes, I feel it." We pull back and he cups my cheeks, searching my watery eyes. His crowfeet deepen and I smile through the pain at the explosions in my chest. "I feel it all with you."

My lungs are working so hard that I can't even see him straight through the tears he wipes away as they fall. I know this won't be easy and will be one of the toughest things we've overcome, but as scared as I am, I'm also happy. And I've longed for that feeling for the past months.

Giulio's hand slips into mine and with a tight squeeze, we climb the stairs to the building. The stark reality of the words we've exchanged excites me, but worry also manifests.

We will find some way to heal from the head down, properly, so we can raise our family.

I'm going to win you back, Lencia.

One of these days you will be mine again.

Dr. Michael Eross welcomes us in. The intimate studio has been my second home within these last few months. Whenever I step inside, any heaviness I feel escapes me. I feel heard. Instead of trapping the words inside my mind for the past six months, here they roll off my tongue with no judgment.

Giulio and I tell him everything. The progression on The Window Case, how we want to concentrate on finding a balance between good communication and getting our diverse points across without the arguments. Then there's the other issue: how to separate the disappearance and our broken marriage.

Michael advises us that instead of constantly concentrating

on both issues and getting overwhelmed, we need to identify boundaries and triggering sentences that onset the arguments. *It is vital to remain proactive instead of reactive. Identify that there are two individual issues to sort through and prevent combining them into one.*

"Improving this aspect is what will determine whether you file divorce papers or resume your marriage. I would suggest initiating the process and creating a plan. Now, I want to ask a rather direct question; at this point, is there any possibility of resuming your marriage?"

There is a flicker of hope in our fickle inferno game when Giulio and I glance at each other with a burning desire.

"Yes, there's a possibility." I don't know which one of us says it, but I know we both mean it.

Something's changed between us, whether it's the additional time we spend together, the way we tend to understand each other even through our opposing views or how everything clicked for me with that sweet dreams spray because I realized the kids need him as much as I do, but there *is* a change and I want to hold onto it for dear life.

Giulio is what I want, even during the war.

"I'm trying to be a good single mother. A good woman. A good worker. But I'm struggling with juggling all of it and I feel for the twins. I really do."

Giulio inches closer to me, his hand wrapping around my shoulder. There's a tight squeeze there that resonates inside me. "That's not true. You're a sensational mother."

"You don't see what I feel."

"I see how much you love them. I know how much they adore you."

"It's inside, Giulio." I shake my head, rushing my fingers through my updo. "I'm getting better. I feel myself getting happier and when I'm with you...I feel so much more like *me*, but the depression still sinks in and when it does..."

"Valencia, concentrate on your breaths," Dr. Eross warns, noticing my angst. "What is going through your mind?"

Too many thoughts.

I feel lightheaded and tingly all over. When I grip the arm of the couch to stabilize myself, Giulio's hand slips under my cropped leather jacket and rubs circular motions against my skin.

"Before...I was close to asking for divorce. Now...this doesn't feel like falling out of love with Giulio. Is this how it's supposed to go? Or are we destined to smile at a distance and love our kids with a barrier? What is our new normal? I don't want to lose him, but at the same time I'm so scared of what comes next if we do attempt to restart things."

His hand on my back slows.

Dr. Eross nods. "What exactly are you scared of?"

"I'm scared of loving. I fear that we'll be okay for a little while and then our diverse views on Addilyn will cause yet another breaking point. I can already hear the tear in my children's hearts and I don't want that. I would rather sacrifice and end it all then go through this pain again. I don't want anybody hurting more than they already are right now."

"It's normal to be scared, Valencia. In fact, you are *traumatized*. You both are. Sometimes in life, we ponder too much. We think everything has to have a solution when it doesn't. Sometimes the best thing to do is to live in the moment and watch what happens. Often, the best things in life are unplanned. Do you know the most important person in this equation?"

"Me."

"Tell me again. Look me in the eyes and believe it this time."

"Me. I am."

"Exactly. It isn't selfish to take care of your first in order to take care of others. It is *okay*. It is *normal*. It is both necessary and a healthy thing to do. It means listening to your heart because, in the end, it's the most delicate piece of us." The therapist pauses to slip off his glasses. When he does, he leans closer to us with a soft smile. "Valencia, I know you're scared. You care a lot about others, especially your children. You're scared to hurt them if you were to get back together and then something were to happen to fall back apart. But guess what? Life will *always* be a gamble. That's what makes it interesting. That's what makes it an adventure. That's what makes it *life*. You're hurting yourself more if you don't give yourself that chance to get back together. Your children love you both and will forgive you if things were to ultimately not work. They know that either way, you will both continue to be in their lives. I see the love between you and Giulio. I *see* it. Those seven years can be seventy. Don't let fear break you. What does your heart tell you?"

Everything Dr. Eross says resonates deeply, outlining the reasons for my fears and why I should just go for it, why I *need* to go for it.

I flick my gaze to Giulio's and find that he's already looking at me. His hopeful eyes are my reckoning. If I don't say it now, I don't know when I ever will. "My heart says that I want to try harder for you. I want an *us*."

"And you, Giulio? What does yours say?"

"That I was a fool to let the love of my life go and I will do everything to have her back." I forget how to breathe. Giulio wants this. He wants me. Our hands intertwine and he kisses my knuckles. "I want the good and the bad with you, Valencia. I want it all, whatever the cost. We don't know what will happen until we try and I so desperately want to try. I want no regrets."

Dr. Eross nods, noting something down on his paper. When he looks up, there's a wide smile on his lips. "Valencia, can you tell me a part of yourself you feel you have lost touch with since the beginning of the abduction and the separation?"

"My happiness."

"Okay. What is something you love about yourself?"

"My children."

Dr. Eross draws a finger to the center of his mouth, not seeming too pleased with my response. "All good mothers would say that. So for the moment, I want you to detach them from you. What is something else you love about yourself?"

It isn't easy for me. "I really don't know"

Dr. Eross turns to Giulio. "What is one thing you still love about Valencia? Something that is a reminder of who she truly is."

"Her resilience and strength. I think she is much stronger than she gives herself credit for. Her dedication is another thing I admire. She's far more dedicated than I ever could be."

"So, what you're saying is despite your separation, this is the type of woman Valencia is?"

"Correct."

"And if I were to say, what was the core of your marriage breaking down? Do you believe it was her dedication and your incapability to grasp that dedicated hope that led to it?"

"Definitely." Giulio's assertiveness has me turn to him. Even his profile is attractive. That straight nose, perfectly stubbled jaw, and those mesmerizing lashes. "When you love somebody, there is no greater pain than being witness to them falling right in front of your eyes. Reaching out isn't good enough. You need to pull them out and I was incapable of doing so."

"Do you blame yourself?"

"Yes."

I clear my throat. "None of this is entirely your fault. It was both of us."

"No, maybe it is my fault." Giulio presses his lips tightly together. "I admit it. I'm to blame. Maybe if I tried harder to believe in Addilyn we wouldn't be sitting here right now."

"There is no way of knowing that. There are so many other factors."

The therapist cuts in. "What I am seeing here is a passive argument. They may be healthy, but it's still something we should seek to eliminate. Are you both willing to change that?"

"Definitely."

"Am I allowed to say hell yes in here?" Giulio's question has us laugh and exchange an amused look. *We agree on just about everything tonight.*

"Okay, then I have two projects for you. One to tackle the arguments and the other to work on the closeness. Now, I understand you both have busy schedules, but when I say close-ness I mean simmering the tension to reach the level of what you both once had." *I'm prepared for anything.* "A dance lesson. I understand that everybody's different, but dancing focuses on in-timate closeness. That confident and comfortable connection is what you both need. I want you both to also try compliments. Before one feels an unnecessary argument spark, defuse it by tak-ing note of something you love about each other. Instead of es-calating a conversation, defuse it."

Giulio and I leave therapy committed to attempting to reach a new level in our relationship. There have already been so many discoveries today and while we may not be able to assist in the process of Addilyn's case, we can improve the way we treat each other.

When Giulio doesn't make the first turn off to Helena's house, confusion entraps me. "Oh, you're not taking me home?"

"I am. I just want to take the long way."

"And what if I had other plans, Mr.?" I playfully tease him.

"Hmmm, and what if you didn't?"

"Well, you didn't know that for certain, now did you?"

Giulio takes his eyes off the road. The way he sweeps his tongue over his lower lip with that hot gaze on my mouth... *damn.* A wide grin overtakes him. "I appreciate your courage."

Huh? My courage?

My eyes narrow until I realize what he's attempting to do. He's attempting to implement Dr. Eross' advice on saying a com-pliment to defuse a brewing argument. *Or in this case, banter filled teasing.*

I smile through my laugher. "Thanks. Now all eyes on the road, Mr. Giannotti."

"Damn. I forgot how strict you can be."

"Shhh, you secretly like it."

He winks. "You know it."

"Giulio! Eyes on the road!"

Giulio's grin expands when he presses cruise control and turns his body towards me. Both hands leave the leather-wrapped steering wheel and rest behind his headrest, involuntarily flexing his muscular arms rather dramatically through his navy dress shirt. *Not only is his gaze off the road, but EVERYTHING is! He still needs to move the car with the wheel!* Those light eyes sparkle, infusing me with nothing but pure mischief. "So, darling…you were saying?"

"Smartass."

"Huh?"

"I said smartass."

"Huh?"

"I said I appreciate your generosity."

"Aww, how sweet of you!"

My face brightens in amusement and we can't help but laugh. *It feels so good to be like this.* At some point, Giulio leans over and kisses my forehead. When his thumb caresses over my parted lips, he whispers two words that have my entire world spin for all the right reasons.

"Soon, baby."

There's a burning smile resting upon my lips the remainder of the drive. Dr. Eross is right. *Sometimes the best thing to do is to live in the moment and watch what happens.*

This is just a phase in our life. We're going to try again. It's all going to be okay.

That voice inside my head comes alive…

It has to be okay.

The following day Giulio doesn't enter until two o'clock. I already sense something's wrong by the dark sunglasses he wears when he passes me. He *never* wears sunglasses inside the office; just last week he warned Marcus about it.

I follow behind and shut his office door.

Giulio's already laid out on his sage ottoman bench with his hands covering his face. The action forces the edge of his charcoal cashmere crewneck sweater to inch higher up, exposing the smallest edge of the black band boxers I already know are Armani. His six-foot-one sculpted frame has his feet perched on either side of the bench.

"Giulio, what happened?" My brows crease and I don't think twice before closing in and sweeping my fingers against the hem of his sweater.

He gently clasps my wrist to brush me off. "I'm okay, Lencia."

I beg to differ.

His face clenches as if he's in pain and that concerns me.

"Please…let me see." I slide off his sunglasses for him and he tenses at the action.

Oh my god!

A loud gasp escapes me at the purplish red bruise across his left cheekbone. Thankfully his eyes seem okay and there's no inflammation or deep cuts, but this is still serious. My heavy breaths intensify when Giulio can't meet my gaze, and so I caress my thumb under the blemish for a little while before asking the only question I have. "Who did this to you?"

Giulio gives me nothing and so my fingers leave his face and resume down to his sweater. There's a small division between the hem and his black leather belt and dark slacks. I overlook the position of my hand so close to his crotch and lift the cashmere material.

He groans and I immediately apologize. My words are followed by an immediate frown at the sight. His impeccable olive skin is marred with a collection of dark bruises. They span from his chest to his toned abs and diagrams to his right side.

"Please," I whisper. "Tell me who did this."

"I can't."

"You can't or you don't want to?"

Giulio reaches up with his thumb to wipe away my tears. "I don't want my opinion on the person to influence yours… Darling, don't cry for me." I don't miss the sorrow in his tone or how he grimaces, as if the concealment of truth is toiling with him.

It has to be someone I know.

"When did it happen?"

"Yesterday. Before therapy."

"But I didn't see any bruising yesterday. Why didn't you tell me at therapy?"

"I didn't want to worry you."

I lean my head into his hand, needing his touch to cure all the explosions and tattered feelings inside me. The warmth he gives can raise me out of this mess. It *will* raise me up.

"Whoever did this is not on my team. Not when they do this to you."

"I promise I'm okay."

"Was it Bryce?"

He shakes his head.

"A client?"

Another shake.

"Marcus?"

Giulio tightens his jaw and it's the only answer I need.

What. The. Hell.

Marcus could not get away with something like this! Beat up his own brother? *No.* No, that doesn't sit well with me. Not one bit. I'm incapable of staying reserved. Not under this circumstance.

"Why would Marcus do this?"

"I don't really want to talk about it right now. I didn't retaliate, maybe I should have…"

"No. You did the right thing." My fingers slowly glide a path around the bruises, across his chest, down his abdominal muscles and toned obliques. "Was it because of me?"

Giulio's eyes drift from mine. I can see the agony in them, no matter how hard he attempts to downplay the hurt with his hand outstretched and caressing my hip bone. "It was because of our father and also something else."

I feel for him. I really do. Although Marcus and I are on civil terms now, it still worries me that Giulio's only sibling is doing this to him.

My hand fans out by his navel as I lower my head. My lipstick proves its transfer proof, not once spreading its creamy rose pigment as I slowly kiss my way up across all of his torso. Moans escape his throat. Ones so sensual I continue up his neck, but purposely skip his face to meet his right ear in a hot murmur instead. "I understand that this is between both of you, but I will always be here for you when you need it. Even if I will never be able to walk in your shoes, I will listen."

Giulio stands up, takes my hand and walks to his leather chair. With his free hand, he combs through his tousled hair. I rarely see him like this, so split between the two men he is. The invincible businessman everybody sees and the generous, tender man reserved for the ones closest to him.

My doubt washes away. I don't regret a single thing when I straddle him and he simply holds me. I make sure not to put too much pressure against him but Giulio creates it anyway, ignoring his hurt. Separated by fabric, his hands draw circles my lower back, inches from the zipper of my black square neck jumpsuit with ruched long sleeves.

I melt as he nuzzles into my neck and presses a long, sultry kiss against the base. *I melt.*

"I know you will always be here to listen." His stubble grazes against my delicate skin as he pushes back my straightened hair and peppers kisses up my neck. My body throbs deeply for him, that it plunges me into ecstasy. *I want him.* "You've always helped me, Lencia."

"I'm sorry you had to go through it alone."

"Don't be. I wasn't alone. I had you in my heart."

The kisses stop and we stay like this, desperately holding onto each other. I never want to move. I think he needs this embrace as much as I do. Giulio always presents himself as this fierce, powerful man, but I relish the times he lets his guard down.

Sometimes it's salvation.

Giulio feels so damn familiar because he *is* familiar. I'm enticed by the smell of fresh, masculine Versace cologne and *him.*

The way he was kissing my neck, the softness in his touch, the look in his eyes prompting the electricity sparking through me... it's all *him*.

"Do you think I could have killed Bryce that night?"

I cup his jaw and the Italian man who stares back at me is all I know. "No, of course not."

"He hurt you."

"Yes, but not to that extent. You know I've always believed in justice for any sort of vendetta. Letting justice play its part is exacting the best revenge."

Giulio swallows loudly. "I know."

I will never get sick of the forehead kisses he gives. Of all the tenderness and affection it projects. Even in this uncharted territory, they bring me back to life. *Back to him.*

"But I think I could have. If he went any further, I think I would have."

Oh.

I rise up from his lap and glance out the window behind him. *Is Giulio really capable of killing somebody?* No. He wouldn't ever do that. He wouldn't cause further suffering for Oscar and Slonne. Yes, I admit that maybe when it comes down to protecting family maybe he...*no.* There is always a line to cross. The line of ending somebody's life is an irreversible move he wouldn't commit.

To me, justice always overrides death. When Addilyn's abductor or abductors are caught, I still wish them justice. I do not wish them death because that is the easy way out.

"I'm sorry." Giulio stands abruptly and lets out a frustrated sigh when he reaches the floor-to-ceiling windows by the sage bench. "Fuck, what type of man am I? When I say things like that, how can I possibly be proud of myself? I'm just a sorry excuse of a role model."

No, honey. You're not.

I edge towards Giulio in time for him to slide his hands into his pockets with a locked jaw. There is something on his mind. I just feel it. Looking out onto Seattle, cars pass down below us.

In the distance, trees dance with the wind and the city buildings create a mesmerizing display.

I don't want him hurting and it destroys me that he's feeling this way. When Giulio's head lowers and I touch his back, I see his fear. I see a strong man break in front of me. The one that has attempted to hold it together all these months. For the first time since Addilyn's disappearance, I'm a part of his vulnerability in the space we share.

My fingertips act on his tensed muscles, trailing against the soft fabric of his sweater. I step in front of him and when his glassy eyes move to me, I can't see past the aversion.

"Everything that happened with Bryce and whatever resulted in those bruises is not your fault."

"It is."

I shake my head. "You are a good man, Giulio. You protect our family and you protect us well. Because that is what we are, *family*. If one of us falls, we all fall together and then we find the strength to rise again. We've all taken a tumble with Addilyn. We're still on the ground, so let's not cause more agony to ourselves before we get back up."

A sad smile crosses him. "We haven't called ourselves that in a while."

"A family?"

"A family."

Even with my heels, I have to rise on my tippy toes to reach his height. My lips meet his cheek and I kiss his soft skin. "We will always be a family." I come down and our smiles extend into a sense of *home*. "That will never change."

"Never." Despite his battered skin, Giulio's arms tighten around my smaller frame and he buries his head in my neck. "Does that mean that if I were to ask you to go out with me on Friday night, which I am, you would say yes?"

My heart beats like a drum.

Holy hell!

"Yes! Of course I will, Giulio."

I cannot be any happier. His touch chains me to a feeling of warm comfort. It's a place where nobody can break us. A part of me wonders how long we can stay like this, but I listen to my heart instead. I stay in the moment.

It takes a moment to realize the tears trailing down my neck are not mine but his. Giulio's body shakes and his chest vibrates against mine. He's holding onto me for dear life, as if he's afraid of something that's lurking inside him. I find myself clutching onto his sweater in need of giving this much to him.

My fingers weave through his hair and I whisper comforting words that eventually ease him. Giulio has always been here for me in my darkest moments. He's been my shining white knight. Even when all we wanted to do was turn away, he has always been there. *Here.*

I want him to know that I will always be here for him too.

I will always be the mother of his three beautiful children.

I will always care for him.

"This feels like the calm before the storm."

"They say no storm lasts forever." I push down the knot in my throat. "But I fear it too."

"Then if no storm lasts forever…the sun will soon come up again and kiss our skin. We'll see the other side of this. Let's not fear anything anymore." Giulio pulls back and looks at me with a newfound faith. *Hope.* Our fused tears are a delicate rendition of us. "As long as I'm here, never be scared. I've got you all. I *promise.* I've got you, Lencia."

I smile softly. "And I've got you too."

I never want to let go of Giulio Giannotti.

Never.

Dear God, please don't take him away from me.

CHAPTER FOURTEEN

AS MUCH AS I'VE BEEN ATTEMPTING TO LIVE IN THE PRESENT, SOME days it's hard not to swivel into the past when your daughter's life is in danger. *But I'm learning.* Learning to smile and enjoy my first night out in months. I agreed to go out with Kayla tonight because I've missed the old times when we used to hang out and simply *live*.

My parents are okay.

The twins are okay.

Giulio is okay.

After my moment of tenderness with Giulio this afternoon, I passed by Marcus in the lobby. I don't know if he caught onto my hesitation but until I learn the full story, I can't accept what he did leaving Giulio all battered and bruised.

Ever since therapy, the dynamic with Giulio has been smooth sailing. Whether it's a saving grace or the calm before the storm, I'm beginning to appreciate and accept it either way.

Helena joins Kayla and me and brings along her kids. It's somewhat of a family affair with me bringing the twins too. Oscar has questioned everything on the menu twice, while Slonne has submersed herself in watching Frozen with Daisy on my phone.

We have spent the last couple of hours at Zeluci, a chic Italian restaurant near work. It's filled with chattering diners, clinking metals, and bolts of laughter. Exposed charcoal bricks cover each wall and dark décor piping adds to the industrial feel. Helena opted for a table at the front of the restaurant, where the aroma of the immaculate rustic food doesn't reach us. *She's just gotten a fresh blowout after all and doesn't want her hair to smell.*

Comfort greets me in Kayla's company. It's just like old times.

Frequently I find myself looking over at my twins, niece, and nephew and then back at the women. Ever since Addilyn was stolen while I was in the house, public places have caused great pandemonium inside me. I'm constantly preoccupied that in the blink of an eye one of them could be taken too. I know I need to stop thinking like this, but the letter threatening that Oscar and Slonne were next doesn't help.

There's this thing about living in strife. The longer I adapt to that twisted feeling inside me, the longer my demons blindfold me in a game of chance. It's a wicked thing.

"Valencia?"

Both Helena and Kayla are staring at me. My sister is to my left and sits beside Daisy and Slonne, while Weston and Oscar are on the adjacent sides. Weston's head is down alternating between his sugar free dessert and homework, while my son observes his cousin's schoolwork. Kayla, who sets down her coffee with a smile, is directly across from me. The head of the table to my right is vacant.

I blink uncontrollably to steady myself. "Yes?"

"How are things with Giulio?" Kayla asks. "Did couple's therapy help in any way?"

"It did! We're getting closer and this afternoon he asked me out on a date on Friday night."

Her jaw drops. "Oh my god! Yes!"

Helena playfully pokes my side. "Yes, girl! And you're only telling us now?!"

I grin at their enthusiasm. "It only happened today! We've had a few moments over the past week and the arguments are simmering down. My therapist shined some light upon us and suggested a new strategy. I think...I *hope* it's a good thing for us."

"Oh my god!" Kayla adds, "I really do hope it works out well."

"Me too. We need to be united against all the chaos."

"Does his opinion on Addilyn's case still stand?"

I nod. "Both of us are still adamant in our views. Working a way around them will be difficult, so I don't want to get too ahead of myself before the night actually happens."

"Girl, I'll take care of the kiddies." Helena winks smugly. "You two need the break!"

"Thank you, that means a lot."

"Anytime. I'm so happy for you both!"

"So am I!" Kayla grins and we raise our beverages to cheers together. "To hopeful beginnings!"

The night goes well. It's fresh air from the past few months. I finally feel parts of the real me returning, the one before all the stress got in the way, and it feels so good. But just like sometimes in life, it comes to a premature end the moment Kayla's eyes widen. "Oh my god."

"What is it?"

"Uh, Marcus and Bryce just walked in!"

What?

She's right. A beaming Marcus strolls through the restaurant doors with Bryce by his side. This is the first time I've seen him since our drunken incident exactly a week ago and I don't know how to feel about it. Giulio told me that he wanted to apologize but I thought he meant in the office, not in the middle of this dinner! Bryce McCarson being *right here* is an uncanny coincidence.

"That's Bryce?" Helena grits, grinding her teeth together.

"That's him."

"What an asshole!" Helena proceeds to slide down in her seat, smiling sinfully. "What? It's not like we want them to see us."

I groan. "They'll still see us. We need menus, you know like in those detective shows."

"They'll see the kids and then they'll see us maniacs," Kayla admits.

"Don't look at him! Eyes are like freaking magnets."

"Mommy, why are you all underneath the table?"

"Because I lost my purse, Daisy."

"But it's here on the table."

"Uh…" Helena stumbles for words. "I meant Auntie Lencia's purse."

"It's on the table too!"

It's absolutely laughable. Three grown ass women halfway down their seats in a game of avoidance. "I can't do it. My back kills me like this." I suppress a chuckle and slide back up in my seat before tucking a tress behind my ear.

Daisy points at my bag. "See. It's right there!"

"*Oh*, yes. Thank you, honey."

She shakes her head and turns back to the movie. "Silly, Auntie."

"Kayla? Valencia?…Helena is that you?" *So much for attempting to save our asses!* Marcus is who I see first. His eyes dart between us with a prompt smile on his lips. "Hey, mind if we join you?"

Kayla shrugs with a sigh. "Not at all."

My sister throws her a look, but what was she alternatively going to say? *No, you can't sit with us.* We aren't in Mean Girls… *well, maybe in some profited spinoff of Mean World.* After all, even though they've both witnessed Marcus and Giulio's tension either at work or during family occasions, they don't know any-thing about the younger Giannotti's attack on Giulio.

Marcus waves at Kayla, greets the kids and me with a side hug, and then flashes a smile over at my sister. Helena looks the other way as he pulls up a chair and takes a seat.

Then, here comes Bryce *cocky cockney* McCarson in the flesh. *There's something wrong about the sentence.* I don't even have the decency to backtrack. *Hell no,* not when Bryce rounds the table and takes the seat right beside me at the head of the table.

He wears an American Eagle black tee and dark washed jeans. That familiar bergamot scent with a hint of spice gets me for a moment.

Bryce gives me his undivided attention. "Long time no see, aye?"

"I really would prefer if we don't go there."

"Okay. We won't go there." He swallows and motions beyond me. "Are they ya kids?"

"Yes, that's Oscar and that's Slonne with the magenta coat."

"They look like you...and Giulio...*Oh,* shit! They're twins?"

"Uh, yes..." I find it only fitting with Helena's gaping stare on him to defuse the animosity. "And this is my sister, Helena. Helena this is Bryce McCarson, an interior designer at the firm."

"A pleasure to meet ya, Hele—"

"Oh, cut the crap you jerk!" I tug at Helena's side praying for her not to go any further. Not here in front of everyone. I don't want to cause a scene but she does, leaving me to hopelessly glance at Kayla. "You fool around with my sister and then have the audacity to sit by her and act as if nothing happened? As if kissing her neck when she tells you to *stop* is nothing? Save yourself the time and leave...don't stare at me like that...boy, I said LEAVE!"

"Really?"

"Yes, *really.*"

"Where do you *suggest* I go?"

"I *suggest* you go to anywhere on the East Coast; there's a sale going on at the moment." Helena motions towards the door.

A travel agent sugar-freak telling *Bryce McCarson* where to go. "Boy, I said leave. Move, hop, jump, sprint, fly…do whatever it is you do but get the hell away from my sister before I send you on a one-way plane to Timbuktu!"

Those distant green eyes don't leave her for a moment, but when they do and they land on me, I look away for my own sanity.

"Okay, Elaine." He scoffs, pushing out his chair. "I wasn't here to talk to you anyway."

"My name is Helena and good riddance!"

As Bryce stomps towards the exit, Marcus groans. There's fury written on his face, one I failed to see when they initially stepped in. "Why couldn't you just let it go?"

"Let it go? How can you seriously say that?" Helena hisses. "Did you not hear what he did to my sister?"

Marcus leaves the questions unanswered and bids us a quick goodbye.

Breathe.

"Hell yeah, ain't nobody speaks to my baby sister like that!"

"I appreciate it, but I could've handled it. I don't want this to lead to yet another thing Bryce gets hung up on about me. It's not the best look stepping forward whenever he does return to work."

"He deserved it! Anyway, I'm going to the bathroom."

Weston glances up from his homework the moment she leaves. "Who was that other guy?"

"Just a man who works with Kayla and I."

He nods and glances back down at his work. I frown but summon the courage to fake the optimism when his gaze returns to me. "Hey, can you help me with something art related? My teacher is challenging us with trivia, but I can't remember the last design principle of art."

"Of course, go on."

"Well, I have balance, contrast, emphasis, and repetition… what's missing?"

"That would be unity, buddy."

Unity.

Weston jots it down and smiles over. "The perks of knowing a pro art teacher."

Oscar glances over at me just as I turn to him. I wink, handing him a marshmallow that came with my hot chocolate. He nudges Weston's arm and I give my godson the other. It's quick and all accomplished behind Helena's back. *Aka the sugar freak!* They both grin and turn back to their papers, chewing away at the soft pink clouds.

Kayla and I distract ourselves by helping Weston out with his homework. It doesn't last long and I feel so bad for it, but I don't catch patches of what he's saying because all I can think about is Bryce and the way he made me feel *that* night. How violated I felt and what seeing him tonight makes me remember.

The tension within the room is so tense. I should have acted differently. I should have spoken to him and told him exactly how I'm feeling.

"Has Helena always been like this?" Kayla asks.

"Always. When I began dating Giulio she was adamant to know everything. She sat him down in a full on interrogation, and mind you, he's two years older than her. They've been so close ever since but you know her, needing to make sure he had the best intentions."

"Aw, I can absolutely see her doing that! I'm sorry, honey, but…" She nods towards the door and in comes take-two. "…They're here again."

Marcus is dragging Bryce by his tattooed bicep even though McCarson is a tall, broad guy who quite frankly could pick up my brother-in-law by his pinkie.

"We don't run away from our problems. We face them," Marcus grits and shoves McCarson in Helena's seat beside me. Slonne scoots away from him, closer to her cousin.

I don't blame you, girl.

"I'm not a dog," Bryce threatens and flips him off. His elbow brushes against mine in the process, prompting him to glance over at me. "Right?"

"Then stop acting like one," Marcus spits.

"I'm not acting like one!"

"You're right. You're not *acting* like one because you *are* one. Now shut up and do what you came to do. Speak to her!"

"Marcus, I can't exactly *shut up* and *speak* at the same time."

"For the love of god, someone remind me how to breathe."

"Absolutely, positively, one hundred percent no." Helena returns in a huff. Her jaw drops not only at Bryce's presence but at the fact that he has stolen her seat. "Are you serious? You're like a cockroach; you think you've killed it but then they spring back to life. Go! Vamoose!"

"I have to tell ya sister something."

"Go ahead. Anything you can tell her, you can tell me." Helena crosses her arms and raises a confident brow. "Come on. Show me what you've got, McCarson."

Bryce's nose flares and I jump in to defuse the growing flames. My smile is flat as I come in the middle of them with a solution. "It's okay, Helena. We'll talk alone outside. Just watch the kids for me."

McCarson and I make our way out.

The icy air blows through my curled hair and down the back of my leather jacket. The city streets are lively as always. Cars zoom by and a group of people walk past us, cheering and laughing.

Bryce doesn't seem to notice them.

He doesn't seem like the type of man that takes in the little things. *The details.* Instead, he pulls out a cigarette and lights it while his eyes remain on a woman in a belted trench coat. She stands at the edge of the sidewalk and glances side to side with a glowing phone in hand, evidently waiting on a ride home.

Bryce stares at the back of her head, and it takes everything in me not to speak up. It all seems to happen for me when a Porsche pulls up to the curb and all of a sudden she's beaming. The car reminds me of Giulio's, the only difference being this one's red.

A man steps out of the driver's seat and greets the woman

with a long passionate kiss. Bryce shakes his head and turns to me while taking a long drag of his cigarette. His cockney accent comes next. "The Porsche drivers always get the women, right?"

I don't respond.

"So ya sister's something else…isn't she?"

"She worries about me."

"Hmmm." Bryce pulls out a second cigarette and waves it around. "It's yours if ya want it."

"No, thank you."

"Of course." He mumbles under his breath. Taking another drag, the glint of the death stick illuminates his arcane eyes. "You're too good for it. A mother and all, aye?"

My rapidly beating heart comes second against his larger than life ego. I've had it with him and snatch the second cigarette, lighting it with the tip of his. Inhaling, I draw it to my trembling lips and take two long puffs.

It doesn't last long.

You went way too bold, Valencia.

I cough through the clouds, the nicotine essence enough to turn me off. "Satisfied?"

Bryce has no words. A part of me wants to say I'm proud of his shocked, parted lips. *I did that.* I guess he wasn't expecting that ballsy move out of me.

Sometimes going bold adds up!

The cigarette crushes underneath my pivoting ballerina flat and I shove my hands in my Levi's for warmth. "So, what is it that you wanted to tell me?"

Bryce rubs his short beard, erasing the disbelief. "I want to apologize about the other night. I went too far, right. You were drunk and vulnerable and I was feeling the same…Looking back I see I took advantage of that. I should have stopped when ya were telling me to."

I nod. "Is that all?"

"Yeah…"

"Okay. I'm going back in."

"Wait, I just worked up the courage to apologize to ya.

The least ya can do is…I don't know, give me some feedback or something."

"Bryce, you're trying to bullshit me."

"No." His accent softens and he shakes his head. The furrowing of his brows and forehead causes a creased line in the middle of his eyebrows. "That's not it at all. I want to apologize for all the pain I caused. You and Giulio are both suffering an incredible loss and I should have been more considerate."

"Okay, but what happens three days from now? Huh? What happens in two weeks when you pull the same act? How do I know that you're not going to try something like this again?"

"I'm very capable of treating a woman right. Don't get it twisted," Bryce grits, tossing the death stick away to enter my personal space. He lowers his head to meet mine and all of a sudden I'm staring into pained eyes. "Just because ya had a bad introduction with me doesn't mean I'm not worthy of some type of forgiveness or a small smile."

"Listen, I take full responsibly for the drinking aspect. I should have limited myself and I don't know why I didn't. But that night last week after Giulio took me to his house, it brought back a lot of heartache for me, the same heartache I'm attempting to suppress to help myself. I thought I could trust you. I wanted to help you with the designs so when you began… when you did *that*, it brought back the feelings I attempt to get rid of every day. The violation. The feeling of not owning my thoughts and feelings."

Bryce takes a step back before looking away.

He has nothing for me.

I can finally breathe without inhaling a gulp of his cologne. The truth was eating me alive and so it feels exhilarating to have finally opened up.

I take one last look at Bryce McCarson, at his dark brown hair and that golden complexion. He's only wearing jeans and a t-shirt and I question his warmth inside my head. That's the mother in me. *Put a jacket on, you'll get a cold.*

I reach for the door handle, only for the Englishman's voice to vibrate every single plunged piece of my soul I left behind here on this Seattle sidewalk.

"I grew up with only my mother. She raised me into the man I am today. She did the best she could as a single mother. Working three jobs and constantly long hours to help others, now she can't even help herself. I'm not proud of some of the things I do, but I always admit when I'm wrong and I just did that. I'm not *that* type of man and yes the alcohol fucked with me, but I still know what I did was wrong. I'm sorry. I really am sorry I did that to you. No woman deserves that and I feel terrible I hurt you. But don't ya act like you've never done something you've regretted doing in your life."

"I have."

"So let's hear it. Come on, we'll go for a short walk and maybe you'll start to realize that you and I are not that different."

It starts, the gripping at my chest that pleads to be freed from everything he is offering. *I have to trust him on this.* And so we stroll against the soft whistling of the wind.

I know Bryce is waiting on my response. "The last time I saw Addilyn. That's my regret. Giulio was in London for work and I had invited my parents, Helena, and Marcus over for dinner. I set Addilyn down in her bassinet and was in the living room when Addilyn began crying. At times, it settled down. The baby monitor wasn't on and so when she quieted down, I didn't check on her until after we walked outside to say goodbye to Helena. My parents, Marcus, and I...we couldn't believe it. She was gone. Cameras show somebody broke the window in the split moments we were outside and just as we came in a masked figure jumped the side fence with my daughter into a waiting car. We didn't hear anything. If I had checked on her earlier, I could have stopped the abduction. It kills me because I was right *there*. Addilyn would be with me right now. I regret not checking on her. It keeps me awake and haunts me in my dreams."

Bryce is silent for a moment. "I cannot imagine what you went through, or should I say are still going through. But I do know that you cannot pin the blame on yourself. What happened was a freak accident. Something unprecedented."

"And yet blame myself is all I do. It's my fault." My heart clenches and I deflate. "It *is* and that's what hurts the most. The outcome could have been so different…"

"You don't know how it would have gone, Valencia. Even if it didn't happen, even if ya prevented it, it doesn't mean that something else wouldn't have happened to Addilyn down the path. Perhaps it's fate, right? Perhaps it's what's in God's plans. Perhaps what happened protected her from something worse. At least this way you can still have hope, that's something, right? Sometimes, as I said, it's God's plan and ya just have to trust it'll all be okay."

Bryce's encouraging words are something I didn't expect. In the office, he's always sarcastic with snide remarks. Ever since last Tuesday night, I thought that was all this man could be. But right now, walking by him and listening to him, I notice there's truth to his words. Perhaps I've overlooked him. Perhaps he does deserve a second chance, just like my marriage.

"All my life I've had to trust that it'll all be alright," Bryce admits. "I get angry and snap when I shouldn't. My father abandoned me before I was even born. My mother came to the States and met this man. It was a holiday fling that resulted in me. When they found out, he bailed and my mother had to return back to London for work. That made me feel…I don't know. He didn't give two shits and I've never met or seen him. I've never wanted to."

"I'm so sorry to hear. Do you know where he is?"

"Don't apologize for a fucking selfish man. I know where he is now, but I'll never meet him. It works me up. It ruins me and so I coax myself to drink and smoke. To forget it all. That night with you I wanted to forget myself. I know it's not a good enough excuse for what I did, but it's all I have. I don't have a lot of people around me here. Marcus, my mother, and a few friends back home are really all I have who care about me, so having you that night meant something."

I find myself nodding at his words. I realize I didn't know a single thing about Bryce up until now. Nothing at all. No matter the situation, his father should have been there. "I'm sorry, I didn't know any of that."

Bryce chews on his lip and we make a left turn by the Seattle Waterfront Park on Pier 57 and cross the road into the park, walking by others who are out enjoying their Wednesday night. The glowing Seattle Great Wheel and moon etches an optical glow of silvery red across the waters. It's there where we stop by the walkway and I'm mesmerized by the night sky and how darkly it glows.

Bryce keeps his eyes on the water and rubs his hands together. "When I was younger, my mother often couldn't afford meals for the both of us. She didn't work the best jobs, but they were the only ones she could get. As I grew older and college was on the horizon she became desperate for money. I was working too but it wasn't enough. Without my notice she got involved in a scam and lured millions from people. It was more than we needed, but I don't think she could stop. Until one day…yeah… the world made it stop for her."

I feel for him. I really do.

I swallow hard, my hand finding its way to his shoulder to give it a slight squeeze. *He's freezing just as I expected.* "I'm so sorry to hear that, Bryce."

"No," he turns to me and his eyes wash over my face. "She didn't die. I worded it wrong."

My hand slips. "What happened then? Is your mother here?"

"No. She's back in London, but she can't work. She has a condition. A mental condition. It had her avoid jail, but she needs to pay back every single pound plus interest. So I had to move away from all the negative and find myself again. All my paychecks go directly to her. I need to help my mother now, just like she helped me even when she didn't even want me. I need to help her…I *do*…especially now that everybody is against her in our town."

"That's a very generous thing, to do Bryce."

"People wouldn't associate that word with me."

"Maybe they don't know this story."

"Ya think you're special, aye?" McCarson holds my gaze for a split moment and a ghost of a smirk works its way on his lips. The same one that has been absent all night, rendering him almost unrecognizable. There is barely any of the sarcasm that Bryce McCarson is known for. It's just his soft voice and growing honesty.

I like this side of him.

I take Bryce's smirk and carve out my own smile. "No. Not special."

"I was kidding. Don't knock yourself down, you're an incredible woman. You really are. A pure rare sight that can have angels sing down at you."

"Now you're exaggerating!"

Bryce's hand hesitantly reaches under my chin and raises it higher to meet his gaze. He's serious now. "No, I truly do mean it. All the single parents out there are incredible. Although you and Giulio may be working things out, I know from experience that you're both strong enough to carry the weight of a broken spirit. It's not easy and it doesn't get better. I'm an asshole, but I notice that much."

"I appreciate it."

I cast a glance to the water one last time and we pick up our pace back to Zeluci's.

"Were you born here, Valencia?"

"Yes. Born and raised. What part of England are you from?"

"Hoxton. It's by the East side. Are your parents both American?"

I shake my head and pull my long waves to one side. "My mother is, she's been a Seattleite from day one. My father's from Vienna, Austria. He has a twin brother there who he's currently visiting for a little while. My mother would have joined him, but their greeting card business demands one of them to stay here."

"That's cool. And Giulio? Well, I know his father's Italian because of the last name."

"Yeah, both of his parents are Italian. His father was from Sicily and his mother from Genova in the north. His parents both moved to New Jersey young and they met there. They returned to Italy for a few holidays with family. It was actually during one of those holidays in Genova where Giulio was born prematurely. They stayed there for a while before returning."

"So, he was born in Italy?"

"He sure was. Why did you move to Seattle?"

"Well, some of us are born in Seattle, others have this desire to escape it all and move here. I did what was best for me. I was a bartender back in London but had a degree in interior design. Seattle was my calling. Much more opportunities and all that. So I said fuck it, I'm thirty and never have been to America before, let's do it. I befriended Marcus at a bar one night and he helped me get my job. I actually bartend at that bar some nights a week for some extra cash. I can't lose my job at Notti Designs because of my mother, but I keep on fucking up."

"Giulio just looks for honesty and loyalty. Give him that and everything will be fine…I've never seen this side of you. I didn't know any of that before."

Bryce meets my gaze. "You've never asked."

Fair point.

"I'm sure your mother is grateful for what you are doing for her. At the end of the day, all we have is our family."

"Yeah, family and a couple of friends." He throws his head back in laugher with his hand on his chest when my brows raise dramatically. "Don't worry, I wasn't referring to you. Not just yet. Do you forgive me?"

For some reason it makes me smile. I nod as we reach the restaurant and stop by the door.

"No, not about that. I mean do you forgive me about what happened earlier last week?"

Some people deserve a second chance.

"I forgive you. I don't want any unneeded animosity between us at the company."

"Thank you." He sighs in relief and reaches for the door with a glint of happiness. "I'll never let you down again, Valencia. You have my word and I never back down on my word."

"Maybe this will be a good thing."

"Sure will be. Can I ask if we can…bring it in?"

I bite back a soft giggle as Bryce crushes me in a bear hug. This time as I wrap myself in that bergamot, I have no hesitation. There was something in his voice tonight that screamed truth and in his own words; *sometimes you just have to trust yourself.*

Unity.

It's all I want. For every single one of us to be united and thriving.

That includes my sweet Addilyn too.

When I dive under the sheets that night, Helena knocks on my bedroom door in tears. She doesn't need to say a word—*Ben*. I hold her tightly and comfort her like she always does for me. I don't want her to be alone with her own thoughts. Not tonight. To avoid spiraling out of control at this stage is vital.

I turn to my side and Helena spoons me from behind, slithering her arm around my waist. I squeeze her hands, knowing just how important she is to me. After this exhaustingly thrilling day, I need her with me too.

We hold onto each other just like when we were little.

I can feel the gaping hole in her heart. *She misses him.* Ben was an amazing man to her. A heroic firefighter. A proud father. For the past seven years, Helena has been unbelievably strong. I'm so damn proud of her. She's my saving grace. Even through hell, we always find a way to pull each other out and that's all I've wanted—*to get through it.*

"I'm so glad I have you, Helena."

"Likewise," she sighs and holds on tighter. My sweet Marc Jacobs perfume mixes with her rose scent. "Nothing will ever break us. No crime or man will ever come between us."

"I promise. We've gone through too much to allow that to happen."

"We've got to get out of this mess, Lencia."

She's the only one who calls me that besides Giulio.

"How?" I ask into the darkness.

"By keep on keeping on and putting ourselves first for once. We need to begin choosing our own lives."

When Helena's breaths soften and her hand falls limp, I know she's asleep. *And I know she's right.* Maybe it's Bryce's words about strength, or how I fathom my heart sinking if anything were to happen to Giulio, or the way life can flash before your eyes at the most unexpected moment…but I reach out to my bedside table and pick up my phone.

They say you never know what you have until it's gone, and the second Giulio and the fantasy of marriage were stripped from me, I *knew*. I learned of the suffering rage inside my chest personally customized for me. I know what Giulio means to me. What he's always meant to me. He means *home.*

Valencia: I want to make this right for us. I want it all for us. I appreciate you so much. I can't wait until Friday night and what it will bring. Goodnight, Giulio. xo

A silent sob devours me, but it's mended with a smile the second a reply appears.

Giulio: Lencia, I am going to regift you the entire world and this time we'll be stronger than ever. This time we'll make it right. We'll fix it all. I appreciate you too, so damn much. Friday seems like a dream. Miss you. *Sogni d'oro.* xx

That night I don't have any trouble falling asleep. I don't wake up at odd hours. I sleep right through, dreaming of our entire bloodline.

United.

Returned.

Unbreakable.

CHAPTER FIFTEEN

Giulio

ALL MY LIFE BEFORE MEETING VALENCIA, I NEVER EXPECTED TO FEEL A deep love like this. As she cradles Addilyn in her arms, a warmth spreads across my chest. The same warmth that appeared when I married the love of my life and when Oscar and Slonne were born.

Addilyn is ours.

Sinking onto the edge of the hospital bed, my slacks press against the crisp sheets. I kiss our newborn's forehead and then turn to my darling. I could not be any prouder to call Valencia my everything.

Kissing her slowly in the midst of tears, I thank God that she's safe. That they're both okay after the anxious emergency cesarean. I haven't stopped smiling since I heard Addilyn Giannotti's first cries. I cannot describe the love I have for Valencia. She's my best friend. The woman of my dreams. The one I know I can always trust and confide in.

Nothing will ever break us.

Nothing.

"I'm so proud of you." The words escape me in a whisper. "You did it, amore."

"Well, you made this possible too."

"And don't you ever forget it."

She reacts to my wink in cute laugher. I love how she shuts those immaculate hazel eyes mid laugh. How her dark hair, which is tied in two French braids, cascades to her ribcage. How her courage has me honored to be her husband.

"I never will."

"Good. I love you so much."

"I love you more."

"Impossible," I murmur softly. "You are my air."

Valencia's soft lips press against mine, increasing the beat of my chest. Here is everything I ever wanted. Everything I ever needed. Family.

We pull away grinning.

"Amore, do you want to go to Daddy? I think you want to go to Daddy!" Lencia gently hands Addilyn to me and I cradle her in the solace of my arms. I'm mesmerized by her. After five years, I'd forgotten how little they are. Her hand clenches against my pinky finger and she stares up at me, seemingly mesmerized by this big world around us.

"Hello, my angel."

Her big hazel eyes with specks of blue fill me with adoration. They're a mixture of both of us. She has her mother's cute little nose and full lips. Her hair, the cause of Lencia's heartburn, is dark and soft with the slightest waves. She's a happy, healthy baby. It's all we asked for.

I love Addilyn.

I love Slonne.

I love Oscar.

I love Lencia.

I love us. Unconditionally.

"My sister's going to tell the twins in the morning. They're going to be over the moon."

"I can't wait for them to meet."

"Me too. I can't believe she's ours."

"I know." My pointer caresses my daughter's button nose. I can't wipe away my smile and I don't want to. "She's our forever and nobody will ever be able to change that. Ever."

I spring out of my bed, clutching my heart. *Fuck.* The bruises. I can't catch a break. My sweaty palms rush through my hair, stabilizing myself from the memory of Addilyn. It's not even 5 A.M., but I can't lie here any longer. I opt to hit the home gym to ease my mind.

She's ours forever and nobody will ever be able to change that. Ever.

Oh, how I wish I could take that March night back. I should have never left for London. I should have stayed with my family. I should have been there and confronted that face of evil.

Regret laces my memories. The same one that has been there ever since Valencia and I took off our rings. That night shut off the light inside me and slaughtered me whole. This morning that light flickers at the thought of Addilyn and my date with Valencia tonight.

Addilyn.

That memory of the first time I held her in my arms brings back everything to me. *The feeling of her being ours.* For six months I have accepted she's dead, but that memory…

I miss her so much.

Have I been wrong? Has my lost faith in Addilyn been based upon a lie? I know why I believe it, but now…is it enough? *We need Addilyn in our lives.* Could it be true she's…still with us?

Valencia.

I need to make it right with her tonight. Last night her text was so unexpected. My heart is rejuvenated reading those words over again. Knowing she wants tonight to come as fast as I do, that she wants this too, is an incredible feeling. Tonight needs to go perfectly as it may be the only chance I have at winning Valencia back.

I want all of her.

The longing in her eyes whenever she looks my way. The stolen glances we share.

Her gorgeous smile. The way she comforts me.

The strength.

The vulnerability.

The forever and always.

Her.

I will take the good from the bad, just like I promised on our wedding day. *Valencia Giannotti, I vow to try harder and be the man you need. Because fuck, I need you.*

After my workout, I take my thoughts to the shower. It's there where the memories of Valencia deepen and manifest in forms I cannot comprehend. *It's her.* It's always been her and to-night I'm going to show her the exact reason why.

Steam fogs my vision and the water slides down my chiseled jaw to my body. It has me slick back my wet hair. I can feel my heart beating wildly for her. My hands tense against the wet tiles to the flashbacks of Lencia and I that cross my mind. They run chronologically through every stage of our life—all seven years.

Lencia is so fucking vivid and I wouldn't have it any other way. The way she overpowers my every thought. The way my breaths deepen every time she steps into Notti Designs. The way I always feel happily secure when I'm with her.

Today, Friday, the twins wake up to the delicious smell of blueberry pancakes. It's a rarity during the week with school, but today there's a reason to celebrate.

Oscar helps me make the last batch as Slonne steals my phone and puts on her playlist of favorite songs. We're all danc-ing to the hot mix just after 7 A.M. I lift my son off the counter and we all get *so* into the Latin beat that the pancakes almost burn. *Almost.* We continue laughing and dancing, and I send an impromptu video of us to Lencia.

Giulio: Getting our Friday off to a good start...Wish you were here!

She replies with a selfie of her in Helena's kitchen with her sister, Daisy, and Weston in the background. She's a gorgeous natural beauty with a top bun and grins while pointing to a pan on the stove with batter. *She's making pancake too!*

Valencia: Ooo, do I smell competition? Great minds think alike. Our Shakira tunes are better than yours!

Giulio: In your dreams! See you at the office—the kids say hi! x

Valencia: Kiss them for me! See you then! x

⁂

Seconds after the twins walk into school, I bump into Helena saying goodbye to Daisy in the parking lot.

"Hey, stranger!"

My sister-in-law whips around and begins laughing at the grin on my face. "Oh my god, it's you! This is so crazy. It's never happened before!"

"It's definitely one for the books." I crouch down and Daisy runs into my arms. Spinning her around in circles with me, her giggles provoke a small chuckle of my own. "Morning, Diasy! I heard you made some killer pancakes this morning. Slonne, Oscar, and I made some too."

Daisy smiles. "Yes, Aunt Val showed us! But ours were SO much better!"

My next question is still directed at my goddaughter, but my gaze averts to Helena. "Really, angel? That's impossible without the SUGAR!"

Helena dramatically sighs. "Look, I put in a little cinnamon. I'm allowing that at least!"

"This fad is going to decline in no time. When it does, I'm going to smother you with homemade cannoli and you're going to love every second of it, you watch." I wink, loving the amusement on her face whenever I tease her on the subject.

"Ahhh...don't talk about cannoli! I'm feeling weak and in need of sugar today!"

"Well, well, well. Is that so?"

"Yay! Cannoli!" Daisy's cheers, her mouth meeting my ear as she asks in a soft whisper. "Can you make me some this weekend and not tell my mom? Pleeeeeease, Zio Giulio!"

"Sounds like a plan!" I press a kiss on her cheek before setting her down on her feet as she grins in victory. "Have a good day at school, darling!"

"I will! Bye, Zio Giulio! Bye, Mommy!" And with one final hug from her mother, she skips off into the school.

I grin over at Helena whose eyes don't sway from me. "I think I deserve a 'hell yes' for converting Daisy to my side of that sugar debate in less than sixty seconds."

She laughs, crossing her arms over her chest. Her hair sways in the cool morning breezy wind and I can't help but notice the brighter than usual nice, healthy glow on her. "Look at you, Giulio. You settled down on a date with my sister and now you've become the happiest man alive."

"That's how Lencia makes me feel."

My sister-in-law nods. "I can happily report she was the same this morning! I'm so happy for both of you! The moment I saw her this morning, it was like she had a sex glow without the sex."

"I'm happy too, Helena...Speaking of sex, am I wrong or do you have that glow too?"

Helena's cheeks blush at my words and she concentrates on a spot beside us, that growing beam impossible to ignore. "What? Me? No, I don't have a glow..."

My jaw drops when she can't quite meet my gaze and falls silent. *That only means one thing.* "Oh my god, you do! Whose ass do I have to bust?"

"Ugh, why can't I ever keep a secret from you? I swear you notice everything, dude! Not even Lencia picked it up yet. Why are you acting like we're on the Real Housewives?"

"Not Real Housewives; we've gone full on terminator because I want to make sure whoever the guy is, has the best of intentions. Now tell Zio Giulio, who do I have to pull aside today and warn that they'll be answering to me if they hurt you in even the slightest?"

"Nobody! Goodbyeeee, I have to go to work!" Helena laughs and pulls me in a goodbye hug. "And for the record…it's nobody, really. So please don't tell Lencia anything about it. It's honestly nothing at all. Thanks anyway, Al Capone."

"Anytime, Bonnie."

On the way to my car, I notice Zoe walking towards the gates with Samuel. She takes one glance my way, frowns, and lowers her eyes to the pavement…. *Well, that was strange.*

"Giulio!"

Every bone in my body freezes to a halt…*that voice…I know it. No, it couldn't be…*Glancing over my shoulder, nobody is there but then for a second time I hear that wicked, husky shout.

"Giulio! Over here!"

I glance back over the roof of my car, my eyes narrowing down in confusion. *Mind games.* This can't be real. I can't be hearing my father's voice. He's dead. I was right there when it happened…*it's all in my head.*

"Giulio, there you are!"

The hell!

My heart picks up speed as I turn to my side, witnessing a man walking with a little boy. *Oh.* As they pass me, the father explains something to the son…whose name is Giulio…my head needs a minute to take that in. God Damn, he sounded so much like my father.

For a moment I thought it was him, despite all the odds.

An unwanted memory washes over me in the driver's seat—*that dreaded Thanksgiving night.* The frown grows. It needs to be flipped upside down by the time I reach the office, this is supposed to be a happy day, yet I give myself the time to bottle away every last thought I have of my Pietro Giannotti.

"*Pour yourself another glass,*" *my father hisses, the wine bottle slamming against the oak dining table in a vibrating thud and missing my plate by inches.*

I speak the first words since entering this house two hours ago. "No, I'm okay."

"Pour it."

"My glass is still full."

My father takes one good look at me and chuckles coldly. Cocking his head, his gaze averts to Marcus on the other side of the table. "Can you believe this bastard of your brother? He thinks that I..." he scoffs and turns to me with a screwed up face of vengeance. "You think I put something in the wine? Huh? You think I'm fucking with you, is that it?"

I stay silent and turn my gaze back to the television. They're doing a Thanksgiving special on some channel I don't care about. I shouldn't have come. I don't know why I thought for the slightest second it was a good idea to travel back to New Jersey this Thanksgiving with hope that my father has changed. It's only us three men as Clare is at the hospital working. It's the first time I've seen my father in three years and the bitter man hasn't changed a bit.

"HEY! I'm talking to you!"

"I never insinuated you put anything in it; I just don't want another drink."

"You don't want another drink?"

"No."

At the head of the table, Pietro Giannotti scoffs and grips the neck of the bottle. "Sure you don't want it in your mouth? Cause it'll be smashed on the side of your head in a minute. POUR IT!"

Clenching my jaw, I down the wine in my glass, snatch the bottle, and pour myself another one. I down the second one in a flash and turn to Pietro with a pointed expression. "Happy?"

"You think you're a big shot now, huh? You think you can move to Seattle and study to be a worthless architect? You won't ever fucking make it, Giulio. Always dreaming too hard just like that darn mother of yours used to. CEO of my ass. You worthless weak shit."

I wish I could say he's even the slightest bit drunk. Nope. This is how it is.

Adjacent to me, twelve-year-old Marcus smirks with challenge. "You don't have what it takes."

"Exactly. At least you understand, Marcus." My father pours himself the last of what's in the bottle. "The most Giulio is set out to do is walk out of this front door alive."

"That's it, I've had enough. I didn't come all the way here just to hear you go on and on again. I was hoping for some type of apology, but I should have known you haven't changed." The wooden chair squeaks as I push back, scratching a stream of white lines onto the chestnut floorboards. I pat down the lapels of my blazer and take my leave for the front door. "A Dio."

I don't make it three steps before I'm slammed against the wall.

My father's musky scent traps me between the reality I'm facing and my past. I'm twenty-one, but the days after my mother's death are vivid reminders of the day Pietro Giannotti stopped being my father.

"You wanted an apology?" He grips my blazer, his curled fists inches from my face. "Weak boy, I'm not sorry for a damn thing I've done to you or your mother. What you gonna do about it, huh?"

I'm not that kid anymore. I don't submit to his torment, which is why I push myself away from the wall, grip his collar, and violently slam him against the opposite side of the hallway. My father's head hits a picture frame and it slides down the dark navy walls from the force until I hear the crunch of glass beneath my feet.

"What fucking photo was that?" My father growls, jerking his body towards mine but I have the upper hand and slam him back again.

"Don't know." I bite back in fury. "Perhaps one of you and your beloved Clare. Wouldn't be one of Mom, would it now? I will never forgive you for what you did behind her back and mine. You're a selfish freak."

"Oh, so I'm a selfish freak now?"

"Yes, and that's sugar coating it. You were with another woman while my mother was dying. I was a fool for believing you had changed. Spending this Thanksgiving with you is a joke to humanity. You, Pietro Giannotti, are a joke to humanity."

His jaw tenses, that five o'clock shadow reminding me very much of my own. I'm grateful that's where it stops and I more resemble my mother. I wouldn't know how I would be able to look in a mirror every day and see him in me.

"You think Clare's the only one?"

My jaw ticks and I fist his collar tighter, constricting his breaths as I hiss, "she better be."

My father laughs in my face like this is some type of joke; the cackle shoots straight to my heart. "Oh weak boy, when are you going to learn that no man ever stops at one? There's always more. Always. Before Clare… and even now. At least Clare gets it."

"You should be ashamed of yourself."

"Or maybe you should be for being the worthless piece in our lives…" Marcus' words have me look to my left. He's standing by the end of the hallway, simply watching.

"You stay out of it."

"Can't. I fit the family perfectly. You're the one that doesn't…remember?"

All the bottled up rage spirals inside me. I decide this is the last time they get to treat me like this—the very last time. I let go of my father's shirt and pivot to my half-brother. Just over half my age and he thinks he can ruin me with his words alone. He won't ever break me.

I'm striding towards Marcus when I hear it. The cocking of something that has me halting. A sinister smirk rises on my half-brother's lips as the tip of cold metal presses against the nape of my neck.

Oh, Dio.

My father digs the gun so deep I'm convinced the finger brushing against the trigger isn't having second thoughts. "Step one foot closer to Marcus and I will end you. Just like I wanted to since you were nine. I swear on your mother I will end you if you hurt my son."

The raging heat circling my neck is enough to haunt me. I raise my hands in surrender because it's the only way to communicate I'm listening without the wave of emotion getting to me.

Pietro Giannotti is forgetting everything. He's forgetting that I'm his son too. That I was his first. That he used to tuck me into bed and tell me he'd protect me from the world he's now going to end for me. That I used to look up at him and see my idol.

He's forgetting it…because he never loved me.

Mom…wherever you may be up above watching over, please save me from him tonight.

The memory fades the second I step inside the office to a grinning Valencia. One moment wrapped in her arms is enough to take away the thoughts of my father and replace them with my adoration for her.

The feeling is reaffirmed during the day and right now when I press her doorbell. I've been waiting for 6:30 P.M. all day and now that it's finally here, nerves begin to rise like it's out first date. Well, this *is* our first date night in over six months. This is us starting over.

A slow, sexy smile grows at the sight of Lencia.

The bouquet of roses almost slips from my grip. Inside I'm celebrating like Italy won the World Cup all over again. She looks fucking beautiful as always. I adore everything about her inside and out, but I'm mentally lying on the ground in a pool of green, white, and red streamers because she hasn't backed down.

She wants this with me.

Valencia has a dark red number on. I remember the dress *very well.* It's my favorite on her and she knows exactly why. We bought it on our honeymoon in Fiji where we must have both forgotten we live in one of the cloudiest states in the USA.

We were a little distracted to say the least.

Now the love of my life stands in front of me. The v-neck long sleeved silk dress is tight against her breasts and waist, and loosens a fraction by her hips and legs. The hem cuts above her knees and she's wearing tortoiseshell pointed heels, compliment-ing her glowing skin.

Her chestnut brown hair is curled to one side, exposing her bare neck. It puts me in a sensual trance I can't let go of. Not with the red lipstick across those perfect plump lips. This is Valencia starting anew and I fucking love it. I've been dying to kiss her, es-pecially when she bites her lip so enticingly like she is now. I need to wait until the perfect moment.

"You look impeccable, Lencia."

"Thank you," she grins. "So do you."

"Let's get the night started."

Valencia Giannotti stole my heart the first day I met her. She's continued to steal my heart every single day in these past seven years and she continues to do so now. I can't help the way I feel for her. I want to be there with her through it all; the adoration, the depression, the *hope*.

This is why I cannot let her go. *And I won't.*

I survived my horrid past and was rewarded with pure gold.

She owns my heart, mind, body, and soul. She never stopped owning them. Her initials are deeply etched into me. So deep that I cannot be myself without her or our children. She's my air. The heartbeat in my chest. The very thing keeping me afloat.

My savior.

My one and only.

Valencia Giannotti is my entire life.

CHAPTER SIXTEEN

Valencia

OUR DATE HAS ONLY STARTED AND ALREADY THE ENERGY BETWEEN us is like no other. Giulio wanted to keep the plans for our date a surprise. It triggered my curiosity and thrilled me all at the same time. When we arrive at the dance studio for a private lesson, I am in awe. This is what my therapist, Dr. Eross, suggested.

I lift my head to Giulio's allusive gaze and feel warm all over from his sexy smolder. He looks sensational in that black dress shirt and those dark slacks. A couple of buttons are undone, exposing his smooth, olive skin.

Rodrigo, our dance instructor circles us again. "The Rumba with Cuban Rocks is all about holding the gaze. It's sexy.

Ruthless. Unforgiving. Just like love. The dance is about falling down, but always getting back up. Closeness seems to be an issue with you, may I ask why?"

"We've been living separately," I say. "Previously we only saw each other to swap custody of the kids. We work together now and are attempting to give our marriage a second chance."

"Okay. Giulio, what is the sexiest thing about her?"

"Her mind."

"Modest man." Rodrigo chuckles and slaps his shoulder. "Come on, I mean on her body. What did you love the most about her?"

"Her smile."

"And you?"

"His eyes."

"Alright, you both need to keep your focus on those two aspects. I want to try something before we implement the dance steps. Now, fall into each other."

Giulio and I press in chest to chest and I worry about his bruises. He doesn't seem to mind, and his touch seeps through my dress, awakening new sensations.

His eyes flicker to my lips and my heartbeat grows rapid. Desire for him flourishes, especially when the action surges him closer and his eyes turn hooded. I feel him all over, just like the other night. I see Addilyn within him and it only makes me want to clutch him tighter.

He's half of her.

"Perfect. Clasp your hands and have them up, up...no, not quite like that. The sexual tension is there. I can feel it. Transfer it into the way you hold each other."

I take in a deep breath, feeling his heart against mine.

I can do this.

Giulio's head lowers, unconsciously teasing me with his masculine scent. It brings me back to life—a constant reminder of who he is and what he means to me.

The way we're looking at each other is so pure...so blinding.

Rodrigo's voice blurs in the background as Giulio's fingers

leave mine and raise to trace the outline of my lips. His thumb rests at the center of them and I involuntarily kiss it. My nipples pebble, poking against my dress at the mere sight of the erotic red painted on his fingertip.

We step out of our trance and the instructor teaches us the basic steps of the Rumba. It takes a few tries for me to execute the slow backward/forward step and two quick side steps.

Giulio has always been a good dancer.

Our locked gazes barely drop and when they do, it's to Rodrigo who stands by the dancer studio's exposed brick wall with an encouraging smile. He observes us from a distance, opting to strengthen our pace to the rhythm of the percussive music.

It was only weeks ago when Giulio and I struggled with words and a lost connection. We could barely speak to each other without negative tension. Now, we blossom in overflowing chemistry. Our silence is powered by our desire. I want to be a better woman for myself—for him—for my children. I need to find my confidence and be comfortable in trusting myself again. It's why I chose to be bold tonight with my dress and push the limits with the lipstick.

An alluring fire rumbles across the springwood dance floor. It intensifies at every slow, sultry, sexy rhythm. Giulio and I begin to transform into the husband and wife we once were.

Our marriage is very much like this dance. It cannot be executed well as a solo. Both of us have to partake, locked in an enraptured hold and compromise. We have to express emotion through it, go in time with the music, and unlock a part of ourselves that we only have reserved for our love.

We seem to do all of it perfectly.

We execute every spin, sway, and pointed step. All except for one. The smooth, sedate Cuban Rocks. The fact that there is a gap between our bodies should be easier, instead it proves to render us incapable of us swaying our hips while looking each other in the eye.

To specifically work through both the syncopated and basic Cuban Rocks, Rodrigo has me turn to face the wide wall mirror.

Giulio is behind me, so close that we're pinned together and his hands grip my hips, aligning them with his. We move to a sensual rhythm, one that has Giulio's lips brushing against my neck.

The warmth between my thighs intensifies and I can't help but smile at how we're carrying through. When I meet his gaze in the mirror, I note his hardness pressing against me and my new-found boldness has me pushing myself back to feel him deeper.

"Baby." He chuckles at my playful taunting, rushing his hands to my thighs. "That's a very dangerous move you're making…"

I grin. "For me or for you?"

"For *us*."

"That's it." Rodrigo urges us on. "You've got it. Build that confidence. Yes. Exactly like that."

Giulio's hot breath tickling my neck has me resting my right hand by the back of his, drawing him closer. We've strayed from the Rumba, but that doesn't stop us. His free hand takes over for me, fanning out across the length of my body in passionate urgency. We're scorching fire as our bodies harmonize together.

Holy hell…

A moan escapes me and I'm not even ashamed. Not when the warm lights dim and Giulio cups my left breast with desire surging in his light eyes. The same desire that has me throbbing. We fuel each other's heavy breaths, taking us to a whole new level of connection.

"You've got this so well," Giulio whispers in my ear.

"You think?"

"Mmhmm. Down pat."

"Sexiness is all through the eyes. Confidence is sexy. I see it within you both." Our instructor reminds us. "I want you to level your gaze higher in the mirror. Remember why you first fell in love, not why you fell apart."

Desire burns through my eyes, especially when Giulio's gaze drop to our movements and a soft curse word falls from his lips. I bite my lip and snicker at the following louder curses.

Rodrigo chuckles. "Alright you lovebirds, let's get back to the Rumba. You're both experts at executing the Cuban Rocks now. Valencia, if you could turn around now and from there, we can create that gaping. Let's do this!"

I submit and Giulio holds my hips securely. I can't stop smiling. This is such a passionate dance and exactly what we needed. *Giulio chose it right.*

"Now, incorporate those sleek sways in the dance…slower, one, and a two…three, four…yes, perfect. One and a two…three, four…, one. Look at that. You're naturals now!"

Giulio's hips follow mine and our motions falling into a slow, sleek flow. My eyes stay burning into his and our hands lead the dance. The entire hour lesson is a complete dream and when Rodrigo's phone rings and he excuses himself to answer it out of sight, the dancing fades out.

Giulio and I are alone and I want him *so* badly. We move closer until our noses brush and my heartbeat thuds to the delicacy of our citric and sweet scents merging into one.

"Lencia." His voice is low and for my ears only. "I want to devour you."

"Mmhmm, I'd like that."

"Darling…you are *killing* me."

That makes me smirk. "What? Am I *stiff* competition, Mr. Giannotti?"

"Definitely *hard*, baby. Very *hard*." Giulio hums, reeling our sexes closer. "But if we're talking competition, it depends on which game we're playing, Mrs. Giannotti."

"I'm up for anything."

"Ditto. I'm up for anything tonight with you."

"Just tonight?'

"No. Not just for tonight, for every single day for the rest of our lives."

Time stops. His naked eyes give me everything I need.

"I never want to let you go, Giulio."

Just then Rodrigo steps back inside the room and cuts the music. "Sorry about that. Alright, lovers, that's the end of the lesson! Sensational job. You should both be very proud."

"Thank you, Rodrigo. Thank you more than you will ever

know." And then Giulio takes my hand and leads me out of the studio in a sprint. Halfway down the first set of stairs, he scoops me into his arms bridal style and rushes us down the remaining three flights so fast I cling onto him tightly, afraid we'll tumble down.

"Oh my god! Why have you turned into Speedy Gonzales?" I ask through my laugher.

Giulio beams and just like that the sexual tension between us escalates even more than it already was. "Because I don't want to waste another second. Not tonight. Not ever, baby."

We make it outside and he sets me down by his car. I'm hot all over, still catching my breath. Giulio is all I see. All I need.

"What are you thinking about?"

I bite my lip. "You."

"Oh, really now?"

"Mmhmm."

"Tell me about it."

"Make me."

Giulio provides the solution we both desperately crave. One sharp stride and everything becomes worth it when he crashes his lips onto mine. Our kiss is hot and so passionately driven that I feel for his collar and draw him even closer, moaning at the pleasure.

Yes. Yes. Yes.

In one solid motion, he lifts me and my legs automatically wrap around his waist. Giulio's sensual touch has me kissing him back harder. He leaves me so breathless—and healed. I graze my fingers over his stubbled jaw and appreciate the way he breaks our kiss with a smile, only to say. "You're my air, Lencia."

My heart clenches at the phrase he always used to say.

This is more than just a first kiss in six months between a separated husband and wife; this is an emotional battle and physical torture.

A slow, sensual kiss follows. Giulio's warm lips awaken every nerve ending within me as he leans me against his car and we savor the way our tongues dance their own style of Rumba.

I forget everything we're battling.

I forget our damned separation.

I forget our split views.

Both the arguments and the investigation. I forget it all and for the first time in my life, I turn selfish. I do this very thing for *myself*. I'm uplifting happiness *for me*.

It feels so right with Giulio.

So right.

Like there's no better way.

Resting our foreheads together, we pull away panting heavily. *My god.*

"I promise to try, and although I know this won't be perfect at the beginning, it will be beautiful in its own way."

"Lencia, I will make up for all the months I was supposed to be kissing you. All the months I was supposed to be right there beside you. All the months I was supposed to wake up beside you. To love. To protect. To simply be. I will make it up to you, Lencia. My whole existence was made for tonight with you… and the rest of our lives together with our children."

"And so is mine because I wouldn't have it any other way."

Our grins widen and he pecks my lips before setting me back down. "Come on, baby. Let's go. Our night is far from over."

During the car ride to the next secret location, I make a vow to myself that whatever happens from here, I will never forget the way he makes my heart so full.

⸺⟨∞⟩⸺

Giulio takes us to Cœur d'or, the very restaurant our entire history was whisked in fate during our first date. Now seven years later we are recreating it. The name of the French restaurant translates to Golden Heart. The burgundy walls spread passion with a lick of ambiguity and the sleek decor remains the same, a frozen piece of the past. There's also a fascinating private gallery I love located upstairs that changes out their art every month.

Upon entering tonight, it was the first place we went and every single painting was so sensational and...*inspiring*.

Now, we're downstairs in the restaurant. Couples dance across the circular dance floor as the harmonious live silk-voiced male crooner warms the ambiance, each note tugs at my heart and spins me in a vortex of verses. I'm reminded of the people we were those seven years ago and the people we are now.

Both versions are perfect with Giulio Giannotti.

Giulio reaches over the table and my hand follows, merging the softness of our skins against one another. His thumb caresses that spot between the end of my hand and start of my wrist. "You don't know how nervous I was on our first date."

"You seemed so calm!"

"No, I was the complete opposite inside." He shakes his head with a chuckle. "I remember picking you up and the moment we entered this restaurant, I kept on saying to myself it felt like a dream. One that I never wanted to wake up from. Then when you told me trivia about that painting by the entrance, that Monet one, and I just knew you were going to be important to me. I could hear the devotion in your voice and how enthusiastic you were to describe the history to me. I saw the teacher in you and then you looked at me and I felt different. A good different. I was right about just how important you were going to be to me, because we connected so well. Spending time with you made everything okay. You made me accept my fate, my flaws, and that love goes beyond. We've made some bold decisions together, but bold decisions pay off."

"Exactly! They're the best type of decisions. I mean, I met you the day of my twenty first-birthday during my first year of teaching! We were married after a little over two months of knowing each other and had Oscar and Slonne all before I turned twenty-two. It all panned out that way because we were the perfect soulmates."

"We still are, darling. I don't want to lose that. I don't want to lose you forever."

"Neither do I."

"Then let's not."

My painted lips have not stopped pulsing since that kiss. It's awoken an exhilarated sensation inside me.

Our conversation and banter throughout dinner soothes me. I love the time we share.

I've missed it.

Our longing stares cannot be mistaken for anything that they're not. It runs so deep that after Giulio orders us Crème Brule—exactly like our first date—I bite my lip and we fall straight back into the questions of our past, powering them with ones of the current and future.

When he grips the neck of the wine bottle, I try to release our intertwined hands so that he isn't holding the bottle awkwardly with his non-dominant hand, but Giulio only squeezes my hand tighter, a silent protest that he doesn't want me to let go. He then pours us another glass with his left hand and sets the bottle down.

Giulio zones back into me, giving me his undivided attention and everything becomes clearer. "When we met, my father's suicide was still fresh in my eyes. Drinking became a habit, never to the breaking point, but it was there. It was never for my father's pain, but more my mother's. It brought back a lot of my childhood grief. When I saw you, something inside me changed at the glowing aura you brought into my company the first day we met. For the first time that night, I didn't drink."

"I didn't know that..."

Giulio nods and swirls his glass. "I know. I'm sorry. It's not something I've ever been proud of admitting. Being with you from that point forth taught me it's okay to be vulnerable, to be emotional, to cry. I could confide in you and you would listen and understand me. You loved me, even on my worst days. On the days I would come home stressed from work, one single glance at you made it all disappear. That's healing. That's love. I chose to devote my life to our love because apart from the good, I knew we would conquer the bad hand in hand...I just never expected our child to cause that bad."

Neither did I.

A knot forms at the back of my throat. "I'm sorry, Giulio. I'm so sorry I let you down."

"You haven't. None of what's happened is our fault. During these past months separated, I have attempted to find healing, but I haven't been able to find it…you know why? Because *you* are my healing."

"You're my healing too. Now that our fate has reeled us in closer, we can change it all."

"I look forward to it." Giulio reaches across the table and kisses me hard. "I want to take away all the bad, I really do. Through it all, all I've ever wanted was to be with you. To be a family again. I don't think I can ever stop those needs."

"Then don't."

"I won't." A smirk appears as he leans back in his seat, eyes flickering to my dress for a second. "I've always loved red on you."

I grin smugly. "See? From time to time I listen."

"I never want to take you for granted ever again."

I tell him my truth without hesitation. "Neither do I. We need to try. Despite us still not viewing the abduction in the same light, I want to be with you. I want us happy."

"I want that all for us too, darling"

"It hurts less when I'm with you. The pain that is."

"That is exactly why we both needed tonight. I need you, just as much as you need me." He motions towards the dance-floor. "Now let's be bold. Excuse me for a moment."

Giulio approaches the jazz band and I glance over at chattering diners. Some with families, others obviously deeply in love with their stolen glances and wide smiles. Suddenly…I'm not thinking about the worst-case scenario in public. I'm breaking away from that and thinking about the good.

Frank Sinatra's 'It Had to Be You' begins playing and Giulio returns, extending his hand to me. "May I have this dance, *amore mio?*"

The dancefloor clears and everybody in the restaurant

quiets except for the band as they continue to play the soft melody of the song.

Our wedding song.

Our slow dance steps are natural, as if they are a part of our soul. With my head resting in the crook of his neck and his hands securely around me, we move in time with the smooth saxophone, piano, and vocals. I feel as though I'm floating in the solace of his arms, wrapped in a classic black and white Hollywood film with a spotlight over us as we sway our way into the night.

This is much different than our last dance. I feel even more connected with him, if that's even possible. The romantic lyrics are a perfect rendition of who we once were and who we are now. I look up in adoration as Giulio's hot gaze burns through me. His smile lines deepen and the thumps transform to a bittersweet ache.

I realize something I have been avoiding all evening until now—*our differences.* There must be a way to respect each one and live this beautiful life with him despite our split views.

The song draws back every single moment of our wedding night. I kiss him softly as diners clap and cheer for our magical moment. We're partaking in one of the most romantic dances of our lives and my heart…it's stolen at the mere sight of Giulio Giannotti.

I've given him my all during our last dance and this one right here. Every single moment crossing the dance floor outlines a stage in our lives together. The day we met. The day we brought our first house. The proposal. The wedding. The days I gave birth. The laughter. The crying. The sex. The abduction. The separation. The agony. The faith. The false hope. The determination. *The love.* It's all here within this very dance, in our eyes, and in our hearts. A rapid reminder that we have gone through an entire war together.

Maybe if we are together in this, on the same side, then we can get past this.

As the music fades, signaling the end of the song, people

clap and cheer around us. Tonight, wrapped in his arms, I come to realize two other things…

One: I *love* Giulio Giannotti.

Two: We need to get out of here. *Fast.*

And we do just that.

CHAPTER SEVENTEEN

Valencia

GIULIO CARRIES ME INTO THE HOUSE WHERE IT ALL HAPPENED. The eerie feeling tugs at my soul, but then I am reminded of what it felt like when Giulio and I purchased this house. Before children. Before the stress. Before it all. How it wasn't just a house but a home. Now it's filled with heart clenching memories that if I think too hard about will bring tears to my eyes.

"Darling…"

Our kiss is hot. Needy. *Potent.*

Giulio sets me on the marble kitchen counter and my eyes shut to savor the erotic kisses peppered down my neck. They rush through my cleavage and down to my legs. I love how he crouches down to bunch up my dress and starts up my right inner thigh, sexily nipping at the delicate skin. His tongue twirls inches from meeting the rim of my panties, teasing me as he bypasses them to work his mouth up my left thigh.

"*Yes*, Giulio…" I moan the moment his hot mouth presses a delicate kiss at my heat through the lace panties. *This right here is heaven on earth.* My hands rush through his soft hair, driving him closer to where I need him the most. "Don't stop."

"Baby, I've missed these sounds so damn much."

"I've missed you."

"I've missed you too." Giulio comes back up to kiss me again. Our hands roam wildly, leaving no inch of our backs not warmed by each other's touch. "So. Damn. Much. Baby."

I kick off my heels and wrap my legs around his narrow waist. It's in that exact moment he flickers his eyes to my dress and he bites down on his lip. "You don't know what you're doing to me in this dress."

Grinning, I surge my hips forward to grind on his hardness. "I think I have *some* idea."

"Baby, you have more than *some* idea. You should wear this dress every day."

"Oh, really?" I tease. "I don't know how my boss would feel about that…"

"He'll love it. Trust me."

"Mmmm, even if I wear it into work for my last few weeks?"

"Fuck yes, but only in *my* office." He growls seductively. Pushing my hair to the side, he aggressively lowers the zipper of my dress. "And only if you kindly reschedule my work calendar for the next three weeks—cancel that—this entire *century* to private meetings with this sensational woman named Valencia Giannotti. I don't even mind working overtime."

When my dress is flung to the other side of the kitchen and his dress shirt follows suit, I can't help but laugh. *Always so eager.*

My palms rush over his torso, carefully avoiding the bruises, and my voice drops. "Done. What about undergarments in your office?"

"Well, if they're anything like the panties you're wearing right this second I don't want you to change a damn thing. It's perfect the way it is."

"So you want them to be mandatory?"

"Mmhmm, just like they used to be."

"And how will you know I've complied?"

"I'm glad you asked. Firstly, I'll set you down in my office chair…" Giulio lifts me and walks us over to the dining table. It's there where he sets me down on the plush dining chair and drops to his knees in front of me. I lean forward and am about to cup his stubbled jaw when he restricts both my wrists with one hand. The other gently grasps my throat as he inches closer, his lips brushing against mine in a hot smirk. "Just like this, baby. Next, I'll do this…" His raspy voice alone drives me to arch my back at the rough kiss on the lace above my clit. "And then, something like …"

Our six months break has accumulated a buildup in our sexual frustration. It's confirmed the moment he tears my panties, throws them across the room, and buries his head between my spread thighs. Suddenly we're free falling, making up for lost time.

"…*this.*"

Yes!

Moans escape me and I throw my head back as Giulio's mouth ravishes my pussy, his stubble teasing me further. My fingers grip the chair's arms, melting at his touch. I'm confident he can hear my rapidly beating heart when those soft hands glide up my stomach and cup my breasts through my bra. One hand undoes it and dives inside, his fingers elongating the tips of my erect nipples.

"I want you, Giulio."

"Baby, you already have me."

I look down at him, and our gazes lock as his tongue erotically draws circles on my throbbing clit, he then works it down lower to my glistering center, teasingly licking and sucking before burying his tongue deep inside me. My heavy breaths have him spreading my legs further apart and his moan like hum vibrates through me.

The moonlight cuts through the open space, rushing across my body, and illuminates the way he makes the six months wait worth every single second. I get lost in his masculine scent and eyes that have me wanting to preserve the way he's looking at me. How he throws my legs over his toned shoulders to deepen the sensation and pleasure me faster and faster.

"Oh my god!" I'm in sweet desire. I feel it across my entire body as the feeling builds inside me. It feels so good. *Too good.*

Giulio replaces his swirling tongue with his fingers. They taunt me ever so slowly until I'm moaning loudly when he pumps the same two fingers in and out of me in a curled, rhythmic delight.

Yes. Don't stop.

His vigorous motions deepen, becoming unapologetically harder and stronger.

Holy hell…

All I want is him.

"You like this, hmmm?"

I caress his chiseled jaw and respond by pulling him up to kiss him. *Yes. I love this.*

Giulio grins. "How much do you want this, baby?"

"I'm so close…"

His fingers dramatically slow in rhythm. *No. No. Keep going!* A cunning smile pulls on his lips before he teases me further by nibbling on my earlobe. His free hand runs across my breasts, edging me further into pure ecstasy. His voice is so fucking hot and sexual when he murmurs the question once more. "Darling, tell me. How much do you want this?"

I rock my hips against him eagerly. "*Please*, baby."

His fingers stop altogether. *No, Giuliooo!* "How much, darling?'

"So much."

"*How* much?"

I can barely keep my eyes open from the pleasure. "I want this as much as I need you in my life."

I forget how to breathe straight when Giulio kisses me. "And as much as I need you in mine." And then he replaces his fingers with his mouth and swirls his tongue inside my pussy, flickering it ruthlessly as I feel myself begin to quiver.

It doesn't take long before pleasure overtakes me in waves as his tongue consumes me whole and I climax hard, screaming out his name. Giulio builds me back up the second I recover and fucks me with both his mouth and his fingers all over again until my moans echo around us.

This is what love does to me.

It consumes me beyond repair.

And now that Giulio is mine again, I never want to let go.

Beaming, I glance down at him as he strokes my hips with a wide grin. "Wow, that was...*wow!*"

I'm still catching my breath, my chest rising and falling hard as I come down from the orgasms. It's the first time we've been intimate in months and *oh my god, how I've missed it.*

Giulio watches me from under his lashes with darkened eyes of desire. He rises up, his arms flexing as he grips the chair's arms and kisses me so sensually, as if we haven't been consumed by each other for years. My head falls back in bliss until he grips the back of it with one hand, deepening the kiss. I taste my sweetness on his tongue and the emotions swirled in it.

"You're sensational, Lencia."

"You are." I'm mentally pinching myself to verify this isn't a dream. "So much so."

"We'll get through this together. We're stronger than whoever is doing this to us." Giulio promises and takes my hand. "I have something to show you. Come with me, darling."

Giulio leads me to the back of the house and into the bedroom. I'm giddy, fully naked, and grinning when he glances my way. I feel free in this house tonight. I feel like myself again.

We come to the French doors by one side of the bedroom and step outside to the courtyard and outdoor staircase. Instead of extending the luxurious single story house, years ago we created this house with a rooftop balcony among sleek outdoor furniture and a wooden deck to look at the mesmerizing sky—it's where Giulio leads me. Tall Hemlock trees hide away Seattle streets, creating our own private oasis where nobody can see us—rather *me* in my nakedness.

Situated near us, is a telescope and a red gift box on top of the outdoor furniture.

What does he have planned?

I arch my brows. "Woah, what is this?"

"You'll see soon enough. Close your eyes, darling."

I do as I'm told and it's silent for a few moments until he bids me to open them. I smile, staring up through the telescope at the section he points to in the night sky. Four stars stand out and shine brighter than the rest of them all.

"Those stars are ours!"

"Ours?"

Giulio chuckles at my curiosity and reels me in closer. Shadows of the night cross his body, pure silver outlines against his olive skin. Angels of darkness that navigate me to him.

"*Amore*, I registered with an official organization, and that star you see over there is named Addilyn. See that one right by it and the other to the left? That's named Oscar, that's Slonne, and the one slightly below it, it's us. Together. This way whenever we look up at the stars, we have our angels guiding us."

Holy cow!

He bought us stars!

"Oh my god! Wow! You did that? That's incredible!"

I'm in awe at the official paperwork and can't stop grinning when I turn back to the night sky. Giulio wraps his arms around my waist from behind me and my head falls to his chest. "This way Addilyn is always right here with us. She's burning bright in the sky and will manifest into our greatest legacy. The twins are right beside her, protecting her. Our presence will shine forever up there."

"I love it!" I turn to hug him properly, failing to suppress my tears. "Thank you so much."

"You're more than welcome." And then Giulio sighs and says something that has my heart clench. "Come back home, Lencia.

Please. It doesn't have to be this house. We can buy a new one. One where we can see those stars and dance through the heavy night. One where new memories can be born. One where we never have the fear of losing anybody ever again."

Come back home.

I back away from his touch and grip the steel balcony. Our stars shine brightly against the dark, ominous Seattle sky. There is so much beauty in his gift. So much opulence and...*hope*.

"Apart from the other night, you haven't slept properly in this house since Addilyn went."

"And I don't know if I will be able to tonight."

"I will be here for you, *with* you. Just think about the idea of a home, darling. You do not need to tell me now. I will give you all the time you need and deserve."

My chest expands.

Of course I want to live with him again. *But there's something in our way...*

"This is all of me, Giulio. This is where I want to be. With you. With our entire family. The five of us," I say, my voice breaking while wiping away tears. "What will it take to convince you Addilyn is alive? I will do *anything* at this point, baby."

"I don't want to hurt you more. I know I might if we talk about Addilyn."

"No hurt. I will listen with no judgment tonight. I promise."

Giulio sighs. "It will still hurt you."

"I can carry a heavy heart."

The rumble of the city so close drowns out the heavy fluttering of my anxious mind. Right now, there are so many things I feel for him that have taken months to come to light. It's only in these past three weeks working for him where everything has begun falling into place.

In slow, delicate steps he approaches me from behind. My heart is set on fire.

Giulio doesn't need to say a word.

He knows me.

The warmth he provides with his bare chest against my

exposed back can save me from a rising tide. When he sweeps my hair off my right shoulder and hugs me from behind, I smile against his secure touch. This is exactly where I want him. How I need him. Why I love him.

"But I want to carry the heavy heart *for* you, baby."

"Do you not believe Addilyn is alive because of your mother?"

"Yes," he whispers and rests his chin upon the edge of my right shoulder.

"During this time I've learned that concealing the past leads you nowhere. We have to confront it with fresh eyes and…I want to understand you. Let me in."

"I try my best to be the man she would have wanted me to be, but I keep failing."

"I beg to differ. She would be so proud of you."

Giulio sucks in a breath. "My mother is the reason I don't believe Addilyn is alive. I have the perfect fantasy that they're together. That they're happy and have each other. Without the fantasy, I lose myself and don't know who I am anymore. Without it, my mother is alone up there. I can't have the agony of waiting it out. I need a solution to this madness and acceptance is what I resorted to these past few months."

It makes sense for him. That's the architect in Giulio; needing everything with precise solutions and followed through with accuracy. I understand it perfectly now.

"My solution is courage to keep believing. I need to find her, even if I'm the only one."

Usually, this would spark a circular debate, but tonight everything is different. "I've tried, baby. I've tried so hard to believe it too. Of course I want to believe it, but in these last months, I've been incapable of doing so and it ruins me. It ruins me because I know how greatly you want her and I want her too. But there's this…toxin inside me that doesn't let me grasp it."

"Let me be your cure."

"Convince me to change. Maybe if you convince me then…" Giulio's desperate lips brush against my neck, electrifying every sensual kiss. I ease back, rolling my head to the side to deepen his access. His stubble grazes my skin through every peck. "Convince me, *amore*."

"There will be no battlefield. We can exist in a way that isn't just memories. We don't have to...hold each other accountable. We don't have to have this divide. I understand your fear and your reasoning. Let's say Addilyn is with your mother now and she's guiding her, but what if you hold onto hope for Addilyn and she can be returned to us *with* your mother's safe touch? I love your mother, Giulio. I never met her, but I know I love her because she made you into the man you are. You carried her wisdom and warmth. Her courage and strength. You took her greatest hidden agony and you protected her. You stood by her even when she wasn't able to do so herself. That doesn't only take a man, it takes a *good* man, and that is what you are. She would want us to be happily thriving in life and for us to never lose faith in her granddaughter. She would want Addilyn to be back in our arms...if we're united, we can make that happen."

"You don't know how much that means to me." I'm relieved that through his pained voice, he holds onto me closer "I don't want to spend another second losing you, Lencia. You and our kids are the best things that have happened to me. Without you, I would have nothing."

"We need each other. I don't want to spend my life without you, Giulio."

"And I need you in mine. As my wife, as my one and only. You can rely on me, *amore*."

Inches apart, I turn to face him. "You can rely on me too."

"I don't want to be scared anymore. I believe it, Lencia. I want our daughter more than ever. Let's find her, because now I realize it's not false hope; it's the *only* way. I believe it now." Giulio's eyes allow our greatest vulnerability to be exposed as he cups my face ever so fondly. "I love you. I love you so much, Valencia Giannotti. I always have. I always will."

My entire world comes alive. "I love you."

Giulio crushes his lips on mine and hoists me to his waist in the same second. He blindly navigates the stairs down until we stumble into the bedroom, where he kicks off his shoes and I lower to strip his clothes in our fiery passion.

It can't be more perfect than this—*Giulio trusting hope.*

He devours every inch of my body with tender kisses to prove just how much he means it. Emotion blooms inside my chest when I fall back against the soft gray sheets and he shows love to my cesarean scar. The warm saturated glow cast down from the ceiling illuminates every scar of our past. I love us more for it. *He believes in Addilyn. He believes in me. I believe in me.*

Yes!

I love the way he knows my body and I know his. How he whispers sweet nothings in my ear as he molds my breasts, twirling his tongue over my nipples before sucking to build the sensual elation of what's to come.

Hope of a better tomorrow.

"I have an idea..."

Giulio arches a suggestive brow. "Really now?"

"Yes, turn us around."

When he does, I sit up to straddle his waist and grin at his enthusiastic sexy smolder. Giulio props himself on his forearms, those heavenly biceps and abdominal muscles tense at the motion. "So, what's going on in that sexy mind of yours?"

"You'll know soon enough," I giggle, pecking his lips before saying. "I'll be right back!"

I'm out of the bedroom and return from the kitchen with a jar of wildflower honey. I rattle it upon entry and Giulio grins widely. "Come here, baby. Remind me how wild we get."

A passionate fiery kiss follows until I straddle his waist and playfully shove back his shoulder. "Hands above your head, Giannotti."

Giulio lies down on the king sized bed as I unscrew the lid. I dip a finger into the golden honey and pop it into my mouth. The taste is light and fruity, yet richly flavored at the same time as I whirl my tongue around.

The way Giulio is looking at me...*Damn, I'm in paradise.*

With his hard cock pressed against my core, I tease him a little longer. I generously dip in two fingers and trail the lustrous honey from his base to a paved path around the bruises and then his lips. There's something about the way he rebels against my hands-off command by sexily holding back my hair and those curse filled moans that have me suck, lick, and swirl away the sticky spread off his body faster.

Erotically, red lipstick along his body replaces the honey. The moment I reach his mouth, Giulio swiftly spins us around so he's on top and pins me to the bed. Instead of devouring his honey lips, he has me share the experience through our long passionate kiss, that familiar electric charge between us intensifying.

"*Dio mio*," he murmurs with a smile, setting the jar of honey on the bedside table. "The things I'm going to do after that sexy stunt you just pulled, Mrs. Giannotti."

My entire body is throbbing for him as he rubs the tip of his cock at my wet pussy, so damn hard and ready for me. His sexy smolder has me grinning. "You make me so happy, Giulio."

"So do you, my angel."

"I'm still on birt—"

Giulio doesn't wait to hear as he thrusts inside me. I moan out his name, the word velvet against my lips. A mystified scent of vanilla and rich oak surrounds us. There's a fire circulating my heart that reaches across every single nerve ending.

I cannot stop grinning against every motion.

Neither can he.

I adore his smile lines and the way it charges the atmosphere around us further. He takes my left hand and brushes it across his chest. I know it's bound to hurt with the bruises. "Your touch repairs me."

The thrusts deepen.

The pleasure builds.

It's so intimate and loving. *Oh my good God.*

"*Fuck.*" He curses against my mouth. My legs wrap around his waist where I lock my ankles as his hands hug my waist. I'm in awe of the way he lifts us up to his knees and pins my back against the fabric upholstered headboard while thrusting.

"Yes, baby." My nails run across his muscular biceps until my hands wrap around his neck for support. This long-awaited moment has been worth it. Our bodies connect so perfectly. It feels as though mine is floating in the air with his enduring hold. I want this sensual moment to last forever.

Every second looking into his bluish-gray eyes and witnessing desire deepen makes me surge faster in rhythm with his hips. We're smiling amid jagged breaths, our romantically tender gazes on one another urges our motions even more intense.

"*Oh*, baby…we're so lucky this headboard is wall mounted."

The reality of his words makes me laugh. "You did it on purpose!"

Giulio winks with a sexy smirk. "Shhh, our secret."

Our pure bliss has me shutting my eyes in pleasure of the fire burning all over my body. The size of the void Giulio fills is so vast. A sticky sweetness hits my bouncing breasts and my gaze opens to honey dripping from Giulio's pointer and middle finger. Still rocking into me, I'm further turned on as he teasingly rubs it all over my breasts and watches me suck his fingers clean before he lowers his head to lick away the glittering golden honey against my skin ever so slowly.

My racing heart explodes. "Don't stop, baby. Don't stop."

"Never, *amore*."

My continuous moans have him flicking his tongue over my pebbled nipples, He intensifies our hot sex by biting down hard on them with a sexy, dominant growl and just the right amount of pressure to pull me under.

I love this man. I love him so damn much.

"You're my air, Lencia."

"And you're mine."

"You're so fucking beautiful. It feels like a dream having you here."

That velvety voice…

"A dream I never want to wake up from."

"We don't have to," he breathes. "Not anymore."

"There's nothing more I want than this life with you."

My nails sink into his skin and it only takes a few more thrusts for me to come undone at his touch. His kiss swallows my moans as I clench around him and lose myself in the new world we have created for ourselves.

It's him.

It's always been him.

Giulio Giannotti is my healing. *My everything.*

Wherever this night takes us, I know I will remember it forever. Because this will not only be a memory, from this point forward this will be *our life*.

Moments later his face falls into the crook of my neck and he kisses the base, all while moaning along to every slower thrust as his warmth spills inside me. Moments pass before Giulio lies us back down and hovers over me. All it takes is giving Giulio *the* specific look and grin for him to sling my legs over his shoulder and pound into me hard and fast again.

We turn the previous urge to make love into fucking mercilessly for all the days we've been without each other. We don't stop at twice. We keep on going into the night until we're beaded in sweat with all positions exhausted and our panting melting into one. Here on this bed, we drive each other to the most intense orgasms of our lives.

I smile at him in pure happiness, easing down as dusk turns to dawn around us.

Now. That. Was. Hot.

Giulio chuckles at our giddiness and kisses my forehead. Still wrapped in each other, we catch our breath. "This is the first dawn of our new lives together."

"And I couldn't think of any other way to spend it."

"I love you so much, Lencia."

"Love you more."

"Impossible."

CHAPTER EIGHTEEN

Giulio

H*OLY HELL.*

Just when I thought I couldn't fall any deeper in love with Valencia Giannotti I'm proven wrong. My heart hasn't stopped exploding with joy since the moment she told me she loves me too. It's one of the best feelings in the world—to keep another's heart safe.

We made love into the early hours of the morning and now as I lie here beside her, I cannot be happier with my decision to trust life and hope for Addilyn. *Trust life*, just like my mom used to tell me.

These past days have brought everything into perspective for me. *My mother will be okay.* She will always be my guardian angel. Her death is irreversible but with Addilyn there is hope.

I know this now.

Valencia's right. She's been right about it all along. I've been so blinded within these last few months, attempting to protect myself from being vulnerable, when all along I should have believed. I could have been with my wife all this time instead of backing away. But I have her now and will never take advantage of our second chance. *Never.*

I've been staring at the dresser across from us for the past few minutes. Inside the third draw, pushed to the right corner is a teal box. It's where our wedding bands rest. I feel so complete knowing that it'll only be a matter of time before we're back to normal.

Before she's officially mine again.

A lump forms in my throat at what else is hidden at the back of the drawer…what Sandro gave me. Valencia has no idea, and until I need it…I'll keep it that way. She will understand.

Silvery shapes of the moonlight slither across Lencia's face, enough to make out she's peacefully asleep. I snuggle her closer and my eyes trail to the night sky through the French doors. Our stars are further east from where the frame cuts off, but my heart warms just the same.

Our love will never fade.

"Thank you for making me believe," I whisper. "Thank you for everything, Lencia."

❧

Sobs wake me and I immediately thank God for being a light sleeper. Pulling Valencia to me, I rub small circles on her bare back. Her pain is my pain. My heart is racing, pondering the first and worst thought in my mind.

Is she crying because of Addilyn or… is she crying because she regrets what we did?

Her breasts press against my chest, sending me a heavy reminder of earlier. I can't see the alarm clock from where I am, but the red-covered dawn skies confirm it's sometime past five o'clock.

"I'm sorry. I dreamt that Addilyn got returned to us and it… affected me."

She doesn't regret it.

Thank God.

"It's okay, darling. It will happen in real life soon, I'm sure of it." I kiss her forehead, the reassurance I give her cures a part of me too. *Yes. In real life. In this life.* "It'll all be okay."

Valencia is quiet for a moment before she says, "I want to go in the nursery."

She hasn't been since the beginning of the case as it evoked too many memories for her every time she attempted to step inside. I get it, but in these past few months without both my girls, that nursery has brought me a sense of comfort.

"You do?"

"I need to force myself. Have you been in?"

"Almost every night. I fall asleep in the rocking chair, only to wake up to a stiff neck and a heavy heart."

She reaches forward to cup my tense jaw and when she does, there's a soft smile among the tears. "Will you come with me?"

My heart is beating out of my chest. I analyze the havoc within her eyes and just how nervous she seems. I don't want her flushed or anxious. "Of course I will, *amore.*"

I slip on my boxers and we retreat to the nursery door.

Lencia's skin glows at the peeks of the morning light down the hall. I take her hand, ignoring the way her sculpted nakedness has me yearning to claim yet another one of her orgasms. *Soon. Now is not the time.*

Lencia's fingers brush against the nursery door, but she steps back. There's a resistance within her that wasn't there before. Her boldness has worn off. *There's no way in hell she is backing out of this now. Not with me present.* I told myself I was going to help her overcome the doubts that cluster her mind, and now is a perfect time to be proactive. She needs to do this for *herself* and I'm going to be right here to weather her storm.

"We'll come out if it's too much."

She shakes her head. Trembling overtakes her body as she

hugs her waist and steps back further. "No, I can't do it. I thought I could, but now that I'm here I can't."

"Yes, you can."

"No, no I can't see inside."

"Baby, relax." I take her waist and kiss her softly. Her entire body relaxes in my hold and it's exactly what she needs. "We've suffered through so much, and from experience, I know at times it's easy to think you're battling alone in a war. It's not true. That only means you haven't looked beside you, because while you're distracted by the lurking evil, support has been marching in to tame the bad. Let me be that support. I'm going to be right beside you. We'll keep the lights off, okay? I'm right *with* you. You can do this."

Valencia sucks in a breath, gathering her strength while I massage the kinks in her tense shoulders. "The thoughts in your head are only illusions. You're stronger than you think, baby. Come on. Let's do this."

Those hazel eyes meet mine and the fury begins to ease. She nods, wets her lower lip, and steps in as I hold the door.

A light whiff of air greets us. It's always been so much colder in here. We don't need to see a single damn thing to know where we are in the room. The slightly ajar door gifts me Lencia's outline. She feels her way inside, gripping Addilyn's bassinet that hasn't been moved. The shades are drawn. I had the window bolted with steel from the outside days after the disappearance.

This is the room I was proudest to have designed, and although a part of me says *it still is*, deep down I know it's done its time. As much as we can stop fearing or find refuge in this room, it will always be the last place we saw Addilyn in.

Valencia nears the rocking chair.

"How is it?"

"It's…overwhelming."

I lift her and she straddles my waist as I sit down. Taking advantage of the dark, her arms wrap around my neck and I kiss her forehead. "It was the same for me at the start. Then day by day it began to be a little easier."

We stay in a comfortable silence for a while, soundlessly reflecting on everything that has been. It must be going through her mind too, or else her breaths wouldn't be this shallow. They match mine, falling into synchronized rhythms and so I focus on that.

It calms me.

Stabilizes me.

A good ten minutes pass before we make any further movement. The memory of Addilyn burns deep inside me. Her cute little smile. Those eyes. Her presence in our home.

Tears roll down my cheeks.

Fuck.

Back in the bedroom, I give Valencia nothing but my raw honesty. "I know that was an important moment for you. I'm so proud you were able to step inside and place your feet on the same floor where somebody destroyed our happiness."

Lencia looks up at me and it's a new awakening for me. Those doe eyes sparkle as she wipes away my fallen tears. "I should be thanking you. You encouraged me."

"You stepped in. That is much more significant."

"I beg to differ."

"*Oh,* disagreeing with me so early in the morning, are you?" I grin, arching a brow in protest at the soft giggles escaping her. "It's never too early for you, is it? Hmm?"

"Never, darling," she teases, tracing the band of my boxer briefs.

"Never she says. Definitely too early for disagreements, but it isn't for something else…"

"Point taken, but you may still get an eye roll out of me if you're lucky."

"Oh *amore,* I'm always lucky when I'm with you."

<hr>

"Thank you for coming in. Please make yourself comfortable."

Instead of in a *chair,* Bryce sits on the edge of my desk. *I let it go.* This is Bryce McCarson we're talking about after all. I should have expected that even if he did assist in my recovery, that doesn't exactly mean we're instant best friends. No. We have a long way to go. *But we're getting there.*

He downs his soda and throws it across the room. Somehow it lands perfectly in the trash and he beams with raised hands. "Now that right there is what I call a shot of a champion!"

I clear my throat and drum my fingers over my laptop. "Bryce, I have a meeting in exactly fifteen minutes and so I'm hoping to get through this as quickly as I can…" I trail off.

"Perfectly alright with me." Bryce brushes down his olive sweater and falls into the guest seat adjacent to me. "How are them bruises? The one on ya face doesn't make ya look too bad. Ya just look like an Italian that came back from a mafia gang war."

I smirk.

Hold up, *smirk?*

Damn, I've been so much happier since working everything out with Valencia that I'm even giving into McCarson's sarcasm. "The bruises are fine. Are you calling me a gangster?"

"Not necessarily. I think that we're all gangsters in our own way. We may not be part of an organized crime syndicate, but we've got those dark, dark secrets that we don't want certain people to bring to life. And let me tell ya something that'll surprise ya…The good guys, right, they always have the darkest. You just don't see it because they conceal it, they're good at that, but they have the darkest even if they seem the brightest. Remember that when you put me down for worst employee of the month."

I raise my eyebrows and Bryce chuckles. "My verdict is in. You're quite an inspirational guy when you're not busy being infuriating."

"If that's your way of saying ya love me, I'll take it."

"It's my way of saying there is no worst employee lists. Not that I love you."

Bryce laughs. "So, are ya going to tell me what you and the Mrs. have decided on?"

Saturday morning when I woke up beside Lencia for the first time in months, we had a slow-paced day. For once, neither of us were rushing to make lunches, getting the kids ready, or pulling into work like a dear in the headlights. Instead, we arrived at Helena's and spent the entire weekend with the twins, Daisy, Weston, and my sister-in-law making cannoli and rejoicing.

It was a novelty to be a family again. *Pure bliss.*

Today before work, Valencia and I had breakfast after taking the kids to school *together* and so many things eventuated from it. All of which are positive beacons of hope. One of the topics we discussed was her plans when my assistant returns in three weeks.

"Painting."

"I didn't know you were painting again."

"Oh, I'm not. Not for now anyway." Valencia goes on to explain how she desperately wants to get back into painting, but the motivation falls short. I can't blame her with all we're experiencing. First Addilyn. Then the letters. The sighting. The vandalism. That reminds me, I need to contact Lance regarding the process of the assisted retirement village project.

"How are you going to make it work?"

"I'm not entirely sure but I need to force myself out of this rut."

"The motivation will come in time. Your paintings were always so magnificent!"

She turns bashful and retreats from my hands. *"You're just saying that."*

I catch her wrist. *"Take the compliment, Lencia. You're a sensational artist. I know it can be hard, but sometimes all you need to do is take the compliment and say thank you, baby."*

She swallows hard. *"Thank you."*

"Huh? I didn't hear you."

"Thank you, Giulio."

"What?"

I love how those lips curl up. *"I said thank you, Giulio!"*

"One more time for the people in the back!"

"Thank you for the compliment, Mr. Giulio Giannotti. Thank you. Thank you. Thank you."

"Now that one was a bit excessive, nah?"

Lencia giggles and shoves my hand away playfully.

Another topic we discussed was Bryce. Valencia gave me some insight into his apology, struggles with his parents, and how he is working a second job as a bartender some nights to support his mom. Collectively, we opted not to fire him and instead give him one final chance.

I give Bryce the run down and by the end he's pensive, stroking his scruffy beard. "So you're going to keep me?"

I nod sternly. "Yes. It's what Valencia wanted and I will always stand by her judgment."

"Thank you. I really do appreciate it."

"She's the person you should be thanking. She made the reasoning passable."

A lopsided smile appears when he extends his hand. "I will. Have I ever told you she's a keeper?"

What did I just agree to?

I shake his hand and breathe through a stiff smile. "Well, welcome back to Notti Designs...I guess."

Outside, Bryce stops by Valencia's desk and a fist bump is exchanged. "I don't know what ya said, but thank you. You don't know how much it means to me to start over with you."

Lencia brightens and looks between us. "It's okay. We'll all be one happy family if we all stick to the rules, right?"

"Well, what can I say? I do like breaking the rules..."

"McCarson," I warn.

"However, on this special occasion..." Bryce smirks mid-sentence and casts an honest glance my way. "For this work environment, I can make an exception. I'll be good, you have my word."

We've made the right decision.

I know we have.

Valencia's wisdom and guidance matters to me. If Bryce

McCarson genuinely needs my paychecks to assist his mother out of the scam she conducted in England, I will do all I can, *however* he must also hold up his end of the deal by being more industrious and less apathetic.

"Hey stranger." I grin at Lencia once he's gone.

She responds and my heart continues to expand. It's only been a few days since we both vowed to take our marriage off life support and finally breathe together again and *damn* how good it feels. "Could you kindly make a reservation for four under my name?"

"Of course. When and where?"

"6 P.M. tonight and anywhere you wish."

Lencia stares down at her notepad. *Oblivious, baby.* "Well, if it's an important meeting I would suggest The Gravel. There's a private dining—"

"That's perfect."

"Okay. Which clients do I need to contact?"

I can't hide my grin anymore. Lencia glances up at me and the first thing I do is kiss her. She doesn't remember that we were going to tell the twins about *us* tonight.

"The clients to contact are a Mr. Oscar, Miss Slonne, Mrs. Irresistible Giannotti, and me."

———❦———

The twins erupt in cheers at the news. A few people turn towards our table but Oscar and Slonne don't even notice. I cannot stop smiling at my family the entire dinner. All I can think about is how perfectly poetic it would be if Addilyn were here.

Slonne gives us a beaded bracelet she made for all of us in her class. I help Lencia with hers and wear my bright pink one with pride. Oscar makes a face, not wanting a part of it.

I watch them all so beautifully together and make an oath to myself.

Here in this restaurant, I vow to not rest until we have our baby back.

Until we're a whole family once again.

Until I hear the word *Dada* spoken…

"I still can't believe you ate all that yucky broccoli."

"Cause I'm cool!" Oscar beams, showing his sister his nonexistent biceps. "See, just like Iron Man!"

Slonne rolls her eyes and glances outside her car window. "More like a goldfish."

"Hey! I heard that…well at least you said I'm gold!"

"Eww, no. I take it back."

"Can't. You already gave it to me, *amore*."

"I'm not, *amore*. Only Daddy can call Mommy that."

Lencia laughs while I take my eyes off our children in the rearview mirror with a smirk.

"How about this, if you both compliment each other instead of fighting, we can watch a movie at home with Daddy?"

I turn to Valencia. *Our therapy suggestion.* She's bringing our story full circle by implementing something for our children that helped us. I love it when she's happy. It's all I've ever wanted our family to be—*happy.*

"Only if we get to watch one of the Mission Impossible movies with Tom Chris tonight!"

"You mean Tom Cruise, buddy." I laugh at his persuasion skills. *He's getting good.*

"Those are pretty long ones and it's a school night. Plus, there are some violent scary parts in it. Maybe when you're both a little older."

"But I'm a big boy! I want to see the scary parts!"

"No, I want to watch Frozen!"

"No!"

"Yes!"

Valencia turns to them in the backseat with a smile. "How about we decide when we get home?"

"Yay! Okay…I LOVE YOU SLONNE!"

"LOVE YOU OSCAR! MOMMY AND DADDY LOVE EACH OTHER TOO."

I wink at Lencia. "We sure do."

"Very much so."

The moment I pull into Helena's driveway, worry erupts. Marcus' Toyota Camry is parked there. Call it instinct, but I can already sense something is off.

Why would he be here?

My thoughts are confirmed at the front door by Marcus and Helena's screams which overpower every stable thought in my mind. Valencia's eyes widen. I hope my gut instinct is wrong, but I fear drugs have to do with this. Marcus came into the office late today, disheveled and on edge.

Valencia quickly unlocks the door.

"WHY WOULD YOU DO THAT?"

"WHY WOULDN'T I?" Helena screams. "WHAT WAS IT? TELL ME!"

"IT WAS HEROIN, OKAY? ARE YOU HAPPY NOW?"

Oh, shit.

I forget how to inhale properly, but Valencia doesn't. She hurries the twins down the hallway to their bedrooms, acting as a barrier between the tense scene. It's evident when I turn the corner and survey the commotion in the kitchen that I no longer know Marcus' capabilities.

He's staring straight through Helena, who's hands are trembling over her face. A phone is discarded on the floor between the barstools and the dining table. My heart sinks at the sharp knife discarded onto the granite kitchen counter-top.

Oh, Dio.

They can't see me from where I'm standing.

Helena steps back. "I'll call the police if you don't leave my house right this second!"

"Are you crazy?" My half-brother scoffs. "You don't even know half the story!"

"I know guys like you. I do not give a damn who you are; I want you *out*."

"What gave you the fucking right to put it all down the sink anyway?"

"Her sensibility, that's what," I grit. Both of their heads snap my way, and just like that, Helena rushes past him to collect her fallen phone. "Hey, are you okay?"

"Yeah…just get him the hell out of here before I return for my coffee." Tears stain her cheeks when she rushes past me and down the hall. I cannot begin to explain my fury at Marcus as he grinds his jaw and stares down at the knife as if it's nothing.

"What the fuck did you do?"

"I wasn't going to hurt her."

"Bullshit! Answer me."

I can't believe it! Here I was having one of the best nights of my life with my family and Marcus just has to ruin it.

My half-brother stands frozen as I round the counter to put the knife away. My heart breaks for Helena. She doesn't deserve this inconsiderate bastard threatening her. Nobody does.

"I don't even know why you're still here. This doesn't involve you!"

"You best believe it fucking involves me. Helena is my sister-in-law and Valencia—"

He cuts me off. "Is your wife? Don't worry, I get it."

"No. You don't get it or else you would have left when Helena asked you to. What did you do to her?" I cock my head, throat hoarse at the next question that falls. "Are you on something?"

"No." Marcus' eyes darken and I notice their reddish tinge. It's all the evidence I need to know he's lying. "I was in the area and wanted to see Helena. So what if I had heroin on me? I'm not using, I wasn't going to start using here! She saw it, fucking lost it, and put it all down the sink. Do you know the street value? I lost thousands in seconds, Giulio! Thousands!"

I have no sympathy for him.

None.

"You've lost more up here." I tap his head, fuming. "Shame on you. That's all I can say."

"Get the hell out!" Helena screeches when she reenters with Valencia by her side. "I said out!"

"You're a bitch!" Marcus erupts with a pointed finger. Redness rises from the back of his neck to his head. "I'm glad all we ever did was fuck because you're not worth it. You're not worth the time nor the effort. You deserved your husband dying all those years ago because at least—"

"You finish that sentence and you won't like the results," I threaten. My blood is boiling as I grip his collar with no intention of letting let go. "I don't care at this point, I *will* call the police.

"Oh you're defending her now, huh? Being the golden god in *Valencia's* life isn't enough, you have to go on and be *her* protector too?"

Ignoring Marcus, I apologize to Helena and Lencia on his behalf and drag him out of the house.

Helena and Marcus were seeing each other? That day at school drop off she was hinting at seeing somebody…but…I never suspected that it would be my half-brother. It's news to me.

The old me would have driven Marcus home and ensured he made it there safe. Tonight…he's pushed me past the point of empathy. I can't control him. I've tried and tried with him. I can't change him. It's up to him to be willing to change, no matter how many times I've hoped he would choose me as his anchor.

"One day you are going to see the consequences of your actions and you'll wish you had listened to me to seek some help. Because after what I witnessed tonight, you need it more than ever."

"I don't need help or anything else from you!"

"Not even your job?"

"I'm only there to keep up half of my deal. I don't give a shit about representing your company. I do it for the clients and I do it because YOU. OWE. ME."

"You only need me because I owe you?"

"YES."

"You don't need me for support?"

"NO, I DON'T."

"Not even for the money I give you?"

The same fucking money he uses to traffic drugs, instead of investing in his future!

"NOT. EVEN. THAT!" Marcus screams in my face, shoving my chest with glassy eyes at each staccato word. I don't budge, but if he wants to get started tonight, I won't be as lenient to his blows as I was last week. Marcus has disappointed me beyond repair. I can't do it anymore. I can't have him here.

"You're fired!" I grit just as he slams his car door and drives out of sight into the dark night.

Arrivederci.

Roaring thunder aids his farewell as the sky opens up. Heavy rain droplets pelt down with a distant earthy smell permeating the frigid air. My anger deflates, yet the disillusion remains. It won't ever fade. Not with him.

"Yeah…I'm going to need a drink."

CHAPTER NINETEEN

Valencia

The way Giulio palms his forehead upon reentering, I already know the situation must have escalated between him and my brother-in-law.

Hard 'pit-pat' rain rushes down against the ceiling as I offer him a sympathetic smile. The strife is nothing compared to the gust of wind that slams the door shut for me. It suggests a storm is brewing. *Not that one wasn't already…*

I don't know what's happening with Marcus. Helena needed a moment to herself when they left and so I made sure the kids brushed their teeth and then tucked them into bed with the promise of watching a movie later on in the week instead.

Marcus has always been a good man in my eyes, a dedicated

individual who strives to follow in Giulio's footsteps, but somewhere along the way, something happened—and now…*heroin?*

"I'm going to make a coffee for Helena, do you want one?"

"Yes, please." Giulio pecks my lips, the sensation still so new and warming. "But with a touch of whiskey in mine, please. I need it. Do you mind if I kiss the kids goodnight?"

"Not at all. I'll make the coffee." I sort through the mugs, mentally preparing myself for the unraveling of Marcus Giannotti when an electric heat spreads against my shoulder blades ending in a tender squeeze. "Thank you, baby."

"For?"

"Everything that you do. The kids are lucky to have a mother like you."

"They're lucky to have you too! Seeing you as a father makes me even prouder to have you by my side."

I feel Giulio's hot gaze penetrate through my entire body and all I want to do is make love to him all over again. *That* and reverse our legal separation. I know it's still early but it feels *so* right. These past few days have been incredible with him. I'm loving every moment of our new vow. Giulio believing in Addilyn only reaffirms my beliefs—making me the happiest woman alive if our baby were to be found and placed in my arms.

"Our family is the best thing that has ever happened to me. To *us*. I will never walk away from what we made. Lencia, I promise you that." Then he kisses me again. It's much slower, so beautifully sensual. We're not tearing each other's clothes off; we simply *need* each other to pull through.

We part at the sound of a thunder clap.

"I will never walk away either," I murmur, stealing another small peck.

The desire is there to continue but tonight everything has become much more complicated. Whatever happened between Helena and Marcus is serious and we need to sort through it with her.

"I'm worried about Marcus. I don't want to lose him. I don't want it to escalate to that."

"Do you know what happened?"

"I don't know what happened with Helena but for a few months now Marcus has been dealing drugs. I have been trying to get him off but it's all too much for him. He borrowed money from me that I was crazy enough to believe would be spent on something good. It wasn't and he never repaid me. I don't care about the latter, but he could've used it to save himself. He stopped for a while, but last week I went to his house and found his coat closet filled with pills and powders. He said he's only dealing. I don't believe him nor am I happy about it."

"It's not safe…why would he do it? If that's the case, I don't want him near the kids."

Giulio nods. "He hasn't been staying with the kids, well not alone anyway. I know he wouldn't hurt them, but I want to be sure. I don't know why he's doing this. He doesn't talk to me about it. I guess I won't be getting much out of him anyway seeing as I fired him out there."

Oh.

This is far worse than I originally thought.

"Is this what you wanted to tell me the morning after the bar incident with Bryce? Remember how Marcus cut you off when you said he should tell me about something…?"

Giulio swallows thickly. "Yes. I've been meaning to tell you, but up until this point, it was his battle to fight. I've told him numerous times that I'm here to help him but he doesn't want my help or any professional help. What more can we do? And what hurts me the most is what he said to Helena and how this was supposed to be a perfect night with our family."

"None of this is our fault. It's just how the night was supposed to go. Helena's a strong woman and we'll be right here to help her through this…Why don't you go to the kids now? I'll make those coffees and your special whiskey order, Mister."

"Thanks. I appreciate it, darling." Giulio winks before disappearing down the hallway.

Helena blinks away a few tears, glancing down at the freshly brewed coffee in her hands. She reminds me of myself in this moment. I see my broken soul within her. I see the fight. The resistance. The pain.

I hate all of it.

This isn't *her*.

Helena Holmes is the life of the party, a sassy soul, and the person everybody wants as a best friend. I never suspected her to be involved with Marcus. *They hid it so well!* It hurts to know Marcus drove her to this point. She doesn't deserve it after everything she's been through, but I know it will only be a matter of time before she bounces back.

"Trust me to find a lunatic to break my dry spell! No offense Giulio."

"None taken. Trust me."

"And Marcus is even seven years younger…I don't know what I was thinking!"

I reach out to hold her hand. "Hey, this isn't on you. You never expected that he would storm in here with drugs and almost reach the point of violence when you threw them out. You did the right thing, but you should have called us, honey."

"I know. I didn't want to disturb your night out together. I mean it *still is* ruined and for that, God, I feel terrible! But I'm so happy that you've both decided to work everything out. You both earned tonight and I'm sorry it was cut short."

"Lencia and I have all the time in the world. Please don't drag yourself down for his idiotic games. You're not to blame." Giulio's pledge is all heart. "And he's not worth the thought either. You deserve so much better."

"Have I told you how much I love you guys?" She glances between us with smile. "Soooo, have you two finally put the G in Giannotti? How's the revival treating you both?"

We all laugh at how quickly she changes the subject. One minute Giulio's grin is in sight and the next the room dramatically dims. The lights are cut and the fireplace becomes the only source of golden saturation within the room.

"What the hell! Do you think it's because of the weather?" Helena asks.

"Could be. I'll go out and check if the other houses have their lights on." Giulio stands and exits into the horrid Seattle night with furiously blowing wind and rain pelting down to investigate.

His absence has me inch closer to Helena who I can just make out the silhouette of.

"Giulio and I are in a good place. It's you I'm worried about. Are you sure Marcus didn't hurt you?"

"He didn't hurt me, honey. Just scared me a little when he got that knife but it was only a scare tactic. God, I can't believe that I even....my head hurts thinking about it. I'm sorry about earlier, Lencia. I didn't mean to push you away. I didn't tell you about Marcus because I thought it would make things awkward; also because I'm partly ashamed it had to be *him*. I mean come on, he's so different than me! I've been struggling through my emotions which is why I was so fired up when Bryce and Marcus appeared that night with Kayla. My mind has been an absolute mess..."

I feel for her.

Marcus' words only had one intent—to hurt. That doesn't sit well with me. Helena's husband dying young was a tragedy. For years she's battled it on her own and finally, when she was ready to take the next step, somebody dragged her down. It's so uncalled for and so unlike the Marcus I've known.

"It wouldn't have been awkward." I pull her into a tight embrace and comfort her like she always does me. "I want to be the person you come to first. You are always there for me."

"You're right, I should have. You know me, I don't get involved with men because my kids are my priority. Maybe later down the road...but right now I don't need any man. I guess Marcus was familiar to me and a few weeks ago one thing led to another. It was only casual. *Very* casual. God, I hate him. I swear I would have called 911 if he woke up my kids. What an ass! It's safe to say we've both been fucked over by the Giannotti's, literally and figuratively."

Laughter lightens the mood. "I think we're on the verge of becoming supermoms with all this strength."

"Speaking of which, you don't know how excited I am about you and Giulio! I'm happy at least one Giannotti is a man of gold!"

I'm about to respond when the lights come alive. Seconds later, Giulio bolts through the door. I await a smile; instead, his face is pressed. His wet hair is violently tousled and his drenched slacks and now transparent white button down cling to his body. It's only when he steps forward that my heart sinks at the knife gripped in his right hand.

Something's happened.

Something bad.

"We need to call the police."

My eyes widen in panic as I bolt up. "What happened?'

"It wasn't the storm…It was a man…waiting by the circuit box. I fought him off until he ran. He…" Giulio's jaw clenches in defeat and the bombshell drops. "He wanted one of us…dead."

Every time I step inside the police precinct, the same sensation accumulates—misery. It's the fear of the unknown that eats people alive and I am no exception to the feeling.

With Giulio's attacker on the run, the stakes are higher than ever. When Giulio went to the circuit breaker box, he discovered an unmasked man who pulled a knife on him. He had been the one to turn off the electricity, not the weather. It was calculated. The attacker was ruthless in fighting Giulio, but luckily, he managed to steal the knife. Yet the man remains at large.

Seattle Police have managed to obtain a considerably clear visual sketch of the alleged attacker. A Caucasian man in his mid to late twenties with jet black hair, brazen eyes, a solid build, and he has a deep scar between his eyebrows. Unfortunately, the man wore gloves, so the only prints on the knife were Giulio's.

The digital sketch of the man bombards the media. Every

time I see it, it's like a kick to the stomach. For the rest of the week, the media remains constantly in our faces, hoping for exclusive statements or pictures. I despise seeing them as much as I appreciate that they are only doing their job, knowing that *our* story is being flashed around Washington only welcomes stares and hushed whispers behind our backs in public.

My saving grace is my family.

Giulio and I have been showing the children our stars every night since the surprise and they adore it. My family is one of the only escapes I have. Just one glance at them and I know everything will be okay. Giulio and I have become a whole lot closer too. Almost two weeks have passed since we told each other those three words and we haven't been able to stop saying it since. Being bold is one of the best things we have decided for ourselves.

It's led us this far.

For the past week and a half, we've spent the days in the office as giddy professionals but at night we dance passionately in the sheets. I still have my belongings at Helena's, but the twins and I have been staying at our old home much more frequently. For the entire end of September and now the beginning of October, I sleep through the entire night and wake up in Giulio's secure arms.

Ever since he eased the tension of stepping inside Addilyn's room, some of the unease has faded. If it wasn't for his encouragement and my moment of confidence, I don't think I would have ever stepped foot inside the nursery again. That night Giulio helped me demonstrate my capabilities.

Giulio has been surprising me with outings for lunch during the week whenever he has an opening in his schedule. Yesterday, we went to art museums. It feels just like old times and a way to take the edge off chasing his attacker.

SPD believes it was a targeted attack most likely related to Addilyn's case. And so, as much as I love every single moment I spend with my family, there has also been mass devastation circulating my mind. *Will these crimes bring us to another breaking point or will we survive it?* Every time the thought comes, Giulio kisses away my fear and reminds me to focus on the present, and I have been.

Kayla brightens every morning for me with a ginger tea by my desk and I preoccupy myself with tasks set on Giulio's action plan at the Tate's. I only have a week and a half left at Notti Designs and although it saddens me to leave, I've also had the best time of my life here. This is where Giulio and I met for the first time and also where our second chance has resurrected.

On this sunny Wednesday morning, a new shipment has been ordered into the large industrial warehouse and I offer to pick it up seeing as I'm ahead of schedule. Some interior designers are by the entrance, huddled in a small staging meeting. Other workers in visibility vests walk around and organize each of their appointed sections. The warehouse is filled with stock; countless wrapped pieces of furniture and unopened boxes.

I'm here for a marble side table, and while I attempt to figure out its exact location on my own, I'm struggling. It must take me at least twenty minutes as I glance over my sheet of paper at the barcodes on each shelf. *I'm beyond lost!*

I pass Marcus on one aisle and my body involuntary tenses.

The following day after the drug incident, he came into work even though Giulio had fired him. Marcus ignored me, even after the brothers had a private boardroom discussion. Giulio exited not looking the least bit pleased, but explained he decided to give Marcus one last chance. I didn't dig any deeper to uncover his reasoning, I just trusted his judgment.

I tell myself to continue looking for the piece of furniture but just as I note that none of the descriptions match, I feel Marcus' eyes on me.

"Valencia?"

"You know I would have always been here to listen," I blurt out, aggravated that he's still made no contact with my sister. "I would have helped you, but pulling a knife on Helena is something I can never comprehend."

His mouth parts but quickly shuts. There's a look of pain in his eyes that dissolves with a blink of an eye. Marcus takes one step my way and I walk straight by him. I cannot get caught up in his mess.

Not today.

I need to find this darn marble side table!

I make it to the next few aisles and do a happy dance when I'm faced with a medium sized cardboard that matches exactly. *Not so fast.* As I grip the box, I instantly stop and groan at the strain on my back. The box recommends two people pick it up, *it is heavy Italian Marble after all,* but I give it another shot because I'm adamant to prove it wrong.

I've given birth to twins, I can certainly push past this!

Or so I thought.

Letting it go, I step back to kick the edge of the box. *Piece of work!*

"Yeah. I think ya gonna need help with that."

Bryce.

I swallow and swing the purse of my crossbody bag to my back. *I'm not giving up.*

"Thank you, but I can do it. I used to do CrossFit and if I've learned anything, perseverance is a mindset."

I grip onto it tightly and uphold momentum.

"Why did ya stop?"

"I'm just readjusting myself."

"No, I meant the CrossFit. Why did you stop?"

"Kids. Work. My drive left me after what happened. It was doing me more harm than good. Yoga helps better." I manage to get the box off the wire rim and crouch down to push it against the polished concrete floors. Bryce is beside me, mocking me with a slight chuckle when a set of stairs face me. "Yeah, there's no way in hell I can get this down."

"Now what, babe?"

"Now..." I groan, propping my hands on my knees for a quick breather. "Now we wait for a miracle to happen."

"Then you're in luck because miracle is my middle name." Bryce takes a hold of the box without any protests from me. The idiot is grinning as he holds it casually against his chest, *as if the box is a stack of papers.*

I guide him to my car where he wordlessly sets it inside the trunk. When it's all done, he stands with his hands stuffed inside the tight pockets of his jeans, simply waiting.

"Thank you for that."

"It's nothing." He gestures back to the warehouse. "Do ya have anything else to collect?"

"Yeah, my stamina."

Bryce laughs with a hand to his chest. "Don't worry, the way you and Giulio can't take your eyes off each other suggests ya stamina and his are perfect. Ain't nobody that happy at 9 A.M. Ya know what I mean, right?"

I bite my lip, failing to suppress my smile. My eyes should have rolled at McCarson's comment, but instead, my heart warms with the reminder of my husband this morning. "I guess you're right."

"Yeah, I *definitely* know I'm right after what I heard early this morning. I wanted to talk to Giulio but aborted the mission so damn fast seconds before knocking on his office door."

Mortified, my jaw drops. "Huh? Don't tell me you heard us when…"

Bryce snickers. "Oh yes, I did."

"Oh my god! Really? We were trying not be loud on purpose!"

"Well, you two reckless lovers fucking failed. Now, that's what I call a sensational fuck."

"Bryce!" I snort, playfully shoving his chest.

He chuckles, dramatically stumbling back with raised hands. "Damn, girl. Look at that shove. Ya like it rough, huh? Giulio better watch out."

The laughs only get louder.

When we calm, he points towards the box. "So, where's it heading?"

"The Tate's. It is one of the final pieces needed before the design team takes over."

"Ah, yes. Look, I've been an absolute dick to you. I know that now. It was never my intention and I'm glad we're in a good space now."

Everything has simmered down dramatically between us since our last heart to heart chat. Ever since the apology, Bryce has been incredible. I appreciate his company, especially in a time where there is carnage everywhere I look.

"We just started off on the wrong path, we're working on it now."

"We are." A prominent smile curls his lips, just like mine. "Aye, let me know if you do end up needing help moving any items."

"Will do!"

"How's your sister? I heard through Marcus that…well…you know."

"She was a bit shaken up but she's okay now." Although the memory will last a while, Helena is back to her bubbly old self. "Thanks for asking. I'm sorry about how you two had to meet. Helena was just worried about me that night and her motherly instincts kicked in."

"It's alright. You sure both had them young."

A heavy weight stabs the back of my throat. "We both found love young."

"Yeah…ya see, I don't do love. It's not in my veins." Bryce flushes with a distant gaze. It surprises me that only moments ago we were so joyous and now his whole demeanor has changed. He seems…I cannot grasp the right word for his emotion.

"Bryce? You okay?"

"Yeah, I'm alright. I gotta go now. Have a good one."

He disappears before I can say anything else.

⸻⸺◈⸺⸻

"I don't think I'll ever take this off." Giulio shakes his wrist, subsequently moving the beaded bracelet Slonne gifted him. "Pink seems to suit me, don't you think?"

"Everything suits you, baby."

"*Oh*, really now?" He smirks, sliding into bed beside me. Desire pools in his mesmerizing eyes and he silences my laugher with a hot, steamy kiss. "You suit me. I wouldn't have it any other way."

It's Thursday now and all of the days' stress of his attacker still being at large eases with the sensual kisses to my neck. They pull me under to a place where only our passion exists. A place I have been craving for months, and now that we're here, I never want to escape it.

Giulio's comforting. His smells like home. His voice is serenity. I trust him with my entire life. Even after all the uncertainty, Giulio still makes me feel like myself again.

Safe.

"Neither would I. I love you"

"I fucking love you too, Lencia."

"Do you save all your profanities for the bedroom, sir?"

Giulio pulls back with a large grin and the throbbing between my thighs only intensifies at the way he pins his body to mine. "No. I save them for the shower too."

"Hmm, and why would that be?"

"For this exact reason." One minute we're on the bed, the next he has me pinned against the charcoal shower tiles with my legs around his hips. Our kiss is a rapid cure to everything we've been fighting for. Steam fuels the air and I can't help but tease him when we pull away.

My hands spread across his wet torso. The bruises have almost completely healed from the incident almost two weeks ago. "Is that all you've got, Mr. Giannotti?"

His voice grips my heart like a vice. "Not in the slightest."

Shower sex has always been my favorite. Perhaps because we're locked away in pure bliss with nothing but warm water cascading down our naked bodies and moans filling the air.

Giulio lowers me and I spin around to press my hands against the glass.

"Baby..." Giulio rubs my heat from behind, nibbling on my

shoulder as I wriggle in pleasure. "This still isn't all I've got." He replaces the sweet sensation with his cock. "I could make love to you for an entire lifetime. Nothing but making love. I adore all the other aspects of our marriage, but right now…right *now*, I'm going to fuck you so deep, baby." The first thrust is ruthless and shoves me closer to the wall. Our moans don't subside. My breasts press against the shower glass and his hands cover mine against the glass. I smile as he fucks me hard while making love to my neck with his soft kisses. "Just like this, Lencia. Just like this."

It's just after eleven when we make it out of the shower. An hour passes with nothing but countless wild orgasms followed by a legit shower that only leads to more pleasure.

Giulio and I check on the twins before deciding to end our night with some coffee. He's a true Italian after all, and he has somehow recruited me into his 'caffeine before bed does nothing to me' club. *I like that club.*

"So, I've been thinking about what you said the other night… about finding a new house to live together and beginning a new story there."

That slow, sexy smile takes over. The one I love and adore. He sets his coffee mug aside and takes his hands in mine. "Yes, baby?"

I mirror his joy. This is something I've been thinking about and I truly do want it with Giulio.

He's all I want.

"I would love to find a new home and become a family again."

"Oh my god! Are you serious?"

"Yes! I want to make this work with us and our family."

Giulio picks me up and I squeal as he twirls us around the kitchen. "You don't know how happy that makes me." He sets me down with a kiss. "Stay right there. Let me get my laptop and I'll show you the house I was thinking of."

Grinning, I cross my legs in my silk pajamas. "I've got nowhere to run off to, baby."

"Good." Giulio winks before heading down the hall.

I'm giddy as I take a sip of my coffee.

This is it.

This is exactly where I want to be.

This is a miracle.

Late night cravings have me opening the pantry to raid it with my coffee mug in hand. There's nothing I want and so I settle for an apple in the fruit bowl. Peeling it, I hear Giulio's footsteps approach from behind and can't help but smile.

I have my back to him, but just from the presence alone I can imagine his heart exploding with the same thought as me—we're in this *together*. I love him dearly and finding a new house with him is the best beautiful fresh start.

"Remember when we went to that apple picking farm with Oscar and Slonne last year?" I shake my head, laughing at the memory as I continue. "Remember what Oscar said? God, it's been in my head ever since! We were laughing for days about it! I swear he gets his wildness from you…it's a good thing though, because I'm crazy about you, baby."

My brows furrow at the silence as I set down the peel in the sink. "Giulio?"

His firm body presses up behind me and bewilderment fades into a smile. *That's better.* Shutting my eyes in pure bliss, I let the back of my head fall to his warm chest. "I love you, Giulio."

But his cologne…I don't smell it like I did earlier tonight.

This…This *isn't* Giulio.

Oh my God.

A static tension crosses my frozen body as I flutter my eyes open to my gravest fear.

No. No. No.

My mug smashes to the ground in tiny little pieces, accompanying the spilled coffee. Then…I feel it. A cool metal viciously presses against my spinal cord.

A gun.

It's a gun!

Panic festers inside me; it never wavers, not even when I grip the edge of the sink to stabilize myself.

"Quiet," a voice grits, the pressure of the firearm deepening, "or it all ends right here."

No.

My. Good. Lord.

What the hell is happening?

CHAPTER TWENTY

Valencia

I WANT TO SCREAM OUT OR RUSH TO THE END OF THE HOUSE, BUT I'M numb and my throat is closed.

"Turn around, real slow. Hands up where I can see them."

I have to be my own savior. It becomes a chant in my mind as I spin around with my trembling hands raised in surrender. The man wears all black. The solid color covers every inch of his skin and the balaclava only makes this a whole lot worse.

Delusion sinks my heart; I can't believe I thought it was Giulio. *Can't believe it.* How and when did the intruder enter? While Giulio and I were in the shower…? *It must have been.*

Why can't I scream?

It doesn't come out no matter how hard I try.

Move, Valencia! Move!

The intruder stares down at me, and even though I can't see his eyes through the mesh piece covering them, I can just imagine how lethal they are. *It's too late.* The barrel of a gun raises to my head as he steps back to create distance. All the while I'm shaking, unresponsive to the terror he is inflicting.

"ON YOUR KNEES! NOW!"

My throat opens to a weak whisper. "Please, don't do this."

"Do you need me to do this first to Addilyn? Huh? Or wait… did I already do it?" A cold mocking laugh escapes him.

Addilyn.

He has Addilyn!

Gun still aimed at my head, I make a small effort to stumble away around the counter, but it's no use and only agitates him further as he catches up. I'm sure my heavy breaths are obvious to him. He's playing mind games. Testing me.

Where is Giulio? He should be back by now.

"Oh my god!"

"LAST WARNING!" the man shouts, cocking his gun. He slams me against him when I don't comply. The gun slides to the side of my head, digging deep into my skull. "I SAID ON YOUR KNEES!"

Something erupts within me.

My desperation for Addilyn.

My yearning for Giulio.

My continuous hope.

My anti-depressants…Maybe *it is* the fact that this time, I have no idea what my fate is. Adrenalin pumps through my veins and I decide I don't want to be afraid anymore. I need to make a sacrifice. The moment has come. I'm so sick of being targeted. I'm sick of the constant fear and heartache. I'm sick of being dragged under.

No. Not anymore.

"Shoot me," I snarl. My body shakes yet I keep my head high. Fierce. "You are a soulless human, this I already know. So, if this is what you intend to do, do it. Kill me. Then you will stop this game, huh? Will you? WILL YOU STOP THEN? I SAID SHOOT M—"

"SHUT UP!" the man roars and pins me to the floor where my kicks and clenched fists are met with an iron body.

If I scream now, the kids will hear.

I don't want them to see this.

I need to call the police.

The man presses my face to the floorboards with one hand. The barrel of the gun slams to the back of my head with the other. Freeing myself proves no help and the tears begin to fall.

I realize my biggest mistake…

My heartbeat is rapid and then it happens.

Two loud bangs.

No.

Warm liquid sprays all over me.

No.

The loud thud beside me has me moving my head and a displeasing smell in the air takes over. The man is no longer on top of me. He's fallen to the side and his head has hit the floorboard. His gun is scattered at his feet and that's when I realize the blood sprayed on me isn't mine. *It's his.* He's been shot.

It's not me…

I lift my gaze, desperately wiping away the blood on my hands, *his blood*, and then I see it.

No!

Giulio stands a couple feet away, a silver gun still pointed at the intruder.

No.

Waves of disbelief ripple through me as I stagger to my feet. *What is going on?* I'm in utter shock…I can't even blink. My eyes widen at Giulio's merciless, screwed up face. His darkened eyes say it all.

Giulio has killed him.

No!

I don't know what to think. I don't know what to say.

Giulio killed…

He lowers the gun and slips it into the waistband of his pajama bottoms. He doesn't say a word; he only looks at me with his lips parted.

"You…you killed him! Oh my god. *Oh my god!*" My trembling finger points to the man between us. "What di-did you just do? Why did you do that?"

"Valencia…"

"Oh my god, Giulio! We need to call the police!"

"*Lencia*…" His attempt to calm me triggers me further. Air laced with the smell of metallic blood churns my stomach. When my gaze averts to Giulio's gun, a terrifying conclusion consumes me. *He has his own gun.* My chest pinches. *No. No, it can't be.*

"Why do you have a gun?" I stop him when he attempts to step forward. "No. Please stay there."

Giulio raises his hands in surrender and sighs sharply. I don't know who this man is anymore. It's ludicrous to think that not too long ago we were devouring each other and now…*this*.

"Valencia." His tone is softer than I imagine but it does not change a thing. Not a darn thing. *He killed a man. Killed him!* "You know I would never put my children in danger."

"That doesn't answer my question. Why do you have a gun in the house with the twins?"

His lack of response leads me to clutch my throat. "*Oh my god.* You are scaring me, Giulio."

Just then, the intruder groans, and I jolt back.

He's alive.

We can call 911. We can extract information from him and enforce real justice. He knows about Addilyn. He's our only hope. The police can make him lead us to Addilyn. *My sweet Addilyn.*

"Soon…" The intruder's strained voice is weak. Dark blood seeps through his face covering when he coughs. "Soon *it* will happen and…without me…you…cannot stop *it*."

Stop what?

Soon *what* happens? Until Addilyn comes back or until they…

Giulio slaughters my every last faith when he pulls out his gun and without warning fires three rounds into the man's head.

No. No. No.

Holy…

Oh my god!

I stumble to the floor at the side of the counter. Blood. Blood is all I see and smell. I hate it. *Hate it.*

The man is sure to be dead now.

"What di-did you just do?" I'm so distressed, my own voice deceives me. "Oh my…Giulio, please call the police! *Please*! We need to call them right now!"

"No. No, this has to stay between us."

"Ar-are you crazy?"

Giulio's gaze remains distant. *I don't want to believe it.* Giulio being capable of something like this is beyond imaginable. He just killed a man who may have been our only chance of finding our youngest daughter.

He's killed the hope I'm searching for, the same one he claims to be looking for too.

"*Please*. If you don't call them, I will."

"No, we cannot. This has to stay between us."

"No. The kids…what if they heard it all?"

"It has a silencer and I locked their doors, but if they did, we can say it was a car backfiring."

"*That* was supposed to be quieter?" I shriek, shaking my head as the tears begin to fall. I wipe them away and summon the strength to stand back up, away from the lifeless man. "No. You're acting all secretive. I am going to call the police and—"

"We cannot go to the police with this. This has to stay between us, *please*. I'll call somebody to clean up this mess and discard the body. It will be as if nothing ever happened."

"As if *nothing happened*? What the hell you are talking about?!"

"Please, Valencia…" he pleads with a staggered breath. "We cannot go to the police."

"Are you hearing yourself right now?"

"I..."

"Why are you talking like this? Why? Why are—"

"BECAUSE HE ISN'T THE FIRST PERSON I HAVE KILLED!"

No.

I take a step back and hit the edge of the barstool. *No.* The air in my lungs is barely enough to push out a full breath. *No. It can't be true. What he just told me cannot be true.*

"He...he isn't the..." Swallowing thickly, his face falls. "The first person I have..."

Where is the man I fell in love with?

"Valencia?"

Where is the man I love?

"Lencia..."

Where's my love?

"I've killed somebody else," Giulio repeats for the second time. "Please, say something."

This time it feels real. "When?"

"Eleven years ago."

"Who?"

Giulio stumbles on the question. His head is down, as if he's ashamed and unable to find his voice. It's ironic, that the simplest question is also the most complex. When he steps closer to me this time, I have no strength to look away or stop him. I only stare deep, sickened and afraid.

"Who?"

Silence.

"Who did you kill?"

A pause...*and then...*

"My father's death wasn't a suicide. I killed him. I shot him dead."

Tears well in Giulio's eyes and it hurts me, just as much as it hurts him. Because once we were so close. *So united.* I thought this could be forever. I thought we trusted one another. I thought we did not hide anything from each other.

Oh my god.

It feels as though he's ripped my heart out and split it in two, because right here standing in front of him, I am heartbroken. I am lost. And I am being strangled by my own breath.

He lied.

He hid this.

I voice the first logical thought that crosses my mind. "I need to take Oscar and Slonne."

Giulio is desperate to defuse the fire, rushing after me as I sprint away from him and plead for the keys to their rooms. "Valencia, I know how it looks. But I never...it wasn't premeditated! If that's what you're thinking, it's wrong. I did not plan to kill him. My father ruined *everything* for me. When my mother died and it was revealed that my father cheated on her during her last months, it was too fucking much for me. The night I went to my father's for Thanksgiving—"

"Please, stop," I beg him in the middle of tears. "I need the keys. Where are the keys?"

His own tears slide down his cheeks. I cannot mask the way I feel. It's everything at once. The shock. The anger. The betrayal. The pain. This has destroyed *everything*. The intruder *knew* information. He gave us a *countdown*. He would have been a piece in the puzzle to *bring Addilyn back*.

The pain of Giulio's past flashes across his face. I know he's suffering too but his actions here tonight scare me to the point I don't know who he is anymore.

"Valencia, please just hear me out."

"I don't want to hear it."

"That night things went south quickly. My father began insulting me and put a gun to my head when Marcus joined his abuse. My father told me I had another sibling. He didn't get through the first name or any other details. I didn't want to hear it. All I kept thinking was he didn't just cheat on my mother once. He began screaming and told me I was the one who was the problem. He was happy with his new wife and Marcus. My mother was the first issue. I was the other half of the issue. He openly admitted to me that he had been cheating on my mother since the day of her diagnosis."

"Giulio, I—"

"Lencia, it tore at my whole heart. She thought he loved her and went to the grave with this thought. Meanwhile, Marcus was in some other woman's stomach! Valencia, please...*please,* give me some time to finish the story and explain everything."

I slow down in front of Oscar's door. All the information Giulio feeds me is too much and the reality gets worse when every single word takes my already shattered heart and continues smashing it into tiny fragile pieces that cannot be put back together.

"I am scared, Giulio."

"I know you're scared. I am too."

"No. This is different." I turn to him with tears blurring my vision. "*You* scare me."

Giulio drops to his knees in defeat.

Clasping my hands, he pushes them to his chest and I witness the sobs that escape him. It hurts my chest, but I cannot accept it. The back of my throat stings. If we were different people I could hold him and tell him I forgive him for this, but I can't.

"Valencia, I love you. Please, I *love you.*" His fragile words break upon continuing. "I will allow you to do anything. To hate me. To call the police on me. To want to divorce me after this. I will not stop you. The only thing I'm begging you to do is listen to my story. Then, you do whatever you want to do and I will take it. I promise you this."

I make a split decision choice.

Okay.

We step away from Oscar's room and into the bedroom. I sit on the edge of the bed while he paces back and forth with his head buried in his hands. There's a string of curse words through his controlled sobs and after a few moments, Giulio finally comes to a halt in front of me.

"I don't think we locked the French doors before we went

into the shower...I think he came through these doors, heard us, and went beyond."

That only makes it worse. While we were driving ourselves to ecstasy, he was lurking around the house. *Oh...my god!*

Eyes red from crying, Giulio unloads the gun and drops it on the floor between us. Moonlight creeps across his skin, illuminating everything I want to forget. When Giulio lifts his eyes to me, they're no longer warm and bright like they were when I first met him.

They're in agony.

Like mine.

"Marcus was twelve when we saw our father for the last time. My stepmother hated me because I was half of the woman she despised. They brainwashed Marcus to hate me from a young age and he did. My stepmother wasn't there on the Thanksgiving night; she was working the late shift at the hospital. It was just Marcus, my father, and me." Giulio purses his lips, screwing up his face at the thought. "The conversation escalated and as I said before, Marcus began taunting me and I was going to give him a piece of my mind when I felt...my father pulled a gun on me. He blamed me. He claimed I would never get anywhere in life. That I would never be good enough, that I was *weak*."

There's so much strangled emotion in Giulio's face. I realize this must be the first time he's recounting this story—that's part of why it's so hard.

"My father continued to say things about my mother that to this day still haunt me. He didn't care about the time Marcus keyed my car, or when he threw my mother's jewelry away, or set my mattress on fire. He *never* cared once my stepmother came along. Sitting at that Thanksgiving table, I knew I needed to leave and return to Seattle. I turned around and was staring down the barrel. I was certain he was going to kill me. That's the type of man my father was. He never backed down. I allowed it for a split moment. I thought that at least I would be with my mother, that it would set me free, but by the end of it what I needed more was to fight for what my mom would never be capable of doing. So I curled his grip and…we fought with the gun. The barrel continued moving between us. Marcus didn't say anything. He didn't move. He simply stood by the end of the hall and watched…I can still picture it. I had enough of it all…I wanted to eliminate the threat my mother was incapable of seeing and so when I had the barrel to his head, his own finger was curled on the trigger and I pushed his down. The gun went off and…he…was gone.

"The entry wound made it seem like a suicide. That's what was in the autopsy. I never physically placed my hands on the gun and my prints on his hands made it seem as though I was stopping him from killing himself. That's what I told the police…and Marcus said the same. We made a pact that if he forever concealed the truth, I would support him financially and he could work at my company when he graduated. That's why he's always held this leverage over me, because we both need each other. I killed my father. I killed him because if not he would have killed me. Just like the intruder. I lost myself seeing you like that. I know it's not an excuse, but it's the pain that I'm living. I should have handled it differently, but you can't change your past. I'm not proud of it but it's who I was those eleven years ago… and who I was in the kitchen."

Giulio finishes his explanation at the other side of the room. He gives me the distance I pleaded for before, yet his words leave me even more bruised. I need to be strong for my kids *and* for myself.

My eyes drift to Giulio's silver gun. I wonder what ran through his head when he decided tonight he was going to claim a second life. It's too much for me to comprehend. Partly because I can't see past the emotion in his eyes.

Giulio Giannotti is no longer the powerful businessman every single one of his clients and employees see. With me, the façade has altered. That is what made me fall in love with him seven years ago. It's the reason I adore his honesty and his openness to be himself.

Honesty.

He has hidden this from me during our entire marriage and separation. He's hidden this from everybody, but I'm not just an *anybody*; I'm supposed to be his *wife*.

Would he have ever told me?

It places so much uncertainty in the water, making me question everything.

"I'm sorry for everything you have suffered. I cannot begin to imagine what you went through. You did not deserve your father's torment, but we promised not to hide *anything*. Especially not something as big as murder. That man would have spoken. I wanted justice for Addilyn, not death. It's too easy how he died. It leaves us with no prospect of getting closer to Addilyn."

Giulio's head remains low and it is everything confirmed.

I've lost him.

A fool. That is exactly what I am for believing we could make this work. Within this moment I feel nothing. Staring at Giulio reminds me of everything we once were and everything we have just lost. I have tried my best and I know he has too, but maybe our best isn't good enough. Maybe this is all we can give, all we have inside of us.

Our white flag is burning in violet embers and neither one of us is reaching to save it because we both know what it represents...

This is where it ends.

"What are we going to do about that man?"

"I will handle it," Giulio promises. "We don't need to go to the police."

"Are you insane? That man was our only hope of getting further in the investigation. He may have spoken with the detectives, he may have helped in a way that—"

"No!" Giulio cuts me off in the midst of tears. "Did you want him to kill you?"

"MAYBE IT WOULD'VE MADE THIS SIMPLER!"

"OUR KIDS NEED A MOTHER, JUST LIKE I NEEDED ONE!"

My heart breaks.

Again and again and again.

I'm scared the kids will wake to hear the shouts between us. Giulio and I continue standing here, face to face as I suck in a brave breath. "Do we need to change our custody agreement?"

It lights the fire between us. From here on out, it's a lethal time bomb, ticking away.

Giulio shakes his head, his lips trembling from the hurt. "No."

"I need to know you won't pull an act like this in front of them."

"You cannot take our kids from me!"

"Frankly, I do not trust you with them anymore!"

There it is.

Everything spills in front of us. Every single flaw, secret, and lie.

I need to look away from Giulio. I don't know who he is anymore. It's as if I've shot him and the bullet has brushed over every single inch of his body. He's torn. I'm torn. He's broken. I'm broken.

We're not good for each other.

Not now.

"Is this the end? After everything we've been through?"

My chest has never clenched this hard for him. *Please, no.* "It has to be."

"If you leave with them, it *is* the end of us." Giulio's muscles tense, withholding from breaking down again. "If you take our children away from me, there's no more faith in us. It's over."

"I know it's over. We were fools to ever think this could ever work again. We're two broken souls attempting to fix one another. It doesn't work. It doesn't work because fixing it doesn't make it go away forever. Do you really believe in finding Addilyn or is it all just another lie?"

"That is nothing but truth."

"Give me the keys, Giulio."

"I'm fine with the kids tonight. You can leave if you don't

want to stay, but…please don't take them away from me…
Please."

That damn gun between us scares me.

I wish he'd hid it.

I sniffle and glance down at my bloodied silk pajamas. I should change out of them but that would only mean prolonging my stay. And so I sling my bag over my shoulder and cast him a look. "Giulio…once you told me to never be afraid because as long as you're around everything would be okay. That was another lie because right now I am looking at you and all I see is what I'm afraid of—losing control." Tears roll down his cheeks. I quickly wipe my own away and lay my truth right upon the sinful air. "You killed what may have well been the only hope in finding Addilyn. That ocean of mine… the one you take me to when I have an attack…you made it my *cure*. You promised you'd be there for me through the storm. But now I realize the person I needed the most through it all was myself. That isn't your fault. It's mine. You helped me as much as you could, but I neglected every aspect of myself. I let myself go. Not anymore. I need to find myself again. And if I sink, at least I know I am going down for my family with nothing but honesty. At least I have a chance of survival. At least I can claim full responsibility for battling both the tide and the storm…*my way.*"

Rushing down the hallway, I make a stop by Oscar's room. My blurred vision stays on the door handle long and hard. A few minutes must pass before I feel Giulio's presence by my side.

He extends two keys to me, giving me unspoken permission to end it all.

"Take them home with you," he whispers, yet his broken voice contradicts every word.

My fingertips brush against the cool metal keys. All I need to do is take them, *it's what my head says to* do, but my heart…it tells me not to. It screams for me be the bigger person and have a little faith in him, even though I'm distraught. *I have to do it for Oscar, Slonne and Addilyn.* I have to deal with my anger towards

Giulio and what's the best thing for our kids as two separate issues. They can't suffer or be involved in any more turmoil as a consequence to our ruined love. It would not be fair.

"Giulio, I…"

"If you don't trust me with the twins, take them home with you."

I back away from both Giulio and the keys all together. "You know I do trust you with them."

"Then why did you say the opposite moments ago?"

"Because when I saw the gun it was…"

"Too much?" Those glassy eyes of his study me slowly. "Is it all too much?"

"Yes," I sniffle.

"I love our children more than the world itself. As their father, I would do anything to make them happy. You know that. I *hope* you know that. But if I'm wrong…if I'm nothing but a poor excuse of a father, by the grace of god I'll open their bedroom doors for you myself."

The moment our eyes meet, our seven years turn to dust.

After everything that's happened tonight, there deserves to be one truth between us. *At least one.* And so, in the midst of my own heavy heartache, I choke out the only words I have.

"Our children need a father, just like you said they need a mother. Even as heartbroken as I am right now, you deserve honestly. You're not a poor excuse of a father, you never have been …because…" my throat aches. "You are the best father in the world, Giulio. I mean that."

I witness the first tear fall from his eyes and leave this cursed house as fast as I can.

Giulio's tense face and fragile soul remains present in my mind during the entire drive to Helena's. It matches mine and hurts me deeper.

Oh my god.

Giulio killed his father.

He killed our chance at finding Addilyn.

I struggle to release a steady breath. Everything is too

much. *The gun. The secrets. Giulio's face.* That man…he said that soon it will happen. What is *it?*

Helena is filling up a glass of water in the kitchen and leaps towards me the moment she sees me. I fall to my knees, clutching onto her on the way down. I sob for every single thing I'm afraid of because they're all happening. All one after the other.

Just when I fell back in love with him…

Helena doesn't say a word. Her sister senses already know. She simply holds me tightly, despite the blood, and tells me everything will be okay. Everything could not be any worse and the final string holding my heart together snaps.

I vowed to love Giulio Giannotti unconditionally.

I plea for God to have mercy on me…because tonight, I break that vow.

Everything I thought to be true is based upon lies. These are the lies we tell ourselves, to comfort one another, to protect each other and it will be these exact lies that will eventually cost us our sanity.

CHAPTER TWENTY-ONE

Giulio

"A s I said, the earliest I can be there is by 8 A.M."

"Sandro, I'll pay triple. You have my word. He needs to go before my children see him."

"Triple?" A sly chuckle cuts through the line. "You sure you want to hand over that amount of money to me? We're heading into six figures of a no refund deal."

"I trust you."

"Alright. We'll settle for triple then. I'll be there within the hour."

My hands tremble on the phone. "Thank you."

"Wipe the cameras."

"Already have."

"Good."

Sandro hangs up and I sink into the couch, pouring myself my second glass of bourbon. I down it in one go and pour my third. My muscles don't ease. They haven't since I pulled the trigger tonight.

My hands tug through the ends of my hair and I recoil in a pit of pain.

What have I done?

I've lost everything tonight.

The love of my life.

My children.

Myself.

I cannot breathe. The tightness in my throat does not allow it. I cannot fucking breathe.

Face it. Look at what you've done. Look at it.

The blood is dried against the floorboards, but in certain sections, it pools. The man...I can't reach forward without tensing. *I can't see his face yet.* I should have a shower and get out of these blood-stained clothes but I can't. I can't get in that fucking shower because I know I will think of *her.*

I know I have done something tonight beyond repair. Not only did Valencia bear witness to me ending a life, but I admitted my greatest secret...*I killed my father.*

I battle the sobs and tell myself that I need to be strong, but how? How does one *be strong* when they've just lost the other half of their heart? How can *I* be strong when all I feel is weak?

You're weak, son.

It is what you are.

It is what you will always be.

Sandro arrives just after midnight with his crew of three other men. He steps inside with his usual leather jacket, five o'clock shadow, and pointed eyes. He pulls the cigar from his lips and nods towards the intruder while his men begin the process of sorting and cleaning. His New Jersey-Italian accent shakes me. "I didn't think you had it in you. Sometimes you only see the true man hiding underneath when your family is under fire."

I know Sandro's line of duty, but I never expected I would actually be using the gun I bought from him or that I'd be contacting him regarding disposing of the body and cleaning this potent smell in my kitchen.

"I'm not proud of it. I lost Valencia tonight."

Sandro takes a puff. "Nah, you didn't lose her. You were protecting her."

"No. She's right, I killed the only hope we had left. I ruined it all and I cannot—"

"Take it back? No, no that's not how this game is played." Sandro cuts me off and his eyes zone in on mine. The gaze of a man who's seen more crimes in twenty-four hours than others see in their entire lifetime. He points a finger at me, his face stern and tense. "The only thing you can't take back is death. You can't take that back. You cannot take what you did tonight back. Alright? Everything else you *can* change. You love her, I see it in your eyes. You killed him because you feared he would have killed her and she got scared. Let me tell you something, that's a *normal reaction*. If she truly loves you, faith will conquer all. It always does. *Vedrai.* Trust me. The world has a funny way of showing it."

All I can do is nod.

If she truly loves you, faith will conquer all.

Vedrai.

Sandro squeezes my shoulders and turns back to the lifeless man before us. "Now you have to do one of the hardest things, but it's gotta be done before we get rid of him. Look at him. See who it is."

When I slip off the balaclava, my jaw tightens.

Oh...Dio...

It's the man who attacked me.

His eyes are wide open, frozen in time. There's that same scar between his eyebrows. That same arrogant face, even in his death.

I change out of my clothes and give the men the ones I committed the crime in, along with the gun. It has me think of

Valencia. What will she do with her clothes? Will she call the police? Will she tell somebody the truth about my father's death?

Fuck.

I pay Sandro the sixty thousand. It's three times the normal rate and on top of that, I sign the NDA. They're out of the house soon after. There's no sign of death in the kitchen anymore. But I still can't breathe easily, not even after there is no sign of the murder. Not even after I unlock the twins' doors and find they are sound asleep. Not even when I slip into the bed with Valencia's scent lingering on the sheets.

I killed my father and I've gotten away with it for over a decade, *but now…?*

The man I killed tonight…will it be my undoing?

Will Valencia call the police?

Both occasions were self-defense. If I didn't kill the man, he would have killed Valencia and I couldn't have that. *Self-defense,* I tell myself over and over, until I can't take it anymore.

My agitation has me reenter the kitchen to grab my trusty bottle of bourbon and then head back to the bedroom. I step out past these cursed French doors and up to the rooftop balcony. I somehow stumble onto the outdoor sofa, causing the bourbon bottle I'm now drinking out of to slip from my grip and smash onto the decking. Liquid gold spills alongside shattered glass.

"Go to hell…" I grumble at the mess and step over it, unsteady.

The Seattle air feels warmer now and I wonder if it's because inside I feel nothing but coldness. It has to be. It's the only reason, alongside my broken heart. I did this to myself. I've forced this sorrow. I've caused this gaping hole for not only my marriage but for my children.

I don't know if we can ever come back from this…

If Valencia can ever forgive me for hurting her this deep.

If tonight I have killed the last hope of finding Addilyn alive.

I'm sorry. I'm so sorry I let you down, Lencia.

I look up at the stars now—at *our stars*—and for the first time in my life, I wish upon them.

CHAPTER TWENTY-TWO

Valencia

"A YE! WATCH OUT!" STRONG HANDS GRIP MY FOREARM AND pull me back into a firm chest. A car zooms past right in front of me, missing me by inches. I stumble into the familiar scent, shaken by my near-death experience. Bryce looks down at me with furrowed brows, witnessing my anxious expression. "You okay? That was close!"

Too close.

My fingers thread through my hair in a panic. I was so lost in thought moments ago that I detached myself from reality and began crossing the road into the traffic before it was my turn.

"Are you okay?"

"Yes, thank you for that. I just was lost in thought."

Bryce slings a hand over my neck. "Ya know what the trick is, babe? You've gotta wait til' the pedestrian lights tell you to go. Simple, innit?"

"Oh, shut up!" I laugh when his grin expands. "Thank you. I should have been paying more attention. That has never happened to me before…my mind is somewhere else today."

Ever since last night, my mind has been wandering to places it's never been. Nothing makes sense, but I need to put on a brave face today. Not for Giulio, but to spend my last days working with Kayla and keeping my mind occupied. My last day is next Friday and I plan to keep my head high and focus on my job, not the man.

McCarson and I cross when the lights indicate it's our turn. He has this pep in his step that has a few women glance his way with beaming smiles and an extra sway in their hips.

"I never thought I'd see the day where ya voluntarily walked alongside me."

"And yet the day has come!"

"Yeah, I'm going to note this in my dear diary."

I smile through the agony because letting completely go of myself would be equal to losing myself. I meant what I said to Giulio last night. From now on, I *need* to focus on myself.

"I'm sure that would be a good look for you."

"Hell, yeah. Feather pen and all. It'll be a hit in the office, but Giulio would probably kill me."

"No! He wouldn't do that!"

My heart seizes. *Jesus.* I shouldn't have reacted the way I did over the killing comment.

That's what happens when you witness a man shot dead and all of a sudden everything's literal.

We come to a halt in front of Notti Designs and Bryce's face screws up. He observes the scene around us for a second before honing in on me. "Aye…everything alright, Valencia?"

I nod.

Bryce raises a brow, far from convinced. His cockney accent softens. "I've gotten the pleasure of knowing you for over a month now and I know something's off when you don't speak."

"I'm okay." I force a smile that most likely doesn't look genuine. "It's just that Giulio and I are not on good terms. We're not together and so there have been a few things crossing my mind."

"Oh? I thought everything was back to normal. It would be tough, especially with kids."

"Exactly, it makes it much more difficult. We *were* good, but something happened, and now…"

"You don't need to say more than you want to," Bryce offers. "Just give it time, it's all you can do. See this tattoo on me hand? I got this rose, because ya know the saying; to truly love a rose, you've got to accept its thorns. I got it for my mother, but the same goes with relationships. Whatever happened I'm sure it'll cool down. It'll all be alright."

To truly love a rose, you've got to accept its thorns.

"Thank you. I really do appreciate it."

"See? I'm not *that* bad to hang around."

We make it through the lobby and up to the twelfth floor. When we come to a stop in front of Kayla's empty desk, he turns to me. "You know the best way to get out of a rut? B.M Keller."

My smirk lightens the dark. "Oh, is that your stripper name?"

"What? How did you guess?" He gasps dramatically and laughs it off. "Joking. In my opinion B.M. Keller is one of the best country meets contemporary singers out there. Listen to one of his songs, have a cry and you'll feel like a new person after."

Bryce McCarson shedding a tear? I find that very hard to imagine, but I suppose everybody has their breaking point. Giulio and I are the perfect example.

"I've never heard of him, but I'll listen to him now. Thanks!"

"Anytime." McCarson's mouth meets my ear in a low murmur. "And by the way, you'll never know the stripper name I go by." I gape at his words. *So, he really does strip?* Bryce rushes a hand through his dark brown hair, winking with that signature smirk of his. I laugh as that same hand descends down his torso. "Never, babe, *never*." And then he's striding away.

Well….that was certainly something else.

The last person I expect to see when I turn around is Giulio.

His somber eyes are lasers towards the space Bryce occupied seconds ago. In one single glance, I am transported to last night and everything it means. To all the feelings of uncertainty that lay between the echoes of gunfire and the unofficial countdown the intruder stated before dying.

Soon it will happen and without me, you cannot stop it.

When is soon? Today? This weekend? Next week on my twenty-eighth birthday?

How can we be prepared if the police are not involved?

My paranoia peaks at the thought of somebody watching us this very minute. I haven't slept a wink and I know it shows. The darkness underneath Giulio's eyes suggests the same.

My stomach churns at our locked gazes when the moments leading up to the death repeat in my mind, along with the fleeting trust. We continue to stare until a phone begins ringing and Giulio steps inside of his office, shutting the door and our past seven years behind him.

⸙

"Just know I'm here when you do want to talk." Kayla smiles, handing over my coffee. "And even if you don't want to talk and it's just silence, that's cool too. I just hope that they find who attacked Giulio sooner rather than later. Do you believe it has to do with Addilyn?"

I give her hand a final squeeze and step inside the hair salon. "SPD suspects it does and so I would have to say yes. I will take any chance of seeing her again at this point."

"I would be the same, honey. It's the only thing we can do."

I took both Bryce and Helena's advice during my lunch break. What is the best way to get out of a break-up kidnapping rut? B.M. Keller and a killer blowout. So when Kayla mentioned she already had an appointment at a chic salon a block away from work, I was all in.

Kayla scurries off to her booking while a middle-aged lady appears from the backroom. Her dark hair is tied back in a high bun and she greets me with kind features and a wide smile. There's a calming presence I get from her, like the comfort of my mother's rose and cinnamon scent or the warm apple and blueberry pie she always used to make on my birthday as a kid.

"Good afternoon, what can I do for you?"

It's been me and my long dark brown tresses for the better half of my life and right now, I'm dying for a change. The sharp sounds of the blow-dryers and client's chatter deter me.

"Good afternoon! I'm sorry…" I smile apologetically. "I'm always so indecisive when it comes to things like this."

"You and the rest of my clientele. Don't stress, let's see what we can do." She steps forward and glides her fingers through the ends of my hair. Her slate eyes meet mine. "Oh, are you Valencia Giannotti?"

The yes gets caught in my throat.

She shakes her head in apology. "Sorry, I don't mean to be intrusive. It's just that I've been following the case on the news. I have been in your position. Twenty years ago my son was abducted when he was two and the investigation was very much like yours."

"Oh, I'm so sorry to hear. Have you…found him?"

She nods. "We found him alive a few weeks before his sixth birthday. It was four years of agony but the moment he was returned to us was the best day of my life. It was during those years I became a hairdresser. I felt something so liberating and freeing about altering appearances. I see how hopeful you are and I was exactly the same. It broke my marriage too, but we ended up coming back together sometime after our boy was returned. I learned to love myself in those years and trust myself. Valencia, I can tell you're strong and so you're halfway there. We should liberate you today."

Tears blur my vision and I can see her glassy eyes redden as well. Without any warning I pull her into a tight embrace. The lady rubs small circles on my back and I connect with her on a mental level as well as an emotionally exhausting one. She'd battled through this hell for four years.

I can do this.

All I need to do is start believing in myself again. *You're strong.* I am halfway there. I will find my daughter. *Love yourself. Keep up the hope. Trust yourself. Don't let go. I CAN DO THIS!*

"I think I know what I want to do."

She grins and we turn to the mirror. "Go on, honey."

"Let's cut it all off to my shoulders."

⸻⧫⸻

"I can't get over how good it looks! I loved it before but *wow*, short hair suits you too! How do you feel?"

"Liberated in some sense. It makes me feel like...a new fresh start!"

"That's exactly where you want to be!" Kayla cheers me along when I run my hands through my new cut. I love the new feeling. It just reaches my shoulders and feels as though a weight has been taken off of me, *literally.* "You don't know how proud I am of you!"

It's the motivation I need to push myself to the limit and understand that *I am* capable of this all. I am strong. I am determined. Nothing will get in the way.

Kayla and I split up as she needs to mail a letter to her boyfriend in New Zealand. They're the true romantics. It makes me think back to the amounts of letters Giulio and I have given each other. There is something about his hand-written cursive that makes me...*Stop!*

Do not think of him.

Breathe.

I stride into Notti Design's lobby just before 2 P.M. Lee greets me with a salute. "As a man obliged to notice his wife's haircuts or else I sleep on the couch, I can confidently say it suits you well!"

"Thank you, Lee! You're a good man."

"Try to be. You don't know how uncomfortable our couch is! Bricks would be better!"

My smile drops at the sight of Marcus waiting by the elevator. His back is to me and he's typing away on his phone. This is the first time I've seen him since learning the truth last night.

I control my breathing and squeeze out a goodbye to Lee.

Be strong.

Stay confident.

I want to fix this between us. It unsettles me that I am at a current crossroads with both Giannotti men. It's not how I want the family to be.

"Afternoon, Marcus."

He completely ignores me when I stand by his side.

"Hey, can we talk for a minute?"

"Don't wanna talk." He jabs the elevator button a dozen times and proceeds to curse when it still doesn't open.

"Please. You're one of the last people I want to be fighting with."

"I don't want to talk about it. When are you going to get that through your thick head?"

I'm taken aback because I haven't done anything to him. *Where is this coming from?* Not only is my marriage slaughtered with Giulio, but it's as if I'm breaking away from all the individuals surrounding him.

"Is that how you got your job here, Marcus? By not speaking? Hmmm, yes. You begged Giulio for it, didn't you? Actually…no, *bribed* is the correct word. Isn't it?"

Marcus scoffs, his stare piercing through my soul. "So, he finally told you?"

"He did."

"Good on him. No more secrets and lies. I don't need your help, I don't need his help, or anyone else's. So do me a favor and wait for the next elevator ride."

"Woah, woah, woah." In a striking gray suit, Lance Hilton steps between us with caution. "Marcus, are you really speaking to her like that? Your tone is unacceptable!"

"Yeah, I really *am* speaking to her like that. Get out of my shit, Hilton. I don't answer to you," Marcus spits, storming into the elevator with his back to us as the doors shut.

"That was uncalled for. I apologize on his behalf, Val."

"You didn't do anything."

"Oh, I like your hair! It's new! When did this happen?"

A knot forms in my throat as I stare at Giulio's right-hand man.

Did he tell him about …?

"Lovely, what's going on?" Lance frowns when my lips part to no words. "Giulio hasn't been himself all day. He didn't tell me anything, only that he ruined everything. Did something happen between you two from yesterday to today?"

"You could say that."

"Am I imposing if I ask what?"

I attempt to explain it the best I can without revealing too much. "It wouldn't be imposing, but it's complex. I wish I could tell you, but I don't think it is the right thing to do. Not by him."

There's a ghost of a smile on his lips and it encourages me to be better. Close friend and business partner to Giulio since college, Lance Hilton has always been supportive of us. They've known each other for fourteen years and throughout the past seven years I saw him every week; Lance and I have also become close. I know I can always trust and rely on him.

Does he know about what really happened to Pietro Giannotti?

I don't think Giulio would tell him. Last night he said nobody else knew except Marcus and me. And so I take my losses and block the thought that Lance could have been misleading me this whole time too.

"Look, I'm on both of your sides. Ever since I met Giulio, all he has ever wanted to do was protect the ones he loves. I remember even before he proposed to you, how he told me how much you were his savior. That you were the woman he wanted to create the family he never had with. A stable one. A united one. He sees refuge in you and is hopeful about Addilyn now. Giulio never stopped loving you. I can't tell you what to do but I can say that this past month he's been happier with you around more. If something happened last night and you're both looking at divorce…I hope you two find a common ground because I love you both together."

Lance gives me a side hug before we step inside the now vacant elevator. I attempt to hide the tears burning down my cheek, but the pain is carved on my face and it caves me in.

Everything follows me with a shadow of doubt.

Every single thing.

"Thank you. I needed to hear that."

"You're welcome. Giulio didn't tell me to say any of that, it just felt right for me to say. I think back to that night he brought you home after that incident with Bryce…and I remember seeing the pure love in Giulio's eyes. I don't think he'll ever be able to stop loving you, but if I'm wrong, if this *is* the end…then I'm sorry, Val. I'm sorry that it has to come to this."

"So am I."

———⊰❈⊱———

"That one was funny! Let's watch that one again!"

When Slonne's sparkling eyes meet mine, she has no idea of the pain and torment I have been through overnight. She knows none of it and it *needs* to stay this way. While Oscar is helping Giulio in the kitchen on popcorn duty, my daughter and I decide on a short film. We're going to be watching the movie I promised last week when hell hadn't broken loose yet.

If I've learned anything, it's to not catastrophize on the future. To take it day by day and concentrate on what I *can* control. *Just like it was stated in his handbook.*

During the time Giulio and I were good, my depression eased. It returned in small waves, but there was this blanket of security over me. Now that our family is broken again, I've been attempting to summon my strength to concentrate on the silver linings, but it's difficult to do when you feel as though there's a gaping hole where your heart is supposed to be.

Giulio and I haven't spoken a word about the events that went down last night. He is the last person I want to see, but between work and the kids, it's inevitable. When he presented himself at my desk after my lunch hour and stated how the twins want me to come over in the evening to watch a movie, I couldn't say no to the thought of their cute faces.

We have to put on brave faces for them and act as if nothing happened.

Giulio's eyes couldn't even meet mine after I agreed and that became our only conversation the entire day. When I arrived at the Madrona house less than twenty minutes ago, the silence continued between us, even as the twins ran up to me and complimented me on my hair.

The reality is *everything* happened.

Last night ruined *everything*.

The pain has me gripped and I continue losing my breath remembering that Giulio killed that intruder. Although I know it was to protect me, he didn't need to extend the torment in ensuring he was dead. I accept that killing his father was self-defense and a fight or flight moment; I accept that he was protecting me by pulling the trigger…but when we saw the man was *still alive*…when we heard him *talking about Addilyn*, why did he have to shoot him *dead* instead of calling the police?

As Oscar rushes into the living room and his father trails behind with a large bowl of popcorn, I give Giulio a good look while he's distracted with the twins. I do my best to ignore the fire in my heart and between my thighs. Just then, I'm reminded of Lance's words, and that sense of security vanishes; *Giulio never stopped loving you.*

How many lies has Giulio told me? Was this the first?

Who got rid of the body for him?

We should have gone to the police and pleaded self-defense!

Giulio falls into the seat beside me. His scent has me sinking further into the couch and crossing my arms and legs. Slonne is on his left and Oscar is on my right.

Charlie Chaplin's 'One A.M.' begins playing. It's a black and white short film from 1916. A silent film with antic sated music. It's been one of my favorite comedic malarkeys since I was their age and I've watched it regularly with Oscar and Slonne in these past few months to add some laughter to our home. There's pure joy in introducing the twins to classic short films and movies I loved. Their riotous laugher always has me smiling.

Halfway through the slapstick comedy, Giulio's arm slides behind my backrest on the couch. An involuntary habitual action that has him retreat less than a second later. I feel his hot gaze burn through my side. I want to concentrate on the television, on the warmth my twins give the room, on how today I finally did something for myself which resulted in a new beginning, but Giulio derails me.

We play a game of cat and mouse. He turns to the movie when I look at him and he looks at me when I look away. *I see how it is.* I find this a better moment than ever with the music acting like a buffer to maintain discretion from the twins noticing.

I lean forward, my lips brushing against his ear. *"Cosa hai fatto con il corpo?"*

What did you do with the body?

When Giulio turns to me, our lips almost meet. *"Ho assunto qualcuno."*

I hired somebody.

Hired somebody? My eyes widen and I need to swallow roughly to douse the fire burning up my throat. It doesn't matter *who* he hired; how can we trust them to keep secret what we did and not turn on us or give the police a tip? We simply can't.

"Chi?"

Who?

"Non devi preoccuparti. É tutto fatto."

You don't need to worry. It's all done.

I turn back to the movie just as the twins burst out into uncontrollable laugher. *I don't need to worry.* Is he serious? What is *all done* supposed to mean? How can he be sure the person he hired won't rat us out? *Is the dead man in some river or did they...*

I feel even more sick than when I lay awake all night at the thought.

"Who was the guy? The one you...*got*," I whisper.

Giulio inches closer to me, his lips meeting my ear this time. It's such a soft whisper that I don't anticipate biting my lip. "The man who attacked me that night by the circuit breaker box. It was him. Scar and all. What did you do with the clothes?"

His response has me spellbound.

"He could have told us so much. He said that we wouldn't be able to stop what is happening *soon* without him. We could've been one step closer to finding Addilyn. We can't even go to the police now! Not now that others are involved. Why would you hire somebody?"

"The clothes?"

"I burned them."

His hot breath hits the back of my neck when he sighs in relief. "Perfect."

Perfect? Nothing about our situation is those two syllables. Not even close!

"I don't know who you are anymore."

"I am the same man, only now you know the truth."

"That's what hurts the most, you lied about it the whole time. Then when he..." I shift closer to Giulio's fresh cologne, desperate for the twins not to catch on. "When he began speaking again about danger coming you finished the job when we could have gone to the police! I get it was self-defense. I do. But killing him when we saw that he wasn't dead...that's murder!"

"That's why I've changed my mind."

My heart sinks. "On what?"

"On everything."

We pull back and I stare at his clenched jaw, left to decide what exactly he means. I can't press him for information, so I turn back to the silent film. Giulio and I remain motionless, frozen in time as laughter rumbles from both sides of us like two lethal rising tides that swallow us whole.

Giulio is right about one thing.

Everything's changed…

For the worst.

CHAPTER TWENTY-THREE

Valencia

I WAKE UP DISORIENTED TO MY BEDROOM DOOR BEING BUSTED WIDE open. I make out a frenzied shadow rush towards me and all of a sudden brightness fills the room. *What is going on?*

My sensitive eyes blink away the light until my vision eases to complete confusion at the sight in front of me.

He is right here.

Giulio hovers over my bedside with worry written all over his face. His eyes are wide, giving the illusion of the illusive gray deepening and the powder blue concoction dissolving.

My first thought is the twins.

"Valencia." His raspy voice is urgent. "Is everything alright? Are you okay?"

"Yes…what time is it? Has something happened to Oscar or Slonne?"

"It's 4 A.M. The twins are perfect, but are you okay? What's going on? Is the person still here?"

What person? I don't get it….

What does Giulio mean by *here*?

"It's okay," His head swings towards my door. "*Oh*, out there?"

I take hold of his wrist before he can make the move, my fingers brushing against the pink beaded bracelet he's still wearing. The one I am too. "What are you talking about?"

"You messaged me saying you needed help and that somebody is here. Are they out there?"

I take in Giulio as a whole. His short, dark stubble which trickles down to his neckline. Those untied charcoal sweatpants. Looking closer I notice his white t-shirt that fits him so perfectly is inside out and my breath stutters. He must have dashed here thinking the worst…*but there's a problem.*

"What do you mean a message? I didn't send you anything."

"You sent me a text not too long ago. Here…" He pulls out his phone and shows me.

He's right.

According to his phone, I sent him a text a 3:45 A.M. stating I needed help because somebody was here. But that doesn't add up. *It doesn't make sense.*

I sit up and the sheets lower as a result when I reach over for my own phone. "I couldn't have sent that. I was fast asleep." I show him my phone and just as I said, there's no sent message on my end.

What the hell is happening?

"This doesn't make sense."

"I thought somebody had come in and injured…" The words fall silent as Giulio begins pacing with hands rubbing over his face. "Oh my god. I can't believe this. What's going on?"

It hurts.

It hurts to see him *here.*

It hurts to see him *like this.*

The truth of the matter is I have nothing to say except that somebody must have hacked one or both of our phones. But how? Why? *And most importantly who?*

A mix of agitation and defeat takes over Giulio's expression. He's at a total loss and it shows, partly because I feel the same knowing he thought somebody was here hurting me.

This isn't easy on any of us.

"I'll go, seeing everything is okay."

I cannot take his departure lightly. I cannot take the coldness. This break up has me testing my every single word and movement, like my choice to follow him out. We pause by the front door where his spare key is inserted. My nipples respond to the chilled air outside, poking through the silk fabric of my pajama shirt as my arms cross over my chest.

The pitch black sky is accompanied by a full moon and several hopeful stars.

Ours are out there somewhere.

Giulio's gaze locks on my left hand and mine falls there too when I realize what it represents. I swallow hard, so loudly that I swear he hears and is bound to witness my heart protrude out of my chest any minute now.

The tension between us is thick. It opens new wounds I've been attempting to compress ever since Thursday night. It's the early hours of Monday morning now and the abrasion to our love is bleeding. Giulio takes my hand in his with an aching sigh, and his thumb brushes over the patch of skin my wedding ring used to be.

How do you respond to this?

What do I say when my heart has been taken away by murder?

There are too many questions. Too many thoughts. The intruder was the man who attacked Giulio and so Seattle Police are on the case. What if somebody heard the gunshots? What if whoever Giulio hired didn't cover up everything? What if the countdown of *soon* is in response to Addilyn?

I recoil in a pit of lethal illusions the second Giulio looks at me, his pupils glimmering in the moonlight. His voice is soft and still affects me. "Telling you my father committed suicide was the only lie I've ever told you. I wish there was a way to take back what I did. To take away all the pain. I didn't mean to hurt you. I didn't mean for it to go this far. There are a million things I want to say to you because I know an apology isn't going to fix this. I'm not that man. I'm not a gangster. I know you're scared and you have a right to be…this is all my fault, Valencia."

"I'm not angry at you. I'm angry at myself because I knew something would happen to jeopardize us but I let myself love you all over again anyway."

Giulio's lips meet my ring finger and I snap my eyes shut at the long kiss.

No. No there is no coming back.

"Goodnight, Valencia."

"Goodnight."

I think it's safe to open my eyes after counting to five, but it's not. His regretful features linger until I step back. "How can I make this right? Please. I will do anything."

I miss him.

Strong. Be strong.

"Goodnight, Giulio."

He nods in defeat. As Giulio turns towards my driveway, his entire body freezes. His perfect jaw drops and that leaves my mouth gaping at the sight before us.

"My car…my car! It's not here…the twins…OH MY GOD!"

My heart aches for something I already know the answer to. "Giulio, please do not tell me that you brought the kids with you…" His lack of response kills me. Somebody stole his Porsche with Oscar and Slonne inside. *No. Please, no. I can't go through this again! Please, God. No!* Nothing can brace me for the eeriness that takes over once the distressed scream escapes me, one I cannot control as my body begins to tremble. "Why would you leave them in there? Why didn't you bring them inside?"

Giulio tugs at the ends of his hair, cursing along with every breath. "I thought something happened to you and I didn't want to risk it. They were asleep and I didn't want to wake them. I thought it would be okay for a split moment."

"Giulio!"

"I didn't think somebody would...*Fuck!*"

"Oh my god, I cannot believe this! This isn't real! It can't be!"

There's no luck for us as our feet slap against the asphalt driveaway and continue looking around our street in panic for any evidence of our twins or the car. We break in front of each other, tears accompanying our every heartbeat. This is our worst nightmare come to life again.

This can't be happening for the second time in my life.

Somebody stole our children.

All three.

I'm the one to make the 911 call on Giulio's phone. After explaining everything, the female operator ensures us that police will be here shortly.

We head back inside the house to the kitchen after our search leads us nowhere. From all the commotion between us, Helena comes out of her room clutching the center of her dusty pink robe. "Guys! What on earth is going on?"

"Somebody stole his car with the twins asleep in it!"

"Tell me I didn't hear that right. Tell me." One look at our faces confirms it. She shakes her head, tears welling in her eyes. "How the hell did it happen?"

The weight of the agitation I feel is so crushing, that I'm glad Giulio takes over to explain.

"You left the engine running?" My sister screeches. "Why would you do that?"

"I was so worried something would happen to Valencia that I wasn't thinking clearly...I thought I could handle who was in here."

My words are out before I know it. "How? By shooting whoever you thought it was dead?"

His silence does nothing to console my emotions. I know he's the victim in this too, but I am so fired up. If only he didn't leave the keys in the car or nobody was out there to destroy us in the first place, we wouldn't be turning on each other like we are.

"You should have stayed home and let me handle whatever was going on by myself. Slonne and Oscar would have still been with you! Everything would have been okay."

"I'm sorry I cared!"

I fall silent, unable to comprehend such a punctured hole in my chest. *I cared.* I blame myself. I don't want to blame him also, but within this moment I physically have nobody else to pin it on. Giulio should have known leaving the kids in his luxury car alone in the dark was the worst possible idea.

"Did you bring it, huh? The gun? Were you going to shoot this guy too?"

"I disposed of it."

"Were you going to call whoever you hired to dispose of the body too?"

"Valencia…" my sister says.

"No!" My finger is trembling when I point at him. "For the last few days I have been trying like crazy to come up with a way to justify your actions, but it is too much for me to take in."

"I'm hurting for what I did, just as much as you are. But I did what I had to do to protect our family. That's what parents do and that is what we are. *Parents.* You and I. Together. United in this. So continue blaming me for this."

A pulling sensation overtakes me. It fights against me, desperate to take a hold of my entire person. It drags me to my knees and I clutch my chest to ease the pain.

Slonne and Oscar are gone.

Addilyn is gone.

Gone.

The unknown, the fighting, the continuous consequences… it's all ruining me.

Helena crouches down beside me, rubbing circles on my back in a desperate bid to calm my shaking body. I have always hated the eeriness of the early morning. Now I know why.

"My father was right. All I am is weak." Giulio's defeated tone rises from the disturbing silence. "His death protected my life. He hated me for being my mother's son and proved it with years of tormenting me by hitting me and taunting me with cigarette lighter burns. They were never enough to create scars, but enough to scare me as a child. I *am* weak…After all, all I'm ever good for is ruining everything. I am the curse that runs deep within this family of ours. Maybe it should have been me that died that night with my father. Maybe I shouldn't have stopped him when he had the trigger to my head."

"Please don't say that."

I mean it.

I don't want these thoughts in his head.

I don't want these thoughts in *anybody's* head.

Giulio sits on a kitchen bar stool. One foot rests on the rail, the other long leg is outstretched towards me. I unravel his anguished expression. It only intensifies the pain of losing the twins.

"It's true." His mouth quivers. "I would have never had a track record. I would have never met you. I would have never married you. Our children wouldn't exist. We wouldn't be eating each other alive because of all the pain. Addilyn wouldn't have been abducted. Oscar and Slonne wouldn't have been stolen. I wouldn't be your husband and maybe that is a good thing."

I don't like the rawness of Giulio's words. They are harsh and precise. Sharp enough to puncture the remaining piece of my heart. The piece that is specifically still for him, even on a night like tonight.

Helena holds onto me tighter, reminding me her quietness is comforting enough.

"You would have met somebody else," Giulio continues with a low, strenuous voice. "Somebody who doesn't have any lies attached. Somebody who isn't so fucked up that he can't keep his marriage together. Somebody who you can have children with without the fear of losing them. He would have told you all the right things, and made you smile every single day. Because in the end, I failed as a husband. I failed as a man. I failed as your best friend. All I ever wanted was to live the rest of my life *with* and *for* you. I wanted to make you happy, but *look at us*, look at what we have become. What happened to *us*? Fuck. You deserve a man better than me, but just know that through it all, I never once regretted the way I feel about you. Alongside our children, I will never love somebody the way I love you. I will forever be sorry for everything I've done. I'm sorry my actions have caused our marriage to fade. I'm sorry it took me so long to support you with hope for Addilyn and that my stupidity caused us to lose our three beautiful children. I'm sorry I turned out to be the weak man my father always told me I was."

Police sirens ring in the distance. They're close but not close enough to blur the resounding alarm in my head. My heart has never hurt this deep. I have never felt this lost in my life.

I have never wanted him more.

Giulio steps outside and my sister smiles sadly before I rush out behind him.

I never wanted this to happen.

I need to fix this.

I need him to know that everything he said is untrue before it's too late.

The sirens intensify as Giulio sits on a porch step, head in hands with shaking shoulders. I don't have to see his face to know he's sobbing. His attempts to conceal it fail.

This is real life.

Right here.

With him.

The pain in my chest deepens when I gather myself and take a seat in the space beside him. My arms wrap around his torso and I hold him tightly to me. Giulio's attempt to refuse my closeness by veering away doesn't go unnoticed. "No. Please, don't. Not when I'm like this, Valencia."

I ignore his masculine resistance and listen to his broken, pained voice instead. I continue to embrace him, and this time he wraps his arms around me as well. We take refuge in each other.

I am still confused about how I feel, but we're miserable apart and so I concentrate on that for now.

"It's *okay*, Giulio. You don't need to hide from me. You never need to hide from me."

His body goes limp against mine.

He allows me to hold him.

To touch him.

To be the strong one.

I hold him closer and one hand slides to the back of his head. My fingers weave through his smooth hair and I kiss it. It proves to be all he needs because he holds my waist, gives in to me, and nuzzles his head in my neck with tears rolling from his eyes to my skin.

"I have been unfair to you. I want you to know that none of this is your fault," I whisper, swallowing the fire bellowing at the back of my throat. "I want you to know that you *matter*. You count. You are not weak. You are not a curse."

"But I failed you, Lencia. I failed every single thing."

"No, you didn't. None of this is your fault and I'm sorry for blaming you. Yes, it was simpler for us once, but that's life. That's marriage. This is us perfecting our epilogue and we're giving it our all. We'll get through this because we always do. We'll find our kids. You are their father. They are half of you. But..." I breathe in an extra breath. "You are all of me."

Giulio pulls me closer. *Even more desperately.*

Tears overtake me at the thought of losing him. I don't know what this means for us; if it's the beginning or the end, but what I do know is that my healing through all of this has always been my family. Giulio and I have been fighting for the solution when it's been right in front of us this entire time. Although I'm still shaken by what he did, I shouldn't turn on him in tough times.

I'm learning to be *me* again.

I'm learning to ease my depression.

I'm learning to be strong and strength means never backing down from what you truly love, especially in times of hysteria, especially from those thorns.

The sirens are blaring. The police must be at the end of the street. I only have a brief moment before they arrive.

"I never want you to ever talk about death like that again. *Ever*. Your father was a toxic man and was wrong. You turned your life around. You are a fighter, Giulio Giannotti, and I will not allow you to stand down now. I share your last name and that makes me proud. *You* make me proud. So don't give up, especially because of me. Never because of me. Without you, clients would never live the lives they deserve. Without you, this world would be a whole lot emptier." I smile because the words run straight to my heart and put back all the strings in jumbled places. *But at least they're back.* The order of each chamber can wait. "Giulio, without you my heart would not beat the same. The world needs you in it. *I* need you in it. What has happened to us is unimaginable and it will take me time to understand what is best for us now, but there's nobody else I would want to go through this with but you and that's why you matter."

Passion blooms in his gaze, alongside that small smile in the midst of this fury. "Thank you. Those words bring me strength. I will give you all the time in the world. I promise, Lencia."

Thank you for making me believe, Giulio.

I will never abandon him because that would only mean abandoning myself *and* our children. I haven't come this far to crash and burn. I need Giulio just as much as he needs me. But I need to sort out my head first. I need to comprehend how witnessing a life end in front of me really makes me feel.

All the words I spoke were bound in truth. I want him to know it all. I'm his only family this very minute and I desperately need him to know just how important he is to me. By the pained smile on his face, I know he understands.

Giulio has always been there for me. He's supported me. Rallied me on. Gave me a job. Helped during my panic attacks. Defended me. Lifted me up. Made me believe that I, Valencia Giannotti, will get through any inferno because I am capable of rising out of the embers.

Flashing red and blue lights blind me. Two police cars park

in front of the house and cut the sirens. I hear Helena's steps behind us.

I have to face this all by myself, but I'll continue holding on. The enemy will not beat us. The abductors of my children will come to light. They'll never win. *No.* Not anymore.

Game on.

Giulio and I share one final embrace before I give over my tattered soul to the investigation. I'm committed to face it all. The hurt. The pain. The fear. The glory.

We need our three angels. I'm not backing down without a fight.

As the officers near, I take one long glance at Giulio. I take in his sunken eyes and pursed lips. His beaten body and his glistering tears. His inner demons and the exposed lie. Yet, all I see are his beautiful silver linings. His love. His hopes. His ruthless sacrifices for his family.

With all his vulnerabilities and our passionate reckoning unveiled, it dawns on me that our story isn't over. I still want this. *I still love him.* In fact, I don't think I will ever be capable of not loving Giulio Giannotti.

The hunt is on.

Officers. Volunteers. Search parties. Media coverage. Helicopters hovering in the skies. Once again our family has been thrown into the deep end. Oscar and Slonne used to be my lifeline and now they've been stripped from me. SPD made it clear that what happened in the early hours of yesterday morning could be one of two things. One, a random carjacking and the perpetrators didn't notice the children. Or two, another vendetta trap in line with Addilyn's disappearance. Deep down I know it's the latter. There has to be a connection.

The tragedy binds us all together.

Kayla and Lance came to see us the moment they heard the news. It surprised me when Marcus and Bryce also joined us on day one of the search yesterday. *Well, mostly surprised about Marcus.* They encouraged us and when my brother-in-law saw me, he pulled me into a hug and apologized for acting the way he did. He even went as far as to clear the air with Helena. Tension will always remain there, but at least now it's simmered.

Somebody else that I didn't expect to hear from was *Zoe.* She had heard on the news while driving Samuel to school and somehow found my number to extend her best wishes, alongside an apology. After Giulio laid out our situation straight, Samuel and Slonne remain friends, but she isn't disturbed with unwelcome kisses anymore. Zoe admitted that she crossed the line and after more moms at the school began avoiding her, she apparently went through some inner soul searching. *And who was I to complain?* I've learned some people do deserve second chances; I mean, I never expected to be friends with a sarcastic Englishman, but life works in strange concepts. So when Zoe mentioned that once this is over she wants to have coffee and start from zero as a peace offering, I decided to give our relationship a second chance.

Naturally, none of us attended work on Monday or today. Giulio made it clear that until Oscar and Slonne are returned to us, Notti Designs will have to run without us. As much as emotion paralyzes me, the entire two days I haven't shed a tear. Not because this doesn't affect me but because I'd been too worked up with dismay and exhaustion over constantly being faced with such trauma.

Experiencing this for the second time has destroyed me, but it won't kill me; that's what *they* would want. Whoever is behind this wants us to suffer. *I'm not going to allow that to happen.*

Once again, the search today is called off just after 7 P.M. These thirty-seven hours without Oscar and Slonne have been hell, but Helena and I return home to hope with a vegetable casserole made by our mother. Given everything going on, Helena thought it would be safer for Weston and Daisy to stay with their grandma in Belltown for the rest of the week while my father's still in Austria. I couldn't agree more.

Helena and I talk of every single possible outcome over dinner together. Not *if* but *when* the twins will be found safe. I take my anti-depressants after the meal because in the commotion of these past two mornings, I've forgotten.

When Helena retreats to bed, I stay in the living room. My mind doesn't stop ticking. When I'm not thinking of the twins, I'm thinking of Addilyn, and then Giulio. I try to understand why he shot those final shots. Every time the feeling becomes overwhelming, I take a sip of my ginger tea.

When midnight strikes I know I should get a couple of hours of sleep because if I'm not energized in the morning it'll be impossible to continue the search.

My phone vibrates to a message from an unknown number.

Unknown: Oscar and Slonne Giannotti.

My fingers slap against the screen.

Valencia: Who is this?

Unknown: Come outside and the twins are yours.

What?

If I wasn't on edge before, I certainly am now. I rush to switch off all the lights and peer through the living room window. My breath staggers at a man leaning against a silver car, a cigarette in one hand, and a phone in the other. My mind jogs back to six weeks ago when I first saw this man across the street. It seems like the same car and it's no irony that it would be the same guy too.

Oh my...

My first instinct is to call 911 but then another text appears.

Unknown: You're afraid. You should be.

Attached is a picture of Slonne and Oscar with tape across

their mouths. The terror on their faces says it all. *My babies…he has my babies…*

I almost drop my phone to the floor…*almost.*

Valencia: Who are you?

Unknown: Come to the car, do what I ask and the twins are yours.

Valencia: You haven't answered my question.

Unknown: And your husband killed one of ours. Hurry up, Valencia.

He knows.

I back away from the window and don't think twice. I'm out the door with a clenched jaw and have no idea if this could escalate, but this is for my children and I will do anything for them. I'm still in my Levi's and dark top from the search this morning. Thoughts of a shower and a change of clothes evaporate as I approach the man.

He looks me up and down as I slide my phone into my back pocket.

The man's smug smirk grows when he takes one long drag and crushes the death stick underneath his shoe. "Ah, well if it isn't *the* Mrs. Giannotti."

"Where are they?"

"Ease down. We've got all night."

"No, we don't. I want to know where my children are and I want you to return them to me, *now.*"

I analyze the unfamiliar man's every detail. I'll need it if I ever have to describe him to the police. Dark blond buzz cut. Light, fair features. Lethal blue eyes. Dark garments. The car is a gray Mercedes and I memorize the license number as inconspicuously as possible.

Blue Eyes scoffs and scans my body one final time, slowing

at my legs before nodding behind him. "Get in the car. I have something interesting to show you."

"That photo you sent…I'm not going anywhere until you confirm they're still alive."

"Get in the fucking car."

"No."

Blue Eyes launches forward and grips my forearm. "Now, I am going to say this once and only once. You don't step inside the car and your husband dies. I have him, Mrs. Giannotti."

"What? Giulio?"

"Yes. I tracked him down and let's just say…you're not the only one who wants your children back. So, this is what you're going to do. You're going to get in the car, I'm going to show you your *beloved* husband, and then we'll go from there."

He doesn't give me any choice, and soon I'm strapped inside the car before he takes off at high speed. My heart is racing. *Does he really have Giulio? Are Oscar and Slonne okay? Jesus, I should have told Helena. I should have called 911 when I had the chance.*

Shit. Shit. Shit

Blue Eyes comes to a stop in a dead-end alleyway.

Nightfall has taken over and darkness blankets us as he drags me out of the car and shoves me towards the last building before a tall brick wall. We take a left and resistance overcomes me as a steel circular staircase leads to a metal door.

Blue Eyes unlocks the door with a key and instantly I'm hit with a distinct metallic smell. My gaze remains on the door-handle, even after he threatens me to step inside. By the third time he grips my chin and snarls coldly, "Step the fuck in or there will be consequences."

I grind my jaw, hiding the fear behind my disgust. "I hope you rot in hell."

I venture into the dark walled room. There are no windows or rooms beyond these four walls. Bile rises to my throat as my flats slam against the concrete floor as I hurry to the other side of the room.

Giulio is bound to a chair with rope restraining his chest,

ankles, and his hands are tied behind his back. He raises his head towards me and I see the bloodied cuts on his face. A mix of metallic from the blood and his masculine cologne welcomes me. He's been slashed twice by his cheekbone and the blood pools. My entire body heaves as I look around for something, *anything*, but there's nothing and so I scrunch up my long sleeve shirt and dab away at the crimson.

When I cup his jaw, I'm careful to miss his wounds. "You're okay, I'm going to get you out of here, alright? Everything will be okay."

Giulio seems disorientated at first, before that familiar warmth blends in his eyes and he smiles softly through the torment.

"Don't speak too fast." The door slams shut and coldness seeps straight through my bones. It's a confined space and the way Blue Eyes grips my neck from behind to make me stand and turn around makes it tinier. "I pulled the same stunt on him that I pulled on you. What? Thought your kids were here? You think a mere photo is enough to make a deal?"

"I'll do anything, just please don't hurt him or them. What do I have to do?"

"A very simple thing." Blue Eyes responds to my urgency with a sinful chuckle. "I'll lead you to the twins but you need to do something for me first."

"What is it?"

"I'm a very sentimental man and so when individuals *interfere* with my process, I feel it right *here*." His gaze lowers and finger brushes against my breasts, landing at my heart. "Your husband killed one of my men. Even if I didn't see it, I know he did. So there is only one way to go about it. Once it's done, then Oscar and Slonne are yours."

"No! Please, don't kill him!"

"Don't worry. I'm not going to kill Giulio Giannotti...*you* are."

I have no air. It's cut. Nothing travels to my lungs. My head shakes over and over. Tears spill over as I step away from him.

Giulio doesn't say a word. When I turn to him and find he's staring down at the concrete floor, it's as if fate has already claimed him.

"No. No, I'm not doing that."

"You will." Blue Eyes pulls a gun from the back of his waistband. "This is how it's gonna be. These are soundproof walls. Kill Giulio and your children will be returned to you. If you don't pull the trigger, I will kill you first, then him, and then…I will destroy your children one by one."

"You can't do this!"

"Oh yes I can, sweetheart. Don't waste all your impeccable beauty in a morgue."

The weight of the gun is heavier than I expected when it's placed in my hands. Blue Eyes grips my shoulders, turns me to face Giulio, and directs me on how to hold the weapon properly. My hands are shaking. Everything turns black and white. I look at Giulio and all I see is my life.

I don't want to do this.

I cannot do this.

Tears blur my vision when Blue Eyes retreats, I wipe away the wetness and take in Giulio. The man cocks another gun and aims it at me. "I'm going to count to twenty. By the end of that, you take off the safety and you pull the trigger. Fail to do so, and my first bullet goes straight into you. I'll let him watch you take your last breath and be helpless to save you. Understand?"

"How do I know you will actually give back my children?"

"Well, that's a little game called trust." He smiles wickedly. "*Twenty.*"

My heart explodes.

NO. NO. NO.

How can I get out of this? How can I get out of it?

Giulio swallows, his gaze pooled with agony. "It's okay, Lencia. It's okay."

"No. I can't. I won't do it."

"It's okay, Lencia. You will get the kids back. It's three lives against one. If this is the way it needs to go, then it's almost perfect. I'll be alright. I promise I'll be alright."

The knot in my throat swells. I'm burning.

Tears cascade down, dripping to my neck. I cannot feel my heart beating. It's numb. Just like the rest of me. "I can't do this, Giulio."

"*Sixteen.*"

"Darling, look at me." His voice is so soft and calm, as if he isn't in a life or death situation. When I do, Giulio manages to smile through his tear-stained cheeks. An angel amongst this hell. It warms me but doesn't settle my uneasy breaths. "You need Addilyn, yes?"

I nod.

"Do you need Slonne?"

Nod.

"*Fourteen.*"

"Do you need Oscar?"

Another nod.

"Then this is the only way out. I'll be okay."

"But I need you too. I need you with me."

"I will be with you, baby. Just in another way."

"No. I need you to hold me. I need you to hold our kids. You can't do that if you're…" My voice breaks and I cannot get the word out.

Giulio looks down at his lap but it's not enough to conceal the pain on his face he so desperately wants to keep in. It's true. *I need him.* This cannot be the last time I see him. I refuse. I refuse to let it end here. To let go of a feeling so strong. To really lose him without the choice or chance of repairing our marriage because we would be in another world.

"*Nine,*" Blue Eyes snarls. "Click off the safety."

Oh my god.

"*Eight.* Click off the safety. DO IT!"

I do as I'm told.

I will never forgive myself if I do this. Our children will have to live with this. There needs to be another way. There needs to be. There always is.

"I'm so sorry, Lencia. I'm sorry for everything I have done. I didn't mean to ruin us and I hope you can forgive me. I hope you can understand that all I ever wanted was to make you happy and protect our family. That's all I ever wanted."

"*Four.*"

"You do make me happy. I'm so sorry too. I want you. I want you, Giulio."

"*Three.*"

"I want you too, baby. Show Addilyn the stars. I'll be there."

"Giulio, I—"

The man cuts me off. "*Two.*"

"I can't do it."

"Yes, you can. You need to do it." Giulio nods bravely. "You're my air. You always will be, even *after*. Tell our children that I will always love them. Always. Okay?"

"*One.*"

"Okay." My heart aches. There is nothing but passionate love burning in his eyes and mine mirror the same. *This is the love of my life. The only man I want. This cannot be the end.*

"Zero." Blue Eyes snaps his fingers. "Do it. Pull the trigger."

I can't.

"SHOOT HIM!"

My finger brushes against the trigger.

"DO IT!"

"I love you." Giulio holds his breath and now fear is all I see in him. "It doesn't matter where I am. I'm yours, Lencia."

"I love you too."

This is not the end.

"DO IT!"

No.

"PULL THE TRIGGER! DO IT!"

It can't be...

"SHOOT HIM! DO IT! DO IT NOW!"

I jerk the gun to the left, aim, and pull the trigger.

Blue Eyes drops his gun as he falls to his knees and clutches his chest. Dark crimson pours through his garments and without thinking I shoot two more rounds. He stumbles back and falls to the ground with a heavy thud, his head cracking against the concrete with a reverberating echo.

Dead. Lifeless. Gone.

Oh my dear god.

I let go of the hot silver gun and rush up to the love of my life.

Our victory kiss is hard and fueled with the awareness that we're both still alive. *We made it.* The adrenaline continues to pump through me even with his comforting presence and I pull away in tears. "I love you. I love you so much, Giulio."

"I love you more, Lencia."

"He's dead. He won't hurt us anymore."

Tonight, I have saved a man and killed another, all within the same minute.

Giulio leans our foreheads together. "We'll get out of this mess. Everything will be okay. It needed to be done. We've both made scarifies to save our family now and we can't go down for them. We need to be *here* for our children."

"This has to stay between us."

I am a killer.

Pulling that trigger wasn't right but it was the only solution. As I help Giulio out of his restraints, I realize that I am no different than him. In fact, I am exactly like him. Only now do I truly understand why Giulio did what he did. Killing in self-defense makes sense. It's clearer what must have gone through Giulio's mind when he killed his father and the intruder. It must have been the same thing that ran through my head seconds before I shot again…*protecting the ones we love at all costs.*

This is a part of the 'whatever it takes.'

I saw the father of my children, the man I love, and everything that I am…and I reacted.

Now, both Giulio and I have gambled with the fate of our children to save each other. This isn't the point where I give up. This is the point where I continue running to the finish line. Because I know that even if I have lost everything tonight, I have gained Giulio.

He is mine again.

We've been shattered by the outside world and turned on ourselves when we should have sought healing in each other's arms instead.

When Giulio's free, we share a tight embrace. The one that was supposed to be goodbye turns into one that says, *I love you. I need you. I am sorry. I want this. I never want to let go.* It's everything at once and is the perfect symbol of *us* and just how far we are willing to go to keep our family safe.

"You saved me. *Thank you.*"

"We saved each other, Giulio. I understand why you did it now because I know why I did it. I don't regret it. I can never regret it with you. I'm sorry I blamed you. I'm so sorry I walked away from us when you needed me the most. I never will again. Not after this. Never after this."

Giulio kisses me slowly and it's all I need to know that I made the right decision. It feels like thunder's pulsing through my veins when he looks down at me and smiles. "Lencia, I don't care how hard life gets, I still want you. Over and over again I will still choose you. I will still choose our beautiful children. I still want to experience the world with the woman I married. The woman I love. That woman is you. Valencia Giannotti, thank you for giving me life."

And I would do it all over again in a heartbeat.

CHAPTER TWENTY-FOUR

Giulio

THIS HAS BEEN A NIGHT I WILL NEVER FORGET.

Tonight reaffirms that when it comes down to the wire, our marriage can withstand any lethal threat. Our separation has taught me love on another level. It has taught me how to resolve any tempest coming our way. That love truly does conquer all. That home can have a heartbeat. That healing can be found standing by somebody.

My somebody is and always will be Valencia.

Stepping out of that alleyway, we are stronger than ever. Sandro does his job efficiently. His men clean up, takes the car, and of course, the dead fucker too. Sandro drives us home discreetly and doesn't make me pay. He says we've endured enough pain and we say farewell with a solidifying handshake.

Valencia doesn't ask many questions and I take that as her way of telling me that what will be tonight will be. That soon the moon will fade and the sun will rise to a new reaffirmed hope and a strengthened bond. One that is unbreakable. *Unapologetic.*

When we arrive at our house in Madrona, Valencia disinfects my wounds and then we attend to our clothes. As she takes a shower, I discard our garments in the backyard fire pit and watch as they burn. The orange embers glow wildly until the only thing that remains is ash with a tattered story nobody else but my wife and I will ever know.

Sandro won't say a word. He's a respected and reliable contact. I trust him.

There's a tugging tension in my chest when I step back inside. A gloom. Our marriage is restored but it's not over for us. Our children are gone, *all three of them,* and that makes me feel helpless. I'm a meticulous man and all I want are my girls and my special buddy safe.

I miss them so much.

When the man Valencia killed presented himself on my doorstep I was ready to call the police until he mentioned the intruder I killed and showed a photo of the twins as evidence. I was on a conference call with Lance, Marcus, and my client, Tate, when it happened. *And damn how I was lucky to have tapped the mute button prior to answering the door.* I believed the man and was willing to take the chance to save them… I never expected to almost die doing so.

I share my somberness with Lencia when stepping into the shower behind her. My hands wrap around her waist and I hold her through the tears. It reminds me of the night she was with Bryce at the bar.

I'm in awe of Valencia. She has been so strong throughout all of this and tonight was the epitome of her dedication. The same one I shared with her. Tied down to that chair, I was willing to risk it all and sacrifice myself for the greater good, so at least she could have our children. But right now, as I hold her, I'm glad I'm still breathing. I never want to stop feeling my adoration for our family. I never want to stop living in a life with them.

"We'll get through this together. It's what we were born to do."

"I know we will. I just miss them so much. This will be our secret. Helena knows about the intruder and your father, but she won't tell anybody. Can I...ask you something?"

I kiss her neck and nuzzle my nose into her hair. It smells of my fresh, woody shower gel with a tinge of her own scent of vanilla. I love the way she's cut her hair. It only barely touches her shoulders and makes me think it's like a new beginning. "Of course, darling."

There is a brief pause until I twirl Valencia around. Warm water licks our skin as I hold her closer. Those gorgeous hazel eyes stare up at me and amongst the havoc, I find courage in them. "When you killed your father and the intruder...how did you feel after?"

"For a few moments, I was in shock and then I felt...liberated in some sense and heavier in another. But with my father, it soon faded. You need to forgive yourself to find closure. The man you killed deserved it, darling. He would have killed us both and then gone on to kill others. Sometimes we resort to desperate measures because we *need* to. We just need to continue to be strong, even after we have our three musketeers back. Can you do that for me, baby?"

"Yes. A million times over."

Yes.

I'm amazed by her resilience. Her bravery. Her devotion.

I cup her face and kiss her passionately against the shower wall. It's foggy when I pull her away from it and note the most impeccable silhouette of her body. When I smile at Lencia, my eyes stray from the fire in her eyes to her natural curves, those beautiful breasts, and killer legs that step even closer to me when my stare lingers.

Holy fuck, I'm spending the rest of my life with this woman!

Her wet hand eases down my abdomen and out of desperation I crush my mouth to her full lips once again. I love her. I love her so fucking much. Valencia Marie Giannotti is my air, my home, my everything. She amplifies the idyllic feeling of being alive over and over again for me—*until I believe it will never end.*

"We're going to be okay. We're going to make it out of this hell."

"Lencia…even through this hell, we still found our life. Heaven is a place I go when I'm with you and I never want to stop visiting."

"Then don't stop."

"I won't."

I catch her smirk and take the moment to take her all in for the millionth time tonight. I could look at her for a single second and find a billion things I love about her. I could continue looking for centuries upon centuries and still find those things.

"Please don't ever feel as though you are alone in this, Giulio. When the days get hard, we can talk about it. You're not alone in this. You never have been and never will be. I've got you."

My heart cannot stop flipping for all the right reasons. Valencia is happy and that is all I have ever wanted. However, there are three more things we need to make this complete. *That* and uncovering who is behind this.

In the middle of bathing, we make love against the shower glass. It's just after 3 A.M. when we enter the kitchen, just as Valencia's phone begins ringing. She hits speaker and our hands intertwine.

"Mrs. Giannotti?"

Sergeant Flynn.

"Speaking. Giulio is here too."

"I have developing news regarding the kidnapping of Oscar and Slonne. We have located the Porsche. It was torched just a few miles away from the scene, and unfortunately it's a write off. No bodies were located which gives us extreme optimism your children are alive. Witness statements are currently being taken. I do suspect this will soon escalate into a ransom... Mr. and Mrs. Giannotti, we're going to need you down at the precinct."

CHAPTER TWENTY-FIVE

Valencia

ONCE INSIDE THE POLICE DEPARTMENT, WE FOLLOW SERGEANT Flynn's orders and hand over our phones to be hooked up to a monitor so if a ransom call is made, the chances of identifying the caller will be significantly higher. The memory of the oak desks in the precinct reminds me of the night Addilyn went missing.

"What are you going to do about the car?" I ask Giulio who is pacing.

"Oh, it doesn't bother me. I just want our children to be okay."

"I al—"

I cut myself short at my blaring ringtone. *It's an unknown number.*

My mind begins spiraling. "Could this be it?"

Detective Brigs signals to Sergeant Flynn who gives me a nod towards the phone. "This very much could be. I would like you to answer. Do not sound nervous or give any indication you are with us. Everyone else is completely silent, okay?"

Giulio falls into the seat beside me as I answer with a sharp breath. "Hello?"

I tap the speaker button and set it on the table.

There is a soft crackling on the other line before a highly distorted voice speaks. "Valencia Giannotti, I have your children. I have them and I will kill them if you do not listen to what I say very carefully."

Panic in my voice cannot be defused. "*Please.* Please, don't hurt them!"

"Listen to what I say very carefully. Are you listening, Valencia?"

Sergeant Flynn gives a thumbs up. My eyes meet Giulio's helpless ones and he squeezes my hand tighter with a nod. *I can do this.* "Yes. I'm listening."

"Two-hundred-fifty-thousand dollars in cash and you will have your children back."

My heart falls to my feet. There's no way in hell we have *cash* like that laying around.

"Wait a minute. I can't..." Sergeant Flynn instructs me to continue talking. "I can't withdraw a sum like that in the early morning. I need to request it from my bank first."

"That is not *my* problem," the distorted voice hisses. "Two-hundred-fifty-thousand dollars or I start with the pretty girl first. Trust me, she will not be this pretty when I finish up. Is that understood?"

My baby. *My Slonne.*

With his free hand, Giulio covers his mouth in a tight grip. It restrains him from saying a word, even though it's evident something is threatening to slip out.

It's as if I've been thrown inside an inferno, forced to accept the consequences of a deal I'm sure we won't be able to complete. "Okay. Okay. I can give you the money. Two-hundred-fifty-thousand dollars in cash. Where do I meet you?"

The man states a Seattle address causing Sergeant Flynn to glance over at Detective Brigs. She points at something on her computer and he nods at whatever he sees.

"I want you to hand me the money, Valencia. Only you. I do not want anybody else to be there or to know you are coming here. Am I clear?"

"Yes."

"The moment I see somebody else, I will break every bone in your daughter's body and I will make your son watch his sister die a long and painful death. Is that understood?"

"Yes! I will have the money! That will not happen. It will just be me."

"For your own sake, it better be. You have thirty minutes or it's over for your family."

That's until 4 A.M.!

My voice wavers. "Okay, I'll have it. Just let me talk to my kids. Let me tell them—"

"Twenty-nine minutes now. *Alone*, Valencia."

"Please can—"

The line goes dead.

Shit.

I have never felt this kind of nervous determination in my entire life. If this were to have happened with Addilyn, I would have crumbled. This time around I want to scream in anguish at the person.

Giulio massages the tension away from my shoulders. "You did well, baby."

We wait in anticipation for anything the detective can give us. Detective Brigs collects something from the printer and when Sergeant Flynn's eyes find ours, they're promising. "I can confirm the location the person provided is legitimate. It is where the call was made. We tracked the number throughout the call and have pinned a man."

"Nick Conrad," Detective Brigs says, setting down the printed photograph. "A twenty-five-year-old male originally from Kent. He was arrested and jailed back in 2011 for accessory to murder. Following his release, it didn't take him long to venture into house invasions, battery, and assault."

Oh.

My.

God.

The man in the picture—*Nick Conrad*—is the man who attempted to attack Giulio by the electrical circuit breaker box, the same man who's sketch is plastered across the city—and who Giulio killed when he broke into the house. He's far younger in the image, but there is no mistaking it's *him*—scar and all.

It couldn't have been this man's distorted voice on the line. Somebody else must have his phone because this man is *dead*.

Giulio doesn't stiffen behind me, but the slower rubs on my shoulders are a stark indication that the same thing is going through his mind. Now is not the time to prolong the thought. *We need to act normal.*

Sergeant Flynn scratches his jaw as his eyes narrow down on the photograph. "We have the sketch on file and we'll have to identify him with AI tech, but this seems like the same man who attacked you. Isn't that so, Mr. Giannotti?"

"Yes, I'm certain that's the man. Please do your best to find him."

We both know there won't be any *finding him*. This man, Nick Conrad, is dead...because of us.

"Of course, Mr. Giannotti. And to confirm, you haven't seen or heard from this man since the attack, correct?"

Incorrect, we have.

"That's right, I haven't."

"Neither have I," I lie.

"Ok." Sergeant Flynn turns back to his team. "We'll have some officers escort Valencia to the location. Lin, ensure a top of the line hidden tracker is placed on Mrs. Giannotti prior to action. Joan and Brigs, search Conrad's house. Detail anything that relates to the case in the slightest. Valencia, how do you feel about this?"

"I can do it, I just don't have that type of money lying around."

"We need to move fast. The location is already a ten-minute drive from here. In this instance, I can see what we can do about the money. Given it's—"

"I have the money." Giulio's voice comes out as barely a whisper. His distraught face twists the moment he drops back into his seat. "I have safe money. All cash. I will cover it."

"Where exactly is this money, Mr. Giannotti?"

"Work." He recoils, pushing a desperate hand through his black hair and pulls at the tips. I wish the opposite would have come out of this mouth, but in this moment of truth, everything is on the line. *Every single thing.* "I don't like this. I don't like this at all."

———◈———

We're speeding to Notti Designs. As we cut through city street, my gaze averts from the car window to the time to the hidden tracker in the hair tie on my wrist, and then to the anxious Giulio sitting beside me in the backseat.

24 minutes.

My heart pounds to the rhythm of the countdown. It has me unable to feel my legs as Giulio and I sprint through his company building. We're vigorously punching security codes, switching off alarms, unlocking doors, and flicking on lights as we make our way to his private bathroom at lightning speed. Giulio stands on top of the vanity and reaches up towards the wood ceiling, presses on it, and a section of the plank wood lowers down.

"Here." Giulio hands me a single black duffel bag and jumps down.

"How much is in here?"

"A quarter of a million exactly, but we should recount it. There's another three other bags up there. Remember I did this last year? It's safe money in case anything happens with us or the company."

The memory comes back to me and I nod without any further questions. Giulio sorts out the money, working at a vigorous speed to count it twice over. I simply watch him, noting how his chiseled jaw remains clenched, activating the muscles in his cheeks, all while he divides his hard earned money for some lunatic who has taken our twins.

This isn't fair.

My love for him is burning bright. It has been ever since I shot that man dead tonight and saved Giulio. I need him in my life and recognize that sometimes we need to endure pain to continue living. I'm so in love with him. We can battle anything because he is my everything. My soulmate. My reason to simply *be*.

Giulio earns this money from being the successful businessman he is. I only hope this all goes to plan and the distorted voice on the other line stays true to their word.

We're running out of time but we'll still make it.

In the time frame of a few hours, everybody's life has been placed in my hands. This could all go horribly wrong or...*right.* *Yes, it will be alright.*

I'm mesmerized by Giulio's every feature. A flawed man stands in front of me...*I love him even more for it. Bryce is right about those thorns. I've accepted the thorns and why they need to be there because I have them too. I know Giulio accepts mine too.*

His tired eyes meet mine in the mirror. "Darling, why are you looking at me like that?"

"How am I looking at you?"

"Like this is the last time."

I swallow thickly and soundlessly take the hefty duffel from him. *Because it could be.*

We rush outside to Sergeant Flynn who leads me to a car that isn't a police vehicle and hands me the keys. Giulio stays by my lowered window, his forearms resting by the rim as his head pokes through.

The duffel sinks into the passenger seat.

17 minutes.

A male detective rushes beside Giulio. "You must ride with

us, Mr. Giannotti. We will be following at a distance. The less conspicuous we can make this, the better. Valencia, we will stand down for twenty minutes. If the operation is successful, we will meet back here or at the hospital if needed. However, if we suspect the operation is a bust we will storm the premises. Okay?"

"Perfect. Thank you."

"We have just under seventeen minutes. Let's go, Mr. Giannotti."

The look in Giulio's eyes is terrifying. This whole situation *is*, but we have to meet this deadline and stay strong for our twins. Whoever is doing this want us to crumble; instead we must rise.

"May I talk with her for a brief moment? Just one minute?"

"Make it fast. Then come to the closest car." The officer leaves.

"I don't know what they're going to do," I admit openly. "I don't know if the money is enough. Even if it is, we are still missing a child."

"Why are they doing this to us? Why are they fucking doing this?"

"I don't know." I don't want to see the pain in his face. It is too much. I need to preserve the tears. "But the one thing I know for sure is that I'm not afraid because there is no plan B."

"You're all I have. If they take you now, I'll have nothing. Absolutely nothing. I'll be a lost man. I...I can't lose you. I can't fucking lose you too."

"You're all I have too." Letting go of our intertwined hands, I pull him into a warm hug through the window. Our hearts beat wildly together. "But this has to be done. I'm yours, Giulio. You are not going to lose me."

There is no way out of this.

I have thought about the possibility that this could be a deadly mission, but the thought of reuniting with my children gives me all the hope and determination to continue fighting.

The male detective returns to us and announces our time is up. Giulio buys us another desperate minute and the detective steps back with a sigh.

"Lencia, *please*. We have to find another way to do this. We have to."

"What other choice do we have?"

"I just…I want to apologize again. I'm sorry for everything I've ever done. Every single thing. I really am. I'm sorry I lost you—"

"I forgive you, Giulio. And I hope you can forgive me too. I know how much you were hurting and I reacted upon my own fears to shut you out. I know you were scared to give us a second try. I was too. Now we know it's the only way to live. We're okay now. I lied too, we both did when we said it was over between us."

"You don't know how much that means to me. *Amore…*" We pull away and his thumb outlines my lips. "Please don't leave me alone. I'm so scared of losing you. It…it cannot happen…" Raw urgency laces his voice. "Not when we just fixed it all, Lencia."

We share a tender smile. *An uncertain one.*

Giulio is my life.

My rock.

"I love you, Giulio. I'm not going anywhere."

"I love you. I love you so much." And then we kiss and it's a bittersweet passionate type of perfect. It's so different from any other time. So unique because our circumstances are deteriorating. Up until this moment in our life, we have been fighting separate battles on the same team, now within this moment, we melt into one another.

We are one.

United.

Just like we should have always been.

I savor every last part of him. Just as quick as it started, the kiss ends, but it's all for the right reasons. *I need to get our children back.*

15 minutes.

"I will never stop loving you, Lencia. I will never leave you." He promises with a forehead kiss. "Please promise me the same—"

"You're with me. *Forever.*"

Giulio gives me one last glance.

It's a look that says it all…

Come back to me.

The car's GPS states the address provided in the ransom call is approximately ten minutes away. I need to get there in time.

I need to save my family.

⸎

My feet bolt across the muddied front garden of the unfamiliar house. Flowerpots are overturned and half of the wood panels on the exterior walls are missing, as if in the midst of a renovation. Windows have bullet holes and the entire atmosphere of the abandoned premises is cold and eerie.

The force of my knock has the front door creak open. Inside, complete darkness faces me.

"Hello?"

Nothing.

In the bleak distance, there's a streak of warm yellow light. It entices me to continue. The floorboards squeak under my loafers, stringing the silence within each step. It's there where I stop by what I assume is the basement door. There's a flashlight carefully placed against it and its flickers match my heartbeat.

I take a chance and hold the flashlight with my free hand. The duffel bag becomes heavier by the second. *Well, there is a quarter of a million in here!*

My thoughts of a basement is confirmed by the steep staircase beyond the door.

"Hello?" My question transforms into a petrified scream as a hand grips onto my right forearm.

"Continue walking," a deep male voice I don't recognize commands.

He urges me down the stairs with an abrupt nudge. It has me clutching the handrail to stabilize myself, but the flashlight tumbles down the stairs, its crash landing has the light vanish.

The door shuts to pitch black. I feel the man's hushed breaths behind me "Walk."

"I can't see the steps."

"I said walk!"

"I need a second to—"

"I SAID WALK!" The cool tip of a gun nuzzles into the back of my neck. "One at a time. That's it. Your children did a better job."

"Are they down here?"

"GO!" He pushes me aggressively and my head is the first thing to smack against the staircase. *Jesus.* My hands involuntarily respond by clutching it with a groan as I continue to fall until I eventually come to a stop. I need a moment to recollect myself on the concrete floor and search for the duffel bag I lost during the fall.

The staircase squeaks from behind me and a gun cocks in the distance. It could be that man's...*or somebody else is down here.* I can't see a damn thing and that concerns me more than the cunning chuckle echoing in the basement.

He's nearing.

"Who's going to save you now?"

"Myself." I grit and hold the duffel to my chest. "You deserve to burn in hell!"

"Now that isn't very nice."

My backward steps lead me to an icy wall. *Perfect.* A dead end.

Just then a light flashes in my direction and I squint at the brightness. All I can make out is the man's hands covered with black leather gloves. *Just like the man who broke into Giulio's house.* The man is adjacent to me when he veers the light to my right, pointing his gun towards two small figures in the corner of the room.

Oscar and Slonne.

My heart burst and all I want to do is hold them.

My babies.

They're lying next to each other with shut eyes and a blanket supporting their heads.

This man must have given them something.

"Go to them!"

I rush to my twins before the command, only making it in time to witness their rising and falling chests before being slammed against the wall. The duffel is ripped from my grip and a gasp escapes me at my aching back after catching the heavy blow and slamming against the brick wall.

"Bad move," the man snarls coldly. "Did you really think I would allow that?"

"Who are you? What do you want?" I push away the tears that threaten to fall. *I will not cry. Not here. I need to continue being strong. I need to do this for my family.* "I have the money, isn't that what you want? What did my family ever do to you?"

Foreign hands blindly grip my wrists and slam them above my head to urge my stillness. I wish I could see who this repulsive person is as the bridge of his nose brushes my cheekbone.

"Did you come alone?"

This man's voice is different. It does not belong to the man pressed against me.

Somebody else is in here...

I can't see him either, yet I recognize his voice as the one from the ransom call. It remains distorted with something most likely covering his vocal cords.

"That's what the doctor ordered."

"Now is not the time to act smart," the guy pressed against me growls.

"I have the money here with me! Please, just give me my children back!"

Footsteps fade away but the man restraining me remains. I can't tell if anybody else is in the room with us now. *Or if a weapon is pointed my way.* All I know is that I need to get out of here with Oscar and Slonne as soon as I can before the twenty minutes SPD gave to raid it.

It feels as though years pass being pinned against the wall with this disgrace of a man. He prevents me from moving. During the wait, I hear Oscar's murmurs before calling out for his Mommy and Daddy and that's when I break. Tears run down my cheek, accompanied by the acid rising up my throat when the man covers my mouth and slams my head against the wall as I attempt to bite against the leather.

Shifted movements come from behind me and Oscar's voice fades until complete silence. The fact that they are so close and I am helpless makes this so much worse.

Footsteps return and the distorted man's voice returns. "We have a problem."

The man beside me drops his hand from my mouth. "Go on."

"We're twenty-thousand short."

"That is *impossible!*" I hiss. "We counted it ourselves!"

Silence…

And then… "*We?*"

Oh. My. Dear. God.

My heart drops to my stomach at my deadly mistake. *No. No. No. I did not just say that! I did not just give it away! No!*

"So you told somebody? Hmmm?"

"No. No, I—"

"You DEFIED us!" the man who has me pinned yells, forcing my back to him. "We had a fair deal, but you couldn't keep it. Do you know what happens when people defy us?" He grips my throat and again the gun digs deeply into the nape of my neck. My breath staggers; it becomes hard to breathe against the constant pressure. "ANSWER ME. I SAID DO YOU FUCKING KNOW WHAT HAPPENS WHEN PEOPLE DEFY US?"

He's going to kill me.

Panicked, I attempt to free myself from his hold but it only tightens. "No. It was only me. I promise. I counted it and it's the amount you asked for. I didn't mean—"

"I don't believe you."

"I promise. *Please!* Count it again. I assure you I counted it right!"

The man grips my short hair and turns my head so that my left cheek presses against the wall, scraping it in the process.

"Sorry, beautiful. That's *not* how we do business."

The metallic weapon is replaced with something wet covering my nose and mouth. It's drenched in a sweet yet toxic odor on some type of cloth. I thrash around. *HELP!* Another pair of arms restrain me as the man presses the fabric deeper. Powerless, I feel myself slipping and am forced to breathe in the chemical.

My family…

The men force me to the ground as my eyes begin to feel heavy and my body weakens…*I'm numb.* I'm nearly paralyzed and in my last bid of strength, I reach towards one of the hands that press me down but can't get them off.

I've failed.

My eyes slam shut.

No…

This is no time to die and yet, it's darkness that greets me on the other side.

⎯⎯⎯⎯⎯⎯⎯⎯⎯

Darkness blankets my vision. There's a coldness running through my entire body prompting sharp chills. *What's happening?* All I know is that my body is being moved, *lifted.* I'm wrapped and bound in something that blocks me from the outside world. I can hear a motor running, roaring in the depths of my soul.

"Quick, we have to do this fast. They'll catch up."

"Come on. Let's move. On the count of three."

I'm lowered and my head drags along something hard. It aches at the additional pressure. *Where am I? I was in the basement. They drugged me. I blacked out.* These people, whoever they are, are going to kill me.

Right now.

The pressure subsides as I feel myself being lifted. Trying to thrash doesn't do anything. I'm flung—I feel momentarily weightless—and I attempt to scream but my mouth is tight. There's a splash at impact and I'm drifting lower.

A freezing liquid seeps into what is wrapped around me. It overtakes me as I sink. Deeper and deeper.

Water.

I'm in water.

It blankets my body but I'm able to kick away whatever binds me. *The twins. Giulio. I'm not going to make it. I'm not.* My lungs are aching as I rip the tape off my mouth. *My...God.*

I don't know when I made the grave mistake of trusting people, of believing they would return my children. I slipped up with my words and now...now I'm struggling to survive. I don't know how much fight I have in me, but I must amplify it.

My biggest fear is that I'm not alone down here.

I can't lose Oscar and Slonne.

Not like this.

Not ever.

I still have the tracker on, it's my only hope that the police are alerted and on their way, but my chest burns from the anxiety just the same. I persist, kicking my legs frantically to swim down the deepest I can. I want to get up for air, a single breath, but I need Oscar and Slone more. *I'll never forgive myself if they're...*I fight against the freezing water yet can't feel anything from where I am. The additional fear factor is all I see is darkness.

Are they here or did SPD get to them?

How long has it been?

I surface, gasping for air as I brush my short hair out of my face. My top and jeans cling to my body. In the far distance, there's a small white boat speeding away from me, and that's when it dawns on me that I must have been thrown off by the culprits.

They left me to die.

I'll never make it to them. Not with their quick departure, and especially not when the boat turns and disappears behind a bend.

My shattered heart oozes in these clear, reflective waters. I could be at some lake, but I don't recognize it. I can't see anybody. The eerie, bracing breeze makes the dark skies more ominous. I glance at the stars and immediately remember what I'm fighting for…

Giulio and our children.

Freezing water surrounds me for miles. *I can't do this.* My energy is fading. There's no pier or sense of impending rescue and while my main objective is to not stress because my ability to swim will weaken, I'm still stuck in the middle of nowhere, treading water to stay afloat.

Breathe.

What if Oscar and Slonne are here too? What if they need me?

Fuck.

I plunge underneath one last time. I feel nothing again and it ruins me because all I want to do is find my babies but can't. I come back up, struggling to breathe. *Maybe SPD saved them. Please.* They don't need this memory to hold on to. They're too young and are already fighting through so much.

I resurface and scream out for help, praying somebody can hear me.

A motor roars in the distance. *It's them.* They're coming back. They're going to finish me off. I can only barely see the boat coming up behind me. They've done a loop—*Wait. Wait a minute.* A floodlight blinds me for a moment and then…*flashing lights.*

Red and blue flares illuminate the water's surface. Coast Guard—*police!*

An angel has answered my prayers.

My angel.

"VALENCIA!" I recognize Giulio's shout of haunting desperation. "LENCIA?"

"I'M OKAY! DO YOU HAVE OSCAR AND SLONNE? ARE THEY SAFE?"

"THEY'RE SAFE. WE'RE COMING TO GET YOU, BABY."

They're safe.

Thank God.

Coast Guard inches closer and a man speaks to me through a megaphone, promising everything's going to be okay and giving instructions on the next step. A lifesaver is thrown into the water, but I can't summon enough strength to reach it as my heartbeat grows thick in my ears…and then I feel myself going under.

I'm drowning.

I want to hold on.

I want to have enough fight in me. *I need to,* but my limbs are numb.

Hold your breath, just a little longer.

And then I feel it. Somebody sinks down beside me. I can't see who it is. I'm pulled up until we surface and I'm coughing out water.

Giulio.

He holds me flush to his chest and pushes back my hair from my eyes. His own is slicked back from the plunge. Water drips from his face as he frantically looks me over to ensure I'm safe. *I am now.* Against the moonlight, a gentle smile crawls up my lips.

He saved me.

We're going to be okay.

Giulio's terrified gaze meets mine and without saying a single word, he kisses me. Desperately. It's everything I need and more. *We have our twins back.* I have him—*forever.*

"Oh my god, I thought I lost you. I thought I lost all of you. When SPD entered the property they had already taken you but left the kids. I thought you had—" His voice breaks, incapable of continuing. I'm right here with his every emotion. "I thought you had died."

"I'm here. I'm right here. Don't ever let go of me, Giulio."

Those bluish-grays light up. "I never will. You are mine, Lencia."

"And I am yours. Until death do us part."

"No. I'll be haunting your dreams even then, darling."

We manage to break out in a small laugh through our heartache. Our intimate embrace only intensifies. We kiss. Again and again. The sensation is indescribable.

I can't believe he's right here.

Giulio Giannotti makes me feel so damn complete.

We share an agonizing stare, realizing this is far from over. Our story doesn't end here. *Addilyn.* Why couldn't she have been with the twins? Why do we still have this agonizing hole in the middle of our hearts?

But we're closer to the finish line.

I can taste it.

The events of tonight only mean one thing; soon the final showdown will come.

Giulio reaches out for the lifesaver and holds onto it as they pull us to the boat. He then hauls me into the arms of one of the Coast Guardsmen. Sergeant Flynn pulls out his hand to pull my husband on board, all while the team quickly wraps my shivering body in a warm blanket.

The boat turns around.

Giulio sits beside me and when he hugs me to his chest, I open the blanket to cover him too.

"You were so strong for the twins. You got them back. You saved them."

"It was teamwork."

"It's us, darling," he whispers against my lips. "It's you and I. It's us."

It always will be.

"I want to spend the rest of my life with you."

That smile I adore breaks out on his lips. "I love you, Valencia Marie Giannotti. I love you and our family. You're all I ever want. I'll continue being in awe of your bravery every single day."

I am willing to fight through it all for him.

For our children.

For myself.

I am.

———◆———

"*Amore mio?*" That voice I adore soothes me awake with a kiss to my forehead.

My eyes flicker open to Giulio's compassionate gaze. "Hi."

"Hey there. How are you feeling?"

"Not too bad. Did I…pass out?"

"You were explaining to Sergeant Flynn what happened and by the end of it you passed out in my arms. Apart from a few bruises, the doctors cleared you. They did run tests and found chloroform in your system. He said within a few hours under observation you'll be okay and be discharged."

"What time is it?"

"Just after noon."

Noon? A third of the day has passed since I entered that basement at 4 A.M. this morning!

"Could you…" My throat is parched. "Could you please turn on the light and get me a glass of water?"

Against the drawn shades, brightness fills the sterile hospital room. Giulio returns to my bedside and I thank him when he hands me a cup of water. The liquid purifies me.

The two reddened cuts by his cheekbones where Blue Eyes sliced him yesterday are closed wounds now. Emotions still consume me because of it—also because of his red glassy eyes.

He's been crying.

"Lencia, darling. I…" Giulio exhales a sharp breath, his face crumbling.

I pat the sheets beside me and he carefully lies down. His head rests upon my stomach as my fingertips slowly run through his thick black hair. It's enough to bring an optimistic smile to my lips.

They tried to kill us.

They attempted to take out an entire family.

They failed.

"I was terrified, Valencia. My heart broke when you weren't in the basement with Oscar and Slonne. This could have been much worse if we didn't have a tracker on you."

"I know, but I'm okay now. How are Oscar and Slonne?"

Please let them be okay.

"They're both well and are in good spirits. The perpetrators are still at large but they didn't injure or harm them. They're healthy. It's a miracle that they're still smiling. They're with Helena now. She's outside. But I…if you drowned, I wouldn't have taken it."

A groan escapes at the sharp pain to my ribs, causing Giulio to jerk up. "Are you okay?"

"Yes, I just have to get used to it." I rest my head on the fluffy pillow, motioning for him to settle back down beside me. "I'm here now. I'm right here, Giulio. We just need to find Addilyn now and we'll be okay for good. We can't give up on that."

He kisses my hand. "We'll never stop looking for her. I was wrong, Valencia. I was so damn wrong when we decided to get a separation." His fingers weave through mine now and he takes my ring finger, kissing where the diamond once rested. "I am sorry so for everything. I am sorry for hurting you. For the lies. For scaring you. For losing you. For believing a separation would fix everything. I never thought it would come down to this."

"Baby, we've already gone through this. None of this is your fault."

"Then why do I feel like *it is* my fault? If I believed in hope from day one we would have never spent these past months apart instead of spending them together."

"We don't know that. There may still have been issues. Addilyn could have still been missing. The ransom call could have still occurred. You could have still lost your car and money. I could still be in this hospital gown."

"That's true…I guess the most important thing is somehow we found a way back to each other." Giulio shakes his head. "You're too good for me."

"No, I'm not." My chest rises and falls with passion. *Passion for him.* "You were scared and your childhood is a big part of what made you into the man you are today. I understand that now. It will always be a part of you, but you need to have some acceptance and empathy for yourself too. You went through hell and back, Giulio. You deserve to clasp happiness now. It's your birthright."

My voice lowers as a nurse passes outside. "You have three

beautiful children and an alright wife. We're your life now. We're together in this. We'll never suffer alone. I want to be a part of your past, your present, and your future. So when you are feeling this way, when the anxiety sinks in, talk to me like you always encourage me to. Talk to me baby, because you mean the world to me."

The healing has been within each other's hearts this entire time. We were both hurting and instead of confiding in each other, we built barriers. We needed this separation to understand just how deeply our love runs and just how connected our hearts truly are.

The devil laced us with evil but goodness always seems to find its way back to us.

"Thank you." Giulio looks at me as if nothing else matters. "I don't want anybody but you, Valencia. After these past twenty-four hours, I know we can surpass anything. You're the only one who understands me for me."

"You're the only one I want. Nothing matters more than family."

"Thank you for saving me last night."

A crooked smirk pulls on my lips. "And thank you for saving me this morning."

"I'm so proud of you. You're a fighter, the way you risked your life for me and the twins…"

"It's a mother's instinct."

Giulio grins. "And you're more than just 'an alright' wife; you're the most beautiful person I'll ever meet, inside and out."

"I'm looking forward to starting this new chapter of our lives."

"As am I. We began believing in ourselves and each other, and we conquered. The past twenty-four-hours only confirm just how short life is and how unfinished it would have been if we didn't grasp our second chance."

I want to hold on to his words forever.

They unlock a world of emotion within me—*good emotions*.

I want this. I never want to live without this feeling in my chest ever again. The adoration laced in his eyes is a replica of mine as our smiles entrap us in a world of hope.

"I hate life without you. I haven't wanted anything more in my life. Except, of course..."

"I know." Giulio understands perfectly. "And we *will* get Addilyn back. Even if the night terrors never go away, we'll be right here holding each other to sleep. We'll overcome this. I know we will. It's you and me against the world, *amore mio*."

He seals his promise with a kiss that has me grip his damp t-shirt to pull him closer. I cannot stop smiling through it.

Yes, baby. It's you and me against the world.

"Aye, who wants me handmade extra sweet bread and butt'er pudding with raisins?" The familiar voice has us breaking away and we turn to find Bryce entering the hospital room. He's grinning wolfishly with a cake box in hand.

The moment my sister trails behind him, Giulio seems to already smell trouble between them as he averts his gaze to me, smirks and resumes kissing me wildly. We rebel against the audible distraction that works as a soundtrack to our kiss.

"You're the worst, Bryce!" Helena gasps. "I have a sugar free zone. It drives the kids wild!"

"How about I drive ya wild instead?" Bryce chuckles loudly.

"Yeah, have fun attempting that. I swore off interior designers the moment you arrived."

"Damn, sweetlips. There's nothing sweet about ya these days, innit?"

"Never *ever* call me that again."

"Alright...*sweetlips*."

Giulio and I pull away from each other in laughter.

Bryce and Helena continue their bickering until Giulio clears his throat and their attention snaps to us. McCarson hands over the delicious smelling pudding with a wink and a side hug. "Hope ya feel better soon, Valencia!"

"Thank you so much. Wow, you made this?"

"Sure did, you'll love it! Just hide it from this sister of yours; she's turning me into a nutter."

"You already are a *nutter*." Helena glares up at him, popping out her hip towards his before she turns to my bedside. "Honey, how are you? I've been worried sick since the news!"

I go on to tell them both I'm doing well. The feeling intensifies when Oscar and Slonne run inside my room and into my arms with wide smiles.

"Mommy!" They gently climb up on the bed and I pull them into a hug. A damn tight one. I could have lost them today. Kissing the sides of their heads, I thank God that they're okay.

"I've missed you both so much. I love you all."

"Me too, Mommy. I was scared but not anymore!" Slonne smiles cutely, brushing a few strands of her soft brunette hair from her face. "Daddy said you saved us. Thank you, Mommy."

"I did all that I could, but I think we all saved each other out there."

Oscar beams, curling his nonexistent bicep. "Yeah, I was like Spiderman out there!"

We burst into laughter and I pull them in for a second embrace, knowing that I will never take a precious moment like this for granted. It will take a while in therapy for them even if they seem okay now, but soon we'll all achieve that ultimate healing.

"Group hug!" Giulio wraps his arms around all of us while Helena rushes to set down her bouquet of yellow roses.

"Wait for your favorite aunt! Yes, now it's perfect!"

There's a knock on the slightly ajar door. "*Almost* perfect. How dare you all forget me!"

It's Lance's voice that has Giulio turn his head towards the door. "Hey, aren't you supposed to be on the work site across town?"

Lance smirks before joining the group hug. "Well…it's a good thing my boss isn't a big pain in the backside and won't fire me for skipping work for family. Isn't that right, *boss*?"

"Giulio, don't answer, it's a trick question." Kayla's voice enters before she does. She sends a playful wink our way, sets down *'Get Better Soon!'* yellow balloons, and joins us too.

I cast a glance at Bryce who stands awkwardly with his

hands inside his jean pockets in the corner of the room. Just then Marcus steps in with a bouquet of lilies. They acknowledge each other with curt nods before looking our way.

I smile and through my intertwined hands wave for them to partake in our embrace too.

They do but with reluctance. After all, we *are* family, and Bryce…well, he is somebody that I have learned to trust and appreciate over the past six weeks working with this entire crew.

My eyes shut and I take in their comfort.

I believe in myself.

These people here believe in me.

We will be okay soon. I just feel it.

We will find Addilyn and it will all be okay.

All of this supportive warmth around me right now is not an illusion, it is not a curse or *too much*—*it's enough.* It's enough because *I* am enough. This is *my* life…*and I love it dearly.*

Giulio

"**D**O YOU TRUST ME?"

"Well…I've been blindfolded for the past ten hours, so I'm obliged to say yes."

The twins giggle in the backseats at Lencia's response. I'm left smiling, crazy in love with us. Fanning out my fingers against the heated leather-wrapped steering wheel, I touch on the brakes at the end of the cobblestone driveway and kiss Valencia softly. "More like twenty minutes. You have nothing to worry about, *amore*."

Today, Friday the fourteenth of October marks Valencia's twenty-eighth birthday and I went all out. We're on Mercer Island and this luxurious modern house in front of us…it's *ours*.

Of course Lencia doesn't know it yet, but Oscar and Slonne do. It's been our little secret for the past few days as we recover from the shocking aftermath of self-defense, kidnappings, car theft, and attempted murder.

The twins' eyes widen in awe through the car windows. I ended up getting another Porsche Cayenne. The dealership and my insurance had an incredible turnaround time after my last car was found torched.

Our kids rush out of the car as I round Valencia's side to help her out. The silk blindfold prevents her from seeing anything. *It's perfect.* Her right hand laces with mine and Oscar rushes back to hold the other.

Ah, the perfect chivalrous gentleman in training.

My heart's never raced this fast or felt this full. For the past six months, I've been directing the design of this home through my business with a contracted agent to sell, but with every single detail, I found myself architecturally customizing this house for *my* family. Our marriage was broken at the time, yet I made the leap and bought this house with the hope that if we were to fall back together…this would be our forever home.

Away from the city.

Away from the panic.

Alone on our little island.

"The suspense is killing me!"

"It's worth it, Mommy."

I guide her forward until we reach Slonne. "Okay…you can undo it now."

The blindfold is stripped with a loud gasp as a shocked Valencia stares up at our new contemporary home. "Oh. My. GOD!"

"Welcome home, baby!"

We step inside onto the white oak floors and soaring ceilings. The theme of white, Pietra gray, sleek black, and brushed gold are consistent through the elegant architectural design. White panel walls and polished rich finishes greet us. Her favorite pieces of artwork illuminate particular walls. Tempered glass pocket walls compliment the open plan style living area and aid our top of the line security alarms. Our *home* is complete with sophisticated imported Italian furnishings I personally custom designed.

Excluding our master suite, there are five spacious bedrooms and four baths. Aside from our master bath, we have a sophisticated glossy charcoal tiled shower room with a ceiling mounted, brushed gold square rain head, a detachable showerhead, and three body spray jets.

The home is three stories, each level with a full wraparound balcony to complement the scenic views of Lake Washington and the mountains. The house is elevated and while the east wing leads to a large backyard with evergreen trees and mountain hemlocks, at the west end there is a different type of picturesque scenery with the clear blue water.

It's there by the expansive dark composite deck that reality really seems to sink in for Valencia.

She looks at me with the biggest grin. "You're joking, right?"

"This is ours! Coming back together doesn't only mean starting over again, it means starting off stronger. We even have our own makeshift ocean with Lake Washington for when times get tough. See? The water doesn't have to represent the pain of the past, it can represent the calm tranquility of our future."

"I love the sound of that. This home is sensational!"

"Is that a yes?"

"YES!" Slonne and Oscar scream in unison, jumping up and down in pure joy. Their happiness means the world to me. They're incredibly strong little renditions of us. "PLEASE SAY YES, MOMMY!"

"Yes!" Lencia embraces me and that damn vanilla scent electrifies my body.

"Happy Birthday, baby!"

"Thank you. I cannot believe this is ours! Wow! Thank you so much, Giulio," she whispers by my lips before sealing her appreciation with a sensual kiss. My already skyrocketing desire ruptures at her single touch. Mommy and Daddy *definitely* need some alone time, away from our children who watch us intently.

I hope bearing witness to their parents falling back in love will always be something significant for them. I hope this teaches them that love can conquer anything. For now, I want to show Valencia something of her own first.

I crouch down to Oscar and Slonne's height with a smile. "Hey angels, why don't you both check out the bedrooms again? They were pretty awesome!"

They disappear in seconds.

I chuckle at their new tendency to get along. The tragedies in these past few weeks have drawn them closer than ever before. The sibling rivalry is still there, but they know that in the end family is most important.

Those gorgeous hazel eyes I love sparkle. "Hmmm, I know all your tactics. What exactly do you have planned, Mr. Giannotti?"

"A celebration of your existence, but first, there is one more room I'd like to show you." Without warning her, I scoop her into my arms and move through the house. Her sweet laughter is a cure for part of the remaining agony in my chest. *The one that's there for Addilyn.*

We'll find her too.

This house isn't complete without her.

In our office, there is a door that's sealed off with a large ceiling to floor wall art. I set Lencia down and her jaw drops when I push on the frame, revealing a secret door.

"Woah…Are you going all Mission Impossible on me now?"

I lead her down the hallway to another secret door. "I'll leave that up to you to decide."

"What's in there?"

I fail to keep a straight face. "Uh…no idea…"

"Yeah, right! You lie, boy. You lie."

This is what I crave—our laugher. Our happiness. *Us.*

A beaming Valencia tugs the door open. "Oh my god! You did not!"

"*Oh*, yes I *did!*"

It's an art studio.

A gray marble countertop runs down the center of the room. On the right side, printing machines and drying racks are stationed. Whitewood cabinetry with painting tools inside line the back walls separated with their own specific stations. Easels and canvases can be easily stored inside them too.

What I love most about this studio, apart from the warm lights that give the room that moody ambiance I know she loves while painting, is the floor to ceiling window that looks out to the mesmerizing skies, mountains, and hemlock trees.

We can't be afraid of windows because of our traumatizing past, so this will be a simple way to learn to adapt and remember the beauty they *can* give—*a mesmerizing view.*

I know Valencia hasn't had the inspiration to return to her love of art between Addilyn and losing her job, but I want her to know that she has the choice to start again when the time is right.

I used to love watching her eyes light up whenever a stroke of inspiration hit and her dedication to not rest until the artwork was perfect. To me, they were always flawless, even as initial sketches.

"Oh, wow! This is perfect. You didn't have to do this; it's too much!"

"You're welcome, darling. Nothing is too much when it's for you. Seeing as it's Friday and Amanda returns to the office next week, I thought it would be a good idea if you had the chance of remaining tied to the company in some way. After all, you'll always be a part of Notti Designs. I thought that if you truly want to let go of teaching and when that passion returns to your heart, perhaps you can have your own division at Notti Designs. You could create artwork for interior design clients and naturally your own independent clients too. You would receive the entire profit, plus a normal salary. Even if you don't know now, the offer will always stand."

I want nothing more than for Valencia to be a part of Notti

Designs permanently. To run the chance of seeing her for more hours of the day and collaborate with her on business projects.

"That would be *perfect*. You're spoiling me!"

"I'm not spoiling, baby. I'm just giving you everything I can because you deserve the world." I pick up a small canvas from the drying rack. "I painted something for you."

"*Oh?* This day just keeps getting better!"

"Mmhmm, never doubt my artistic hands."

Valencia bites her lip. "I prefer those hands when they're on me..."

I arch a suggestive brow and smirk. "As an architect, I'm obligated to ask you the following question. You prefer my hands on *what specific* parts of you, Mrs. Giannotti?"

"On *everything*, Mr. Giannotti."

Hell yeah, baby.

"Well...it's your birthday so be careful what you wish for, darling." I come to a stop in front of her with the canvas behind my back. "Okay, promise you won't laugh?"

"Promise."

I haven't even shown her the painting for a split second before she's shaking with laughter. Blends of pink, red, and yellow spread across the top of my canvas, creating a dawn sky. I've also painted textured green hills, but I know for a *fact* that they're not what has her so flustered. Holding hands on top of one of the hills are five stick figures. It's supposed to be our family, *however they're stick figures and practically have no identifying features at all...yeah, not my proudest moment!*

Valencia points at what is supposed to be her and happy tears flow. "Oh my goodness! Why are we stick figures? I can't get over the fact that the only thing differentiating me is the ponytail!"

"You said you wouldn't laugh!" I tease through my own laughter.

"I'm so sorry, I can't help it! This is gold! You're supposed to be good at drawing!"

"Darling, this was my third attempt!" Our bodies continue

to rumble as I pull her closer to me. By the end of it, I'm wiping away both of our happy tears. "It's a masterpiece, no?"

"Hmm, I'm afraid you won't be taking Monet's crown anytime soon, Mr. Giannotti."

"Oh, what a shame!"

Our banter brings back so much. It's so refreshing to share moments with her like this.

"Have mercy on me…" I playfully murmur against her pink, full lips. "For tonight I'll show you all the other things my hands can do, baby."

CHAPTER TWENTY-SEVEN

Valencia

I'M STILL IN AWE OF GIULIO'S SURPRISE EARLIER TODAY WHEN I PARK in the driveway of our new home. I cannot believe it's ours. I've been beaming ever since. This represents our fresh start. *A better start.* The home we'll bring Addilyn to live happily in.

I love everything about Mercer Island. It's a beautiful neighborhood, the security and the fact it's only a short fifteen-minute drive to the city. The grass is much greener for me on this side of Washington and not just metaphorically. Every single one of our neighbors has a blooming rose garden running up their drive with hopeful tinges of scarlet red.

I prefer it here. I love the serenity, the privacy, and most importantly, the fact that the tight feeling isn't in my chest anymore.

It hasn't been there ever since my life changed for the better. I'm a million percent devoted to the love of my life and my new-found self-confidence.

Today, my last day at work, which is also subsequently my birthday, goes by so fast. I honestly enjoyed working with this team. Giulio is thoroughly blessed to have such passionate employees. Giulio not only blocked out our lunch hour schedule, but also Bryce's, Kayla's, Lance's, and even Marcus' for a joint birthday celebration at a nearby café.

I would like to say that the relationship between us and Marcus is better, but it isn't. There's still tension due to everything that's happened, but today's my birthday and so we put it aside.

Just as I set down my menu, Helena struts into the café grinning with killer heels and pledges she has plans for the rest of the afternoon with me before the kids get out of school. And so that's how it goes. I have the most beautiful lunch surrounded by the people I adore before being whisked away with my sister.

I never thought it would take me twenty-eight years to have an enzyme facial, but Helena's peer pressure is worth it. The entire afternoon we spend pampering ourselves with chilled mimosas at the beauty spa and hair salon where blowouts and manicures are hot red on our list of must-dos.

With everything that's happened during the past seven months without Addilyn, neither Slonne nor Oscar have been interested in any extra circular activities. But now they've been wanting to try it out and so it's better late than never, even if they did both miss the initial lessons.

During our lunch, Giulio stated he would go personally to enquire about a later start at both the soccer club and dance studio before taking Oscar and Slonne to the final site visit he had for the day in Ballard. Then they would come home. This way, *as Giulio claims*, this entire birthday weekend is exclusively for discovering Mercer Island. His analytical mind has timed everything perfectly and when I offered to pick up the twins instead to save him from going up and down, he simply blew me a kiss and practically whisked me away into Helena's arms.

When I return home after my lovely afternoon with my sister, it's just after three. I'm greeted by a man with an earpiece and holster in a dark suit just outside the front door.

He extends his hand and we shake. "Good afternoon, Mrs. Giannotti. My name is Raj."

"Hi, Raj. It's nice to meet you."

Raj goes on to explain that Giulio hired him and how he rotates eight-hour shifts with two other men, seven days a week. It's far safer in this house with high end security.

When I step inside and text Giulio a thank you, he replies with words that make my heart swell. A single rose is laid out on the kitchen counter, beside it is a flute of champagne, and a thin gold wrapped dark chocolate. I bring the chilled glass into the bedroom and take a sip of the bubbly livener. The suite is much brighter than our last with the northern sun brightening the dark, but it's the large midnight blue box placed on the bed that sparks my interest. A card and a white rose rest next to it, alongside another box situated at the foot of the bed.

I take the card on top of the larger box. It has swirls of vibrant crayons and my lips tug up at my children's masterpiece. In the center, Giulio's cursive handwriting reads; *Happy Birthday to Our Hero!*

I open the card.

HAPPY 28th BIRTHDAY AMORE MIO,

Happy Birthday, Lencia! We hope you're having a beautiful day! Always know that I will risk it all for you. Our journey this year hasn't been one without grit, but it has led us to this point right here and for that I am grateful. I am grateful to have you by my side. I am grateful for our children. I am grateful for loving you with no boundaries and all of our beautiful merciful vows.

I love you with all my heart. Here's to your birthday and many more years to come! Here's to all my infinite years with you. Darling, here's to our whole lifetime together.

Tonight it is for us. Us and the twins. These pieces are for you—we hope you like them!

We love you and cannot wait to see you! Happy Birthday into infinity (and beyond!) P.S...We can always rely on our kids for the Toy Story reference, I was peer pressured I tell you, haha!

Yours Always,
Oscar, Slonne, Addilyn, and Giulio xx

I chuckle even more at the last part.

P.S.S You're almost in my club! Can't wait for you to be thirty and dirty with me in two years...not that we aren't the latter already! HAHA, the kids are gone and so I'm just rambling. Ahem...can we kindly hide this from their existence? Thanks, darling! Ciao! ;)

P.S.S.S Hi! Hey! Yes, I'm still here giddy about how much I love you. My heart can't function without you. You're my air. My cure. My everything. Ti amo tanto.

I open the first box to the most beautiful cream silk dress. Its entire make is divine. A lacy white thong is underneath the dress and I bite my lip with a growing smirk. There is no bra accompanying Giulio's gifts and so I take it as an indication not to wear one. The silver shimmering Jimmy Choo heels in the second box complement the dress further.

My phone rings as I step out of the shower.

"Happy birthday, sweetheart! Wow, I cannot believe it!"

"Thank you, Mom. I really appreciate it!"

"I'm so happy you've both settled everything! I know it's still a long road ahead to get Addilyn back, but you're both stronger together and that's all that matters. Plus, that house is purely sensational!"

Wait a minute.

How did she know about the house?

Well played, Giulio. Well played.

"He hid the surprise well. Everybody knew except me!"

She laughs joyfully "That's the exact purpose of a surprise. You don't know how glad I am you have each other again. You complement each other in the best way."

My mother stating the very words I feel only reaffirms just how much Giulio and I both want this. "Mom?"

"Yes, my love?"

"I just want to say how grateful I am to have you and Dad in my life. Your unconditional love towards each other made me the woman I am today. Although at times I'm not perfect, I think I have found my rhythm. It's important to me."

"I see you're blooming now for the better. I'm so proud of you and love you so much."

"Love you too, Mama. Oh, is Dad back from Vienna? I tried calling and texting but it's been switched off and I haven't gotten a reply yet."

"The idiot lost his phone the other day and needed to get an emergency one. He has a new number, but it won't be for long as he'll be back next week. He'll be sure to call you soon with these time zones. Such a typical move he'd make. I send him to Vienna to see his brother after so many years and he's in such a hurry to sustain twin telepathy he loses his belongings. Talk about men driving us crazy!"

I smile to myself. "But we love them for it in the end."

"That we do. Anyway, I'll let you go. Enjoy your dinner!"

"How do you know about that?"

"Now, Valencia. Don't be jealous of our mother and son-in-law relationship. I know more than you think. For example, what exactly he'll *do* after dinner." I gasp but before I can say another word the line goes dead with my mother's laugh drawing a smile to my lips.

There's nothing like healthy family rivalry.

Forty-five minutes later, I'm slipping on the Jimmy Choos when the front door clicks open. Little feet patter across the hall and burst inside the bedroom. I pull Slonne and Oscar close to me. "Hey lovelies, how was school?"

"It was so good! I learned a new rhyme." Slonne doesn't even wait to proceed with it and I clap, swaying side to side and cheering her on.

By the end, Oscar joins along too. "Yeah, I only learned the last part. It's the best part."

I kiss their foreheads and grin at their cuteness. "So tell me, am I looking at the next champion soccer player and dance superstar?"

"You are! Daddy spoke to them and they both said we can join. Slonne starts dance after school next Tuesday—"

"No." Slonne interrupts her brother. "She said next Thursday, remember?"

"Oh yeah, whoops. Yeah, Slonne has dance on Thursday and I have soccer on Wednesday."

"I'm so happy for you both! I'll be sure to talk to Daddy about it. Why don't you both get ready for dinner now? I'll come to help in a minute."

Slonne shakes her head. "Daddy said he'll help us and to let you finish getting ready."

"Well, that was very kind of him. Okay. Tell him I'll be finished soon, alright?"

They nod and skip out of the bedroom hand in hand.

Addilyn. My breath staggers. *The final piece of the puzzle.*

We'll have her soon.

In the bathroom, I decide against my normal lipstick and choose the deep red one instead.

"Amore?" Giulio calls from outside the bathroom door, his husky voice shooting electric sparks across my body. "Sorry, I

couldn't come in earlier. I'm halfway through making dinner. Everything going okay?"

"It's no trouble! Yes, I'm almost done. You can come in."

"No, not yet."

Snickering, I draw the lipstick away from my full lips. "Why not? It isn't as if this is the night before we get married and you can't see me or my dress."

"That night was pure torture without you."

"Ditto." I rub my red lips together. The dress hugs me in all the right places, accentuating my legs and cinching my waist. "Is that why you picked white?"

"I guess that's for me to know and you to find out."

I'm having the time of my life and the night hasn't even begun. For the first time in ages, I feel like myself. When I step out of the bathroom with a hand running down my smooth thighs, I find Giulio sitting on the edge of the bed wearing a dapper tuxedo. White tuxedo dress shirt, dark silk bow tie, a finely pin-striped black vest with matching slacks, and a *hot* blazer.

He looks elegantly sexy, *as always*.

"*Oh, Dio.*" His jaw visibly drops. "My god, Lencia. You look so stunning, you always do. Those red lips…your hair…*wow*."

I run my hand through my short hair. I've curled it into loose waves tonight. "You really like it, huh?"

"I *love* it. I think you're ready for world domination."

I laugh at his comment. "If you say so."

"It suits you so well. New beginnings, huh?"

"New beginnings."

Giulio stands and motions for me to step forward. Head high, I stride towards him. We're grinning from ear to ear as he takes my left hand and raises it over my head. "Spin around for me, baby."

I do. *Slowly.*

"I love everything about what you're doing. I know what it means and could not be prouder."

Leaning forward, I steal a peck on his lips. It's short, yet enough to signal just how grateful I am. Our grins deepen, proving difficult for me to wipe away the scarlet transfer on his lips. "Keep still, baby."

"Impossible." He kisses my thumb. "By the way, the kids helped me pick out the dress."

"Aww, really?"

"True story." Giulio's hands depart from the dips of waist and I laugh when he softly spanks my ass before giving it a tight squeeze. Then he dips forward and in a sexual, deep voice he teases by my ear, "But those panties were all me. They're *mine*. And don't you forget it."

"*Oh* I won't, Mr. Giannotti."

"Good."

⎯⎯⎯⎯◆⎯⎯⎯⎯

I'll never forget this birthday.

Giulio has turned the luxurious rooftop deck on what is the fourth level into this mesmerizing wonderland. Flickering candles guide the path to the large rounded marble table. Adjacent to us are lounges, a hot tub, and a dreamy rooftop pool with views of the mountainside. Below, in our backyard, fairy lights wrap around the soaring trees, gold balloons align the fence, and everything I could have ever wanted is here underneath the pink hued sky.

All except for one.

Dinner outside our new home is something special to me. The rustic Italian food is divine and the orange flourless cake is to die for. Later, we switch to wine as the kids sip their hot chocolates. The conversation flows easily from topic to topic, and the outdoor gas heaters blanket us in sweet serenity. It's simply perfect.

As the stars begin to show, we navigate the skies until we find ours. They're impeccably aligned and the twins are completely mesmerized, just like they are every single time we show them...*and* every time I see them too.

"Why don't you get Mommy's gift?" Giulio says.

"Oh, yeah!" Oscar rushes down the outdoor marble steps and into the house with his sister hot on his tail.

Giulio rounds the table and moves his chair next to mine.

"Thanks for everything today. It's truly been one of the greatest birthdays I've ever had."

"Better than that Beyoncé concert years ago?"

"Smart move." I nuzzle into his chest. "Better than the Beyoncé concert."

"Helena will never forgive you for that answer."

"I don't think I'll ever forgive myself if I don't choose you over Queen B. There's no better healing than when we're together."

"I would do anything for you, and you know I'm not just saying that. You're the only woman I want, and I'm glad we have overcome our version of hell."

"Same." I'm hot all over, loving the way our citric vanilla scents mix into one as my lips trail down his neck. "I could stay like this forever."

Giulio's hands pull me in closer. "Mrs. Giannotti, you're playing a *very* dangerous game kissing my neck like that. The twins will be back any second."

"*Oh?*" I smirk. He's left to witness my hand glide down his chest, past the dark leather Tom Ford belt with a thin golden T-shaped buckle, and resting on his crotch. I give his already semi-hard cock a tight squeeze. "What is it you said about a dangerous game, Mister?"

"Don't tempt me more than I already am," he murmurs softly. "If we were *alone* alone, I would bend you over this table and take you from behind with that beautiful dress of yours bunched up to the sides. How's that for participating in your dangerous game, Mrs. Giannotti?"

Hot...damn!

I arch a suggestive brow.

He mirrors the action and licks his lower lip.

Holy hell!

I'm all flustered and in need of him even more when Giulio kisses my lips with the same passionate urgency I've been craving all evening. The tip of his tongue gently slides against my lips and I part them. His tongue finds mine, softly devouring me into sweet ecstasy. Giulio takes me over the edge as I alternate between slowly stroking his length through his slacks and fast palm rubs.

"That feels so good." He breathes against my lips. "Fuck, baby."

My smile widens. "It's my birthday, I can get away with it."

Giulio is about to respond when the twins come running up the outdoor steps. We separate in a flash. My hand moves instantly to my wine glass while he groans in a mere whisper to me, "*Dio mio*, you tease. I'll get you back. You just wait until later. Just *wait*, baby."

Haha!

I can't stop laughing inside at the way Giulio is looking at me—so hot and bothered.

Oh darling, I feel exactly the same…

I clear my throat and face the twins. "That was quick! But you didn't need to buy me anything."

Giulio leans forward, discreetly adjusting himself under the table, and winks at me. "You know that was never going to happen."

He walks towards Oscar, blocking my view of something they exchange. They step apart beaming. My heart seizes as the twins sit back down meanwhile Giulio helps me out of my chair.

What's going on?

We stand in front of the outdoor table, hand in hand, and get caught in each other's warm eyes. "Valencia…we were both fighting against an invisible enemy. Up until a few weeks ago, I thought it would be impossible to ever be with you again. The thought destroyed me."

"The only way we can get through this is together."

"And I am with you, Lencia. I want this for us. I want this for Oscar and Slonne. I want this for Addilyn. After everything we've been through, we deserve that silver lining. We deserve more than ever to find our baby and we will."

There's a pang in my chest at his words, our reality, and most importantly the rebirth of us. Emotions begin to hit me. Somewhere along the way, I began living again. I brought myself back up. *I survived.* This is *my* life. I deserved to live it right. *I am worth it.*

Giulio casts a glance towards the twins and turns to me with a sharp breath. "I met you at a very delicate time in my life. You came into my life and saved me. You've continued to save me ever since. For that, I'll forever be grateful. You're important to me. I love you more than life itself. With all my heart, I love everything about you."

"I love you too."

"Then let's do this the right way, all over again. Valencia, I had the honor of falling in love with you twice over. Not many husbands can say that. Not many children can witness their parents fall back in love again and that is something purely special. I want to find Addilyn. I want this life with you, Oscar and Slonne. I cannot do it without you all. So…"

Giulio grins, dropping down on one knee.

Oh. My. God.

My hands tremble as he reaches inside one of his suit pockets. *A teal box.* He opens it and I understand perfectly what it is.

My Platinum diamond wedding ring.

It's altered because now attached to the original ring is another thin band of emeralds. The color of hope and rejuvenation. It signifies the second time we've fallen in love. Our two stories. We are stronger. Wiser. More compassionate.

"Valencia Marie Giannotti, you're the one for me. Will you be my wife again and together annul our separation?"

"Yes. YES!"

Giulio slips on my wedding ring and pulls open the second box, revealing his wedding band altered with a matching rim of emeralds among the brushed titanium. I slide it on him and the twins cheer loudly as we press our lips together.

Yes. Always yes.

Eagerly tugging his lapels, I show him just how much I mean

it. It doesn't matter how many times we kiss. Every time feels like the first. That fiery devotion. That pooled longing. That warmth in my heart delivered straight to him. Only to him. Always to him.

"I love you, Lencia."

"I love you too, Giulio."

Oscar and Slonne rush to us and we come together in a group hug.

We did it!

Our lips haven't detached once since shutting Slonne's bedroom door. We stumble into our bedroom as Giulio's hands rush through my new hairdo, setting off a moan caught in my throat. It's therapeutic the way one single kiss from this man has enough depth to pull me under.

"God, I will never get enough of you," he whispers softly, slowly pulling off my dress and I grin as it hits the floor. Apart from my panties, I'm bare against his tuxedo. "Never."

"Well, it's a good thing we're married then."

"You see, I missed the sarcasm and those snarky replies too."

"Wait until I'm in my dirty thirties."

"Baby," he whispers, "every day is a blessing with you."

"You're my blessing. You make me feel alive again. I used to feel as if I was constantly fighting to be the perfect wife, mother, sister, and friend… I felt so alone, Giulio…*so* alone."

"You have to be there for yourself first" His soft hands slide against my breasts, his heat spreading with mine. I look at him with burning desire. So intimately. "Lencia, don't worry about being the perfect anything. Perfection is an illusion. Nothing is perfect. All we can be is our best. *That* is fulfillment. But it begins and ends with you, darling."

"I believe that now."

I cannot stop kissing him.

Touching him.

Appreciating him.

He falls to his knees and his mouth brushes against my core. Giulio *knows* my body. He knows of that fire burning inside me as he grips my hips, close to the band of my lacy thong. He knows my body is a perfect reminder of Addilyn—I'm certain of it as his warm lips meet with my white cesarean scar, my heart thudding at the open mouthed kisses.

I'm not surprised that Giulio can sense exactly what's going on with me, even when I fail to pay attention to it myself.

"I really missed you, Giulio," I admit with a puff of air escaping me. My body softens naturally to his touch. "Everything about you."

"I missed you too, baby. It's time we stop blaming ourselves. We'll make this right for our little girl too." Giulio makes his point clear, meaning every single word. "I'm here now. I'm here with you. For you. Forever."

Hot tears trail down my cheeks at just how perfect this moment is.

"Lencia, tell me where you want me."

I tap my heart. "Right here."

Giulio stands tall, overpowering my ability to think straight with his striking masculine Italian features. "I need you there too, *amore.*"

And then his lips are on mine. Hard. Warm. Desperate. I undo his bowtie and pull him closer with the ends. Giulio lifts me in one solid motion, and my legs wrap around his narrow waist.

Giulio has me slipping into his world.

One I never want to escape. Not when he lowers me on the soft Egyptian cotton sheets. Not when he coats every inch of my skin with sensual kisses as my smile widens, not when he stands at the foot of the bed, exerting his dominance as he peels off his pinstriped blazer and vest with his hooded eyes still locked on mine. And especially not when his shirt, leather shoes, and socks follow suit.

It's so sexy watching him undress.

Waiting and anticipating.

Desire grows deep inside me when he sets down his bowtie on the bed beside me. I adore the way his toned arms flex when he bends and his hands press against the sheets by my waist.

"Not so fast." My right heel softly meets his chest to push him back up. "*More.*"

Giulio smirks and clicks his tongue at my demand. "Of course, *amore mio.*"

I kick off my heels and I follow his hands working his belt. My hum urges Giulio to remove his slacks vigorously. The bruises along his chest and cheekbone have faded and are now projected against my own ribcage from falling down the stairs after the ransom call. But overall, I'm okay and in time they'll fade away too.

Giulio strips me of every single dreadful memory.

This is my past, present, life, and future. *With him.*

The second time Giulio lowers himself on the bed, an alluring smolder is in his eyes. I love the way his crow's feet deepen and those smile lines extend.

"You're being demanding tonight, baby." He spreads my thighs and hovers over me. I moan at the sensation of his skin on mine. "And I'm loving every single second of it. I love you, birthday girl."

I smile in the low light, my hands caressing and swirling over his dimples of Venus. "I love you more. I love that tonight also marks seven years of knowing you. I love it all."

His kisses from the crook of my neck to my breasts and down around the bruises.

It's all a part of us. All a part of our story.

When Giulio comes back up, there's a sly smirk on his lips. It has me ponder what's going through his mind. "I wasn't joking earlier when I said I'd get you back for teasing me like that."

Oh, that!

I giggle at the mischief on his face. "What are you going to do about it?"

Giulio bites his lip and nods towards the silk bowtie.

"You want me to…put it around my neck?" I ask.

Head shake. *No.*

"Put it on you?"

No.

"Uh…" I bite my lip, perplexed. Giulio's looking at me with a warm, mesmerizing smile. Those hot lips are potent when he hands me the bowtie. The smooth material sways from side to side between my thumb and index finger. "I don't know what else…"

"Remember Valentine's Day this year?"

When my eyes snap to his, I find we're both smirking. "You want to blindfold me again, Mr. Giannotti?"

"Baby, I want to bind your wrists together with this and blindfold you with something else for teasing me so damn hard." His smooth hand fans out across my body, slowing by places I need him the most. "I want to forbid you from touching me tonight. I want to devour your sense of feeling. I want you to feel it. You're the only one that sets me free."

"Giulio?"

"Hmmm?"

"Shut your mouth and do it *all* to me."

"*Mmhmm,* that I can do. That I can definitely do, *Mrs. Giannotti.*"

Our poetic last name becomes the antidote for our entire past and assurance for our future. The words Giulio whispers in my ear only intensify the warm sensation across my entire body as he puts an end to my wandering hands. We're smiling as he binds my wrists above my head and collects the silk blindfold I had on this morning before he surprised me with this new home.

He winks at me seconds before I'm blinded.

"Safeword, baby?"

Through the darkness, I grin. "We won't be needing one."

"Oh, that confident, huh?" Giulio teases, and I can hear the smirk on his lips. "We'll stick to red if you want to stop, okay?"

"Okay."

I gasp at the sound of him *literally* ripping my panties off. "Giulio! Again?"

"Shhh, I'll buy you another pair."

"*Oh, really* now?"

"You better believe it, birthday girl." Another chuckle rumbles in his throat and for a second I don't feel his touch. His erotic, masculine cologne has my body craving him. "You're so beautiful, Lencia. So goddamn beautiful."

Then just like that he kisses my sex and I begin quivering and moaning. Giulio lustfully growls at my tied hands that have come down to find his soft wavy hair. I guide him deeper and his tongue works all types of magic. It doesn't take long to lose myself in a long, powerful orgasm.

I wish I could see his face when I feel him coming back up to me. My back arches in his arms at the first thrusts. *Yes. Yes. Yes.* Our intimately pinned bodies drive me wild, as our fingers link together above my head and brush against the soft fabric headboard.

"Keep your hands up here, baby," he says by my ear, giving the lobe a rough tug with his teeth before running his tongue over my skin and diamond stud. "Mmhmm, right there."

"I'm sorry...*not* sorry!" I laugh.

Giulio chuckles and I can hear the amusement in his tone. "God, I love you." And then he kisses me so beautifully, swallowing my moans and connecting our bodies even closer as I open my legs wider, giving him even better access to fuck me harder.

Giulio has a way of electrifying my entire body with one single caress, one single word, one single whiff of his scent. He's always made me feel like this, yet right now, the sensation intensifies.

Our wild hearts beat to the same rhythm.

The tinge of vanilla in the air fuses with his cologne, urging me to blindly kiss and teasingly swirl my tongue along his neck before teasingly nipping the skin. Giulio allows it for a split moment until he takes over my mouth with a sweet, unapologetic kiss. It's a giddy reminder of where we are and everything we will be.

Giulio does everything so sensually right. I feel all of him and it's so intense and intimate—*so* good.

Our bodies belong together.

They always have.

Always will.

"I hate doing life without you."

"So do I, *amore*. We never have to again."

The intensity grows and our moans with it until they are the loudest they can be without waking the kids. The blindfold brings sweet anticipation. It's there as his hand glides by my waist, electrifying my tight skin until he grips my jaw and peppers it with kisses.

All of a sudden Giulio's sensational grin is all I see as the blindfold is taken off. We share an extended, beautiful moment of nothing but admiring the rising pleasure. My entire body is on fire as devotion sparkles in his gray-blue eyes.

Our pace quickens and I tell him just how much I love him and how close I am to heaven.

Giulio's husky voice edges me even nearer. "Happy birthday, my girl."

A rush of ecstasy builds and I come undone the second his thumb circles my clit. A few last thrusts do it until his body tenses and he falls into elation, climaxing right with me. Too thrilled by the fact we're now in each other's life permanently, we can't even speak through our panting.

The beauty is that we don't have to, *this*—our love—is enough.

Giulio spins us so we're side by side. Still inside me, he unties my wrists and kisses them a million times over. "Holy fuck, if that isn't up there with the hottest things we've ever done."

"If this is how it's going to be, I should tease you every second of every minute."

"Don't make promises you can't keep, baby…"

"Oh, don't you worry. I'll keep it." I chuckle, so happily in love. "I certainly will."

When we wrap our arms around each other, still buzzing

from the high, he kisses my forehead slowly with the biggest grin and it's all I need to know that everything is going to be okay.

Now, when I look down at our wedding rings, it's a stark reminder this isn't a dream.

This is all real life.

The thought alone has me beaming, knowing that among all the derailments Giulio and I found our way back to each other and have solidified our healing with true love.

All of our past desperation will lead us straight to Addilyn. I sincerely believe it because here in Giulio's arms I confirm that hope is truly a tangible reality and what defines strength, the same strength we have gripped by the horns, is to keep on keeping on. To find silver linings. To never give up. To always see the beauty in every single tragedy.

That is strength.

CHAPTER TWENTY-EIGHT

Giulio

"**A**ND THIS IS SLONNE," I SAY, SMILING AS MY DAUGHTER exaggerates her wave.

My mother grins and picks up her granddaughter. "Aww, well aren't you the sweetest! You're such a good girl, aren't you? Aw yes, you are! And I adore your brother too."

My heart warms at the sight in front of me. There is no fear. No death. No limits. My mother is here meeting the family I have created with Valencia. My mom's right here. She's alive—living and breathing.

"I'm so proud of you both. Look how stunning this house is!"

"It's new. Mercer Island is where our family belongs now."

"My little boy has grown up to be the man I always knew he'd be.

Strong. Dedicated. Passionate in love. You make me so happy every single day. I see it all, amore."

"I love you, Mom."

"I love you too. I love all of you!" My mother sets Slonne down and my daughter rushes away giggling. When my mom turns to me, her rich dark curls fall over her right shoulder. Those silver eyes with a touch of baby blue remind me of my own "But now I need to go."

"Stay a little longer."

"No, amore. I have to go."

"Please, Mom." My heart tugs in my chest. "Don't go yet. Stay for dinner."

Valencia steps by me, glowing as she clasps my mother's hands. "Giulio's right. We would love for you to stay longer."

"I know, dear. However, there's something I must do. I promise I'll come back soon."

"No." I step forward in pain. "No, you won't come back. I need you to be with us. I need to know Dad won't hurt you again. I need to know you're safe. Please, Mom."

"I'm safe, amore. I've been safe for a long while but now there's something I need to return to you. A child. Your child. I've been protecting her but now she must be yours again. Go on without me because I'm okay and she'll be yours again."

Addilyn.

My daughter's name gets caught in my throat.

Valencia looks to me. "Addilyn is okay!"

When we turn back, my mother is gone. We search room after room but she isn't in the house. She's gone. Gone. Gone. But with her departure, she took with her a weight from my chest.

Her words echo; Go on without me because I'll be okay and she'll be yours again.

Addilyn will be ours.

"Baby?"

I rise up to sitting in bed and a hand is circling my back. *Valencia. My darling.* She's here.

Scrubbing a hand over my face, I try to make sense of the dream that woke me. "I'm sorry...I..."

"Are you okay, baby? You were tossing and turning. Did you have a bad dream?"

"I'm alright now and I had the opposite." I breathe and take a second to regroup.

Fuck.

It felt so real.

When I lie back down, I hold Valencia, breathing in her sweet floral vanilla scent that brings me back to real life. "I had a dream similar to the one you had about finding Addilyn. Instead, this one was with my mother. She was visiting us in this house and told us that she couldn't stay, but she was safe and needed to go somewhere. She said that she has been protecting Addilyn but now she must return her to us."

Lencia's fingers caress my chest, drawing long calming strokes. "Maybe this is her way of saying goodbye. You said that you've never dreamt about her since her passing, right?"

"Right."

"Well, perhaps that was your mother's way of saying that she's safe and all this time has been up above guiding Addilyn back to us. Your mother was an incredible woman. A brave one and although I never met her, I feel like I know her."

Lencia's wedding ring catches the moonlight and flares light up inside me. I kiss her ring and then her lips tenderly. When I pull back to brush strands of her hair away from her face, I smile knowing that *it all* makes sense…

That my life has panned out the way it was supposed to.

That life is already written out for us and at times we just have to let go and follow its motions.

That *this* right here is my given custom life and I will love Valencia and my children until my very last breath.

This I know.

I never thought a woman like this existed. Valencia Leitner, now Valencia Giannotti, was never in my plans as a young boy hurting from his mother's death and father's torment. Yet life gave me the most precious gift. The gift of sharing my life with the most inspiring woman and our three loving children. The gift of owning a successful architecture and interior design business. The gift of simply being *me*.

I will continue to thank the world every single day for these blessings.

"You know if we weren't already married, I would marry you all over again."

She giggles sweetly. "You have me, Giulio. You have me."

"Thank you for always knowing what to say."

"Thank you for making me sane."

My lips perk up. "Our daughter needs us and I have a gut feeling she'll be with us soon."

Valencia jumps at my phone alarm that bursts through the room. "Sweet God!"

"Sorry, baby." I laugh, reaching over to my bedside and stop the buzzing.

The smile isn't wiped off my face at the 6:30 A.M. wake up, but rather at three texts from over half an hour ago.

Bryce: Since when did you make six o'clock meetings a part of the job? This meeting better be fucking biblical, mate. It's far too early. Hurry your ass down here!

Lance: We're all here. Just waiting on you, man.

Lance: Hey...you haven't showed. Where are you? Is everything okay?

What on earth are they on about?

My brows furrow as I show Valencia the texts. We share a confused look seconds before her ringtone begins blears. She quickly reaches over and taps the answer button.

"Woah, Helena, slow down..." Valencia's nose scrunches up cutely as silence takes over.

My sister-in-law isn't even on speaker and I can hear her loud, panicked voice. I inch closer to my wife who hits speaker to Helena's frantic words and hands me her phone. "I'm telling you they're showing it everywhere! Put it on the news, it's on right now."

"What's on?" I ask with a raging heart.

"Oh my good god! Giulio, switch on the TV and you'll see it." Helena advises with a sharp sigh. "Please let me know if there's anything I can do to help. I'm just shocked and...so sorry."

I switch on the television to the early morning news and my heart drops to my stomach at what I see. Beside me comes a shocked gasp as Valencia covers her opened mouth.

Oh my...

Fuck.

FUCK.

BREAKING:

NOTTI DESIGN WAREHOUSE ABLAZE AFTER SUSPECTED ARSON.

REPORTS OF FOUR EMPLOYEES CRITICALLY INJURED IN FIRE.

Shit.

Sure enough, the broadcasting is Live from *my* property. There are hovering helicopters shooting footage over the brightly burning design warehouse—*my* warehouse.

Helena hangs up and I remain paralyzed from the heavy words just muttered from the phone in my hands, staring at the television. Valencia is there to take the phone and when my eyes land on hers there is a strain in my heart that projects my greatest fear; more people getting hurt.

Suspected arson.

Four employees critically injured.

With our nakedness colliding, she straddles my hips and says the words I have said to her all along. I shut my eyes at the softness of her hands against my three-day stubbled jaw and the void her touch fills. "I'm with you, Giulio. You are not going through this alone, I'm here."

My fingertips run up and down her spine, awakening my skin further. "I just wanted a weekend without any hassle. A weekend just for us. Why is that so hard?"

"You already gave me everything and more yesterday. I had the best time with you, but your work and employees are just as important. Helena can look after the kids while we head back to Seattle. And don't worry, the goodness will always overrule the bad."

"You're an angel." I look up and find her with a placid smile. "My golden angel."

I see the new confidence in her and I adore it. I love how much we've both grown and strengthened during the toughest period of our life. Our vulnerabilities coming to light have led us to this moment. There is nobody else I want to go through this with but with my Valencia.

"We'll do just that." My lips brush against hers when her hips rock forward. It makes my entire world spin. "But first make me forget, darling. Make me forget every single thing around us—"

Ding-dong.

The doorbell breaks my train of thought.

What the hell is going on?

I can tell by Valencia's wide eyes and my own peculating thoughts that we already know who's at our front door... Is this *the* moment our family has been waiting for, for the past seven months?

I kiss her and tell her to stay in the bed while I rush to slip on my boxers, slacks and creased dress shirt. There's another ring of the doorbell as I'm jogging to the front door, flicking on the lights on my way.

Two officers meet my gaze on the other side of the door.

Finally, some answers.

But then it all stops for me...because the officer on the left looks familiar. *Those deep-set beady eyes that stare into my soul.* I swear I've seen him somewhere before, but I cannot pinpoint where.

"Officers, what is going on? Do you have any leads? Are we going to the warehouse?"

The officer on the left shakes his head and inches closer to me. While I'm the one looking down at him, there's something about him I don't like…*judgement.*

He flashes me his badge. "No, Mr. Giannotti. The only place you're going right now is to the police department for questioning over the suspected arson of Notti Design's warehouse."

What?

My brows furrow. "Questioning? Why for questioning?"

"Mr. Giannotti…" The officer scoffs with an arrogant shake to the head. "You already know what's going on. You *know.*"

"*Know* what exactly?" I glance to the other officer who's taken a backseat to the conversation and instead rakes his gaze from my security guard, to the house and then back to me. "Look, could you kindly tell me what is going on? I just woke up to news that my warehouse is up in flames!"

"We have reason to believe you were in fact involved in the suspected arson, Mr. Giannotti. As I previously stated, we're going down to the police department for questioning."

"You think I did this? I didn't do anything! I was asleep with my wife!"

"That will all be further determined down at the department. Now, are you going to cooperate with us, or are we going to call backup?" He steps closer, trapping me in a whiff of torturing tobacco. His stare burns straight through me, so deep it makes me remember my father. "And trust me, you don't want me to call backup….not when that wife of yours is right *there.*"

I note the presence of Valencia behind me and all of a sudden *everything clicks.*

This officer…he used to be my father's right-hand man— *Craig Jones.* It's been over fourteen years since I saw him last. *What is he trying to do to me?* Pin me for a crime I didn't do in order to get back at me for his corrupt closest friend being dead…?

Try me, bastard.

I'm saved by Sergeant Flynn who steps into the small interrogation room after a solid fifteen minutes of being wrongfully questioned by Officer Craig Jones. My father's friend had been asking me the same few questions and spun them around with hopes I would break. Deep down he probably has some type of suspicion about me after my father's death. But it doesn't concern me and neither do any of his questions regarding my warehouse because I'm fucking innocent.

Craig takes his send off with a death glare and I uncross my arms over my chest when Sergeant Flynn steps in. After much fewer questions, he establishes I wasn't involved in the suspected arson and that I *am* telling the truth, prompting the pending investigation to go forth.

It is brought to my attention that firefighters have been battling the inferno at the Notti Design Warehouse for the past hour. Bryce, Kayla, Lance and Marcus have all been critically injured. Apparently, an email sent from my account urged them there for an early morning team meeting and once they were all inside, doors were locked and an inferno ignited.

When Valencia and I arrive at Notti Design's warehouse, the scene is much more dire than I imagined. Firetrucks, police cars, and the press are warming *everywhere*. The fire is easing, but dark ash and burned merchandise line every step. This clean-up bill will be in the millions, more with all the décor perished, but I don't care about the money, all I care about is everybody being alive and safe.

All I need to know is that they'll all be okay.

We enter the burn unit at the hospital and walk through to the first room the lady at the desk directed us to. This entire situation is surreal, accompanied by a sinking feeling in my gut.

Valencia rushes to pull Kayla into an embrace. Thankfully she's stable and only suffers from a few minor burns to her legs. She was the first person the firefighters located and were able to rescue. She tells us with a bright smile that she will recover soon and none of this is our fault. Her optimism runs deep and she makes a joke about this finally luring her boyfriend to fly in to see her.

Next is Lance Hilton—my closest friend. To see such a dignified man lying in a hospital bed with bandages on his forearms and leg shatters me. I wish I could take away the pain.

I shake my head upon arrival and squeeze his shoulders. "I can't believe this, man. I'm so sorry. How are you feeling?"

"Don't be sorry, this isn't on you. I'm feeling okay, really I am. I suffered some smoke inhalation and these right here are second degree burns. I may need a skin graft but we'll have to see." He remains hopeful with a smile and turns to Valencia. "I'm sorry this had to cut your birthday weekend short, Val."

"Don't be ridiculous, you don't need to apologize!"

"What happened exactly?" I ask.

Lance grimaces when he attempts to push himself upright on the bed. I support his back while Valencia offers her hand. "Thanks, guys. Well, I went to the warehouse because I received an email from your account stating you needed assistance in the warehouse. I thought it was odd, especially because it was so early on a Saturday, and on Friday you were adamant about staying on Mercer for the weekend, but work is work and so I made my way there. The four of us all arrived at the same time so we walked up together and into the warehouse. We were waiting on what was supposed to be you, and out of nowhere, I started smelling this gasoline. Then there were massive explosions of fire. I...I couldn't navigate myself out of there. Bryce had to virtually pull me out because the firefighters were struggling to get to us. I really have him to thank. He risked his life too. If it wasn't for Bryce I really don't think I would have made it...not from where I was in the building."

Valencia and I share a glance.

Bryce?

We need to give credit where credit is due.

I let Lance know that I'm here for anything he needs,

financial aid included, just like we told Kayla, and plan to tell both Bryce and my half-brother. "Thanks, man, but the one true thing I want for both of you is to find Addilyn. That's all I want."

It's what we all need now.

Along with uncovering who the hell sent those emails and who's behind all of this.

Marcus is lying in a hospital bed and staring up at the ceiling when we enter. He's suffered a few first degree burns and is far less interested in our presence. He doesn't seem to care or even notice when Valencia and I pull up two chairs beside his bed.

The room is so clinically white. The tension is thick and the shades are drawn, creating a dark stream of friction. He doesn't react to our embraces. *It's as if we don't exist.* Even after all the arguments and firing him only for him to continue working as if nothing happened, I *still* care for him.

I *still* want the best for him.

Marcus' dark eyes stare ahead, beyond us. "When we were younger, do you remember when we went on that vacation to Rhode Island with Dad and my mother?"

"Yes," I pause. "Yes, Marcus I do. It was just before my eighteenth."

"Then I must have been nine. Do you remember we fought over something? I don't remember what now, probably something…stupid. I stormed off and didn't know it, but you had followed me. I was sitting at the edge of the bay and slipped and you didn't think twice about jumping in to save me, remember that?"

"I do."

"And he did the same thing to save you. Isn't that right, Valencia?"

She clears my throat beside me. "Yes, he did save me."

"Exactly, he saved *you*. *Your* family. I'm not a fucking part of it. I'm not a part of anything. So why come all the way to check on me?" Marcus looks at me to emphasize his point, redness circling his eyes. "Huh?"

"First, you're my brother, and second, somebody torched my company's warehouse. How could we not check in?"

"We're *half*-brothers. Being blood never made anything better between us."

"We still fought the same battles!"

"Yeah, battles *you* created! The ones you fucking built the moment you killed our—"

I lean forward against the bed and cut him off in a hiss. "This is not the time or the place."

"It is! You wanna know why? Because I've made up my mind. I don't want to see you anymore. I don't want to see any of you. I don't want to be a part of your fucking family."

The words leave me uneasy. After everything we've been through, and even though we've never been close, the last thing I want is to lose another person. *I don't want to lose him.* "Marcus, those battles were created the moment our father cheated with your mother while mine was dying. I know it's not your fault. I am not claiming that it is. However, you didn't help the agony. Never did you stand by me. Not even once. You amplified it with your own mind games."

Marcus swallows hard, glancing between Valencia and me with narrowed eyes. "I should have died today. You weren't there to save me this time. It would have been easy."

"Please don't say those things, Marcus."

"You don't know a thing about me, Valencia! None of you do!"

"My wife *knows* you! I *know* you!" I growl, losing my patience. "We have always been here for you. *Always.* Even through the drugs and when the last thing we wanted to do was look each other in the eye. I adhered to your deal after that Thanksgiving night. I did everything you asked me to. I am *still* doing everything you ask me to!"

"Exactly! Why are you? Why are you always helping me? I'm a burden. That's all I am."

"Marcus—"

"I want to be alone." His voice cracks as he shuts his eyes. "Please…just leave me alone."

It kills me. I see the physical reaction in Valencia's eyes. I feel my own composure break. She has *always* been there for him too. Despite it all, we have *always* been family.

My heart breaks and not only for myself. "I don't know where I went wrong with you. I supported you with everything. The grief. The terrors. The obsessions. But *this*, you cutting me out of your life, I will not accept that."

"Then maybe we should end this right here."

"We will *always* be here for you when you need us."

"I don't need either of you, Giulio."

Wow.

I stand at the edge of the bed and Valencia follows suit, massaging my tense shoulder blades through my coat. Marcus avoids our gazes. *So, this is really it.* All I can do is stare at Marcus helplessly. I feel all my past burdens let go. The moment I step out of the hospital room, this will be us giving up on mending our parents' mistakes.

This is our brotherhood burning.

This is our goodbye.

"Let's go. He wants to be alone," my wife whispers.

It takes a moment but when I finally nod I know this *is* it.

Goodbye, Marcus.

We walk wordlessly into Bryce's hospital room. *Perhaps he can bring some light to this situation.* All hope fades at one glance at him. Bryce looks stone cold. The usual spark in his bright green eyes is doused. There's no smirk or sassy comment upon arrival. His dark brown hair is swept to one side, his skin has a reddish hue and he's shirtless with a white bandage on his lower abdomen; alongside it, dark tattoos spread out across his chest and down his fully inked arms.

"Oh, Bryce!" His body tenses at Valencia's concern. "Are you okay?"

He continues to stare into the distance with a nod. His jaw remains tight, frozen in time. Bryce saved Lance and that means a lot to me, so when I extend my hand, I don't expect the wave of resilience as we complete the solid shake.

A moment in history passes between us.

We accept each other.

"I appreciate what you did back there. You're a hero. Thank you. I really mean it, Bryce."

Another nod. He probably just needs some rest after such a torturous morning.

Valencia reads my mind with a smile. "We're going to go and give you some space. Please let us know if there is anything we can do at all, finances included."

Why isn't he saying anything?

I wish I could erase my frown when we say our goodbyes, but I can't.

"I'm sorry, Valencia."

We turn back to Bryce, the words seeming foreign coming from his lips.

"For?"

Bryce's gaze snaps between us as he takes in a sharp breath. "For being part of the reason ya cut your celebration short. I know how much it meant for you to be with family."

"You're the second person that has apologized. None of this is your fault. What happened this morning was a tragic incident and the police will find whoever did it. We just want you to recover and get back to the Bryce McCarson we know and love."

"This ain't my fault." Dropping his gaze to his hands, Bryce repeats Lencia's words as a mutter to himself. "Not my fault."

I've never seen him this low and it's concerning. He's always so lively and resilient. Then it dawns on me that I've never heard Bryce speak about any friends or family here in Seattle apart from those in Hoxton. Could it be that...*he's lonely? Or more vulnerable than we thought? Maybe he really does value his friendship with Valencia and me...maybe we're all he has. He and I aren't really close...but we're something so that must count...Right?*

"Hey, are you sure everything is okay?" I ask.

"Positive." His voice doesn't convince me.

Valencia and I silently communicate to stay a little longer

with him. Perhaps he just needs some time to open up and tell us what's on his mind.

"Thanks," Bryce says in desperation. "Thank you both for being my only hospital visit."

My lips part to respond when the door bursts open. Freezing air floats into the room from the hallway. The last thing I expect are two Seattle police officers. A male officer checks us over and the other is a woman who marches towards Bryce, flashing her shiny badge awfully close to his face.

"Bryce McCarson, you're under arrest for the alleged arson of Notti Designs Warehouse. You have the right to remain silent, anything you say or do will be used against you. Do you understand?"

My heart drops.

Bryce is...

What?

What is going on?

"Aye! What the hell do ya mean?" Bryce retaliates against the officer's handcuffs. "I didn't do it! I swear! I didn't do anything!"

"Anything you do or say will be held against you. Do you understand?"

Bryce shakes his head. Only now does his entire body come alive. His eyes widen in shock as he turns to Valencia and me. "You've gotta believe me! It's not me! I didn't do it! I wouldn't do something like that!"

The male officer steps between us, blocking us from a hysterical Bryce. "I'm going to need you both to step out, Mr. and Mrs. Giannotti."

"He didn't do this. I can see it in his eyes."

Me defending Bryce?

Now, this is new but it feels right.

There's absolutely no motive for Bryce to cause the fire. It was Lance who only just stated he was right there with him when all hell broke loose, and Valencia and Bryce have become so close during these last couple of weeks. I have to listen to my gut instinct.

Bryce could not have done this.

He *did not* do this.

"If it were that easy, you would be doing our job for us."

The initial shock doesn't subside during our drive home. It transforms into a glass jar of emotions that explodes every single time I relive the moment the police stepped inside Bryce's room. The genuine shock in his eyes. His resistance. His pleas.

"He's been set up!" Valencia says. "They must have found some evidence but it must be planted or circumstantial. Who would do that?"

"I have no idea. I need to call my attorney for him." I touch on the brakes as we approach a red light. "I can't believe this is happening."

"I only hope they find who really did this because I feel bad for him. He's suffered a lot. Maybe something to do with his past…with his dad never being there. Would Marcus know Bryce's whole story?"

"Even if Marcus did, he doesn't want to talk to us now." I pull her hand over the console and kiss it. "And Bryce doesn't strike me as the type of guy who talks to his friends like that."

"So, you're saying you believe at times the humor and confidence is a façade?"

"That's what I suspect. Only time will tell, my gorgeous girl, only time."

Valencia smiles through the chaos and is about to say something when her phone begins blaring. "It's an unknown number…"

"Put in on speaker."

A second passes. "Hello?"

"Mrs. Giannotti, I have a message to pass to you." The voice is distorted. *Shit.* It must be one of the men still on the run from the other ransom call. The same ones who stole and burned my vehicle, kidnapped my kids, and attempted to drown Valencia.

What the hell is happening?

Valencia hunches forward in the passenger seat. "Who are you?"

"Mrs. Giannotti, are you listening?"

"You will pay. You will pay for all of this!" she grits, beyond frustrated.

"What do you want?" I growl into the phone seconds after Valencia's threat. My grip tightens on the heated leather wheel. "Why don't you just show yourself? Huh? Why don't you just grow some fucking balls and own up to everything you've done?"

"I have Addilyn, Mr. Giannotti. You should not talk to me like that. Not when you're driving around in your new car with that *irresistible* wife of yours. The fire...the letters...the kidnappings...You have no idea what types of things I can orchestrate. Understood?"

Valencia's mouth drops and I flick my gaze to my rearview. My heart, I can't fucking feel it. Nobody seems suspicious. Nobody is on their phone. Nothing is out of place.

But the person is out there.

I just know it.

I can fucking feel it.

"You're not even close, Giulio. Admit it, we know how to play this game better than you can both ever imagine. You won't beat us. This game was practically *made* for us. Imagine that..."

"What the hell do you want from my family?" I hiss into the phone, blood heating my face. "Where the hell are you? Who the hell are you? FUCKING SAY SOMETHING!"

"Listen, is Addilyn okay? Please. We will give you anything, please—"

Laughter interrupts Valencia's sentence. Haunting laughter that makes my core tighten. "So impatient. Remember, we *control* this game. The next move is made when and how we want it. You have twenty-four hours to find her. Twenty-four hours and then Addilyn Giannotti is no longer. *Only twenty-four hours.* Time starts...*now.*"

"Don't—"

The call ends, leaving Valencia and I searching each other's faces in dismay.

Fuck.

CHAPTER TWENTY-NINE

Valencia

THE PARANOIA KICKS IN INSTANTLY.

Giulio and I spend the entire day attempting to come up with theories. There is only one issue. We can never settle on the culprit or culprits involved. We don't believe Bryce lit that fire. He couldn't have, not after we've grown so close in the last two months.

I notify Sergeant Flynn straight after the call from Addilyn's kidnapper and the stakes regarding the investigation are raised again. Twenty-four hours…*I need my baby back.*

Even when evening falls and there are still no leads, the thought of running out of time is not a possibility. It *won't* go that way. We *will* find Addilyn. Our hope *has to* amount to something.

Just before midday, Giulio and I received a call from SPD stating they have arrested two of the men who allegedly attacked me. Both names are unfamiliar. *But there were more than two people in the room. I just feel it...*

Seattle and Mercer Island Police are doing their best with zero clues and no verbal cooperation from the two men they arrested. It gets worse when they state they cannot track the number who called us as it was a burner phone. It forces us to take a whole step back with less than nineteen hours to go.

It's 2 P.M on this detrimental Saturday afternoon. Something needs to save us before 9 A.M. tomorrow. It's déjà vu, only this time Giulio and I are a team.

I feel better knowing the security at our Mercer Island home now consists of two men keeping guard at the same time instead of one.

Relief floods me when Kayla calls to notify us that she's been released from hospital. She wishes us all the best while she recovers at home with Zac who flew in to see her.

It's different this time for me. No tears fall during this whole ordeal. The fatigue, anti-depressants, and bittersweet moments of the past few weeks have finally caught up with me and all I want is an end to this madness. I don't want any more tears—I just want Addilyn.

"So you knew about this house too?"

Helena grins as she finishes braiding Daisy's hair. Daisy thanks her mother and runs off to play with her brother and cousin. "Sure did. Giulio made me join him to preview it. This confident husband of yours turns into a nervous wreck when he wants to please you."

"Shhh, we all have our weaknesses." Giulio chuckles and pecks my cheek. "It just so happens to be that Valencia is mine. Isn't that right, *amore?*"

"And you're mine."

"Well, now that we've established that you two are made for each other, can we talk about the elephant in the room?" my sister mocks playfully. "I'm thirty and nowhere near being in the dirty club!"

No. Way!

"Oh my god! You read the card?"

"It may or may have not slipped out of the closed drawer and into my hand."

"Look at her!" I turn to Giulio with a wide grin. "We've got our own Sherlock Holmes on our hands. Helena Holmes. The funny thing is that's actually your last name, haha!"

"Yeah, it's a good thing Ben Holmes was my weakness." Her smile flattens as she sighs sharply. "I still feel a little guilty I jumped in with Marcus and lost myself for a little while."

Giulio purses his lips. "From experience, I know grief does not have a time limit. You're a smart woman and your decisions are valid. You made them for a reason and that reason doesn't have to equal guilt."

"You're right. I just…I don't know. It's been seven years since he passed and I feel like I'm ready to find love again. Other days, the whole idea scares me to death. That's why I thought something casual with Marcus would…help…but, well, you both know how that went."

"Sometimes the heart wants what it wants. There is nothing wrong with that." I reassure her. "I mean, look at me! Look at how far Giulio and I have come! We've surrendered to the pain and have committed to make it work again. Somebody will come into your life again and love you for you. They say patience is virtue and with everything that happened with Addilyn, I now know that all the anxious wait was worth it because soon she will be ours. Soon, you will find the next love of your life. You will, honey."

This isn't the first time I've seen her like this.

I can't begin to imagine what losing Giulio so soon would do to me and how it would affect me and my children, but what I *do* know is that ever since Addilyn's disappearance, at the end of the day, those you love will always rally with you.

I will always be here for Helena because she deserves a man just like Ben. One who respects, commits and is devoted to her *and* her children. That's just as important.

"But what if it doesn't happen for me again?" Helena frowns, weaving her hands through ours. "What if Ben was it? I loved that idiot so much. Maybe all I'll ever have are the memories..."

"Ben was your soulmate and you two had a love that inspired my outlook on it. This year it's been important for me to turn *'what if'* into *'will.'* So, if finding love again is something you truly want and you are ready, then with time it *will* come to you."

"And when he does..." Giulio adds with a similar smile, "I'll be right here to sit him down and make sure he has the best of intentions, just like the interrogation you did to me when Lencia and I first started dating, but worse."

And just like that, her sarcasm returns with a smirk. "Gee, thanks *Dad*."

"Giulio's right, honey. If any man wants you, he needs to get through us first."

"I'm only kidding! Thank you. I really do appreciate it from the bottom of my heart." Her smile widens. "Oh, and Lencia? I'm loving the new you. I'm so proud of the new strong, confident badass woman you've become. Not that you weren't it before, but it's amplified. I just love it!"

For the first time in my life I don't feel like hiding away or fussing at the compliment. I want to live in the moment and learn to appreciate it. "So do I."

Giulio kisses my cheek. "And I love it too."

My phone buzzes just as Helena opens her mouth to speak again. *An unknown number.* When I answer, an automated machine asks me if I would like to accept a COLLECT call from King County Jail from inmate... Bryce speaks his name at the pause and then there is a tone. I accept the charges.

"Valencia?"

"Bryce!"

"I can only make this quick," he says, his Cockney accent hushed yet reverent. "You are my only call and I...know ya would listen. I'm being held in King County jail now without bail and my court hearing is tomorrow. They can't find any fucking evidence because deep down they know I didn't do it. I want ya to know that I didn't light that fire. I didn't do any of it."

My breath stutters. "I believe you, Bryce."

There's a long pause on his end. "You do?"

"I do."

There is relief in his sigh. "Thank you…Are you with Giulio?"

"I am."

"Put me on speaker. I have something to say."

Something to say?

I hit speaker and I glance around us. "You're on."

Helena leans in closer, but Giulio remains beside me with knitted brows. "Bryce, do you have a lawyer? I can arrange to—"

"No. No, let them appoint me a public defender."

"But I don't have an issue having my lawyer represent you."

"No, no I don't want that. I don't want to cause any more trouble."

What is going on?

"Valencia…Giulio…I've done things I regret. Things I am not proud of. I did things to both of ya and I know I've hurt ya both. Things revolving around…the investigation."

No.

No.

No.

Heat courses through my veins. "What do you mean, Bryce?"

"Giulio? Do you remember when I told you that the good guys always have the darkest secrets? That ya don't see it because they conceal it well?"

Confusion strikes me when Giulio nods to himself and swallows hard. "I remember."

"Good, because I forgot to add something. That the nutters have the deepest lies. I'm a nutter. Why? Because when I first arrived in Seattle, somebody lured me with a big sum of money. Four million dollars to be exact. I didn't know anything about Addilyn, who she was, or who had her. They lured me with the huge fucking sum of money and because I'm the sick bastard that I am, I took the deal. I took the deal, right, because my mother needs the money. It would change her life and pay off the millions she needs to pay back…"

"Bryce, I—"

"Please listen to me, Giulio. If I don't say it now…I don't know if I ever can."

My husband clears his throat. "Go on."

"So it began and I had to submit to these fucking guidelines, right. Valencia, violating you at the bar was never in any part of my guidelines. That was a pure mistake. A drunken lonely mistake I still regret even though you say you've forgiven me. I fell in love with the idea of you that night…the idea that somebody cared for me even for a split second, because nobody else ever has in that way…I'll forever be sorry for that, even though I already gave you my reasons. I'm sorry. However, Giulio, I *did* purposely act like I was shit at my job to follow my appointed guideline. I…I created those letters and placed them in the mail. I distorted the cameras. I was an accessory to stealing your Porsche, an accessory to Oscar and Slonne's kidnapping *and* Valencia's attempted murder. I didn't touch them or you. I simply was there. Watching. I know it doesn't make it better…I did it all for the money. I began having this envy for you both."

I clutch at my heart, yet cannot feel the beats.

McCarson continues, "But then something changed. Valencia, you forgave me. Even when I wanted you to hate me the most, ya forgave me for what I did. And you, Giulio, that day when your half-brother was beating you up, I had this calling to help you. I was supposed to light the fire. It *was* supposed to be me, but this empathy came over me, one I've never experienced in me whole life. It made me want out. I didn't care about the money. I couldn't hurt ya family more. I wasn't involved in the fire. I wasn't involved in physically kidnapping or putting my hands on any of you five. I was told about the ransom calls, but I never made them. I never saw or was involved in any aspect of Addilyn's disappearance. When I said I wanted out before the fire, I was almost killed. They got livid and framed this on me. Ya see? They framed this all on fucking me and I know I'm not perfect; I'm very much the opposite, but I will not go to my grave without honesty. I'm sick of disappointing others, sick of it because I feel sick to my stomach for what I did. I want to be honest with ya both and I want to help."

The phone trembles in my hands.

No. No. No.

Fear twists in my gut, as if somebody has just punched me right there. *Bryce is involved.* I trusted him. I helped him. I defended him. I feel so betrayed now.

Helena begins pacing up and down the living room, fingers through her light honey brown hair. *Her instincts told her not to trust Bryce from day one...*

Giulio's stance mirrors mine. He remains still, his hot gaze burning straight into the phone with a disheartened grimace. My throat tightens. Anger boils my blood. We're so shocked that we don't even have the fight in us.

"Were you in the basement when they counted the money?"

"Yes. In one of the corners, but I never touched you or your children."

"Where's that money now?"

"Burned. It was destroyed, but not by me."

"All of it?"

"Yes. Initially, I heard it was going to be used to help pay off other people who were hired."

Giulio clears his throat. "And you never saw Addilyn or were an accessory in any way?"

"Never."

"Bryce," I begin, so shattered, "were you pretending to be my friend this entire time?"

"Never. Even though I needed to be pretending, I couldn't with you. The friendship we have...*had*...was an authentically genuine one. I really did develop a bond with you. With ya both, but especially you, Valencia. I...I value you so much and it hurts me to the core that I'm losing my only true friend I have here because of a manipulative game that I thought at the time was—" A jagged breath escapes him and a heart-wrenching cry cuts through the phone. Pain marks his every word. "I can't believe I did it...I want to go back...I don't want to be alone in this world. I swear—I promise, I never knew about Addilyn, only about my deal. I just wanted the money. I *needed* it. By the end I realized just how much it was a cruel and selfish thing to do, even if it did help my mother. I couldn't get out when I wanted to, so they lit that fire and are framing me to prove a point. I deserve all the convictions coming my way...I'm a fucking monster. That's all I am. That's all I'll ever be."

"Bryce?" I whisper, swallowing the knot in my throat.

"Aye?"

"I...*really* valued you too." Tears roll down my cheeks. "What else haven't you told us?"

"I'm sorry for hurting you all and for everything I've done." Bryce's agonized voice breaks into a sob. "I want you both to know this wasn't all on me; I wasn't the mastermind nor have I ever had a vendetta. All I ever did was follow instructions. I need to make up for my sins because only now do I realize how much I went wrong. I lost everything. I *am* a monster. I know it...I overheard a conversation and know where Addilyn is. Please trust I'm telling the truth because it's the last chance to get her back. I'll tell you it all. I promise. I will."

My heart stops.

This is it. This is the moment I have been waiting 229 days for.

"Bryce?"

"Yes?"

"Who has our baby girl?"

There's a brief moment of silence before all hell breaks loose. "Marcus Giannotti."

CHAPTER THIRTY

Valencia

Sickened is not a good enough word to describe how I'm feeling. The revelation that both Bryce and Marcus were involved disturbs me deeply. I don't know what's worse, the fact that I trusted Marcus and grew a friendly liking towards Bryce, or that this was all a game to them.

Bryce McCarson *did* supply us a Seattle address before hanging up. The sound of the line cutting wasn't just a conclusion of a conversation; it was the conclusion of everything we once believed to be true. Now it's all turned out to be lies.

Helena practically shoves Giulio and me out of the door. "Go! Go to the police! You don't have much time!"

I pull her into a tight embrace and smile softly at Oscar and

Slonne who come rushing down the stars behind their cousins. Giulio pulls us all into one massive group hug. When I kiss Oscar and Slonne's foreheads, I tell them everything is going be alright and that we'll get our happy ending.

"Thank you for everything you do for me." I tell my sister.

Helena shakes her head, a tight smile on her glossy pink lips. "Thank *you*. Now go on. Go on and bring her home!"

"Are you going to bring Addilyn home, Mommy?" Slonne asks, her vibrant eyes hopeful.

"Yes, baby. We are going to bring Addilyn home."

Giulio and I take a moment to breathe when we park in front of the police station.

"Do you really think Marcus is capable of this?"

"That's what I keep asking myself too." Giulio sighs, holding my hand in his between the leather car seats. His soft skin relaxes me. "There's only one way to find out."

"Whatever the verdict is we will have Addilyn *and* each other now."

"Yes, my darling. That is the only thing that matters."

When Giulio kisses me, everything slows. Like a rapid reminder of everything that has happened between us. It intensifies into need, as if this is the pinnacle of our existence. Because it truly *is*. This is our reason *why* and soon we will seal our forever with our sweet angel.

On the other side of the sword, if something bad does happen, at least we have *this* and we'll go down as a family.

I will always love Giulio Giannotti.

Always.

The moment we pull away, there's nothing but adoration in his eyes. It resonates within me too. We have just been given a lifeline by Bryce—*a last hope.*

I catch the sight of our wedding rings and my heart flutters. "Through all the crazy, I'm glad you didn't let me go. I'm happy you're here with me."

"I'm here. I am right here and I will never let go. Never again, Lencia."

"We're in this together."

"We always will be." And despite the agony, he gives me that slow, sexy smile. "Let's do this. Let's get our baby back, *amore*."

If somebody told me seven months and fifteen days ago that we'd reach the point that the Seattle police department would be preparing to enter *the* suspected house Addilyn has been held captive in, I would have dropped to my knees. The entire drive behind the police seemed an eerie joy. The reality is this could very well turn into a recovery mission; the police made that *very* clear. We don't know what we're going to find. We just have to brace for it all and *be bold*. It's all we can do.

As the several police cars near this dark unknown suburban home, I hold onto Giulio's hand tighter. Freezing air rushes down my spine as an officer orders us to stay close to our car.

We are early, with eighteen hours to spare.

Five officers march up the dark porch steps. "SPD! OPEN UP!"

One pounds on the door with a thud. At the second attempt, Sergeant Flynn emerges and breaches the door. It flings open and the officers enter with guns drawn.

Giulio pulls me to his side.

The urge to rush inside behind them is there, but we can't just yet. Staying behind fosters agitation to pump wildly through my veins. I need to distract myself and I do so with Giulio's pounding heart against my ear. I listen until our beats merge into one.

Soon, SPD officers emerge from the house with a group of women and men. I don't recognize any of them. Their hands are cuffed behind their backs and their heads remain low as officers place them into the backs of four separate police cars.

Sergeant Flynn is the next to step out of the house.

"Oh my god!"

He's with a handcuffed Marcus.

Sergeant Flynn is met with an SPD detective who gestures towards one of their cars, but he shakes his head and eyes flicker in our direction. Marcus' sinister stare entraps me. I'm distraught as he walks to us with Sergeant Flynn, coming to a halt only a foot from us.

It's true. Marcus is involved. He had Addilyn this entire time.

Trusting him was a losing game.

Oh my god!

Marcus' face remains clenched as he emotionlessly glances between us.

"I trusted YOU!" The pain is written all over Giulio's face as he launches forward, an accusing finger jabbed into his half-brother's chest. "With my kids. With my wife. With my company. WHY? WHY WOULD YOU DO THIS? HOW COULD YOU DO THIS TO ME?"

Marcus flinches. "You think I did this alone, brother? Oh no. Who do you think helped me? Who do you think constructed those letters? We both know I am not a tough or creative guy. Bryce did that."

All the air sucks out of me at the confirmation. The coldness Marcus emits foreshadows the end before he even begins. His words cut deep. *Too deep.*

Why would he do this?

Why would he destroy his own family?

My God...

"We know what Bryce did, but you did the rest. You hired all these people to hurt us. You planned that fire. You kidnapped Oscar and Slonne. You tried to *kill* Giulio and me. You took Addilyn *away* from us!" When Marcus' only response is to look at me, I cannot take it. He gives me everything and nothing. It takes everything in me not to break down in front of him. *He's not worth a single tear.* "You should be ashamed of yourself, Marcus!"

"More than ashamed. Why would you bring Bryce on board?"

"Mr. Giannotti, these questions will be answered by Marcus down at the jai—"

Marcus cuts Sergeant Flynn off. "Because after kidnapping her, I tracked Bryce down in a bar one night in May. He didn't know me...but I knew him. I needed people for phase two and made him an offer he couldn't refuse. I formed a deep relationship with Bryce. I thought I could trust him, but he was just another person in the plan of my defeat. I don't know how I didn't fucking foresee it, but he pulled out at the last moment because he grew a fucking *heart*."

Giulio shakes his head. "*You* made him into the monster. *You* bribed him."

"I did. Jealousy does a lot of things to a person, but envy is a whole other level. Giulio, you destroyed our father and then went on to have the perfect family. *I* wanted that." His face twitches in disgust. "*I* wanted the successful career, the intelligent wife, the children. *I* wanted it all. I needed to ruin you, and ruin you I did. I began with the *weakest* link, Addilyn. It's a good thing my mother and our father deceived you. Nobody loves you, Giulio. *Nobody*."

"*I love him,*" I grit. "Our children *love* him. My family and our friends *love* him. I would die for this man. I would have *died* for him. You are undeserving of every single thing Giulio has done for you. He believed in you when nobody else did, even when you didn't even believe in yourself, he did. And I was there right alongside him, Marcus. We. Were. Always. There. For. You. We've always been on your side, right until this moment."

"Whatever." Marcus chuckles coldly. "I'm smarter than you think. Come on. I was over for dinner with you, Helena, and your parents the night Addilyn was *abducted* to even make it look like I wasn't involved. SPD never suspected me because CCTV proved I was with Valencia, yet *I* hired the abductors. My men did everything to make your life hell and it worked. The pressure made you separate. It made your kids fall asleep crying. It drove you both to insanity."

"Your plan failed. You want to know why? Because now Valencia and I are unbreakable. Unstoppable. We are stronger than ever, all courtesy of your corrupt plan."

"*My* corrupt plan? How about Bryce's plan...or should I say our *half-brother's* plan? Oh yes, that's right. Our half-brother on our father's side is Bryce. Go figure, hmm?"

My eyes widen.

WAIT.

WHAT?

Giulio takes a step forward until they are inches apart. His rapid breathing matches mine. I cannot see his face but already know that this is the final showdown.

Game over for Marcus.

"What on earth are you on about?" Giulio asks calmly, *too* calmly.

"That's right. Remember that fateful Thanksgiving when our father said we had another brother? It's Bryce. He's two years younger than you. That's why the plan was perfect. Bryce always hated the idea of his father because not once did he visit or contribute. You didn't give Bryce a chance to give Father a piece of his mind, did you? You just had to *cut it short*. Well, how's this for short? Our *deal* is *over*. Soon enough I'll make everybody know you kil—"

"YOU RUINED MY FAMILY!"

"AND YOU RUINED MY LIFE!"

"NO, YOU RUINED IT *FOR YOURSELF!*"

The brothers remain staring at each other, rage filled breaths hang heavy in the air.

"Our father ruined it and then you did!" Giulio sneers. "You're never going to change because whilst you're *our father's* son, I am *my mother's* son. And I'm so fucking proud that the only thing I claim from the devil you call *Dad* is his fucking last name. Our father deserved everything that happened to him. He deserved it all and you deserve every single thing coming your way too, *brother.*"

The last word is enunciated so violently slow that Sergeant Flynn attempts to pull Marcus away but he stops. "Before I go, let me hug my sister-in-law."

"No, Marcus. We need to get you to the downtown."

"One. Hug."

My brows furrow and Sergeant Flynn sighs. I remain staring at the man I once called my brother-in-law. So much pride came from the name but none he's earned now.

He did this.

He abducted Addilyn.

He ruined it all for me.

"I can't allow that to happen, Marcus."

But I can just imagine how it would have gone. Marcus Giannotti would have crushed me in the tightest embrace I've ever received from him. My hands would have remained by my sides. I wouldn't have hugged him back. *I wouldn't do it. I wouldn't surrender. Not again.*

He drove Giulio and me into a living hell.

He hurt us almost beyond repair.

He had Addilyn…his own niece and Goddaughter.

'*Get off me*' is what I would have said.

My mouth is dry when Marcus continues studying me, forcing me to stare into those dark orbs. I see a helpless empty soul. "I'm guilty. I'm guilty of everything you believe I've done."

"I will never *ever* forgive you for the pain you've inflicted upon this family."

"I don't expect you to."

"Goodbye, Marcus."

Marcus takes one good look at Giulio, then back at me with the most placid smile.

"Bye, Val…" he whispers.

The weight pulling my chest doesn't leave me because of what happens next.

Maybe it's because of the large police presence that I don't expect Marcus to risk it all. One second his coldness zones into me, the next he makes a run for it in the opposite direction.

There is a scuffle and loud shouts between him and Sergeant Flynn who catches up and drags him to the ground. Other officers rush towards the scene to assist when Marcus breaks loose again and sprints away. It's as if Giulio already foresees what's going to happen as he pulls us back, presses my face to his chest, and holds me there seconds before a loud bang.

He doesn't let me see it.

I press my forehead deeper into Giulio's soft sweater with

my eyes shut and concentrate on my breaths. *In. Out. In. Out.* Giulio holds me tighter, his fingers threading through my hair and across my back. His rich cologne calms me. Giulio kisses the side of my head and we squeeze each other tightly as shouts ring louder in front of us.

Oh my God.

Then there's another fire of a gun, a painful groan and everything simmers to silence before a crashing thud rumbles beneath our feet.

I hold my breath for a moment.

"Is Marcus…?"

"Yes, darling," Giulio whispers, facing the commotion. "He's gone."

Gone.

Dead.

"Did they…kill him?"

"Yes."

We simply hold each other. This right here is the strongest embrace of my life. Right here is a moment I will never forget. A deadly fate has met Marcus in the darkest of ways—the same fate as his father—*Marcus Giannotti is dead.*

"We made it, darling. Don't let him win and get inside that beautiful mind of yours."

I nod, unable to shed a tear. "It's us."

"It's always been us. You're my air."

"And you're mine. Always."

My answer to crimes has always been via justice, but after being the one to pull the trigger on the man who taunted me to kill Giulio, I now see justice in a new light. Some people don't deserve the jail sentence or to continue living. Truly vile people deserve to go out within a blink of an eye; and I'm convinced that Marcus meets that criteria. He threw away his entire life for envy, even when he had devoted people there for him.

I take Marcus' good from his bad and as much as it's shocking, a weight lifts from my shoulders.

It's finally the end of his horrid story.

I feel free.

Safe.

Wherever Marcus Giannotti's soul may be rising now, I sincerely hope he finally finds peace.

My attention snaps back to the house just as an officer comes out. He points at the surrounding guards and snipers to put down their guns.

I wonder why.

And then I see *why*.

The officer behind him points towards Giulio and me with a large grin.

Oh my...

A scream escapes me at who is safely wrapped in his arms.

Addilyn!

Her eyes are warm and twinkling. She has grown so much in the past seven months away from us. She's over nine months old now and with that large smile on her lips, she has no idea what seeing her right now means to me—*to us*.

Giulio and I sprint hand in hand past the police cars and weave through the line of officers to reach her. *This is it*. This is where we are meant to be. Away from our past and right into our future.

Oh my god. Addilyn is here. *Right here*. And she is healthy. And she is ours.

The officer grins. "Here you are! Go to Mommy and Daddy!"

I am breathless and beaming all at once as Giulio and I hold her together.

"Addilyn, I love you! Mommy and Daddy love you so much!"

"And we'll never let you go again. Never," Giulio says with a kiss to her forehead. "We have missed you so much!"

Addilyn smiles between us with two cute little bottom teeth. Giulio stretches his arms over my shoulders and pulls the three of us even closer together. The adoration within my heart and those I see mirrored in his eyes makes me feel alive.

We've done it.

We made it.

I feel complete. I feel like myself. *I feel alive again.*

"You don't know how much I love you, Lencia."

"I think I have some idea. I love you with all my heart, Giulio Giannotti."

His love sends me to a place of heaven. I never want to let go of this warm feeling across my entire body. I never want it to leave me again and what secures me is the reality that it never has to.

Addilyn's presence has me smiling through the tears streaming down my cheeks. *Happy tears.* It's my heart responding to all the joy. Our lives are full now. There have been tragedies along the way and lives lost…but *this*, right there, *this* is how it is supposed to be.

From this moment forward, we will be complete. Nothing will ever stop us again. We will take control of our lives, live them to their fullest, and never take another moment for granted.

I love every single part of the family we've created. I love Giulio Giannotti. Both his good and his bad. Both his flaws and his strengths. Both the pleasure and the secrets we exclusively share. This is what marriage *is*.

All the sacrifice, pain, and glory have been worth it. They've been worth it because it eventuated in this moment, getting our sweet Addilyn back and becoming whole again. I found a stronger version of myself along the way, while Giulio healed from his scars of the past to truly accept himself. We've become indestructible—Nobody will ever change us now.

Right here and right now, I'm clutching onto my greatest reassurance.

My greatest resolved hope.

My greatest truth among the lies.

And they smile back at me in lively colors.

EPILOGUE

Giulio

"I CAN TOTALLY SEE YOU!"

"Shhh." I grin at Addilyn's eagerness. "Come. They won't find us here, *carina*."

She's addicted to this game of Tag, but also too cutely persuasive to get us to ever stop, even during this winter. We tuck back behind the wide tree stump, hoping to be concealed. Across our backyard, Oscar and Weston are hidden behind another tree and every two seconds my son pokes his head out to see if the coast is clear.

Daisy, Helena, Lance, Amanda, and my in-laws are all out in the yard joining us for Christmas, but it's Valencia who finds our giggling ten-year-old Slonne first. Lencia starts a light jog, giving our daughter an advantage as they run around the green grass to pass the tag.

My eyes do not stray from their grins.

I love them so much.

At the point where Lencia closes in on our daughter, her strong arms lift her and they spin around in circles, laughing with pure joy.

A lot has changed since the fifteenth of October 2016—the day we found Addilyn.

Good changes. The ones all families wish to have.

As we mark over four years since our youngest daughter became ours again, I'm still in pure awe at our family's bravery. We've bounced back to a healthy, perfectly normal family and it's all I've ever asked for.

Just over three years ago, Valencia stopped the anti-depressants and visits to Dr. Eross. Her mental health has improved tremendously and it's all due to her strength and that dark void from our past being filled. The twins have stopped therapy, and a couple of months after finding Addilyn we flew our immediate friends and family to join us in Fiji to renew our vows. It was one of the most heartfelt moments of my life.

Naturally, there are also bad days. Those where one of us wakes in the middle of the night to a nightmare. I've had my fair share featuring Marcus. He used to haunt my dreams every single night after he was killed. But as the weeks faded into months, they stopped and I took comfort in the thought that his evil is at peace now. I never wanted it to end that way, but Marcus played with the devil the moment he thought he could rise above Seattle Police. He's with our father now…That brings an odd comfort I don't think I will ever quite understand.

Seattle Police confirmed Marcus Giannotti to be the mastermind behind Addilyn's abduction. He hired a dozen men and women—who are now imprisoned—to aid his quest for revenge and paid them with the profit he made selling drugs and the money he *borrowed* from me. Marcus orchestrated the vandalism at my retirement village project. He was the distorted voice. He threw Lencia into the water. He stole my Porsche and torched it. Hired somebody to abduct Addilyn and kept her in a basement the entire time. His intention was never to hurt her, after all, it was revealed that three nannies signed an NDA and were taking care of Addilyn this entire time. It was why she was in perfect health, and that too brought a strange comfort.

Sergeant Flynn was adamant that if Marcus hadn't died that day, he would have been looking at life without parole. He took the easy way out. That is the coward he was.

As for Bryce McCarson, he was convicted of second degree auto theft, kidnapping in the second degree of Valencia, Slonne, and Oscar, accessory to an attempted murder, and unlawful imprisonment. Bryce pled guilty and was sentenced to six years imprisonment and after completing his prison sentence will serve four years of federal supervised release. He is also ordered to pay restitution.

Valencia and I haven't visited him in jail yet…and I don't know if we ever will.

There's a great heaviness in my chest that always appears at the thought of Bryce. He was a confident, complex man who helped destroy our family. On the flip side, his rage melted into compassionate empathy and helped us reunite our family. I think many people see his tattooed skin and rough exterior and instantly label him a villain. As much as I despise him for what he did, I don't think I will ever be able to say *those words*. I don't think Valencia will either.

Why?

Because ultimately, Bryce was the one who led us to Addilyn.

The two men Valencia and I murdered were never accounted for. Sandro outdid himself and executed such a complex plan that the police believe they fled the country. I haven't seen Sandro since that last time. It will be Lencia's and my secret until our last breaths. In this story nobody is perfect, but we are brave. Our sacrifices will stay with us forever, but we did what we needed to do to protect our family and I will *never ever* regret that.

"Oh no, Daddy! They're coming!"

Oh, hell no!

Loud shuffling beside us has me look there. Oscar rushes around the backyard with a cheeky grin. He must have been tagged in the midst of my thoughts and so I pull Addilyn against my chest, hiding her from visibility.

We stay still at the anticipation of Valencia or Slonne finding us at any moment.

Their nearing voices and the crushing of leaves makes Addilyn muffle a shriek.

"Don't worry, Daddy's not going to let them get you."

Just then Valencia stops in her tracks feet away. "Check behind the trees, Oscar! Maybe they're there."

Darling, I think you just broke my heart.

They're feet away which means we don't have much time. I hold onto our daughter tighter and chuckle against her sweet, vanilla floral, and woodsy scent. Ever since we used Lencia's perfume to help Slonne's nightmares, we've done the same thing for Addilyn as her own type of cure on the nights she needs to get the monsters to go away.

Addilyn's still too young to understand the severity of what happened just yet. And while my wife and I have sat Oscar and Slonne down to ease into the topic, we need to give our youngest more time.

Oscar changes up the game and unexpectedly tags Valencia. She gasps but laughs when he runs off with Weston and Slonne.

Yes! That's my boy!

The moment Valencia lifts her gaze further and sees us, I know it's all over.

"Well, well, well." She grins, diverting our daughter's attention too. "Look what we have here!"

Before I can move she taps my back and I'm the one laughing now.

And that right there is the love of my life.

"RUN!" she grabs Addilyn's hand and they rush through our endless backyard.

All of our laughs merge into one as Slonne retreats off to her grandmother and Oscar joins my team as we try our best to zone in on one of them. The bubbly, bright Helena we all know and love cheers her sister on. I call on Lance to join us but he's too occupied with his fiancé, Amanda, to notice. *That's a man in love right there.* After the incident, I was thankful he made a quick recovery and the injuries weren't as severe as we initially thought. Before he could officially resume site managing, he spent the days in the office. When my assistant returned from leave, they hit it off and now they're engaged to be married next year.

"Let's split up," I call out to my son. "I'll take Mom and you take Addilyn."

"Neverrrrrr!" Addilyn screams in a fit of giggles.

Valencia motions for her to take a left, the safer route. Oscar is hot on his sister's tail. I take the right, well aware of my wife's incredible stamina… *Not today, darling.*

She dashes between the tall hemlock trees, laughing. Just a little further, and we end up in the middle of our patio before the lake before she takes a right. There's a dead end fence coming up soon *and damn does she know it.*

I continue on, sprinting behind her, watching that sculpted ass shake and her short hair sway from side to side. Valencia's kept it this length and I cannot get enough of it—*or her.*

"You'll never get me, honey!"

"Hmmm, I don't know about that."

She has the *audacity* to cast me a glance from behind and wink. "We'll have to wait and see…"

Oh, it's so on, baby.

Pushing forward, I run full speed and leap over our outdoor furniture like I'm in Frogger. I slide through trees and foliage until we reach the dead end that right now is my greatest victory.

A game of Tag has never felt so good.

Grinning, I come to a halt a couple of feet behind her. "Hmmm. It's game over for you, isn't it?"

"I still have a few seconds." Valencia paces up and down the parameter of the black-stained cedar fence which marks the borders. Her smile expands. "And…breath to catch."

I smirk, slowly approaching her with pure amusement in my eyes. *She's still scheming a way to save herself with her hands on those exquisite hips! I have a brave woman by my side.*

I'm glad Valencia took up my offer to join Notti Designs permanently. It was exactly two weeks after Addilyn was returned to us that I found my wife in her art studio painting away. Ever since that moment, she's had her own division in the company where she creates artwork for Notti Design clients and her own too. It makes her happy and that makes *me* happy.

We've surpassed hell together and now we get to enjoy the freedom.

We finally have our deserved epilogue.

"Time's up!" I zone in on her until her back gently presses against the fence. "What are you going to do about it, Mrs. Giannotti?"

I still haven't passed the tag. *Not yet.*

Valencia joyfully beams at our close proximity. The glimmer in my eyes expands as her hazel ones roll at her misfortune.

"I think this is the moment it becomes game over for you," I murmur softly.

"You haven't tagged me yet, so technically I'm still in the game."

God, I love her voice.

"Not anymore, darling."

It's heaven when I kiss her. A moan escapes Valencia and it evokes my own. The passionate kiss electrifies me, leaving me to fall captive to her. My desire for the love of my life has me wanting her even more intimately right now.

This game we're playing…I've already won.

I pull away, leaving both of us wanting more. "Tag."

Lencia kisses me.

Just as I cup her soft jaw to pull her to me, she pulls back with a smug, "Tag right back, baby."

She's such a tease—The type that hastens every beat in my heart ever so beautifully.

I don't mind it though, because we have our entire lives to continue playing this game of love. And we will continue to do so until we reach the stars above and even then I will never let her go. I love Valencia Giannotti and our incredible family unconditionally. I'll love them forever.

Her irresistible hazel eyes tell me the same.

She'll love us forever too.

"Tag. You're *it* for me, *amore*."

And then I kiss her. All over again. Sealing in every one of our merciful vows.

ACKNOWLEDGEMENTS

When Giulio and Valencia's story came to mind, the words didn't stop flowing. Their story consumed me completely and with the central theme of healing, their voices came at a time where I needed them the most. Letting go of Giulio and Valencia feels almost like separation anxiety in a way, but I am beyond grateful and happy they are out in the world and most importantly, glimpses of their story will continue in the following inter-connected novels in The Giannotti World!

I want to extend a big thank you to every single person who has been a part of my journey and encouraged me in publishing my debut novel. Thank you. Thank you. Thank you. I wrote this novel during a very dark time in my life where I needed healing. Grief never stops. It is a heavy weight that stays with you forever. It stays with you forever because you will never stop loving that person, and hence the hurt, delusion and agony in grieving is permanent.

Merciful Vows allowed me to breathe in some fresh hope, and while the small peace we learn to grasp with grief only covers a small fraction of the pain, I found a way to emulate those feelings of love and loss into my novel in a real-life way. My heart is in every single word of this novel, in Giulio and Valencia and in their story. It's all from the heart.

Just as I reached my editor's revisions for this novel, I was once again hit with yet another loss of a very close loved one. All the feelings I was already feeling doubled. Healing never stops, but gratefully for me words unlock a little peace for me. So, here's to all words, to everybody who has supported me by always there for me during Merciful Vows and to many more years of novels!

There are so many people I want to thank for all the love and support.

To Mamma, for everything. I couldn't have done this without you—my best friend, my greatest inspiration, my biggest cheerleader. You mean everything and more to me. I love you!

To Nonna and Nonno, for teaching me a love beyond words. I will love you both forever. Grazie per tutto.

To Kristen Portillo, Gemma Woolley, Stacy Blake and Tash Drake—Thank you sensational ladies for making this book possible. I am beyond grateful for all of your beautiful work and time dedicated to perfecting Merciful Vows from the edits, proofing, interior formatting and cover design. I absolutely adore how everything turned out—thank you!

To Sarah Wendt, for always being there for me with encouraging words and inspiring me to reach the stars. You always make me smile and I am beyond grateful to have met you. Thank you for all the love and support, for always supporting my David Gandy obsession (haha!) and for all of the good times. Our friendship means the world to me. Thank you also for being such a genuine co-host to our Author WIP Challenges!

To Brooke C, one of my dearest best friends and the kindest soul I know. Thank you from the bottom of my heart for your constant support, love and generosity. So grateful to know you!

To Cheyenne Cierra, for your sensational talented work that always inspires me. Thank you for being such a bright, caring and supportive friend. Thank you for all of the advice and love!

To Betty Maxine, for your endless determination and grit. Your constant rallying me on and giving me so much love really touches my heart. Thank you!

To Gabrielle Villalba, for your kindness and all of our epic writing chats. Thank you!

To Rosemary Slade, for all of your support and being one of the very first people to beta read Merciful Vows. Thank you!

To all of my author friends for always being by my side, my Instagram writing community for continuously showing my work so much love and my wonderful people over in my

Reader's Facebook Group: Vanessa Luisa's Lovelies. I love all of you. Thank you for everything!

To all my other family and friends, I wish I could list you all—thank you!

To the bloggers, ARC teams and beta readers, thank you. I appreciate you all!

And last but not least, I want to extend a big thank you to all of the readers because without you all this wouldn't be possible. Thank you for stepping into this journey with me.

Vanessa Luisa x

ALSO BY
VANESSA LUISA

The Giannotti World:
An interconnected series of bittersweet romance
standalones set in Seattle.

Merciful Vows (#1)

DIESEL ROSE:
The poetically tragic rock star and his muse...

Remember I'm Yours (#0.5)

Diesel Rose (#1)

STANDALONES:

Oceans of Us

Kisses in Heartache

Happy reading!
Vanessa Luisa xo

ABOUT THE AUTHOR

Vanessa Luisa is a contemporary romance author. She resides in Melbourne, Australia, with her army of current reads, sassy cat and Tom Hardy...the latter is purely all in her mind, but shh don't tell her! Vanessa adores all things from the Golden Age of Hollywood, Seinfeld and believes tea is a writing essential. Her love of reading and writing have always been with her, and while she has a background in certified personal styling, nowadays Vanessa is turning her dream of being an author into reality. She loves writing swoon-worthy, emotionally gripping stories with passionate alphas and strong-willed women. When she isn't writing, Vanessa is busy running her own business and spending time with loved ones.

Vanessa Luisa loves to hear from readers so feel free to kindly contact her at vanessaluisaauthor@gmail.com for any questions or comments.

Connect with Vanessa Luisa:

Kindly join my Facebook reader group:
www.facebook.com/groups/vanessaluisaslovelies

Instagram: @thevanessaluisa

Twitter: @thevanessaluisa

Facebook: www.facebook.com/vanessaluisaauthor

Follow me on Goodreads!

Website/Blog/Subscribe to my newsletter to stay up to date
for all new releases, behind the scenes and receive exclusive
bonus material:

www.vanessaluisa.com